PERFECTLY MATCHED

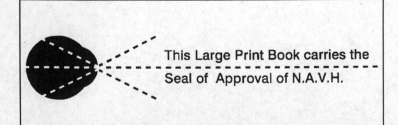

This Large Print Book carries the
Seal of Approval of N.A.V.H.

THE BLUE WILLOW BRIDES

PERFECTLY MATCHED

MAGGIE BRENDAN

THORNDIKE PRESS
A part of Gale, Cengage Learning

GALE
CENGAGE Learning

Detroit • New York • San Francisco • New Haven, Conn • Waterville, Maine • London

GALE
CENGAGE Learning·

LIBRARY OF CONGRESS CATALOGING-IN-PUBLICATION DATA

Brendan, Maggie, 1949–
    Perfectly matched / by Maggie Brendan. — Large print edition.
      pages ; cm. — (The blue willow brides ; book 3) (Thorndike Press large print Christian fiction)
    ISBN-13: 978-1-4104-6343-2 (hardcover)
    ISBN-10: 1-4104-6343-5 (hardcover)
    1. Mail order brides—Fiction. 2. Large type books. I. Title.
PS3602.R4485P47 2013b
813'.6—dc23   2013035152

Published in 2014 by arrangement with Revell Books, a division of Baker Publishing Group

Printed in Mexico
1 2 3 4 5 6 7 17 16 15 14

To Jody, KatyKat, Amelia, and Snowball, my pets, and, of course, Moose, the dog in this story who has joined them in heaven. To the ASPCA, for their dedicated service to all animals everywhere.

Speak up for those who cannot speak for themselves; ensure justice for those being crushed.

Proverbs 31:8 NLT

1

Denver, Colorado
Fall 1888

"Do you, Anna Olsen, take Edward Parker to be your lawfully wedded husband?" Reverend Buchtel cleared his throat and peered over the spectacles resting on the bridge of his large nose. After a moment of silence, he shifted his feet, and the hardwood floor moaned loudly under his weight. He sighed.

Anna stared out the narrow church window, open to provide cross ventilation in the warm sanctuary, and watched a monarch butterfly flit across the sun-kissed lawn. She wished she were outside to catch it. She'd been reading up on wildlife and plants common to Colorado before leaving Cheyenne. A moment later, a black-chinned hummingbird paused to dip its tongue into rose-colored salvia. Oh, how she longed to paint the scene for Catharine's twins!

She turned her attention to her groom. Edward was quite dashing in a cutaway and four-in-hand stretched over his starched white collar. His gray-striped trousers were sharply creased above his polished shoes. The only thing he was missing was a top hat, but Anna bet if it were evening, he'd be wearing one. He cleared his throat and dabbed his brow with a monogrammed handkerchief, then pulled out his watch, and she noticed it was a fine gold timepiece before he slid it into his coat pocket. He turned to face her, his eyes resting on her.

Reverend Buchtel coughed loudly. The sound snapped Anna back from her woolgathering. "If you care to join us now in this ceremony, Miss Olsen, I asked if you take Edward Parker to be your lawful husband," he said in a clipped tone. His warm gray eyes narrowed in question, and his voice conveyed his dismay.

The handful of witnesses snickered, and Anna's face flamed in embarrassment when she glimpsed Edward's face. Her silent bridegroom stared at her in open apprehension. He stood ramrod straight, giving her an annoyed look through narrowed eyes. He seemed to be very serious about everything. She could tell that the moment she'd met him yesterday, when he'd told her the ceremony was already set and planned down to the last detail.

How could she let herself get distracted when Edward was here next to her? He seemed to be perfect . . . perhaps just a little too perfect? His letters, though few, had been careful but not fastidious. Now Anna was beginning to wonder if he ever relaxed. And did he ever laugh?

"I — well, of course I do," she muttered, barely loud enough for Edward and the reverend to hear. She looked down again at the wedding gown that Clara, Peter's mother, had insisted she take when she'd left Cheyenne. Created from the finest Belgian lace over ivory sateen, it fit Anna like it was made for her. However, she knew that it wasn't the latest fashion, and from the looks of Edward's clothing, he would think it was terribly quaint indeed. Anna smoothed her hands over the bodice. It was a dear gift, and it was simply amazing Clara had parted with it at all. A true testament to the depth of their relationship.

"Very well. Let's continue on then," the reverend said.

Anna nodded. How she wished Clara was with her now! Clara, who was like a mother to her, had tried to dissuade her from leaving Cheyenne. But Anna felt stifled in her sister Catharine's farmhouse, and she wanted her own home and family and a chance for adventure. After all, Greta and Catharine both were mail-order brides and quite happy with their new lives. Why couldn't she find the same thing? Leaving Holland had been hard enough, but the experience had given her courage to spread her wings.

Edward watched as his new bride tilted her chin up to meet his kiss after their vows were spoken. He supposed he was nervous as any typical bridegroom. He hesitated briefly. Yesterday, when she'd stepped off the train, he'd been completely taken by this beautiful Dutch woman — slender, graceful without effort, with the most unfathomable blue eyes he'd ever seen. How in the world had he gotten so lucky! He could hardly wait to get her home.

As he leaned down to meet her lips, a spark shot through his bones and threatened to completely undo him. Her full lips were luxuriously warm, sweet, and so deliciously soft that he had to stifle a groan that threatened to slip out. Quickly he took hold of his senses and pulled away, but Anna reached for his hands. Hers felt small in his larger ones, and while he stood smiling at her shyly, he suddenly felt he needed fresh air. It was terribly stuffy in the old church.

The reverend caught his eye and then gave them both a gentle nudge, so Edward turned Anna toward the aisle. They walked past the handful of friends he'd invited, their warm wishes following them down the aisle out into the sparkling fall afternoon. He now had a wife, a helpmeet, a true partner. Life was proceeding according to plan!

Edward was determined he would be a better husband than his father had been to his mother. The shame he felt was one of the reasons he'd decided to seek a mail-order bride, someone who didn't know a thing about his family history — all the drunken brawls, his father's disappearances for long periods of time, and Edward having to work after school at a young age because their pantry was empty. He sighed. Beyond that, he hoped a wife would be a big help with keeping the home tidy, giving him more time to design his timepieces.

Today he would think on his bright future with his lovely bride. He did wonder, however, what other surprises were in store with Anna in his life. When he'd picked her up from the hotel to drive her to the church, she'd been more than fifteen minutes late to receive him. Her face was flushed, and her wedding dress was apparently borrowed. It looked old and a tad yellowed, and while it had a certain prettiness, it was definitely too snug for her womanly curves. He didn't want others staring at her shapely form, but he held his tongue.

From her letters, he knew that she had a good upbringing and her family had once been well-to-do. Perhaps after they got to know each other better, he could guide her in American customs and perhaps influence her manners concerning tardiness and her slightly rumpled look. All in due time, he thought. He just hoped she wouldn't get homesick. He didn't want a baby on his hands, and she looked so young and innocent. It must have been her luminous blue eyes. She'd wound her blonde hair into intricate braids about her head in an artful fashion of which he'd never seen the like. He wondered if her hair was long and hung to her waist. He'd soon find out. He swallowed hard.

The pungent smell of fir and pine — a purely pristine Colorado scent that Anna was now familiar with — refreshed the outdoors. Its bracing effect only added to the anticipation coursing through her. From

14

the time they left the church until they arrived at his sister Ella's house for the reception, Anna felt Edward's eyes on her. The reception was a small gathering, but Anna could tell that Edward was trying to make her feel at home.

"I hope our reception meets with your approval, Anna," Edward said. His eyes held hers briefly. "I had a little help from Ella in the planning."

"Then I'm impressed, Edward. Thank you for making this day special." Anna smiled at him.

"Come on, you two. It's time to cut the wedding cake," Ella ordered. She nudged them in the direction of the table, then handed Anna a knife.

Anna laughed. Slicing cake evenly was not her expertise, but with Edward's hand over hers, she managed to cut the first big slice of white cake. "Open wide," Anna teased as she allowed Edward the first taste of cake.

His eyes lingered on hers. "Your turn now," he said, gently bringing the cake to her lips.

Her sister Greta had told her the symbolism of sharing the first piece of wedding cake — it promised a special bond between the bride and groom. In her heart, Anna prayed it would be so.

The guests clapped, then waited for Anna to slice the cake before Edward handed the slices around.

He'd planned both the ceremony and reception with the aid of his sister. Not at all what she'd expected from her groom. Anna nibbled on her wedding cake and looked at the perfect table setting. Delicate pink roses adorned the center of the oval table, and a crisp white linen tablecloth was set with gleaming crystal dessert plates and silver utensils.

"Ella, everything is just beautiful. Thank you for doing all of this," Anna said.

Ella smiled, then confided, "Oh, goodness! Edward did most of the shopping and the work. I just offered my home. Most of this was his doing, not mine. He's a thoughtful person and kept telling me he wanted everything to be perfect for you."

Anna's heart squeezed. He'd been thinking of her? How sweet. "Well, just the same, I appreciate your helping Edward."

"It was no trouble at all, Anna," Ella said with a wave of her hand. "I pray you will come to enjoy living in Denver. It's an exciting town. If there's anything you need at all, remember, I'm only a couple of blocks away. *If* my brother can bear to part with you!" Her lighthearted laughter followed her tease.

"I'm sure I'm going to like Denver. I think living in the city will be more exciting than the stillness of the Wyoming prairie. I rather enjoyed the hustle and bustle of city life, even when we went to Cheyenne to shop. It's so invigorating."

"Then I think we shall become good friends." Ella grinned.

Anna touched Ella's arm. "I would very much enjoy your friendship," she answered. Ella was friendly and reminded Anna of her sister Greta, and Anna immediately felt at ease.

Edward came and stood next to them. His hand firmly cupping her elbow, he gently guided Anna toward a small group who chatted away. "Anna, I'd like to introduce you to a few of my friends. This is Harvey Thompson."

Anna looked up to an affable older fellow with a beard and a sagging jawline. He greeted her warmly. "I'm so happy to meet you," he said.

Edward paused for their handshake. "And this wonderful lady is a librarian. Mrs. Pearl Brooks."

Pearl stood about an inch shorter than Anna, her ample figure squeezed into a teal day dress almost the same shade as her eyes.

"Congratulations on your marriage to Edward. We've been matchmaking for years to no avail." She smiled through tight lips.

"*Dank U wel* — thank you," Anna murmured under the scrutiny of Pearl's narrowed gaze.

"Oh, you have a strong accent!" a woman with honey-colored hair said, extending her gloved hand rather stiffly. "I'm Callie Holmes, and I'm delighted to meet you." She turned to the gentlemen standing next to her. "And this is Daniel Moore and Christopher Maxwell."

Anna nodded and extended her hand to each of the men. Daniel was tall and good-looking and looked as though he could crush a bear if need be, despite his fancy church clothes. He shook her hand with a firm grip.

Christopher bowed slightly and tweaked his impeccable mustache between his forefinger and thumb, his eyes sweeping over her in appraisal. "You may call me Chris, Anna. If Edward gives you the slightest problem, let me know." He winked at Edward. "His ways can be . . . a little disconcerting."

While she considered a response, Edward took her hand and gave it a squeeze. "I hardly think that we'll have any problems, but thanks for your consideration." Edward shot Chris a look, and Anna wasn't sure if he was teasing or not. "We'd better see to our other guests before we leave. Come with me, Anna."

"It was nice to meet all of you, and thank you for attending our ceremony," Anna said. As her husband led her away, she found herself curious about his friends. Would she and Edward be entertaining a lot? Oh, how she wished she'd paid more attention to Catharine's cooking lessons!

Edward drove the carriage through a stylish neighborhood of Victorian houses not far from Ella's as neighbors and passersby waved to the newlyweds. They could've walked the two short blocks, Anna thought. Edward stopped the horse in front of a wrought-iron fence separating the yard from the street. Little had been said between them on the drive, and Anna took that to mean he was as nervous as she. She watched him out of the corner of her eye as he set the brake, hopped down, and hurried to her side of the carriage.

"Here we are! I'll put the carriage away after I show you where we'll live," he said, smiling up at her. "My jewelry shop is attached to the front side of the house, which makes it very convenient for my work, as well as visible from the street. The house was left to me by my parents after they died, and I added my shop after that."

Anna glanced at the large white painted house and admired the delicate gingerbread fretwork adorning its broad porch. Green plants and potted mums were scattered about, complementing the rockers and a porch swing. The only thing missing from the picturesque setting was a plump dog. *Hmm . . . wait until he finds out about Baby later.*

Smoothing her gown, she rose from her seat in the carriage and stared down at his broad shoulders and capable, strong hands. He reached up for her hand, taking care to keep her gown from getting tangled in the carriage step, and then guided her down to the sidewalk. She was no more than a couple of inches from him, and she could smell his aftershave. She allowed her eyes to travel from his broad shoulders to his chest and then to his narrow waist. He was lean and very masculine — surprising, she thought, for one who worked mostly indoors.

Thoughts of their wedding night sent a rush of heat to her face, and she hoped he hadn't noticed. Edward's steel-gray eyes locked onto hers briefly, but he quickly grabbed her about the waist, scooped her up in his arms, and then kicked back the gate, banging it hard against the fence. Was he going to be gentle with her? Or was this pent-up passion that he'd held back for years? A shiver coursed its way down her spine. Could she meet his need? She knew very little about what a wife was supposed to do.

2

Edward hugged Anna tightly to his chest, and though the fabric of his suit and her wedding gown separated them, the contact from this mere slip of a young woman ignited a flash of fire that coursed through his arms straight to his heart. He drew in a deep breath, savoring the lavender scent of her hair, and noticed that her bottom lip trembled, her hands holding the now-wilted bouquet of yellow mums shook, and her blue eyes were wide. *She's scared! Of all that's holy, I will never harm her or treat her harshly.*

In that moment, Edward decided to set her fears to rest. He swung open the door, but before he set her down, he leaned down and lightly pressed his lips to her quivering ones and said, "Welcome home, my lovely bride."

He marveled at her pale skin with its delicate flush of pink, then watched as she turned to survey what was to be her new home. From behind her, he noticed the many buttons that traveled down the bodice and skirt of her wedding gown. How had she ever gotten into it? Would she be asking for his assistance when she changed? Her slender neck tilted back to gaze up the cherry staircase leading to the second floor, then her eyes swept across the living room and hallway. He was proud of his home. A few of the finer pieces of his furniture he'd acquired from his friend Daniel, whose craftsmanship exceeded anyone's in Colorado. Everything was in place for her arrival, down to fresh flowers on the piano.

"Are you pleased?" he asked.

"*Ja!* You have a beautiful home, Edward." She walked toward the deep burgundy settee placed beneath the front windows, which were ensconced in the same heavy material that blocked out the sunlight. "I'm almost afraid to touch anything, it's so . . . so immaculate," she said, running her fingers through the fringe of a tapestry pillow. "Do you think you could show me to our room? I'd like to change out of my gown." She gave him a frank gaze with those enormous blue eyes.

"It can wait a moment or two. There's something I want to give you," he said, removing his suit coat and draping it neatly across the back of a chair.

Anna's heart began to thump against her tight corset. "I can't wait. What is it?" *Oh, he is so romantic. I love surprises.*

He gestured for her to have a seat in the chair. "I'll be back in a minute." He walked quickly down the hallway to his adjoining shop. She listened until his footfalls became distant. Perhaps he'd made a special piece of jewelry for her as a wedding gift. She twisted the gold band on her left finger. Simplicity was just fine with her. Now, with her sister Greta . . . well, that would be a different story, she thought with a smile. Anna leaned back against the chair and waited for her surprise, enjoying the light scent of beeswax and lemon that hung in the air from a recent cleaning.

He hurried back with a brown envelope and took a seat opposite her. *Just like a man not to take time to wrap his gift,* she thought, nearly giggling. She sat with her hands in her lap and waited patiently, though she wanted to snatch the envelope from his hands. Patience was not a particular virtue of hers. She flashed him her sweetest smile, and his lips lifted at the corners, finally showing his nice, even teeth, though his steel-gray eyes looked concerned. He was probably afraid that she wouldn't like his wedding gift, but she had few wants when it came to material things. It was the fact that he thought of something for her that tickled her.

Edward gave a nervous cough before he opened the envelope now balancing across his knees.

"Well, what is it, Edward?"

"First, I want you to know that I'd like our marriage to start off in the best possible way. We've only exchanged a few letters, and there will be much for both of us to learn. So I've devised a system that will outline exactly what's to be expected of each of us." He slipped out a sheet of paper and handed it to her, then kept a second one for himself.

Anna stared down at a list neatly typed on the paper. As the heat rose up her neck, she wasn't sure if she should laugh or cry. She felt foolish for thinking he'd had some special gift for her. The list read:

Your Wifely Duties

You will serve breakfast at 7:00 a.m. sharp.
We will have lunch at 1:00 p.m. when I break from my work.

Supper will be at 7:00 p.m.

Monday — Do the marketing and plan the meals.

Tuesday — Do the wash. If there is free time in the afternoon, you may rest before supper.

Wednesday — Dust and clean the floors and make sure the rugs are beaten.

Thursday — Do household expenses and other correspondence.

Friday — Do mending or ironing. This is when I have my literary society meeting, so you will have those evenings free.

Saturday — Go shopping, take free time for yourself, or volunteer at church.

Sunday — Attend church at 11:00 and have lunch with Ella.

You'll need to keep the lamps clean and windows washed and weed the garden.

In cold weather, keep the fire going in the hearth and gather the ashes.

Fresh flowers, when available from the garden, should be placed throughout the house.

The consummation of our marriage will take place after ten days to give you time to adjust.

Anna waved the piece of paper in the air. "Ack! You must be joking, Edward! This is an impossible list! I could *never* accomplish all of this on my own!" Her wedding gown was becoming sticky, and her corset was threatening to cut off her air supply. This was not what she thought being a bride was all about. Not at all. "What do you mean about . . . consummation after ten days?" Anna felt her chest expand and did her best to control her indignation. He'd made all the decisions down to the last detail, and they'd only been married a few hours! She started to rise, but he pressed her gently back down into her chair.

"Anna, please calm down." He reached a hand out to touch hers, then quickly withdrew it. "I have my own list here, if you would like to see it. And I can help you when time allows." He shifted in his seat. "I know you'll need time to adjust to me and to being away from your family, as well as to get to know me better. I don't want you to feel pressured."

Confused, Anna stared down at the sheet of paper. "I see." She didn't want to convey disappointment or sound too eager for them to consummate their marriage vows, or he'd think she was a bit loose. "I don't want to see your list. As for mine . . ." She sighed with resignation. "I can try, but I'm afraid my skills will be sorely lacking."

He shifted in his seat, then stuffed his sheet back into the brown envelope and leaned forward with a serious gaze, his hands on his knees. "Can you cook, Anna?"

She suddenly noticed how his dark hair curled into his collar and tried to rein in her thoughts. His frank question was only fair. She *had* answered his ad for a mail-order bride. One would easily assume she was ready to take on the duties of a wife.

She chewed the inside of her lip. "Only a little. My sister Catharine did most of the cooking on the farm."

He laughed. "Well, at least we won't starve. I'll take you upstairs and show you our bedroom, and you can change. I hope the light supper Ella left for us will be adequate for tonight." He reached for her hand and pulled her in the direction of the gleaming staircase.

Anna stood in the center of the bedroom. Edward had left quickly — too quickly — giving her time to freshen up. Their room was decorated nicely with choice pieces of cherry furniture — a sleigh bed and a finely carved armoire. Pink roses with lighter shades of red patterned the drapes that adorned the large window facing the main street. Directly beneath the window, a luxurious rose velvet chaise looked enticing after her long day. The room had such a pleasing and relaxing effect that she decided she wouldn't change one thing about it. Edward had very good taste and had even seen to a dressing table for her. And earlier he'd retrieved her luggage from the hotel while she was dressing for the ceremony.

He *was* very thoughtful, if a bit particular, so she tried to put the list out of her mind for the moment. She did not want to ruin her wedding night or show her disappointment with the surprise list of chores.

Anna selected a dress from the trunk and began the task of unbuttoning the lacy sleeves of Clara's wedding gown. She twisted to reach behind her back, her fingers feeling their way to unhook the buttons, but she instantly knew her attempts were futile. The best she could do was release the pearls from their loops at the top and bottom of the dress, but not the ones at the center. Struggling somewhat, she was able to remove her petticoats and toss them aside, leaving only the thin chemise beneath the silky gown.

Turning her back to the cheval mirror, she craned her neck around to see if she could locate the buttons but couldn't quite manage the task. So instead, she gathered the heavy dress up to her waist, intending to slide it around to the front of her body, but it was more than she could handle and way too tight. In her frustration between the tugging and yanking, her fashionable high heels became tangled in the volumes of material, and she lost her balance and fell sideways against the mirror. It crashed against the porcelain lamp on the dressing table next to it. In spite of her best efforts to save the beautiful lamp, it shattered on the hardwood floor, sending pieces of glass flying across the room, and she landed hard on her back.

A thundering crash from above sent Edward clambering up the stairs two at a time to find Anna with her wedding gown billowed up about her neck like a mushroom. She was lying on her backside, fully exposing her cream-colored heels, silk stockings, and pantaloons. The neck of her dress had slipped off her shoulders, exposing her collarbone. Silky blonde hair, uncoiled from one braid, hung limply against her throat. Struggling up on her elbows, she lifted her head and giggled, but he didn't see anything amusing once he saw his grandmother's broken lamp and a large scratch on the dressing table, made by the mirror's fall.

Edward wasn't sure which to do first — move the mirror or help Anna to her feet. She was a funny sight to behold, and he felt his lips twitch in amusement. He'd never been so close to feminine underwear or ladies' legs and was a little uncomfortable, but at the same time, he couldn't help staring. The outline of her slender form beneath the stockings gave him pause, but he quickly knelt on one knee to assist her amid all the silken fabric. "What in the world . . . ?"

"I couldn't unbutton the center of my dress, and the heel of my shoe caught in my skirts. I'm sorry I made a mess of things."

She took his hand, and with one solid move he brought her to her feet, forcing her to topple directly into his chest. A fit of laughter bubbled from her throat as she steadied herself against him. Edward's hand reached out for her delicate skin where the gown had slipped. She laughed again, and he joined her. *Playful little thing, isn't she?* He suddenly had a premonition of things to come, and he felt like he was losing control. How could a woman with simmering blue eyes and curves cause him to forget who he was?

"Why don't you turn around and let me finish with your gown?" he said after a moment. Slowly she twisted her back to him, and he sucked in his breath. Her white shoulder blades jutted out from her back as his fingers grazed her velvety skin, working to free the buttons from the frogs. As he reached the last button, the front of the gown fell forward. Desire flashed in him, and it was natural to draw her against his pounding chest until the back of her head nestled beneath his chin. He breathed deeply of the smell of her hair and skin, then encircled her with his arms, feeling the flimsy material of her chemise and her warm body beneath.

Anna trembled with a soft sigh, then shifted slightly. Edward stifled the urge to keep holding her and dropped his arms. The next ten days were going to be very long. In two strides he was out the door as if the devil himself were after him.

3

Now where had she put the list? Frantically, Anna, still clad in her robe, dug through the bureau drawer, then looked in the closet, but it was nowhere to be found. Worse yet, she'd overslept because she'd stared at the ceiling half the night listening to the even breathing of her husband lying inches from her. Edward must be downstairs. She'd already been in bed last night when he slipped beneath the sheets in his long handles, but she hoped he might pull her to him despite his "adjustment period" of ten days. She'd enjoyed the feel of his strong arms about her waist for those brief few moments last night when he'd assisted her with her gown.

This searching was useless! Catharine always said she wouldn't be able to find her head if it wasn't already attached. Perhaps she'd left the list on the settee last night. Best to hurry down to the kitchen and see if she couldn't get breakfast started. She could dress later.

Unfortunately, when she swung open the door to the kitchen, the look on Edward's face told her everything she needed to know. A folded newspaper in one hand and an empty coffee cup in the other, he stood staring at her, his eyes flicking over her entire body from top to bottom. Would it always be this way?

"Edward, I'm sorry I over —"

"Well, well, well, good morning. I see you finally finished your beauty rest. I didn't want to wake you. Breakfast *was* at seven, but I've kept some sausage and eggs warm for you on the back of the stove." He moved to the stove and laid his cup on the counter next to it.

Anna felt terrible. "I am sorry, Edward." She accepted the plate he offered and sat down at the table. "I guess I was more tired than I thought."

He set a cup of coffee in front of her, then took a seat across from her. "You'll do better tomorrow, I'm sure," he said with a droll smile.

"I seem to have misplaced the list you gave me. I forgot when you said you wanted breakfast."

The smile became a small scowl. "That

34

can be easily remedied. I'll just type it over again. Not to worry."

Anna breathed deeply. Was a list really necessary between husband and wife? The scrambled eggs felt thick in her throat, but she forced herself to swallow them. She sipped the hot coffee to wash them down and found his eyes on her when she glanced up. She knew she looked frightful — her hair not braided but loose about her shoulders, circles under her eyes — and she pulled the robe tighter. He, on the other hand, was already dressed for his workday in tan wool trousers, suspenders, white shirt, and bowtie. Was he ever rumpled? She doubted it.

"Well," he said, rising from the table, "I should be getting to the shop —" He was interrupted by the door chime. "It's mighty early for visitors. Are you expecting someone?"

"No, not someone, but . . . er . . . maybe something," she muttered under her breath as he strode quickly into the hallway to answer the door. She heard voices, and then Edward's voice grew louder with agitation. Anna pushed back her chair, knowing exactly what the cause of all the commotion was. But no sooner had she done so than Edward thundered through the doorway, followed by a young lad from the rail depot carrying a wooden crate. Anna wiped her damp palms on her robe and then folded her arms across her chest for the battle she knew was coming.

"Anna! What is the meaning of this? This lad said he was to deliver a dog to you." Edward's jaw clenched, and he smashed the newspaper between his hands. "I believe an explanation would be prudent right now."

The yellow-haired, gangly young man grinned and set down the crate. "Yes, sir, this was shipped all the way from Cheyenne. Never been there before, but I plan on it someday. You from Cheyenne?" he asked Anna. "Maybe you can tell me all about it. Is there really a Cheyenne Social Club?" He rattled on as the dog began whining to be let out of the crate.

Anna licked her lips nervously and smiled at the young man while Edward tried to catch her eye. "Yes, the club does exist, but I'm hardly the one to ask about it," she answered as she made her way over to the crate. Baby, her dog, started yapping as soon as she was near. "Shh . . . Baby, it's Anna." She bent down near the crate to re-assure Baby in a soft voice.

"This here is the freight charge. If you'll just sign here that you received the dog and pay the bill . . ." The young man pushed his cap back on his head and rocked back and forth on his heels, his hands in his pockets, while Edward looked over the freight charges.

"Edward, this is my dog, Baby. I had my sister send her to me. I've had her ever since she was a few weeks old." Anna turned to the lad. "Do you think you could pry the crate open for me?"

"Be glad to, ma'am." He fumbled deep into his pocket for a screwdriver, then worked on the nails that held the crate together. By now, Baby was scratching at the wood slats and barking so loudly that it was hard to hear anything Edward was trying to say.

"Why, I never!" Edward sputtered, causing the lad to take a step backward. "I don't know where you intend to keep that dog, but it won't be in this house!"

The nails were off and Baby bounded into Anna's arms, licking her face and hands. She stood, struggling to hold the dog, and lifted her chin defiantly to her new husband. "Baby has to stay with me. I can't turn her out."

"Humph! The dog smells. Why would you think I'd ever consider allowing a smelly creature inside *my* home?"

"Because I'm your *wife* and we are to share this house." Anna could feel tears sting her eyes. Why was he so against having a pet?

"Excuse me . . ." The lad shifted in his scruffy boots, looking uncomfortable. "I need to get on back to the depot. If you'll just pay for the charges, I'll be on my way."

"I'll be glad to pay you for the freight charges, Edward," Anna said.

Edward stood stiffly, considering what she'd just said. Of course it was to be her home too. Didn't he agree to that when he took a wife? But then, he'd never considered Anna wouldn't want to live exactly as he did. He fished in his pocket, took out some bills, and handed the money to the lad, who made a quick exit, slamming the front door on his way out. When Edward turned back around, the dog she called Baby jumped from Anna's arms and hopped around, then stood on her hind legs against Edward's pant leg, her tongue wagging and her friendly dark brown eyes shining. He didn't know exactly what to do as the little dog danced on her hind legs.

"The freight charge is not the point." His jaw muscle twitching, he gave her a firm look of reproach.

"She likes you, Edward." Anna stood with her hands fingering the ties of her robe.

"I surely don't know why." He tried to take a step back, but the dog just followed with a happy bark.

"Didn't you ever want a pet when you were growing up?" She gave him an odd look, and Edward's heart squeezed.

There had been a time as a seven-year-old boy when he'd come running home from school after finding an injured stray kitten. He begged his father to let him doctor the kitten and keep him. Even now, he remembered how his father had snapped that a *real* man didn't like cats. The answer was emphatically no. His mother tried to persuade his father to change his mind, but he wouldn't hear of it. Too much cat hair flying about the house wasn't good for one's health, his father explained. Edward never asked again, but he used to secretly long for a dog or cat to play with.

"Dogs can tell if you mean them harm. She must not sense that with you. I think she just wants to sniff your hand. Why don't you just give her a pat on the head? I think she'd like that," Anna suggested, laughing.

Edward bent down and gave the dog a pat on the head, and Baby licked his hand. He quickly withdrew it. Baby sniffed his shoes, then began exploring the kitchen, poking her nose at the half-opened pantry door.

"See! She likes you, Edward."

He looked at his bride. After her romp with her enthusiastic dog, her hair was disheveled, the belt of her robe was undone, and her pretty linen nightgown was peeking from beneath the robe. Her eyes were large and unsure, her lips a moist pout. But heavens above, she couldn't have looked any prettier!

He sighed heavily. "Maybe so, but what are we going to do with a dog?" If he continued looking into those luminous eyes for another moment, he'd move heaven and earth to purchase the moon for her.

He stifled a groan. He must get back to work. A good hour or more had slipped by already, and he had promised Mr. Hadley that he could stop by and pick up his watch this morning. A clasp on Mrs. Kinkle's strand of pearls needed repair, and he must service the bank's vault. The list went on and on. In hindsight, he wished he'd taken a few days off to get to know Anna. Why hadn't he thought of that?

"Edward, are you all right?" Anna's brows knitted together in question.

He focused, suddenly remembering his immediate problem. "Yes, I'm fine. But I must get to work now," he answered, glancing around for the dog. "Please find your dog and confine her to the kitchen until we can discuss the matter further." He turned and stalked down the hallway to the adjoining shop, calling over his shoulder, "If you need anything at all before lunch, please just come and get me."

Edward unlocked the shop door, leaving it open a little in case Anna walked over later. He supposed he should show her the shop, but there'd be time for that later. He felt guilty leaving her so suddenly — but then he'd not allotted time for that little surprise with the dog. Normally he felt comforted when he entered his store, greeted by the ticking of all the different clocks from grandfather clocks to mantel clocks, but today his thoughts were all a jumble.

He switched on the light at his work counter. Although sunlight flooded the shop, he needed a special concentrated light to work on the delicate movements of the different timepieces. He began to polish the pocket watch he'd repaired for Mr. Hadley, but the vision of Anna's impish face continually interrupted his thoughts.

4

Anna hurried through the dishes and gave Baby some table scraps. She took the dog out to the backyard to do her business and then left her in the kitchen. After hurrying back upstairs, she dressed quickly, donned her coat, and grabbed her straw hat, determined to explore the city of Denver while Edward worked. It proved to be a glorious day, the crisp air chilling her bones, so she quickened her step down the sidewalk past neighbors' homes until she reached Larimer Street bustling with horse-drawn carriages, wagons, carts, and pedestrians. *Alstublieft!* she thought. *So many people!* Cheyenne would be considered quaint in comparison.

The clanging of a streetcar's bell sounded across the street. Should she just take a ride? It would be easier to see downtown in a shorter time frame. Then she could return home and get settled in. The black-and-green car lumbered to a stop, and Anna stepped up the metal stairs to place a coin into the fare box.

The conductor nodded, his crinkling eyes visible just below his black conductor cap, and Anna smiled back and moved into the aisle. A few businessmen looked with interest at her, and one lowered his morning paper to smile at her, but she avoided their gazes and took the first empty seat available. The streetcar lurched forward. Gazing out the window at the different shops and spacious stone buildings, she sat back against the leather seat to watch the busy view.

The streetcar stopped at every corner as people got off or came aboard. This was going to be her town now, so she tried to familiarize herself with its street names as she passed — Speer Boulevard, Lincoln, Logan, Blake, and Wynkoop and 17th, where she had arrived by train at the enormous Union Station just two days before.

Once again the mountain panorama was spectacular with snow-tipped peaks. She shuddered. It must be icy cold living up in the mountains. She thought fondly of her sister Greta, barely wed, and wondered what kind of weather was in store for her. She hoped they would occasionally be able to have short visits. She really liked Greta's husband, Jess, and knew he would take good care of her, if not rein her in a bit.

An older lady took a seat next to her and adjusted the folds of her dress and cape. "Quite a morning chill today," she said cheerfully.

"*Ja,* it is. Would you know if there is a park nearby?"

The lady seemed affable enough and gave her a broad smile. "You're a newcomer to the Mile High City, aren't you?" The lady crossed her arms and turned in her seat to look at Anna directly.

Anna nodded. "I've been enjoying the ride through the city to get the feel of the town."

The older lady clucked her tongue. "Well, good for you! To answer your question, yes, there is City Park — not the oldest, but very large. It was designed after New York Central Park. A pavilion and lake are already under construction. You'll need to get off at the corner of York and Colorado Boulevard — we're nearly there now. You'd better enjoy the park before the snow flies. 'Course, I've seen it snow one day and melt the next. That's the beauty of living here."

"*Dank U wel.* I'll remember that."

They chatted pleasantly until the lady told her the next stop was where Anna needed to get off.

"Bless you. It has been so nice chatting with you," Anna said as she stepped down, waving goodbye. If everyone was as friendly as that nice lady, then she would enjoy living here.

Bright sun warmed the morning to a comfortable temperature, allowing Anna to unbutton her coat as she walked to the park. It was easy to spot the park, with mothers pushing their babies' prams, couples strolling the winding pathways, and small children chasing a ball. Scattered about were benches in the sprawling grassy meadows. A posted sign said pets were not allowed in the park.

From where she stood, Anna had the perfect view in any direction of the Rocky Mountains. Many trees had been planted, some old enough to lend plenty of shade in the hot summer months. Now they created an impressive splash of gold, orange, and red against deciduous firs. Leaves drifted slowly to the ground, and she enjoyed the crackling sound when she walked on them. Anna could already envision herself painting the autumn scene on canvas.

After strolling down the winding path along the perimeter of the park, she finally took a seat on a bench. She hadn't realized how far she'd walked and soon shed her coat, placing it on the bench next to her. She watched as a squirrel dug furiously beneath the fallen leaves, hiding his food for winter.

Leaning back and closing her eyes, she was mindful of nature's song all around — the birds tweeting, the wind rustling the leaves, the distant sound of children's voices. Whether from the long walk or the sleepless night, she felt drowsy and fell asleep from the sun's warmth caressing her face.

A nudge against her shoulder startled her, and she jerked awake.

"I'm sorry, Anna. I thought it was you and I didn't want to disturb you, but I felt like I must. We met yesterday. I'm Callie, a friend of Edward's," Callie said softly, peeking out from her frilly umbrella. Her blonde curls were pulled up into ringlets, and fringed bangs framed her pretty oval face. Her dress was cream silk with accents of peacock-blue along the bodice and shoulders, gathered with fullness with a tuck of blue bows at a point. The back of the dress was slightly bustled. Suddenly Anna felt awkward and plain in comparison, with her Dutch braids and plain Woolsey dress. *Perhaps I should take more time with my appearance. Then I might look as lovely as Callie.*

Anna blinked at her new friend. "Hello. I must've fallen asleep."

Callie took a seat next to her. "You must've been very tired. You were only married yesterday! I must confess I'm surprised to see you at all today." Callie had a worried look shadowing her face, and Anna blushed.

"Edward is working, and I thought I'd take a look around . . . kind of get my bearings," she answered. Anna was not about to tell Callie about last night or the list since she hardly knew her, but something about Callie's sweet countenance made Anna think she could be a trusted friend once she got to know her. "What are you doing out this morning?"

Callie put aside her umbrella. "Well, I like going for an outing or a drive for fresh air. Most of the time, I get out of the carriage and walk for the pure enjoyment of it." She paused. "But it's hardly morning now. It's already one o'clock. Would you care to ride back home with me for some tea and sandwiches? I haven't eaten yet."

"*Ack!* It's that late already?" Anna quickly hopped up and reached for her coat. "Oh no. I must catch the streetcar and get back home. Edward will be waiting."

Callie rose as well. "Oh? Then why don't

you let me take you home. I'll tell my driver."

"You have a carriage here?"

"Yes. That's my carriage parked by the roses over there. I don't mind at all, and you won't have to take the long way home. It's no trouble at all." Callie motioned for Anna to follow, and after a few seconds' hesitation, Anna fell into step with her, grateful for the ride home and wondering how in the world she could've allowed herself to fall asleep. She blamed it on the warm sun.

The grandfather clock chimed one o'clock. The morning had flown by. It was time for lunch now, and Edward's back was aching from leaning over Mrs. Kinkle's string of pearls. At least Mr. Hadley's watch was ready when he dropped by first thing to pick it up. Edward was sort of expecting Anna to at least be interested enough that she would pop in, and he was disappointed when she didn't. He smiled. She was probably just preparing lunch now. He shoved his chair back and left his suit jacket behind, considering whether he should roll his shirtsleeves back down, but it was warm in the shop today, so he didn't.

He whistled as he walked down the hallway, more to alert Anna that he was coming than anything else, but the house was quiet. Pushing the kitchen door open, he glanced around and things were just as he'd left them this morning. There was no sign of food for lunch or of Anna. To make matters worse, the dog, yapping, danced around from her place by the pantry door, which unfortunately had been left ajar. Baby had pulled out a sack of flour and the white powder was all over the place. When he walked over to see the damage, he stepped in a puddle on the floor. Edward clenched his fists at his side, then looked at Baby.

"Shut up!"

Baby cocked her head at him, whimpered, and lay down in front of him with her front paws crossed and her head down.

This was not going to work. He knew this dog was going to be trouble. That's why he liked horses — you could keep them in the barn!

"Anna!" he called as he took the stairs two at a time, but she didn't answer. He checked their bedroom just in case. *Where could she have gone?* Edward had intended on a quick lunch, then a trip to the bank. He paused, scratching his chin. Should he be worried? She knew nothing about the streets of Denver. He decided he'd give a little time

49

for her to return before he started to look for her. Maybe she'd taken a short walk, but if so, he wished she'd at least informed him first.

He headed back down to the kitchen to clean up the flour and make a sandwich, and by the time he started working on making his lunch, he heard the sound of a horse and buggy beside his front gate. He looked out the kitchen window but could only see the back of a carriage. He frowned. It must be Mrs. Kinkle, and she was hours early. With a groan, he stopped slicing meat and set his knife aside.

5

Anna called out to Edward as she entered the house, Callie following close behind. She wasn't sure what frame of mind she would find him in. Would he be furious with her?

"I'm here," Edward answered as he wiped his hands on the kitchen towel. Moving toward them, he smiled brightly at Callie. "Oh, hello, Callie. I didn't know you two were out together."

"Hello, Edward. We weren't, but I thought Anna could use a lift home." She gave him a warm smile.

Anna felt her face burn. "I was out doing a bit of exploring. I'm sorry I'm late. I lost track of time." Her excuse was flimsy at best, especially for a new bride whose husband decided what her every move would entail.

Edward turned back to Callie. "Thank you for bringing Anna home. What do you think of the book we're reading now? Or maybe I shouldn't ask until we have our next literary meeting."

Callie's laughter was gentle and ladylike when she answered him. "Edward, I must confess, I'm rather enjoying it . . ."

Their voices faded into the background while they chatted and exchanged ideas about books, and Anna withdrew into herself. She couldn't help but notice how Edward's demeanor was relaxed and happy as he talked with Callie, whose brilliant smile reflected her good nature. Anna again compared her plain Woolsey dress to the stylish outfit Callie wore and indeed felt like a servant instead of a wife.

Edward turned to Anna, his lips pursed in a thin line. "Perhaps you could fix our guest some tea?"

She shook off her silly thoughts of comparison to interrupt them. "Yes, I will make us some tea," she murmured. But she wasn't sure Callie even heard her, and only a nod came from Edward. She turned to leave, but Callie paused, staying her on the arm.

"Please, no tea for me. I must be going. But another time, perhaps? I'll leave you newlyweds for now. I'm sure you have much better things to do than entertain me — but

I will insist you come to dinner some night in the near future." She raised an eyebrow in Edward's direction, waiting for an answer.

"We'd be delighted. Let me show you to the door, Callie. Thanks again for bringing my wayward wife home safe and sound," he said. He walked her to the door and out into the street where her driver waited. With a brief wave, the driver set off down the avenue.

Land of Goshen, he acts like I've been wandering for days, Anna thought. Then she realized she'd probably resembled a wanderer today. She went into the kitchen to set the teakettle to boil and finished slicing the roast Edward had set out for sandwiches. At least she knew how to make a simple lunch. Anna had seen the disapproving look in his eyes and chided herself for falling asleep in the park. She whacked away at the meat until it no longer resembled sliced roast beef.

"Ahem." Edward cleared his throat when he entered the kitchen, then strode over to take the knife from her hand. "Better let me take over before you slice off a finger."

Anna moved aside, crossing her arms. "How long have you known Callie?"

Edward paused in placing the meat on bread and glanced up at her. "Since we were

53

children. Why do you ask?"

Anna's heart thumped against her rib cage. "No reason, really. Callie seems the perfect lady. She was very nice, bringing me all the way back home."

"Yes, Callie is a true lady. She always seems quite . . . organized in her behavior. Where were you anyway? You should've told me you were leaving. Besides, you don't know anything about Denver. You were gone so long I tied the dog out in the backyard. I didn't know what else to do with her."

"Thank you for doing that. I'll check on her and give her some table scraps, if you don't mind." He shrugged so she continued, though she knew that wasn't the end of the dog topic. "I decided to take a ride on the streetcar through downtown and wound up at City Park. I guess I fell asleep on the park bench after not sleeping well last night. It was so peaceful and quiet."

"*What?* Fell asleep in City Park? Where *anyone* could've seen you?" he sputtered, his steel-gray eyes widening.

Anna pulled her shoulders back and breathed deeply. "I merely leaned back against the park bench to feel the sun's rays. It was all very appropriate, I assure you."

"I can't believe you'd go that far alone in a city you know nothing about." As she was about to retort, Edward stepped closer and stroked her cheek gently with his finger. "That explains the sunburn on your nose and cheeks." He didn't move away but stood looking down at her. "With your fair skin, you'll have to wear a bonnet. Denver is a mile high in elevation, so you're closer to the sun's rays."

"I — I — didn't realize." She touched her fingers to her face. He leaned so close that she could smell his aftershave. "I have several in my trunk," Anna said, lifting her eyes to meet his. She thought he might kiss her, but instead he hastily moved away.

"Good. Be sure to use them when you're outdoors. Now let's have our lunch, and I'll go type up a new list for you. Maybe it would be best if you put the list in the kitchen where you can always find it. Then everything will be just right." He placed their lunch on the table along with two glasses of water.

Anna cringed. He set such high standards for her that she was sure she could never expect to meet them to his satisfaction. "Edward, I will *never* be perfect. God didn't want us to be perfect, otherwise we wouldn't need Him, would we?"

But Edward kept quiet, his arms folded across his chest.

■ ■ ■ ■

On Friday, Anna was perched on the edge of a chair in Edward's study like a schoolgirl summoned by the headmaster after some terrible indiscretion. That morning she'd dressed in a light woolen gray dress with red trim around the collar, sleeves, and waist that further accentuated her figure. She sat with what she hoped was a prim picture of decorum, hands folded in her lap, while Edward stared at her from across his ornately carved desk. Baby sat perfectly sweet next to her feet.

He moved from behind his desk and, with his hands clasped behind his back, began pacing back and forth. His pacing was almost making her dizzy, until he abruptly stopped and expelled a deep sigh.

"I'm afraid this just isn't going to work with a dog in the house. She chews up anything left lying around but seems to have a penchant for my newspaper. I'm finding dog hair on the couch and on my clothing! Baby will have to go."

Anna lost all thought of trying to be ladylike and leapt to her feet. "But Baby has to stay! She means no harm. I've been trying to correct her, but she is, after all, just a dog."

"If you'd spend more time *inside* the house rather than *outside* with the dog, I believe you could get all your chores done. And who names a dog Baby in the first place?"

Is this the way he's going to conduct our marriage? Controlling my every move, including my dog? Well, it wouldn't work. She was sure of that. There hadn't been a hint of this type of control in their brief correspondence. Only friendliness. What had he been looking for?

"I'm finding your list a bit . . . overwhelming to say the least, Edward. I think we need to talk about that."

"I should think you'd be happy to have things itemized so you don't get bored being a housewife."

Anna nearly howled with laughter. "Edward, I'll hardly have time to be bored. There's so much to see and explore here in Denver. In fact, I was just thinking perhaps we could drive to the park for a picnic tomorrow. It's a perfectly lovely spot. Soon it will be too cold to do so."

She gazed up at him. Only a foot of space separated them. His manly presence so close to her — so close but yet miles apart

— created a flush that spread from her neck down to her chest. Were these feelings normal? She'd never had them before, when she'd been to the fall dances back in Cheyenne, where plenty of available young farmers vied for her attention. But then again, she'd been bored with Cheyenne, bored on the farm. Now she was in an exciting, bustling city — and Edward was a part of her grand adventure.

"Well . . ." He stepped a little closer, his lips twitching as he gazed into her eyes. She thought he was going to reach out to kiss her, but Baby jumped in between them, wagging her tail and sniffing, her toenails making clicking sounds on the hardwood floor as she danced around. Edward bent down and patted Baby on the head to calm her at the same time Anna did. They both rose up at the same time, bumping heads with a resounding *whack!*

Anna touched her hand to her forehead, feeling dull pain shoot above her eyebrow.

Edward took her hands, stepping closer to examine her forehead. His eyes narrowed as he tilted his head down for a better look. "Are you all right? I'm sorry if I hurt you —"

With one quick movement, Anna quickly stood on tiptoes and kissed him soundly on the mouth. His lips were warm and full, like they'd been the day they'd said "I do." She would have pulled back, but a sharp intake of breath from Edward stopped her. He pulled her against his chest and kissed her lips . . . then her forehead . . . then lingered near her throat with light butterfly kisses. She leaned back and closed her eyes, dreamily thinking of warm, sun-kissed days in a lush meadow, until she could no longer breathe.

Abruptly, Edward released her and stepped back, nearly tripping on the dog, who was still underfoot. He awkwardly bent to pat Baby's head again. "Sorry, Baby," he said softly under his breath.

"I thought you didn't like dogs," Anna teased.

"Well, I don't — er, maybe just a little . . ."

She saw an odd shadow cross his face as if some unpleasant memory had surfaced.

"If a dog can bring us this close together . . . then maybe I should consider allowing her to stay," Edward said.

She could feel the warmth of his breath against her skin when he spoke, his lids heavy with desire, and he gave her a shy smile. She liked the twinkle she saw in his eyes and knew he'd felt something magical too.

Anna looked at Baby. The dog lifted her head and cocked it sideways as if she knew they were conversing about her. "I rescued her from drowning in Cheyenne. I'll try to brush her more often, and I'll try to teach her not to chew on your things, Edward."

"Well, that's a start." He moved away from her slowly. "Remember, I have my literary society meeting tonight. I'll try to figure out how to make a nice place for the dog off the kitchen hallway, but *not* in our bedroom. Understand?" He yanked his overcoat off the cloak rack as he talked.

"Oh, let me get my coat!" She moved toward the doorway.

"There's no need." Edward donned his hat. "Why don't you just stay here and play with your dog. I'll return in a couple hours." He left her standing rooted to the spot as the door closed behind him.

Well, how do you like that! she thought. *It looks like I'll be spending the evening with my dog instead of my new husband!* Was she so unlovable? She felt patronized being told to stay home and play with her dog like she was some child. Anna folded her arms, drew in a deep breath, and then let it out in agitation. She'd show him! She was not about to sit around alone. This called for another

adventure out, something she never shied
away from.

6

Edward strolled the few short blocks to Callie's where the literary society met, but where it was once Callie who filled his thoughts, now Anna's angelic face was firmly implanted in his mind. It was a good thing he'd left, or he'd have been hard-pressed not to break his imposed rule of cohabitation. It took great control, but he truly wanted to give her time to adjust, and he wanted to get to know her a little better. He knew he criticized her clothing and appearance, at least in his mind, when she came downstairs. He did that a lot. Not a very admirable trait to be sure. Even when he was trying to concentrate on his work, he'd always done things like that. Even as a schoolboy all his sums had to be in a straight line. And when Anna had said that God didn't expect people to be perfect, it stunned him. He'd never considered what God's thoughts were about being perfect —

he just knew he wanted to be.

He sighed. She was right, though, and he instinctively knew he over-processed his thoughts or actions to the point of distraction sometimes. He resolved to do better in the future.

Anna turned the corner, grateful for the streetlights. She had no plan, simply walking. Most of the homes she passed had shining lights and open windows that revealed the sound of children and family in the midst of evening supper time. A strange sensation pricked her heart, and she felt lonely for her family and Catharine and the twins. Hopefully she and Edward would start a family soon — if they ever made it through the next few days!

A wooden sign just ahead boasted MOORE'S FINE FURNITURE. *Could this be Daniel's workshop?* She decided to find out. She walked up the stone path, knocked on the front door, and waited.

When the heavy door swung open, Anna was delighted to see that it was indeed Daniel's workshop. He stood, hands on his hips, a thick lock of hair hanging across his forehead. His shirtsleeves were rolled up to the elbows, displaying his strong forearms, and curly, dark hair escaped his shirt at the throat. He looked a bit different than he had at her wedding reception.

"Anna! How wonderful to see you. Please come in," he said, stepping aside with a sweep of his arm. The smell of wood shavings filled the workroom, and pieces of furniture were in various unfinished stages, and the smell of stain, linseed oil, and turpentine tinted the air. "What brings you over here tonight?"

"Pardon me, it looks like I've interrupted your work," she said, staring at the tool in his hand, then glancing down to his dusty trousers and shoes.

His laughter bellowed. "I'm always working, but I will stop to chat with a lovely lady." His straight, even teeth flashed in a smile, setting her at ease. "Gives me an excuse to take a break. Everything going all right with the newlyweds?"

"Oh yes!" Anna felt her face burn. "I was out walking while Edward attended his literary society."

"I see . . . No, I don't see. How can he leave his new bride home alone the first week of marriage?" He stared, one brow cocked upward.

He pulled up a Queen Anne chair for her, and Anna licked her lips as she took a seat. Daniel flipped another chair around and swung his leg over the seat, sitting backward on it.

"Well . . . we have an agreement to give each other a little time to adjust . . ." She felt her face redden at the implication of her words, surprised that she would even breathe a whisper of this to someone she hardly knew. *What's wrong with me? I seem to have lost all reason.*

Daniel quirked an eyebrow. "What you mean is *Edward* decided on an arrangement, don't you?" He waved his free hand. "I'm sorry, it's none of my business, but I know how detailed my friend can be at times. Would you like something to drink — some coffee or lemonade?"

"Thank you, but no. I was just passing by and saw your sign and was curious. Edward told me that you made most of the furniture in his home."

"*Your* home. Yes, I did. Do you like it?"

She nodded. "You're a fine craftsman."

"I'm not sure that's true, but I do like working with my hands." His eyes searched hers with genuine friendliness.

"I shouldn't have interrupted. I was out for a stroll after Edward made it clear that I wasn't invited along to his reading society." Anna knew the tone of her voice indicated her displeasure.

Daniel humphed. "That group can be pretty exclusive with their ideas about what is literary and what is not."

"Oh? Are you a member?"

His eyes flew wide open. "Me? Not hardly." He shook his head. "I'm not much of a book reader, you see. And you have to be *invited* to join their group. They usually meet over at Callie's house. If you have patience, Anna, they'll probably extend an invitation for you to be a part of the group sooner or later. You are Edward's wife, after all."

"Maybe . . . I expect Callie lives in one of those beautiful houses over in northwest Denver that Edward told me about."

"No, she just lives on the next block. Once they're through, Edward will have a short walk home to you." He smiled over at her as she rose, smoothing down her homespun dress.

"Well, I need to get out of your way and let you work." She walked to the door and he followed.

"Stop by anytime, Anna, and if there's anything you might like to commission me to build for the house, I'm your man."

"Dank U wel," she said, slipping quickly down the sidewalk with a wave of her hand. She'd already decided where she would

walk as soon as Daniel mentioned it. The evening was chillier now, and she was wishing she'd thrown on her coat instead of her knitted shawl, but it was too late now. She'd just have to walk briskly, although she didn't know what she'd do when she reached Callie's. She couldn't just show up unannounced. She told herself she only wanted to see where Callie lived.

The gas lights cast a myriad of patterns from the elm trees arching over the sidewalk as she walked past homes, looking for the names on each mailbox or fence. She savored the crisp, cool night and nodded to a couple who strolled along, wishing it was Edward and her. Finally, she spied the name HOLMES boldly written in white on a plaque across the gate of a wrought-iron fence.

She paused and looked up at the lights glowing from the front part of the house. Pushing open the gate, she wandered toward an open window, hearing voices from within. This must be the parlor, where they met to discuss different books they'd read. Moving closer, she heard Edward's voice and Callie responding with light laughter. She couldn't see inside from where she was standing since a hedge was between her and the window, so she slipped in front of it. A twig snapped loudly and she held her breath, but they went right on talking. Anna heard the tinkling of teacups.

Even on tiptoes, she wasn't able to see the group. She glanced around for something to stand on and saw an empty flowerpot sitting off to the side of the porch. Perfect! She dragged the tall pot over to the uneven ground and stepped atop it, holding her skirts, stretching up to the windowsill. Now she had a clear view of the small group in Callie's lovely parlor — all looking relaxed and cheery. A pang pierced her heart that she wasn't sitting right next to Edward, and she wondered why he really wanted a wife. Was it just to run his household?

But she knew he'd felt something with that kiss earlier . . . hadn't he? She knew she did. But now, glancing over at the pretty Callie, she felt envious. Callie wore a pale green dress that showed off her small form to advantage, and her hair was perfectly coiffed, with ringlets along the crisp white collar of her dress. Suddenly Anna felt very tall and unattractive. Callie had everyone's full attention, and Anna couldn't even concentrate on what was being said once she caught Edward's gaze resting on Callie.

She felt sorry for herself and decided she should leave — she wasn't wanted here in the first place. As she moved to step off the pot, it teetered sideways . . .

"I'm enjoying *A Christmas Carol,* but to tell you the truth, it rather makes me nervous to be in the dark now." Callie giggled. "Ghostly figures . . ." She shivered.

Pearl shifted in her seat on the settee next to Chris. "Exactly my feelings," she said, placing her cup and saucer down on the coffee table.

Edward laughed. "Well, ladies, it'll soon be time to choose another —"

"What's that noise?" Callie sat up sharply, listening, but didn't budge from her chair. "Is someone outside prowling around?"

Pearl glanced to the window with an anxious look. "It's pitch-dark now. Maybe it's children."

"I can't imagine —" Chris began to say when a crash sounded from beyond the window.

"I'll go take a look. You ladies stay here where you are. No need to face any Frankenstein," Edward said. He moved toward the front door, pausing long enough to pick up a poker from the fireplace. "There's nothing to fear, I'm sure." He nodded at the ladies' anxious faces. He was sure it was nothing — a dog or cat — but in this cow town one needed to be cautious, especially since Callie now lived alone following her father's death last year.

Edward slowly opened the front door and quietly stepped down the creaking steps into the darkness. Chris followed with a lantern, lifting it high so they both could see the intruder on Callie's lawn.

"Who's there?" Edward said. No one answered, but a noise from the bushes near the window caught his attention and he moved toward it. As Chris held the light up above his shoulder so they could see, Edward nearly swore under his breath.

Sprawled across the lilac bush, her skirts and petticoats a jumble, exposing stocking-clad legs, was his wife! He had to swallow the sudden surge of desire as he stared at her undergarments, and wished Chris hadn't followed him. Anna scrunched up her pretty face, blowing lilac leaves away from her upper lip, then pushed the strands of silky locks away from her eyes, all the while struggling to free the twigs stuck to her knitted shawl.

"Anna, what are you doing here?" Edward croaked out. He put the poker down and set his hands on his hips. How could it be that his wife was straddling a lilac bush like it was a horse in a riding event? He hurried to her side and helped pull the twigs from her shawl, and she reached up to take his hands. He righted her on her feet, and she hurriedly smoothed her petticoats down, then brushed the leaves from her shawl. She rubbed her backside, looking embarrassed. *Well, she should be,* he thought.

"Anna, what were you doing beneath the window? You just made a laughingstock of yourself — and me!" What would all his friends think? He heard the voices of the others crowding into the yard behind him and was embarrassed by this ridiculous discovery of his wife instead of a burglar. What had she been thinking, spying on them? Or was she spying on *him*?

Anna moaned softly, rubbing her arm, then squared her shoulders and lifted her chin defiantly. "I was curious about your book meeting and decided to see for myself what it was about."

"Well, now you know," he said with a clenched jaw. "And it's not a book meeting — it's a *literary* circle." He took her by the arm, intending to guide her to the gate, but Callie stepped up.

"Anna, won't you please come in and refresh yourself? Our meeting is nearly over," she said.

Edward admired how Callie pretended that seeing a lady snooping in her yard was nothing out of the ordinary. Now *she* was a

71

perfect lady.

Pearl stood near Callie and nodded her head. "We have plenty of refreshments."

"Thank you, Callie, but no. I truly didn't mean to interrupt. I need to get back home and let you all finish your meeting. I need to be looking over my list of chores anyway, right, Edward?"

"I'll come with you," Edward said.

Anna plucked a twig from her hair and patted the blonde strands back in place. "No, Edward, you'll do no such thing. Finish your meeting and I'll see you back at home." Anna turned to the small group on the lawn. "Good night."

Edward watched his wife, looking small and lonely, march down the sidewalk and flip the gate latch, her narrow shoulders back and head held high with what was probably false dignity. On the backside of her dress, below her shawl, a thick patch of leaves moved to the swaying of her hips.

Drawing his lips in a tight line to keep from chuckling, he shook his head and sighed, then said what he knew he should. "Anna, please come back and join our group."

7

Anna stopped dead in her tracks, whirling around. "Do you mean it?" she asked, her eyes widening in delight.

"Of course he does." Callie answered as Edward walked toward her. The other members murmured in agreement.

"Yes, of course I do." Edward latched his hand to hers and pulled her down the sidewalk. "You'll love Callie's hummingbird cake."

"First, come with me, Anna, so you can wash your hands," the capable Callie said to her, nudging Anna inside.

She knew Callie was trying to put her at ease. In the homey kitchen, where the spicy smells of baked cake lingered, Callie handed her a clean kitchen towel and soap.

"Thank you," Anna quietly murmured as Callie turned on the spigot so she could wash her hands.

"Anna, I'm really glad that you stopped

by," Callie said.

"You mean dropped by, don't you?" Anna grinned at her and Callie laughed.

"So you did. I'm sure Edward would have asked us tonight if you could join our group."

Anna laid aside the towel. "You're being nice. I shouldn't have gone snooping like some lovesick adolescent whose beau was courting another lady." She bit her quivering lip, surprised at her own admission of jealousy.

Callie looked shocked and reached to take her hands. "Oh, goodness! You have nothing to fear on that line. Edward and I are just friends. We've known each other since we were children. Please don't give the notion another thought!" she said, her eyebrows scrunching together.

"That's good to know, Callie, because I could use a friend here in Denver."

Callie squeezed Anna's hands. "Then you have one! Now let's go have a slice of the cake I prepared."

The others' conversation was quiet, and Pearl was busy filling the cups with coffee. She smiled at Anna as they entered, and the conversation ceased. Anna wondered if they'd been talking about her behind her back. Perhaps they had — but she couldn't

74

worry over what was done. She took a seat on the settee next to Edward, who balanced his slice of cake on his knees.

"I'll finish serving the cake," Callie said to Pearl, who handed her the knife and then licked a speck of icing on her fingertip.

"As usual, it tastes delicious!" Pearl said as she took the plate that Callie held out.

"Now that we've all settled back, why don't we finish up before the evening is over?" Chris suggested.

"Good idea." Harvey nodded. "Anna, have you read Dickens's book *A Christmas Carol*?"

Anna set her fork down and swallowed her cake. "Indeed I have. Several times. There are many lessons about human nature between those pages, and I felt such compassion for Tiny Tim's character. It brings England's poverty to our consciousness by drawing on our own sentimentality of the Christmas spirit."

There were murmurs of agreement around the room. Edward glanced over at her with an admiring look. Was he surprised at her knowledge of the book?

"Scrooge was a greedy old man, of which there are a few in this town, I'll wager," Pearl summarized. "I'm glad we've been reading this long before Christmas is upon us."

"I couldn't agree with you more, Pearl." Callie bobbed her head. "What about you, Edward?"

Edward was thoughtful for a second. "I'm happy to say I don't think I'm a miserly shop owner like Scrooge who mistreats my clerk like he did Cratchit . . . at least I don't think I'm anything like that."

"Well, of course you're not, Edward." Pearl laughed. "Well, I for one thoroughly enjoyed the book. Who gets to choose the next book?"

"First, I move to nominate Anna as a member of our group." Callie grinned at Anna. "It's obvious that she's quite well read."

Harvey leaned forward. "I second the motion. Anyone else in agreement?"

"I very much agree." Pearl sat straighter in her chair, smiling at Anna.

"Great idea, Callie. Anna will be a lovely asset, but we men better watch out or we'll be outnumbered soon." Chris chuckled.

"It would be nice to have Anna join us. I didn't want to leave her at home," Edward said.

Callie set her cup down. "Good! Then I'd like to suggest that as our newest member,

Anna has the honor of choosing our next title."

Everyone's eyes bore into her, and she was momentarily surprised. Quickly she came up with an idea. Glancing slyly at Edward, Anna answered, "How about the book of Song of Solomon from the Bible?"

A leaf drifting to the ground beyond the window could almost be heard in the silence that followed. Anna felt Edward stiffen, so she risked a glance at him. Seated so close to him, she was keenly aware of his nearness and his masculinity. He wasn't built like Daniel in physical strength, but he had a certain force about him that alluded to the power of his presence — at least in Anna's mind. However, now his jaw was clamped like a beaver trap.

"You *do* read the Bible, don't you?" Anna looked from one person to the next, pretending not to understand the silence. Had she said something wrong?

Finally, Harvey cleared his throat, adjusted his paisley waistcoat over his ample stomach, and pulled out his pocket watch. "We do, Anna, we do. The title just kind of took us by surprise, that's all. Right, Edward?" He looked at Anna's husband.

Edward shifted on the settee, drumming his

fingers on his knee. One thing he didn't know a lot about was Scriptures on marital bliss, and if he remembered right, the Song of Solomon was replete with them.

Pearl clapped her hands. "Oh, I can hardly wait. Every once in a while the reverend touches on the . . . er . . . that particular topic in the book that no one will talk about."

"That's because a lot of it could've been taken out, if you ask me," Harvey commented.

"Oh, you old prude! If it's in the Bible, God must've thought it was good enough for us to study. Count me in. It's a great idea." Pearl sat back in her chair, a pink flush across her cheeks.

Oh dear, what has Anna started now? Edward sighed. Pearl would be interested since she was an old maid, always trying to get Harvey to perk up and take notice of her. Having Anna in this group now gave it an entirely different meaning. But he had to admit, when he'd thought she was lacking in the literary sense, he'd been wrong. Now he felt ashamed that he'd assumed she should stay at home tonight.

Edward's eyes followed the delicate line of her profile, her flawless skin, and her pert nose. He should be flattered that she'd risked looking foolish to see what he was up to. But then, was that a normal way a wife would react, watching his every move? He hoped not or he would feel stifled.

"I'm not sure it's appropriate for our group at this time." Callie's voice faltered. "Maybe another time, perhaps?"

Harvey coughed, and others made inaudible comments under their breath.

Edward rescued her. "I believe you're right, Callie." He turned to Anna. "However, you and I can read it together at home." Her face showed confusion, and he tried to remember that she was young and naïve. "Perhaps you'd like to suggest something else."

His lovely wife's face brightened quickly. "All right. What about *Pride and Prejudice*?"

"Excellent selection." Pearl leaned forward. "You and Edward will enjoy reading the Song of Solomon together, I'm sure."

Anna shot her a grateful smile.

"Harvey and Chris, are you in agreement?" Callie asked.

Harvey and Chris nodded, and Edward felt immediate relief.

"It's settled then!" Signaling the end of their meeting, Callie rose. The rest followed suit and retrieved their coats from the hall tree. "We'll meet again in two weeks."

8

Anna's knees burned from kneeling against the hardwood floor, and she was sure she would have a crick in her back and be bent double for the rest of her life — *if* she ever finished cleaning the living room and hall-way. Loose curls escaped the scarf tied about her head, and she pushed them out of her line of vision, threw the wet brush into the soapy pail, then leaned back on tired legs. Since she had some extra time, she moved Wednesday's chore to today. She'd get her chores done as she saw fit.

The room seemed to have grown to twice its size since she'd started the chore right after breakfast. She sighed, rubbing her wrist. *Drat Edward's list!* She was sure that her sister Catharine had never worked this hard at the farm. *Or did she — while I was chasing rainbows and butterflies to paint?* If she had, then Anna felt shame that she hadn't noticed. Well, the floor looked good enough for her, so she declared the item completed, then shoved a window up to allow the breeze to dry it thoroughly. She wondered about Edward's list.

She dried her hands on her apron and fished the list from her pocket. Today was market day, and she was looking forward to getting out of the house. She'd have time to tidy her appearance, then go shopping. Edward had been in his shop since breakfast, and she longed to have someone to talk to. He'd been quiet when they ate, and she'd watched how slowly and deliberately he'd spread the butter and then the jam on his toast, making sure they spread to the edges, and being certain that the toast on his plate never came in contact with the eggs. Earlier he'd insisted on putting the bacon on a separate plate. She wondered why that was so important to him, but she didn't ask.

She changed from her homespun brown work dress to a woolen navy skirt and stiff Battenberg lace blouse with a navy velvet ribbon tied at the throat. Slipping on sensible walking shoes, she picked up her purse from the dresser, donned her bonnet, and set out for the walk to the store. She drank in the fresh morning air, feeling quite happy to be outside with the sun's rays warm against her face. Late September was becoming colder with each passing day, but she didn't mind. Especially when she'd have someone to snuggle with once the ten-day postponement of marital consummation ended. She almost blushed at the thought and felt a quiver in her belly. She wasn't given to vapors, but the thought of lying in Edward's arms as his wife, and their coming together to strengthen their vows, caused her to be short of breath. *It must be the thin air and altitude,* she thought.

Admiring the fall leaves against the vibrant blue sky with their shades of gold, orange, and red, she walked briskly, humming a tune. The street was a flurry of morning activity, from horse-drawn carriages and wagons to people on foot going about their day-to-day activities. Anna decided that she liked the air of excitement the town had to offer beneath the backdrop of the gorgeous mountain range. It was the best of both worlds — not too far to traipse to the foothills, but still connected to a bustling community.

A commotion across the street caught her eye. A portly gentleman had started up the steps to the bank when a large, reddish-brown dog moved toward him stiffly and began to sniff at his pants. The man shouted at the dog and motioned as if to hit it with his walking stick. The dog stepped sideways but only for a moment, then stood in front of the bank's door. Anna had never seen a dog so large, but she couldn't help but notice its thinning sides and matted, dirty coat. Suddenly the man kicked the dog in the side — not once but twice — and the pitiful dog yelped, then limped down the stairs with its tail tucked under and its floppy ears flat.

Anna felt her throat constrict with pity for the dog and anger at the man. Shopping would have to wait. "You there!" she yelled, waving her hand in the direction of the man. He paused as she hurriedly crossed the street, barely sidestepping a moving team of horses pulling a laden supply wagon. "Wait just a blasted minute!"

The older gentleman peered down at her from the top step while adjusting his finely stitched vest and topcoat. "May I ask what the devil for?" He cocked one eyebrow disdainfully, eyeing her from top to bottom.

"How dare you kick that old dog! Can't you see it's sick?" she spat at him, her voice cracking with emotion.

"I beg your pardon? And what business is it of yours, I might ask?"

"I make it my business if I see an animal

in danger."

The man snorted loudly. "Ha! That old good-for-nothing dog? He's always hanging out around here. It's not good for customers at my bank. Now, if you'll excuse me . . ." He turned to enter the door, but Anna was quicker and put her hand on the doorknob.

"Animals are God's dumb creatures entrusted to our care," she said.

"*Dumb* is right, but not entrusted to *my* care. If it matters so much to you, then *you* do something about it!" He smirked. "In fact, I'll be the first to donate to your cause! The streets of Denver have enough riffraff to deal with without having to worry about stray animals." His mocking tone rose as a man and woman walked out of the bank and paused to stare at them a moment. He doffed his hat at the couple, then glared at Anna and dismissed her with a wave of his hand before waltzing into the bank.

Anna clenched her fists at her sides, muttering under her breath. *Overbearing pig!* She turned and noticed the dog lounging on the porch of the general store, his head on his outstretched paws. Drawing closer, she noted that he had sad eyes and graying hair around his mouth. His thick hide stretched over protruding ribs. Her heart twisted inside. *Why, he's nearly as big as a moose.* Moose! That was what she'd call him. She knelt next to the dog, stroked his broad forehead, and told him to stay put until she came back outside. The dog only closed his eyes, appearing too weary to move.

Once inside the general store, she headed directly to bins that held the freshest vegetables still available and found tomatoes, squash, and potatoes. Anna nodded to the skinny clerk, who grinned at her as she gave a tomato a brief squeeze.

"May I be of help?" he asked, strolling over to her.

"No, I think I've found what I need for today." Seeing his crestfallen face, she paused thoughtfully with a finger against her chin and said, "But there is one thing you could do for me."

The freckle-faced young man immediately perked up. "Anything. Anything at all, miss."

"Do you have bath salts and body fragrances?"

He bobbed his head, and suddenly his pink cheeks flamed red. "Follow me. I think we have exactly what you're looking for, Miss . . . ?"

Anna lifted her eyes to his inquiring ones. "Oh . . . it's Mrs. I'm Mrs. Edward Parker."

The young man's face went blank, and he stammered, "Yes, Mrs. Parker, of course." He motioned her to the counter housing all the sundry items. "Help yourself. We have some nice rose bubble bath or lavender-scented oil," he said, holding up a bottle of liquid for her to take a whiff.

"I'll take the lavender bottle," she said. "And do you happen to know if that dog on the porch belongs to someone?"

The lad shrugged. "Not that I know of. He just hangs around all the shops, looking for a handout. Don't worry yourself none about him. I saw you hurrying to his rescue a moment ago."

Anna paid for her purchases, then said, "Oh, I'm not worrying. I'm going to take care of him!"

"You what?" He shot her a disbelieving look. "He ain't worth keeping. He's got rheumatism and he's old."

"That's just the reason he needs looking after," she said, taking the sack he handed her. "Thank you."

He shrugged again. "Suit yourself."

She started out but stopped to ask, "Do you know that man I was talking to across the street?"

He gave a short laugh. "That's ol' man

Waldo Krunk. He's the president of the bank."

"I see. Well, thank you." Anna hurried out and stood over the huge dog still resting right where she'd left him. She bent down to give him a scratch behind the ear, and he rolled his head sideways to look at her contentedly, lifting one paw nearly as big as the palm of her hand.

"Come on, boy. I'm taking you home with me and filling that belly of yours." The dog blinked and she laughed. "Matter of fact, I've christened you 'Moose.' But we need to hurry," she urged, nudging him up. "Phew!" She pinched her nose with two fingers. "We're gonna need a bath, aren't we?"

The dog rose to his feet, tail wagging, when Anna produced a piece of bread from her sack. She handed it to him and he quickly gobbled it down. Somewhat stiffly, he obediently followed her down the sidewalk in hopes of another handout.

9

Edward glanced up from his work at one of the many clocks on the wall, wondering how the morning could have flown past so quickly. The last time he'd seen Anna, she was knee-deep in soapsuds, creating an image in his mind that he couldn't dismiss. With each swipe of her brush, her backside moved gently beneath her serviceable housedress. Her hips tapered upward to her small waist, and he allowed his eyes to travel to her slender back and shoulders. He stared as if he'd never noticed a female before, then finally dragged his eyes away to retreat back to his work counter. He hadn't interrupted her. Besides, lunch wasn't until later.

After spending time adjusting the delicate ratchet motion of the pallet mechanism for a grandfather clock he'd been putting together, he flipped up the magnifying glass secured around his head with a leather band. Many times, after bending over the parts of a clock or watch pieces, his neck would cramp — and today it was hurting. He rubbed it to loosen the knots and sighed, thinking about Anna. Soon the ten-day waiting period would be over. Then what? Had she adjusted to being a wife? Would she be happy? It would, of course, take time to begin to feel comfortable with each other, though he hoped she was beginning to ease into life here in Denver.

He slid open a drawer under the wooden counter and pulled out the sheet of paper with his list. He smiled. He was continually adding items to it. The list he'd given Anna might have been a little too long, but it was, after all, things that had to be done to run a household.

Baby's barking from the front porch broke into his ruminating. Blast it all! Why didn't Anna shut her up?

The barking continued. He wasn't expecting any customers, so the dog couldn't be barking at that. Finally, he shoved his list back inside the drawer and walked to the front of the house. Through the beveled glass he could see Anna coming up the walk with her market basket. Ah, so that's where she'd gone. As he reached to open the door, he saw the reason for Baby's barking. A huge, ugly dog was trailing right behind his wife. *What in the world?* Baby leapt up and scampered toward Anna, then stood barking at the mongrel hiding behind her skirts.

"Hi, Edward. I've got some fresh vegetables for soup tonight, and I picked up cinnamon rolls from the bakeshop to go with our coffee." Her voice was light and her smile contagious like the crisp fall air.

"Stop, Baby, or I'll tie you up again!" Anna snapped, and the dog quieted.

"I'm glad you did the shopping . . . but whose dog is *that*?"

Anna looked away from him, licking her lips. "Well . . . he's a sweet, hungry dog that —"

Edward held his hand up. "Stop right there. I don't care and I don't want to know anything else about him. He's not coming into this house. One dog is quite enough, Anna!" He spoke loud enough for the neighbors to hear as a muscle in his jaw twitched.

Anna stopped at the porch steps and set her basket down. The huge dog stayed close beside her, cowering at Edward's loud voice. "Oh, I won't bring him inside. He needs a bath first."

"You could say that again," Edward muttered, his nose twitching in disgust. "I don't care how many baths he has, he's *not* coming inside. He's almost the size of a small pony, for heaven's sake. And you are completely ignoring our disagreement about animals in the house."

Anna patted the dog while Baby sniffed and came closer. Anna lifted her head to meet Edward's gaze and smiled. "Edward, he was starving, and the president of the bank, Waldo Krunk, was kicking him in the ribs. I couldn't just stand aside and watch. I had to do something! I'll find him a home, but right now he needs a little tender care, and I'm just the one to give it to him. *Please,*" she begged, her large blue eyes wet with emotion.

What was he to do with Anna? He didn't hate dogs, he'd just never had any chance to be around them. He would admit that Baby was beginning to grow on him, but this . . . this . . . odious-looking creature? This would be the last time for certain.

"He looks like he's ready to cave in, Anna . . . I don't know. Just look at him. You shouldn't have gotten in the middle of this with Waldo." The dog's coat was dull, and his ribs stood out against his hide. Edward could feel his resolve beginning to crumble.

"The dog will be fine if you'll just let me

get some food and water into him." She continued to gaze at him until he thought his heart would melt from her look of compassion.

Edward tightened his jaw. This was becoming a test of two wills. "I insist you put the word out tomorrow that he needs a home. Got it?"

"*Ja!*" Anna ran up the steps, threw her arms around Edward's neck, and kissed his cheek. "I knew there was a soft spot in there just waiting to be tapped," she said. She poked him on the chest with one finger, and the corners of his mouth tilted into a smile despite his trying to be stern with her.

Anna stepped back and adjusted her bonnet. "Oh, by the way, I named him Moose because he's so huge. I saw one in Wyoming once. Such magnificent animals!"

"At least you're not bringing home a *real* moose. And he doesn't need a name if you're going to find him a home, remember?" He shook his head and turned to go back inside. "Next thing I know, you'll be asking me to fill a tub with water so you can bathe him!"

"Oh, would you?" Anna clapped her hands.

He rolled his eyes and hurried inside, leaving her to her own devices.

■ ■ ■ ■

Knowing full well that Edward did not like tardiness, Anna hurriedly ladled the thick soup into bowls, then placed them on the table. She was running late because she'd taken an hour to scrub Moose. She was already tired, and tomorrow was wash day. She was not looking forward to it. But at least he hadn't forbidden the dog from staying — not totally. A small victory for her. She'd noticed Edward giving Baby a scratch or two behind the ears or gently patting her on the head a few times when he thought Anna wasn't looking. Seeing him befriend her dog made her heart sing. Maybe she could change his mind about Moose, whom she was falling in love with. He was a sweet, gentle dog despite his size.

"Soup smells wonderful, Anna," Edward said as he took his place at the table. "Perfect for a chilly fall day. I could smell it all the way down the hallway out to my shop, so I just followed my nose." He smiled at her across the table, his eyes lingering on her.

Anna flushed. "Then I hope it tastes as good as it smells. Would you say the blessing?" she asked as she placed her napkin in her lap.

Edward's blessing was brief but heartfelt. He dove right into his soup, smacking his lips and declaring it the best he'd ever had. "About the dog . . . I think tomorrow you should put some signs up in a few shops and I'll put one up in the window of mine. Maybe he could be a good companion to an elderly person since he seems old himself."

Anna laid her spoon down, swallowed her soup, and answered, "I think he has a bit of rheumatism. I'll try to see what I can get to help him with the stiffness, and I promise to post some signs."

"I think I know how Moose feels."

"You do? What do you mean?"

"Sometimes at the end of the day, I get a stiff neck from bending over the jewelry and clocks all day." He absently rubbed the back of his neck.

Anna scooted her chair back and walked up behind him. "I'll rub it for you. You just sit still." She grinned as a surprised look crossed his face. This was one thing she was good at. She'd had lots of practice when her sister Catharine was pregnant. Rolling down his collar, she went to work massaging his neck and shoulders until he groaned with pleasure.

"Ahh . . . I believe I've died and gone to heaven."

She giggled. "Well, don't do that." She was close enough to smell his aftershave, and she liked how his hair curled at the nape of his neck. When she finished kneading, she let her fingers stroke his neck gently up and down, then trail down to the broad expanse of his shoulders. She wanted to press herself against him to enjoy what it had felt like when he'd showered her with kisses in his study, but instead she sucked in her breath and then expelled it with a sigh.

Edward turned in his chair, latched on to her hands, and pulled her into his lap. "That was relaxing, which makes me wonder what *other* talents you may be hiding from me," he teased.

"I'll have to think about that." She gazed back at him.

He stroked her cheek gently, and her heart stilled. He was going to kiss her and forget all about waiting! She held her breath and closed her eyes, but instead he folded her hands in his and kissed her fingertips. He must have thought her foolish, so she opened her eyes but avoided eye contact.

"How would you like to go to the rodeo?

It's a really big deal here and lots of fun."

"Rodeo? I'm not sure what that means." She pulled back from him, thinking it must be a strange party or get-together that she had no intention of attending.

"It's where cowboys compete for prizes. They rope steers, ride broncos, and there's a lot of food and fanfare. The winners of the events take home a nice prize. Most of the people from all around Colorado and Wyoming attend."

"Oh yes! It sounds like a lot of fun and a great distraction from our daily chores." She pulled herself from his lap, and he dropped her hands. "I'd better get the supper dishes cleaned up. Why don't you go relax so your neck and back feel better for tomorrow, instead of going back to your shop?"

"Yes, I think I will, if you don't mind. I can feed the dogs scraps first if you want me to." He stood up and straightened his collar.

"That would be a big help, and you can get to know Moose a little better," she answered, although she knew that was the furthest thing from his mind. He was just being nice. "I put the dogs in the backyard." She turned to lift the plates off the table, nearly dropping Edward's plate, her hands shaking as she tried to still the rapid beating of her heart.

"I'll get their bowls," he said, moving to the doorway.

She paused and turned around. *"Dank U wel,* Edward."

He grinned. "I love it when you speak Dutch. Your accent is quite charming." He wandered outside to retrieve the dogs' bowls while she stood watching him go in the twilight.

10

Anna braided her hair, twisted it up, and covered it with a wide-brimmed bonnet to shield her face from the sun's rays, which she'd learned could quickly become very warm. Then she donned her apron and brogans since she would be in the backyard. Edward had carried one washtub of water for washing as well as another one for rinsing and then left her to do the laundry. She was glad that it was only two of them to wash for. At least his nice Sunday shirts were sent to the laundry in town. She wasn't sure she could iron them as nicely as he liked anyway. She took the large bar of soap and lathered it, rubbed items against the rub board, then rinsed them thoroughly.

"Ack!" Anna jerked her hands back and wiped them on her apron. The water was hot!

Doing laundry brought back fond memories of Cheyenne and her sisters, Greta and

Catharine. Somehow it was more fun when you had someone to work with and help pass the time more quickly. She was not looking forward to this weekly chore, especially on cold days, but for now she was grateful for the fall weather they were blessed with. Baby ran around in the grass, sniffing and frolicking, trying to get Moose's attention, until finally Moose lumbered over to nudge her playfully. Anna giggled while watching Baby and Moose playing, but Moose appeared only slightly interested. Still, the dogs were becoming fast friends. She'd hate to give the old dog away, but she must try to obey her husband, who'd been kind enough to let her keep her own dog.

A train's whistle sounded in the distance while Anna struggled to hang the sheets across the clothesline. The wind, sweeping down the foothills with a blast, caused the sheets to snap sharply against her face. Baby yapped at her heels and she started laughing, but she couldn't see her for the tangle of sheets.

Suddenly a deep growl erupted from Moose. Whatever was wrong with him? That was the first loud sound she'd ever heard him make. She yanked the sheet from her face, lapping it over the wire line to see what was wrong, and out of nowhere a grimy hand clamped over her mouth.

"Don't make a sound, lady," the intruder hissed.

Anna twisted around enough to see a dirty-looking tramp, who yanked one of her arms behind her back in a vice grip. She could smell his unwashed body and see his tobacco-stained teeth. She shuddered.

"Nothing's going to happen if you do as I say." He licked his lips, then squinted at her. He had bushy eyebrows and a thick beard, and his hair looked as though it hadn't come into contact with soap the entire summer. "I'll bet you've got some cash in that fancy house of yours and your husband's off to work this fine morning."

Anna's heart beat wildly as she remembered that Edward was going to the bank before he started work this morning. Her eyes frantically roamed beyond the man in search of a weapon in the yard, but seeing nothing, she wondered how she was going to get out of his filthy clutches.

"I see you have a little fight in you. That'll make this all the more fun." He leaned in close, jeering at her. "Let's see that hair you have pushed under that there bonnet. I have a fancy for blondes."

Anna swiftly kicked him hard in the shin with her heavy brogan, but it didn't seem to faze him in the least. He only yanked her arm harder and grabbed her around the waist. "It's been a long time since I've had a woman," he said, lifting his hand to crush his lips to hers. Anna gagged from the taste and smell of him and gasped for breath. Finally he pulled back, slapping his hand over her lips again before she could call for help.

Baby was barking sharply, and Moose, seeing his mistress was in danger, snarled then lunged at the man. Standing on his hind legs, which made him nearly six feet in height, he clamped down on the man's arm, refusing to let go even after the man gave him a hard thump on the nose. The tramp walloped the dog again and caught Moose's eyebrow, splitting it wide open. But still Moose held on as Baby chewed on the man's pant leg.

The tramp uncovered Anna's mouth but still held her arm. "Call that blasted dog off my arm, or so help me I'll kill him!"

"Never!" Anna spat, twisting and turning to try to wrench herself free. "Hold on to him, Moose!" she screamed.

The tramp's face was full of fury, and he lashed out against the big dog again, his fist to Moose's side. Moose howled, letting go, and dropped down in pain. Baby let go too and ran to his side. Anna, thoroughly terrified, didn't have time to react or run before she saw Edward storm through the side gate, yelling at the man to stop.

The tramp froze momentarily. He shoved Anna to the ground, then took off running down the alley with Baby right behind him. Moose struggled to his feet, a bit wobbly, with blood dripping from his brow. Edward sprinted after the man once he saw that Anna was all right.

Anna sat up, rubbing her elbow and hip. The wind had been knocked out of her. She wasn't sure why Edward had come back early, but she thanked God for His intervention. Moose hobbled over to her and licked her face.

"Moose, I think you saved me from a worse fate than I could imagine. I'll have to stitch up your eyebrow." She knelt on her knees and wiped the blood around his eye with the bottom of her apron.

After what seemed like an eternity to Anna, Edward finally appeared from the alleyway with Baby running alongside him. "Are you really all right, my sweet Anna?" he asked, pulling her upright to fold her against his chest. His long fingers stroked her head and back as he murmured over her, crushing her tightly to him.

Anna could have stayed there indefinitely with the feel and smell of his strong arms about her, but her nose was pressed into his chest, making it hard to breathe. "I think I will be if you'd let go long enough for me to breathe!" Her laughter rang out in the stillness of the morning.

When he let go, he lifted her chin, gazing at her with tenderness and concern, and her heart swelled. "I'm fine, Edward," she said. "Just a little bruised and scared."

"The man slipped away from me. I think he must've gotten off the train that just passed through and wandered here looking for a handout — and trouble. I'm sorry he got close enough to lay a hand on you," he said, reaching for her hands. He nodded over at Moose. "If it hadn't been for that ol' bag of bones, I'm afraid it could've been worse before I got here." He smiled, his handsome face softening with a gentle expression. "Maybe he's worth keeping after all."

Anna's heart fluttered at his gaze. "*Uff da!* That's wonderful, Edward, but you're really the one who saved me when that man saw you and ran. Why did you come back in the first place? I thought you were going to the bank."

"I forgot my list for watch repairs that I

needed. I'm so glad now that I forgot it, or I'd hate to think what that louse would have done. Come on, let's get you cleaned up and clean Moose's eyebrow," he said, lifting her in his arms. "The wash can wait."

11

Edward's fingers trembled as he unbuttoned the sleeve of Anna's blouse and pushed it up to check her arm. It appeared that she had received only a bruised elbow. Her skin felt soft under his touch, and he marveled at her delicateness as her penetrating blue eyes looked into his. It could've been much worse, and he was so glad that he'd forgotten his list, or . . . well, he didn't want to think about that now. He glanced over at Moose and Baby, who'd followed them inside and were lying nearby. He'd have to attend to Moose, but Anna was first.

Tonight the imposed ten-day waiting period was over, and he could barely think straight. He couldn't wait to hold Anna in his arms and taste her lips . . . feel the delicate skin on her shoulders and back . . . He mentally shook himself. Where was his focus?

"I'm so glad nothing's broken. How's your

hip feel?" he asked, taking over the wandering of his mind.

Never taking her eyes off his, she answered, her voice shaking, "It aches, but I'm none the worse for wear, only a bit rattled. I'm so glad you came back, Edward. I —" Her voice cracked. "I'm not sure what that man might have done." She looked away from his gaze. "I need to get back to hanging out the laundry."

He pulled her sleeve down and buttoned it. "It can wait a few minutes — the sun will be out all day." Edward guided her to the settee, fluffed a pillow under her head for her to lean back into, and lifted her feet onto the settee.

"No, Edward." She struggled against him. "My brogans are too dirty to put on your beautiful couch."

"Then I'll slip them off. And it's not *my* couch," he said. "It's *our* couch." He set about unlacing the brogans, and when she attempted to help he moved her hand away. "I'm going to brew you a cup of tea to calm your nerves. I'll be right back."

Quickly he lit the fire and set the water on to boil. He went to the butler's pantry and fished out his grandmother's Blue Willow teapot and two teacups. He wanted to treat her in a special way.

106

The sweet smile on her face when she saw the teapot let him know that he'd done just the right thing. "Here we go," he said, setting the tray down next to the settee. "We'll have a quick cup, and I'll help you hang the laundry."

"Oh, how sweet of you. Thank you."

Edward couldn't help but notice the tears at the corner of her eyes.

"*Het spijt me* — I'm sorry I've been such a bother this morning and kept you from your work."

"You have not been a bother. I'm thankful to God that I came back when I did."

She sighed and sipped her tea, then set the cup down. "The Blue Willow reminds me of my mother and sisters."

"The tea set was my grandmother's," he said fondly, circling the rim of his cup with his thumb. "I use it on special occasions."

"Am I to believe that this is a special occasion?"

Her tearstained face was flirtatious and her upturned lips seemed to say "kiss me," but he dragged his eyes away. His heart thumped hard against his chest. This week he'd felt they'd become better acquainted, though at times still shy.

He leaned forward and kissed her forehead, answering softly, "Yes, it is, Anna, because you are very special to me."

She lifted her hand and stroked his jaw. "And you are to me, Edward."

He straightened and sat back to sip his tea, wondering if she were thinking about tonight.

"I thought you had to get back to the bank. I don't want to hold you any longer. I can finish up the laundry."

Edward was more concerned about her being alone than his errand. "It's still early, and I had no set appointment."

She shook her blonde curls. "I'll be fine, Edward. He's not likely to return, not after what Moose did to him." Still, her laugh sounded apprehensive. "But I could use some help doctoring Moose, if you don't mind." She implored him with a sparkle in her eyes.

"Not at all. It's the least I can do for him protecting you the way he did." Edward glanced over at Moose, who made a noise at the mention of his name.

"Did you really mean it when you said he could stay, Edward?"

He reached over and pushed a loose curl from her face. "I did say that, didn't I? Well, I'm a man of my word, so I guess the answer is yes." Somehow he knew he was going to regret that promise, but one look at her charming face and pleading eyes and he knew he couldn't refuse.

Anna threw her arms about his neck and kissed his cheek. "Oh, thank you, Edward!" As she moved away, his lips brushed her temple, and he sucked in his breath at the delicate smell of her.

"Drink your tea while I go fetch some antiseptic and a clean cloth for Moose's —"

Her hand stayed him. "Edward, are you anxious about tonight?" she asked boldly. "You know the ten-day waiting period will be over."

Edward felt his neck grow red and his mouth went slack. His thoughts slammed back to the bedroom scene he'd just been envisioning. He couldn't believe she would ask him such a question! My, but she was bold. "Anxious? That would be the word. And excited!"

"Oh . . ." Her voice trailed off and she stared into her teacup.

"And you? Nervous?" He watched her face for a sign that she wasn't ready to consummate the marriage.

"Maybe a little . . . but not scared —"

The sudden ring of Edward's shop bell sounded, signaling he had a customer. "Excuse me. I must see to that. Do you think you can handle Moose's cleanup?"

"I'll be just fine, thank you. Go see to your customer," she said softly with a wave of her hand. "I'll doctor Moose, and if you're free you can help — but truly I'm okay."

He rose, hesitating. "Okay. You'll find ointment in the pantry labeled First Aid, and don't forget to wash your hands," he called over his shoulder. He hurried down the hallway to unlock the door to his shop.

By afternoon, Anna had most of the laundry completed and had convinced Edward to go on to the bank. She wasn't afraid, but she could tell that he was hesitant to leave her alone. The space between her shoulders was aching as she leaned over the washboard, and her hip and side became more sore from the fall with every passing minute. After lunch, she'd hoisted her skirts up and found a large bruise on her side beginning to swell and turn purple. It hurt so badly that she couldn't stand to touch it, and now she was stiff as she tried to rise from the washtub. She hurried to get the last piece hung, then realized that the first part of the wash was dry and needed to be taken down and folded . . . and there was dinner to be started. She was looking forward to the free time on Saturday that Edward's list allowed her. Ha! She had to laugh. She would have to talk to him about his list.

She loved the smell of sun-dried laundry, especially when she crawled into bed with fresh, clean sheets. She'd make the bed right after supper, and it would be so inviting for both of them. Ahh . . . to feel his tender kisses while he taught her the ways of love . . .

She would slip on the beautiful hand-embroidered nightgown of fine lawn linen that Catharine had made for her wedding night. A tingle went down her spine. Would he think she was beautiful? Edward was a man of few words, and it was hard to tell what he thought. She wanted the kind of love her sisters had been lucky enough to find. After his kisses earlier, she sensed that Edward was beginning to relent a little. But maybe she was just a dreamy-eyed girl.

Catharine would tell her that finding love had nothing to do with luck but divine intervention. Anna hoped she was right. She *had* prayed before she'd answered Edward's ad. But she couldn't help wondering now why God had brought the two of them together. They were opposite in so many ways. Yet she was very attracted to him and enjoyed his intelligence. She would need to trust God. And she could hardly wait until tonight when she would become his wife completely.

12

Supper dishes were washed and put away, and the dogs were fed and asleep on the back porch. It would have been better if Edward had suggested they let the dishes wait, considering that tonight was *the night*! Anna sighed. How foolish of her to think he would stray from his routine! She hadn't even had time to put fresh sheets on the bed. That would have to wait until tomorrow.

Pausing in the hallway, she caught her reflection in the mirror on the hall tree. She looked tired and older. How was that possible? She removed her apron and slung it over a hook on the hall tree, patted her hair, and pinched her cheeks to make them pink, then hurried to the living room, where Edward sat reading the newspaper. He looked up when she entered the room, flashing her a quick smile. *My, but he is handsome.*

"Come sit next to me. Dishes all done?" He patted the settee.

"*Ja.*" Anna sat down, making sure she put most of her weight on her good hip by leaning to one side, then adjusted her skirt. She was close to Edward but not touching. It was hard not to think of anything but sharing his bed. Suddenly she became petrified that she wouldn't be all that he expected. After all, he was so particular about his home, his meals, his clocks — literally everything around him.

Edward folded the newspaper and set it aside, turning to face her. "Anna, I'm so proud of all the work you've been trying to accomplish from my list. I think we've grown closer, and you are adapting well to life with me."

"I would agree, or at least I'm trying, Edward." She looked down at her hands, unable to meet his penetrating gaze, and noted that her fingernails were in bad need of attention. She lifted her head. "And what about you? Are you adapting to having a wife?"

Edward lifted one of her hands, rubbing the top back and forth with his thumb. "I am indeed. How could I not with someone as lovely as you?" He leaned over to put his arm around her and pulled her close to his chest. She could hear his heart beating. A few minutes passed and they sat in comfortable silence, then he lifted her head, bracketing her face with both hands, his eyes searching hers with a smoldering look. His kiss was tender and oh so delicious as he pressed his lips into hers — at first lightly, then with more pressure until she returned his kiss with her own and slipped her arms around his neck.

Anna could feel his warm, ragged breathing against her face as he kissed her brow. Finding her mouth again, he nipped at her bottom lip playfully. Her pulse quickened and she felt warm in places that were new to her as he lifted her onto his lap and held her in a tight embrace. No words were needed, just the exploring touch and feel of each other — until the sharp sound of the doorbell and the dogs barking from the backyard interrupted them. Reluctantly they pulled apart, Anna trying to control her pounding heart.

Edward nearly dumped her off his lap in his haste to answer the door, his breathing shallow and his face flushed. "It appears we have guests — don't worry, we'll continue as soon as I can get rid of them."

Mercy! Anna hoped the visitors, whoever they were, hadn't seen their embrace through the living room window. She hadn't had a chance to pull the curtains against the dusk, and the lamp on the table illuminated their silhouettes through the large window behind them.

"Were you expecting someone?" Anna uncurled her feet and dropped them to the floor, smoothing down her skirt. She must look a mess with her hair falling about her face and her cheeks flushed. Of course, Edward looked much the same. She watched him comb his fingers through his hair.

"No, I certainly didn't want the night to be interrupted," he whispered, his lips in a grim line as he strode to the front door.

Anna heard him swing open the door and greet someone, and then she caught the sound of several women's voices. She stood up, her hip causing her to move rather stiffly, when he returned with two older ladies and a younger woman chattering behind him.

"Anna, I want you to meet a few of our neighbors. This is Patty and Polly Holbrook and their niece Sarah Holbrook. Ladies, this is my wife, Anna."

Anna could tell the older ladies must be sisters from their brown eyes and the identical widow's peak above their brows. She extended her hand and Patty, then Polly, gripped it in a firm handshake. Sarah nodded to her and looked as though she'd rather be anywhere than standing here with her aunts. Her hair was the color of ripened wheat and she had large hazel eyes framed with thick lashes. Anna thought she was stunning, to say the least, in the pretty lavender gown that flattered her youthful figure. She looked to be near Anna's age.

"It's so nice to meet all of you. Please, have a seat. I'll make us some more tea. We were just having some ourselves, weren't we, Edward?"

"Yes, dear," he said as the three ladies took a seat on the settee and he sat opposite them.

"We promise not to stay long. We brought a big chocolate cake to welcome you, Anna. It's one of Edward's favorites." Polly motioned to Sarah, who held a covered dish in her lap.

Sarah extended the plate. "Welcome to Denver, Anna."

Anna peeked underneath the cloth. "This looks wonderful. I'll bring a knife and some plates and slice some to go with our tea." She turned and picked up the teapot to head toward the kitchen.

"I'd be glad to help," Sarah said with an

eager look on her face.

"I'd enjoy that." Anna smiled at her husband, who looked less than pleased. But what else was she to do? They'd have their dessert and a little chat and be off before the hour was late. He'd have to wait to finish what he'd started, she thought as a pleasant thrill washed over her.

Two hours later, after they'd heard the sisters' stories of growing up in Kansas and all their trials of moving to Denver, Anna's eyes grew heavy and her hip had a dull throb. Sarah spoke very little, but none of them could get a word in edgewise, and Edward fidgeted in his chair. Once the cake was eaten and the tea drained from the pot, neither of the sisters made any move to leave until the clock chimed the lateness of the hour and Sarah calmly suggested that they ought to be going. Thank goodness! Anna wasn't sure she could listen to one more story about widowed life! But she would like to know more about Sarah, who seemed to be restraining herself as well as a little anxious to leave. Of course, they couldn't know tonight was really Anna's wedding night . . .

With a reluctant sigh, Polly nudged her sister. "I hope we didn't wear out our welcome. It's been so good to catch up with you, Edward, and get acquainted with your new bride."

That's all it took for Edward to hop up, ready to escort them to the door. Anna followed behind.

"Don't forget about the rodeo this weekend, you two. It's a big sport here and plenty of fun," Patty reminded them.

"We'll be there," Edward said rather crisply.

"*Dank u wel* for the cake," Anna said. "We'll enjoy the rest tomorrow."

"Oh, I just love your Dutch accent! Next time we want to hear all about your family, Anna," Patty chirped.

"Yes, again, welcome to our city," Sarah added. "If you need anything at all, we're at the end of the block just across the street. It's the only house painted bright yellow." She smiled at Anna, a twinkle in her eyes.

"I'll be sure to stop in sometime. See you soon."

Edward closed the door on the chattering widows making their way down the sidewalk to their house, and leaned against the door. "Finally! I thought they'd never leave!" he said, loosening the top buttons on his shirt. "They've known me for years, and they mean well, but sometimes they don't know when to quit jabbering." He placed his arm about Anna's waist. "I don't know about you, but I'm ready to douse the lights and go to bed. How about I read some of the Song of Solomon?"

"*Goed!* That would be perfect." The shy smile she gave him caused his heart to beat faster in anticipation.

"Why don't you get changed, and I'll take these dishes to the kitchen."

"Let me help you." She moved to stack the dessert plates onto the tray, but he stayed her hand.

"Not this time. You do whatever you women do before bed. I'll see about these."

"If you insist," she said with a knowing look.

"I do." He touched her back gently, nudging her toward the door, and watched her go, her small hips swaying like a pendulum in one of his grandfather clocks. *So young and sweet, and she's mine!* Was she nervous? Excited? His hands shook as he carried the dishes to the kitchen. He tried to keep his mind from wandering to the lovely vision that, God willing, would forever share his bed.

When he came into the bedroom, Anna was leaning against the pillows propped up against the headboard, looking lovelier than ever, wearing a filmy white gown trimmed in blue ribbons that tucked the material across her bosom. She was holding her Bible and her skin glistened — from a quick bath, he assumed. The vision took his breath away. Edward climbed into bed wearing only his underwear, and she fluffed his pillow so they could read.

"Edward," she said in a low voice, "we both read up to chapter four last night. Why don't we read together? I'll listen to you. I enjoy your reading voice." She held the Bible out to him, and at the light brush of her fingers, every nerve in his arm jolted.

He tweaked her shiny nose and answered, "Only if you cuddle against me like you did in the living room before we were so rudely interrupted."

Her answer came in movement against him — leg to leg, shoulder to shoulder. He swallowed hard, opened the marked passage, and began to read.

" 'Behold, thou art fair, my love; behold, thou art fair; thou hast doves' eyes within thy locks: thy hair is as a flock of goats, that appear from mount Gilead. Thy teeth are like a flock of sheep that are even shorn, which came up from the washing; whereof every one bear twins, and none is barren among them.' "

"Mmm . . ." Anna snuggled closer, laying her hand across his chest, the sweet smell of her hair teasing his senses.

Edward continued. " 'Thy lips are like a thread of scarlet, and thy speech is comely: thy temples are like a piece of a pomegranate within thy locks.' " He paused. "I'm not sure this should be read aloud in our group, Anna," he rasped.

"Continue, Edward." Her fingers trailed his collarbone, gently circling to where his heart thudded. He was beginning to feel very warm and wanted to throw back the blanket, but he didn't. Was it the warm night or his feelings building from the mere touch of her hand against his chest?

He licked his lips. " 'Thy neck is like the tower of David builded for an armoury, whereon there hang a thousand bucklers, all shields of mighty men. Thy two breasts are like two young roes that are twins, which feed among the lilies.' "

He stopped. Goodness! He blinked at the words on the page. "I don't believe I've ever read this before, Anna. Is this what you read for entertainment on the farm?" he teased. He was beginning to think that the chosen selection by Jane Austen was preferable to this.

There was no answer from her, so he continued. " 'Until the day break, and the shadows flee away, I will get me to the mountain of myrrh, and to the hill of frankincense.' "

Edward was beginning to understand the passage, and his desire grew to hold his sweet bride and show her his passion, but a soft snuffle escaped Anna, and her deep, even breathing told him that it would not be tonight. He had his neighbors to thank for that.

He spoke the last line in a hushed tone, feeling sorry for himself. " 'Thou art all fair, my love; there is no spot in thee.' "

He especially liked verse 3 in chapter 6. "I am my beloved's, and my beloved is mine." Edward closed the heavy Bible and set it on the nightstand, contemplating what he'd read. *No spot in thee . . .* The words resonated in his head. He believed in things being perfect.

He lay still without moving until his arm went numb, then he slowly shifted down far enough in the bed so they both would be comfortable. Looking at Anna now, the thought occurred to him that only God was perfect. After much contemplation, he finally fell asleep.

13

Anna awoke feeling refreshed, stretching until she saw that the other side of the bed was empty. The coolness of the sheet told her Edward had been gone awhile. She bolted straight up, wincing from the pain on her hip, as she remembered last night. It was to have been their special night. She was angry with herself for falling asleep while Edward was reading, but she hadn't been able to keep her eyes open. She had devoted extra attention to her toilette and brushed her hair loose until it shone, hoping to look desirable for him. She wished he'd awakened her.

If only the company hadn't stayed so late! Somehow she'd try to make it right. The fresh laundry was still piled in a basket to be put away, and the sheets needed changing. She stripped the bed and decided to put fresh sheets on after she prepared a light breakfast. Hurriedly she threw her robe on and made a beeline to the kitchen. She was sure Edward would already be in his shop, and she was right. Finding the kitchen empty and no evidence that he'd eaten, she swiftly made coffee, toast, and fruit.

Carrying the tray, she hurried down the adjoining hallway and shoved open the shop door with her foot, but he barely lifted his head from his work, a blank look on his face.

"Morning! I must've overslept. *Het spijt me.* You should have awakened me, Edward." She set the tray on the counter. "I've brought you something to eat." She smiled timidly at him, but he did not smile back. Anna thought the air was thick enough to cut with a knife.

"I said I'm sorry." She moved stiffly to the other side of the counter to face him like his customers would. The pain in her hip was bearable, but she made a mental note to find some liniment for her bruise. She hadn't had a chance to look at it in her haste this morning.

"It's no matter," he answered. He continued working on some mechanism he was adjusting on an old mantel clock, using a slender steel tool. "I wasn't hungry anyway, and I have plenty to do if we're going to the rodeo Saturday."

Could it be that he was sulking? She

almost laughed. But he was serious. It wasn't her fault that she'd had mountains of laundry to do yesterday, then was tackled by a tramp and had guests who didn't know when it was time to leave. Did his ego bruise that easily? *Oh, please,* she thought, but dared not say anything. She was reminded of the times her sister Catharine's husband, Peter, would have a spat. She handed Edward a napkin, not taking no for an answer. She would just ignore his attitude and act like everything was all right.

"What shall I wear to the rodeo? What time do we leave?"

"Around three. Just wear something comfortable and be sure to wear a hat." He picked up the toast and took a bite. "I'll close up shop early."

"Mmm," Anna answered. She walked slowly around the room, admiring the beautiful clocks and jewelry that lay behind glass cases. "You do fine workmanship, Edward." When he didn't comment, she continued. "What I would like to know is how in the world you can stand to hear all this ticking all day long." She was trying to start a conversation, but the endless ticking of the clocks drove her insane.

"I find it to be very comforting background noise. Noise that keeps perfect time.

126

Sort of like sand sifting through an hourglass. Peaceful and constant."

She sighed. "Interesting. I suppose one could get used to it." She stared down at the piece of metal and springs on the counter. "I think I prefer the sounds of nature."

Still he said nothing. The air was heavy with silence.

"I'm sorry I fell asleep last night. I was exhausted and lulled to sleep by the gentle sound of your voice. I'm not used to so much work." Out of the corner of her eye, she watched him take a swig of coffee. She fingered a spring lying next to the screws and pendulum, wondering how all the pieces worked, but she knew now wasn't the time to ask. She poked her finger inside the spring and began to turn it tightly around inside itself.

"*Don't* do that!" Edward jumped up from his stool.

Anna dropped the spring on the glass clock face, smashing it. Both pieces fell to the floor. She looked up at him, holding her breath, and the look of horror on his face said it all. She dropped to the floor, scrambling around and scooping up some of the scattered pieces into a corner of her robe. "I'm sorry —"

"Oh, Anna. What were you doing fiddling with the clock pieces I was about to put together? You act like an inquisitive child!" he said, his voice rising as he bent to help pick up the rest of the shattered glass. She saw him glance at her exposed leg underneath her robe, then quickly look away.

That did it! Anna rose and dumped the contents of her robe onto the work surface. Stifling a sob with her hand, she ran from the shop and upstairs into the bedroom. Flinging herself facedown on the unmade bed, she let hot tears fall until her pillow was wet. Everything was going wrong. Maybe they were just too opposite. Didn't he know she hadn't meant to break the glass? She would never touch another piece in his precious shop again! Here she'd been thinking of asking if she could help out in the shop with customers sometime.

She knew she was feeling sorry for herself, and to make matters worse, her hip throbbed.

Edward sighed heavily as he examined the spring Anna had wound tight. He knew he shouldn't have shouted at her. She hadn't meant to drop the spring. Sometimes he held his breath when things were picked up by curious customers or when they picked up one of the smaller clocks to examine it. He just knew that one day someone would either break or drop one of the imported clocks he'd ordered.

He shoved all the pieces of glass to one side. He needed to go see if she was all right and apologize. He had to admit his ego had been deflated last night, but it wasn't Anna's fault. Perhaps he should've never written that list for her, but he had to admit that she had followed through with most of it — at least this week, after a bad start the first week. After all, he had let her keep the dog for now.

He turned the lock on the front door and flipped the sign over to read CLOSED. He'd reopen after he talked to Anna. It was still early and not many were clamoring to order clocks or jewelry this time of day. As he walked down the hall, he thought he heard crying. Now he really felt terrible. He hated to see a woman cry.

Anna was lying on her side on the bed, but when she heard him come into the room, she sniffed into her handkerchief, limped to the laundry basket, and picked up the sheets. She ignored the fact that he stood looking at her as she snapped the sheet open to make the bed. She was lovely to look at even in her anger, with her hair a mess and her face tearstained.

"Anna . . ." He moved toward her. When she didn't look at him, he grabbed her hand still holding the sheet. "Anna, listen to me. I'm sorry. I didn't mean to shout at you." He touched her face, forcing her to look at him. His heart ached when he saw that her eyes were red from crying at something he'd thoughtlessly said.

She blinked. "Truly, I didn't mean to mess up the round spring thing or drop it onto the glass face of the clock." Her glittering eyes held his.

"It's called a mainspring. And I . . . I shouldn't have said you were a child. If I could take it back . . ." he said.

"In truth, Edward, I feel like a child when I'm with you. But I accept your apology. I was only trying to make conversation."

"You're not a child to me. Here, let me help you make the bed. I'm good at this job." He took the sheet from her and popped it over the mattress, and she ran her hand over it, helping to smooth it down. He hadn't said much about the way she'd made the bed last week. He almost had but thought better of it.

Edward watched her struggle to tuck the corner in. It was obvious that she was all thumbs and grew quickly frustrated.

"I'm not very good at this, and you are so particular!" she fumed, yanking on the sheet.

"I'm only particular because if it's done properly, then the ends stay tucked in." He bent down to show her how to corner the ends. Just then she popped up with an aggravated look and smacked his chin with the top of her head.

"Ouch!" He winced. She stood eye level to his chest, rubbing her head, then looked up at him. Suddenly they burst out laughing. She turned back to the bed, but her satin house shoe caused her to slip on the top sheet left lying on the floor. Still laughing, he reached out to steady her, but then they both fell in a heap on the bed, his arm under her. Anna's robe fell open, and he glimpsed her pretty nightgown beneath and her lustrous, pale skin.

Anna didn't move but stared back at him, all laughter dissolved. She was soft against him, and so lovely with her dreamy eyes and her dewy fresh skin that smelled of lavender, that he caught his breath. Her lips parted, and he admired her small, even teeth. She was irresistible. *How did I ever get so lucky?* he thought. He would have to learn how to treat her like the thing of beauty she was. He felt so inadequate. He knew more about the mechanisms of a clock than a woman. *Heaven help me.*

"You are exquisite, Anna," he whispered softly. He drew her closer, kissing the lips he'd longed for during the night while she slept against him, and hot fire shot through him. She returned his kiss with one of her own. "My sweet wife . . . I don't deserve you."

Anna lifted her head, now in the crook of his arm, and reached up to push a lock of hair from his forehead. "I'm ready to become your wife in truth, Edward. Hold me close," she murmured.

In the living room, the grandfather clock chimed seven thirty, but the couple bound together in God's covenant neither heard it nor cared that the sun cast its morning light across a cloudless sky while the streets of Denver bustled with activity.

14

There was no mistaking the air of excitement among the block-long line of people buying tickets for the rodeo. Anna marveled that people from every walk of life were represented today, laughing and talking until their turn at the ticket window.

"I can tell you're surprised at the turnout," Edward said to her. "Just wait until you're in the arena and you see 'em all in one place. Why, the crowd alone is worth seeing. It's always a great show between broncos, steers, and cowboys. The cowboys do their best trying to wrestle the bulls with their rope in the shortest time, and the bucking broncos and longhorn steers do their best to get away." He chuckled. "The lucky ones walk away with a nice purse if they win, so they take it seriously."

"I can hardly wait," Anna said. He slipped his arm about her waist and gave her a quick squeeze just as Ella and Ernie walked up to wait in line with them.

Edward's sister was stylishly dressed. She wore a shade hat of straw that sported a wide embroidered velvet band encircling the crown, from which hung an array of flowers and foliage that fell toward the front of the brim. Anna's simple hat of leghorn straw with a narrow crown of black-eyed Susans paled in comparison to her sister-in-law's.

Ernie stood with his thumbs in his pants pocket, coat open and hat pushed back, greeting half the people around him. Anna smiled. He must know everyone in Denver, and she could see why. Both he and Ella were good-natured, and she was glad they were her in-laws, though she hadn't been around them for any length of time yet. She was looking forward to a fun day in her favorite place — the outdoors. And she had the added bonus of Edward and his family. Her list of chores for next week was the furthest thing from her mind.

"Line seems to be moving now. We'll be able to get our seats soon before the show starts," Edward said. He gave Anna's hand a squeeze, and she gazed up at her husband — she could really say that now — and saw the love reflected in his eyes. His look made her blush, and she remembered how they'd spent that first wonderful time, skipping lunch until Edward reluctantly said he must go open the shop. After the evening meal, Edward had hurried her through doing the dishes, clearly anxious to turn out the lights and gently point her in the direction of the bedroom. He was tender and sweet with her and made her feel like the woman she had longed to be. There was no hiding the smile on her face this morning.

"Is a rodeo always so well attended? I haven't seen this many people since I came through Union Station in Denver," she commented.

"Once a year, cowboys come from all over the West to compete," Edward said proudly. "Denver is making quite a name in the rodeo circuit."

Ernie nodded in agreement. "It's the best entertainment you can get in these parts, separate from the theater, which Ella really doesn't enjoy attending."

Ella poked her lip out in a cute pout and Ernie winked at his wife.

"Now, darling, you know I go with you at least once a year," she reminded him. "Whether I want to or not." She shook her head, then just rolled her eyes at Anna. The flowers hanging down from her hat seemed to nod in agreement. "Come on, Anna. Let's walk over to the arena and wait for the men there since they're next in line for tickets. We can walk past the exhibits."

Anna pulled her hand from Edward's and followed her sister-in-law through the throng of people. Everyone was in high spirits in anticipation of the events, and their enthusiasm was contagious. There were booths with items for sale, from cowboy hats, leather vests, bridles, and saddles to every bit of rodeo paraphernalia one could imagine. Ella bought them both a colorful paper fan, telling Anna that the crowded stands could get warm in the sun.

A few minutes later, the men joined the women, and they moved into the area that was laid out in a semicircle equal in diameter to the length of the grandstand. Anna marveled at the number of the spectators crowding the grandstands and the parade grounds, and laughed at the children who ran up and down the steps of the stands, waiting for the show to start.

Once they were seated, it wasn't long before the show began with much pomp and circumstance. A small eight-piece band struck up "The Star-Spangled Banner" as a cowboy on a white horse, carrying a large American flag, waved proudly when he flew past the spectators. Right behind him were cowgirls and cowboys who comprised the contestants for the various events, wearing brightly colored outfits. Anna rose to her feet, along with Edward and his family, to cheer and yell as the riders all circled the corral then formed a long line in the center with the flag in the middle.

She smiled up at Edward and knew he was enjoying watching her. "This is quite a show, Edward."

Edward swiped the tip of her nose with his finger. "This is only the beginning. There's so much more to come."

"Is that Daniel in the lineup?" She squinted in the bright sunshine at the row of riders.

He laughed. "Yes, my dear, it is. Daniel loves cowboying when he's not woodworking. He grew up on a ranch, and his pa still runs the Crow's Nest. I'm sure he's in the stands today somewhere to watch."

Anna was surprised. Daniel was like a gentle giant whose hands caressed the wood he worked with. This side of him seemed strangely out of character. *This indeed will be fun,* she thought. She watched as the line of contestants rode their horses single file out of the arena.

Over the loudspeaker, the announcer introduced himself as Billy McKinley of Cheyenne, along with judges H. H. Metcalf, Carey Culver, J. H. Gorman, and P. G. Webster, who occupied the stand facing where the events would take place.

"Ladies and gentlemen. We're here for a good time, and today you won't be disappointed. We have some of the best participants this side of the Mississippi." The announcer paused and the crowd roared their enthusiasm. "Without further ado, our first event of the day is bronc roping, so hold on to your hats!" he said in a booming voice. "Remember, folks, these ponies have never felt a rope before. The pretty little sorrel here will be roped by Bill Smith. Good luck, Bill!"

Edward leaned close to Anna's ear when she frowned. "He's right. These ponies are taken right off the range and can be fiery and mean."

"Oh . . . really." She was concerned now for Edward's friend. It had never occurred to her that there might be danger at this huge event. She had much to learn, she realized.

"Yes, it takes a practiced hand and a willing fool to mess around with wild horses or bulls."

Anna watched Bill wave his hat at the admiring crowd then plunk it back on his head, readying himself for the release of the horse from the chute. The wooden gate of the chute was let loose, and Bill pressed forward into a fierce battle, the horse's hooves sending dust flying in every direction. He made three brave attempts to rope the wild horse's neck but missed every single one. The crowd cheered him on, but he never came close to putting a saddle on the pony's back. The buzzer sounded and Bill gave up, shrugging his shoulders as he headed out of the corral.

Anna was caught up in the excitement. She wondered how in the world one rode that hard and fast and roped a moving wild horse.

"Our next cowboy is Pinto Jim," the announcer called out. Pinto Jim was a raw-boned cowpoke anxious for his chance the moment the gate swung open. The bronco burst into the corral, and Pinto Jim made several quick attempts before time was up. The wild horse went this way and that as the crowd roared in the background, but finally it wore down from all the plunging about. Pinto Jim snagged a jaquima on the horse, threw a saddle on him, and was astride the sorrel's back just as the buzzer sounded.

The crowd yelled their approval, and Anna added her voice to the cheers. It was excit-

139

ing to watch as cowboy after cowboy tried their expertise to rope and saddle a wild horse. She laughed out loud and Edward smiled down at her.

"What's so funny?"

"I was just thinking that we're mostly standing rather than sitting every time another rider takes the ring," she said, looking around at the crowd.

He cocked an eyebrow. "Are you tired, Anna?"

"No. Not a bit. I was merely commenting on everyone's enthusiasm. It's very exciting and I'm glad you brought me."

Edward stroked her arm. "And I'm happy to see you enjoying yourself."

Anna blushed, noticing Ella watching them with satisfaction on her face. She was glad that she and Ella were friends. She had so few —

Her thoughts were interrupted by the next event beginning.

"This is the steer roping," Edward said. "I think Daniel is doing this event. He's had plenty of firsthand experience."

"What's he supposed to do?"

"Rope a steer with his lariat, then hop off the horse and tie the steer's hind legs up." She shuddered and Edward chuckled. "Don't worry. No animals are harmed in the events, my dear."

"I'd say he's strong enough to do that, but I know he'd never harm an animal. He's much too kind."

She opened her fan and waved it over her face to get relief from the pounding sun, glad that Edward insisted she wear a hat. Surely her brain was baking.

She turned her focus back to the arena. It wasn't long before one rider was disqualified and another had a bad throw with his lariat, missing the steer. What she found most interesting was how fast the horse and rider and the steer shot out of their stalls simultaneously, with the steer running full speed ahead as if he knew what was coming.

Daniel rode a beautiful horse and dressed in a cowboy hat and leather vest stretching tight across his broad shoulders. He seemed to fit the part of a cowboy instead of a furniture maker, Anna thought. She was impressed with the way he rode, self-assured and tall in the saddle. His muscular forearms stretched out the reins once the buzzer signaled, and he pressed his horse forward. In a flash, he was out of the stall and drawing close just behind the steer. He skillfully swung his lariat, which slid around the steer's head with seemingly no effort on

Daniel's part. The spectators cheered, coming to their feet as they watched him slide down from his mount, tie the steer's hind legs with a leather strap, and raise his hands in the air to signal he was done — all in under a minute and a half.

Anna was fascinated at his skill and apparent ease around the horse and steer, not to mention his natural good looks and brawn. Daniel tipped his hat to the audience and with a sweep gave them a deep bow. Surely he'd win.

Edward whistled for his friend, then turned and followed Anna's gaze clearly directed at Daniel. Her face softened and her mouth slightly parted, but her fanning halted. His beautiful wife seemed mesmerized by Daniel's performance, but there was something else that he saw in her face . . . Was it more than admiration?

Don't be ridiculous! She's just never seen a rodeo before and is impressed, that's all.

Suddenly he compared himself to Daniel, something he'd never done before. But then, he'd never been married before either. Daniel had a rugged handsomeness to his features and was always a bit unkempt, which Edward couldn't understand, but women were drawn to his quiet charm and soft-spoken voice. But outward appearances never seemed to matter to Daniel as far as Edward could tell.

Daniel had told Edward to lighten up about everything being so scheduled and his clothes being perfectly pressed and fresh. That's the way Daniel ran his life, though — doing what he wanted to do when he wanted to do it. Yet now Edward was seeing his longtime friend through different eyes . . . through Anna's eyes. Daniel's body, though lean, was muscular and firm, whereas Edward's was not. How could it be? All he ever did was stay inside at the shop without doing a lot of physical labor.

Maybe Anna thought Daniel was more handsome and more skillful. She'd mentioned his woodworking more than once since she'd arrived and commented on how easy Daniel was to talk to.

Suddenly Edward had a sour taste in his mouth, when only moments before he'd thought things were moving in the right direction with Anna. Especially after last night's lovemaking. Finally being able to hold her and share the warmth of their new relationship gave him a fire in his belly that shot straight down to his toes. But now he felt adrift in the huge arena, despite the hundreds of folks and his sister at his side.

Today he felt somewhat pale and boring in comparison to the virile, dashing Daniel.

15

Ernie had fetched lemonade for everyone during the fancy riding event. Anna sipped the refreshing drink, admiring colorful dyed shirts and fancy boots and hats. She held her breath as several different contestants, including two women, showed off their incredible horse-riding skills. They stood on the horse as it ran around in the semicircle, or they hung from the stirrups of their saddle. Finally they dismounted their horse, which bowed with one foreleg bent low to the ground.

As the day wore on, Anna slipped her free hand into Edward's. He gave her a mild look of surprise and squeezed her fingers in return. This was the most fun she'd had in a long time, and spending it with her handsome husband made today even better. As she remembered last night and how tender Edward had been with her, her heart felt full and satisfied. She wondered what he was thinking. Was he remembering the sighs, their luscious kisses, and the magic they'd created? What if she was pregnant? She felt her face burn at all these intimate thoughts.

Ella gave her a poke on the arm. "I think it's safe to say that you're having a good time."

"*Ja*. It's a wonderful show. Is it over now?" Anna stretched her neck to see around the man in front of her.

"Just one more event, and that's the bronco busting," Ernie answered. "Don't know how those cowboys stay on, much less have the nerve. They have to rope and saddle 'em, then mount them without being thrown. The man with the lowest time wins the purse."

"Looks like Daniel won his event," Edward surmised.

"Yup, he's real smooth-like when it comes to horses. He has a natural knack for handling them. Guess that's why he's been spending the weekends at his father's ranch."

Their attention was directed to stalls where the last event of the day was about to take place. A horse was pawing the ground in its stall and lunging at the side walls.

"That one looks mean as a wild bull! I

wouldn't want to get near him," Ella said.

The rider was announced as Dull Knife from Meeker, and he rode a white pony. Anna couldn't help but notice that he wore a large white sombrero and leather-fringed chaps. He sported a big red kerchief around his neck and a fancy belt that held an ivory-handled gun and knife. He sat perched on the back of his horse atop a hand-tooled Mexican saddle.

Anna watched as a bay was pointed out to him and the catch released on its chute. Then off he went. It wasn't long before the bay bronco, nostrils flaring and tail and mane streaming, was cunning enough to figure out what the horse and rider wanted. Using the natural ability of his breed, the bay dodged Dull Knife, giving him a run for his money and a show for the crowd. For all his flashy and debonair appearance, Dull Knife skillfully caught the horse about the legs with his rope. The bay gave in and the rest was in Dull Knife's hands.

The audience clapped and whistled as the entire group of contestants again rode in, waving their hats at the cheering crowd. Ribbons and cash were given to the respective winners of each event, and Anna was pleased to see that Daniel was among them.

As they made their way down from the

stands, Ella suggested they all go for coffee at her house before going home.

"That's a great idea, sis." Edward nodded. "Is that okay with you, Anna?"

"*Ja,* it would be a pleasure."

Lengthening afternoon shadows fell across the sidewalk that led to Ella and Ernie's house, making for a pleasant walk. Anna had forgotten how homey their house was from the first time she'd been there, on her wedding day. Edward plopped down on the settee as soon as they entered the living room, and Ernie took their hats and hung them up.

"I'll come help you, Ella," she said, following Ella's slender form toward the kitchen.

"Okay, it'll give us time to catch up since you married my brother," she whispered, looping her arm through Anna's and leading her down the narrow hallway to the kitchen.

Smells from a morning breakfast of fried bacon still lingered, and Anna spied a large bowl of apples in the center of the breakfast table. "Do you have apple trees in your backyard?"

"Heavens, no." Ella laughed. "I get those from the local market. I want to make applesauce next week. Maybe you'd like to join me if you have time. I know Edward runs a tight ship."

"You know about his strict rules?"

Anna watched Ella light a match to the stove to start water boiling for the coffee. She turned around with her hands on her slender hips, giving Anna a thoughtful look. "I am his sister, you know. Of course I know how difficult he can be, but he has a heart of gold. It's just a little harder to figure him out."

Anna giggled. "You can say that again. We got off to a strange start with a long list of things he expects of me."

"What? Oh my goodness! Do you want me to speak to him for you?" Ella looked shocked.

"No. I appreciate your concern, but I don't take the list too seriously, though I'm afraid it's getting under his collar, if you know what I mean. I insisted on bringing my dog with me from Cheyenne and have since adopted an old dog that probably saved my life." Ella was all ears, and Anna proceeded to tell her about the tramp.

Ella shook her head of dark curls as she reached for a tray to hold the cups. The coffee began to boil, so she turned the fire down a notch and looked back to Anna. "*Two* dogs? Ha! Never thought I'd see the day that'd happen. Our father would never let us own a dog. But I think you'll be able to stand your ground with Edward. I caught him looking at you with adoring eyes today during the rodeo, so things must be improving."

"They are, especially in the last few days."

"What's happened in the last few days?" Ella cocked an eyebrow.

Anna's face flamed. "I shouldn't have said anything. I . . . we, uh . . ."

"What? Had a fight and made up? We all do that. It's what most married couples do. Makes the loving all the better." Ella paused, looking straight into Anna's eyes. "What?"

"We fully became man and wife — finally."

Ella took Anna's hand and pulled her to a chair to sit. "*What?* You've been married two weeks!"

Anna sighed. "It's because of the notion Edward got into his head that I should have time to feel comfortable here and with him, but it was truly a part of his strict rules — wanting things his way. I had no choice. I thought if I disagreed, he'd have thought I was being loose." Anna stared down at her hands, noticing how bad her nails looked.

Ella's frank, open gaze told Anna she had a friend in Edward's sister. "Edward did that more for himself than he did it for you,

Anna. Trust me in this. He was probably more afraid of rejection than anything."

"Rejection? I don't understand. I wouldn't reject him." Anna couldn't believe that the self-assured and competent Edward would have those ideas in his head.

"Edward always feels like he has to prove himself. I think it really began with our father." She sighed. "Our father was an alcoholic. Why my mother put up with him, I'll never understand. There were times when he would be gone for a month or more and then just show up, only to be taken in by my mother. Edward and I both had our ways of coping as children. He liked to tinker with things that took total concentration and perfectionism. I think that was his way of controlling what he could around him, and he became compulsive about certain things." She stared down at the tea tray.

"Ohh . . . I didn't know. I'm sorry . . . for both of you." Anna's heart squeezed. She wondered what Ella's crutch had been, but she didn't think she should ask now.

Ella lifted her head with a trembling smile. "Somehow when you go through tough events you become stronger for it. It made us who we are."

The coffeepot was boiling again, and Ella

jumped up just as Ernie called out from the living room.

"Honey, where's that coffee you promised?"

"Coming," she called over her shoulder. "Anna, we'll talk again when I make applesauce. Would you put some cookies on a plate for me? The cookie canister is sitting on the first shelf where the canned goods are."

"Certainly," Anna said, quickly moving to the pantry. She was just beginning to understand this sensitive husband of hers.

Anna snuggled close to Edward that night, tenderness for him in her heart. Somehow she must get him to talk about his relationship with his father, but tonight was not the time.

Was he feigning sleep? She touched his foot, feeling its coldness, but he didn't express interest in anything but sleep, which surprised her after last night. But Anna was not deterred. She stroked his arm and felt the quiver of forearm muscles through his nightshirt, then allowed her fingers to trail down to his hand and laced her fingers into his. She heard him take a deep breath.

"Edward, thank you for the lovely day. I'll have to write my sisters about it," she murmured softly.

Without turning, he answered, "I'm glad that you had a good day. But we need to go to sleep. We don't want to miss the preacher's sermon, now do we?"

She gave a soft giggle. "There's no chance of that. You're so used to rising early."

She waited. Still no movement to take her into his arms. Had he been disappointed in her last night? No, he hadn't seemed to be. Maybe he was just tired. *But too tired to hold me in his arms?*

"Edward?"

"What?" he mumbled.

"Would you hold me for a little while? I'm feeling a little lonely and it's colder tonight," she murmured. As soon as the sun went down, the night became very chilly, but it had been too late to have a fire by the time they'd left Ella's and fed the dogs. Tomorrow she would dig some heavy woolen socks out of her trunk, she promised herself.

He yawned, then twisted under the sheet until he faced her. Placing his arm under her head and shoulders, he drew her closer until she could feel the beating of his heart. His manly smell, mingled with his aftershave and body soap, was pleasant to her senses. She turned her head until she could see his profile.

"What are you looking at?"

"You, Edward . . . my handsome husband."

"You don't have to flatter me, Anna. I know I don't hold a candle to those cowboys we watched today, especially Daniel."

She drew back to see him better. "Whatever are you talking about? Who's comparing? Certainly not me." She watched as he slowly turned to face her with a solemn look.

"I am. That's who. You could've had any one of those dashing cowboys out there today." His eyes held hers. "I saw the way you were admiring them. I can't compete with them," he choked out.

She playfully swatted his arm. "Really, Edward, I'm *married* to you! Remember?"

"A friend of mine had a mail-order bride who left after she found something that suited her fancy better."

She couldn't believe he was thinking like this. "Edward, for goodness' sake. Do you think I'm so shallow after the time we've had together?" She propped up on one elbow, laid her other arm across his broad chest, and locked eyes with him.

He rubbed his eyes. "It's just that you're so beautiful. I feel blessed that you even answered my ad at all."

She tweaked his nose. "Well, I fancy you. So there!"

He lifted her chin with his long fingers, stroking her cheek. "Anna, I think I'm falling in love with you . . . I don't want to lose you," he whispered in a ragged voice.

Anna felt a catch in her throat. "You won't, Edward . . . You won't," she breathed. She leaned in to receive his waiting kiss as his arm tightened about her.

16

When Edward looked out the bedroom window Sunday morning, a light dusting of snow resembling sifted confectioner's sugar layered the shrubs and clung to tree limbs, announcing summer's close. He combed his hair in place, smoothed down his tweed vest, and moved away from the window, then stared at his reflection in the dresser mirror while he adjusted his tie. He wasn't sure what Anna saw in him, but his blood had quickened when she called him handsome, since he didn't view himself that way.

Anna was finally dressed for church, after they'd lingered long over breakfast. He smiled to himself as the vision and events of last night filled his mind. She couldn't have been any sweeter to him than she'd been last night as she'd soothed his bruised ego.

They were as different as day and night, he thought as he glanced over at the mess she'd left in their bedroom. She'd gone through several dresses, flinging them on the unmade bed, before deciding on the perfect one for today's cold weather. Her indecision and clutter were hard for someone like him who thrived best on continuity and routine. Yes, she was a little scatterbrained, but he had to admit that made life interesting. He never knew what to expect from her.

Anna walked to the cheval mirror and asked over her shoulder, "Edward, will this do?"

She wore a navy dress that bustled at the back with a matching velvet-trimmed bodice — the dress she'd worn the first day he laid eyes on her. The dress's dark color contrasted with her eyes, making them stand out against her sweeping thick lashes.

"I thought the first outfit you were wearing was equally nice, but that one is probably warmer. I don't want you to catch cold, since it snowed while we . . . uh . . . slept." He coughed slightly, watching her pretty delicate skin turn pink.

"Thank you. I want to look my best. Now, if I can just get my coat, we can be on our way," she said as her lips tipped upward in a smile.

"If you're ready, I'll go bring the carriage around, okay?"

She nodded, and he noted that she'd spent thirty minutes creating blonde curls only to sweep them up to the back of her head in a stylish fashion. Anna turned this way and that as she adjusted her peacock-blue satin hat, which was trimmed in cut velvet with black jet triangles and sat jauntily just above her curls. He almost chuckled, watching her finally tie a satin ribbon underneath her small chin. She looked very different, and he'd never seen her with her hair this way. Very adult and womanly — or should he say wifely? Either way, twenty minutes later he would be happy to escort her to church and see all the admiring looks of men and women.

The Trinity United Methodist Episcopal stone church was a magnificent structure of sandstone, with a beautiful Gothic design, a triple archway entrance, and the tallest steeple that Anna had ever seen stretching toward heaven. She appreciated the church's fine stonework and intricate architectural detailing. She supposed it would still be around after she was dead and gone. The adjacent courtyard begged to be explored, and she intended to do that as soon as she had a chance. Painting this impressive church might be something to put on her list of things to do sometime.

Inside, the church was cold, making Anna grateful that she'd carried a muff to slide her hands into. Edward said hello to folks he saw in passing, and Anna nodded to them. The building was packed with towns-folk of every type today, and they had to take a seat on the last row in the back.

As it had on her wedding day, the beautiful sanctuary with its rich wooden beams and magnificent stained glass and pipe organ impressed her. The church was newly built after the congregation decided to relocate to downtown Denver, and Anna knew it would be a joy to worship here.

Reverend Henry Augustus Buchtel began by apologizing for the cold, saying they were taken by surprise at the drop in temperature overnight. "Our good man Isaac Blake, our music director, will lead the congregation now, and later I'll speak to you about the care of our fellow man and all of God's creation." He stepped back as Mr. Blake walked over to the podium and the organist began to play "Holy, Holy, Holy."

When the song ended, Anna leaned over and whispered to Edward, "What are the boxes of seating near the front for? There's a curtain drawn over them." She'd wondered about that when she'd first seen them.

"Those," he whispered back, "are for the . . . um, ladies who are . . . expecting." He choked on the word.

Anna gave a soft giggle at his embarrassment and said, "I see."

"Shh." Edward put his finger to his lips.

Anna leaned against the pew while the music director led them in two more songs before the sermon began.

It wasn't long before Anna gave the reverend her rapt attention. His topic was caring for not only our fellow man but also the animals that God entrusted us with. He spoke of things she'd never considered before — how God had used animals in Scripture to carry out His purposes. God ordered ravens to feed Elijah. He provided a large fish to swallow Jonah and caused Balaam's donkey to speak. Anna read her Bible, but somehow she hadn't thought about allowing animals a special place in the world, even though she instinctively had a soft spot in her heart for all animals — especially ones that suffered.

She listened intently to the reverend's sermon and thought it related quite well to her way of thinking lately when it came to her focus on animals. As he talked, it inspired her to close her eyes and pray that God would show her any opportunity to help her neighbor and use her affection for animals in whatever way He chose.

Several latecomers arrived, and Anna shivered with every blast of cold air from the open door. During the time of prayers she asked God to bless her marriage, to help her define her role in her marriage and in life, and to be able to accept that role with a grateful heart.

Before communion began, Anna felt something bump against her leg. She bent down to move the folds of her skirt aside and heard purring. Despite Edward's protest at her movements, which knocked her hat askew, she felt around between the kneeling bench and her skirt. Her hat, which at this point was cockeyed, slid off and rolled underneath the pew in front of her just as she came in contact with a soft ball of fur.

A kitten! For goodness' sake! It was a tiny little thing and thin enough that she could feel each rib. A very neglected kitty indeed. Her heart filled with pity as she sat back up. It must be cold and hungry, and it must have slipped in somehow when the door opened. She'd have to remove it before they stood to take communion or she'd step on the little creature. Edward could retrieve her hat for her later.

Edward gave her a sharp look, one brow cocked upward in disapproval, and muttered something under his breath. Anna put her finger to her lips to silence him. Bending down again, she lifted her petticoats and pulled the frail kitty from beneath them. The kitty gave a weak *meow,* but it echoed loudly enough to be heard in the stillness of the sanctuary.

She looked around sheepishly, and Edward threw her an irritated look, clearly shocked at what she held in her hands. She could only shrug her shoulders at him, mindful of the people in the rows in front of them turning around to see what the commotion was about. Tucking the scrawny kitty against her chest, she motioned with her finger that she was going outside. Quickly she picked up her muff and hurried out the back door, being careful to close the door quietly.

In her haste Anna slipped on the slick front steps and fell on her behind, but she managed to keep her clutch on the kitten. A passerby walked over and assisted her up, asking her if she was all right. She nodded and thanked him as he scurried on inside, very late for service. She brushed the light snow from the back of her coat and the kitten meowed loudly, so she hurried past the

162

large wrought-iron gates and down the street to find the place where Edward had parked their carriage. She climbed up, thankful for the top cover, and spread the warm robe across her lap and legs before taking the kitten out from under her arm.

Taking a good look at the pitiful creature gave Anna a pang. Its tiny eyes were nearly matted shut and its fur was dull and sparse. But nonetheless, she could tell it was a pretty little thing.

She stroked its head and it purred loudly. "I promise to serve you some warm milk as soon as we get home, little kitty, and take good care of you until you feel better." A louder purring was the kitten's response. She tucked it underneath the blanket in her lap, and soon it was fast asleep.

Not many people were out on the streets. Horse-drawn carriages plodded to and fro, slowly making their way down the street. The powdery snow skimmed the rooftops and dusted the elm tree limbs to give the street an enchanting storybook look. One that said all was well.

It wasn't long before the cold penetrated her coat and she could see her breath in the air. Hopefully Edward would hurry out as soon as church was over. It was hard to believe that some people discarded animals

163

as though they were rubbish. It angered her, and she thought of Moose. "We're supposed to care for God's dumb animals," she grumbled out loud.

"Who are you talking to?" Edward climbed up, a scowl across his brows as he tossed her hat on her lap.

Anna gave a short laugh. "The kitten, of course." It was obvious that he wasn't happy with her. She'd have to choose her words carefully.

He cast her a dark look, warning her. "What do you think you're going to do with the cat?"

"It's not a cat. See?" She pulled the robe back. "It's just a baby kitten that someone discarded."

"For heaven's sake, Anna. Cats roam the city just like dogs. You can't be sure someone tried to get rid of it just because it slipped into the church sanctuary."

"Well, it sure seems that way, else its little ribs wouldn't be sticking out so."

"Doesn't matter!" He reached for the kitten. "I'm taking it right back to church to let the caretaker deal with it. It looks sick to me."

"No, Edward! Please let me nurse the little thing back to health," Anna pleaded, keeping a tight hold on the little ball of fur in her lap. "I'll find a home for it. I promise."

"When have I heard that before? Anna, we cannot bring home every stray animal you find."

"Why?"

"Well, because . . . I don't know . . . because I said so."

"Well, you'll have to do better than that. How could you possibly leave this sweet, fragile thing on the streets?" She couldn't help but wonder if he was afraid of animals.

Edward rolled his eyes and slapped his hands on his thighs in exasperation. "I never said I would. I'll take her back to the church —"

"Edward." Anna reached to touch his hand. "Please reconsider. The kitten won't take up much space and the dogs will enjoy the company for a little while."

"Oh, sure they will. Dogs and cats just *naturally* like each other."

"*Please* . . . I'll make you apple dumplings." Anna would not give up. She hugged the kitten against her face lovingly.

She caught the look of kindness in his eyes, but for some reason he pretended to feel otherwise. He reached for the horse's reins, turning his head from her. "You win for now . . . but soon as the kitten is better, out it goes, understand?"

165

" 'Course, dear." Anna knew she had no plans to find a home other than theirs for the kitten, but Edward might come to actually like having a cat. *Now wouldn't that be something,* she thought.

"Okay. But I'll be looking for my apple dumplings . . . if you know how to cook them." He clicked the reins with a "giddyup" and headed the carriage homeward.

Anna was already planning how she would clean up the tiny kitten and make a nice warm bed in the kitchen for it as soon as she got home — right after they had lunch.

17

After a hasty lunch of leftover soup, Edward watched Anna hurry through the dishes. "We could've gone to Ella's after church if it hadn't been for that blasted cat," he grumbled as he glanced over by the fireplace where the cat lay sleeping. This was not how he'd planned to spend his Sunday afternoon. He envisioned they'd read the *Rocky Mountain News* after lunch, then perhaps snuggle together on the couch and . . .

"I'm sorry, Edward, but as you can see this tiny one needs some tender care." She frowned as she lifted the kitten from a quilt she'd folded into a bed and smoothed the animal's matted fur. "Do you have a pair of scissors handy, Edward? I think I'll have to cut a few of these mats out before I can brush her . . . at least I believe it's a 'her,'" she said, flipping the wailing kitty over and staring hard.

Edward peered over her shoulder. "Great,

a female cat. I hope you understand you're not going to keep her, Anna." He retrieved the scissors from the cabinet drawer. "You hold her and I'll snip."

Anna's eyes grew wide. "Be careful not to nip her skin. There's only a couple mats, then I'll give her some warm milk."

Her eyes filled with tears, wetting her thick lashes. He knew Anna had a tender heart after he'd watched her gaze at the scrawny thing. What was he going to do with her? But seeing the empathy mirrored in her eyes struck a chord in his heart. There was nothing wrong with having a tender heart, though he didn't want a house overrun with animals.

He sighed deeply. "That should do it," he said, finishing with the scissors and laying them aside. He brushed off the flying cat hair that had landed on his shirt. "This is why I don't care for pets in the house."

Anna poured warm milk into a small bowl and set it in front of the kitten, who was almost too weak to stand. Anna cooed to the kitten and touched her finger to the milk, then to the kitten's nose, urging her to taste it. The kitten blinked, flicked her pink tongue out, and began to quickly lap up the offered meal. A smile flashed across Anna's face, and Edward had to smile too.

"I'm going to wipe her down with warm soapy water to remove the dirt and grime. By then she'll be happy to lie in her little bed." Anna touched Edward's arm. "Oh! I forgot to feed Moose and Baby. Would you mind, Edward?"

Edward's arm tingled where her fingers had touched him, and he grabbed hold of her hand, pulling her to him. "If you promise to make those apple dumplings," he teased.

Anna put her arms around his neck. "I think I can be persuaded, unless you prefer a different type of dessert . . ."

Edward touched her lips with his fingers. "Well, you little minx . . . I won't be long. Hurry with the cat."

She threw him a coy half smile. "I'm not going anyplace."

His heart began thumping hard as he watched her skip back over to the kitten, whose full tummy pooched out. He hurried out to feed the dogs what was left of the soup. As he was filling their bowls while they danced around his legs yapping with glee, he drew up short and thought about what he was doing.

How in the world had he let Anna wind him around her finger this way? She'd almost made him forget what he'd said about having pets in the first place. Just look at him — running out to feed *her* dogs while she attended to *her* waif of a sick-looking kitten whose hair shed all over him and most likely the kitchen as well.

When he was finished filling the bowls, he gave both dogs a pat on the head. Well, he'd just have to set her straight but avoid looking into her pretty little face. That's what always got him into trouble, causing him to drop his usual reserve. The cat would have to go tomorrow!

The kitten leapt around the kitchen like a cricket, exploring every corner. Anna found an old cloth after she heated water for the kitten's bath. From the looks of it, she was a calico, a pretty white one with black and orange spots. Her nose had a black splotch that appeared to be dirt but, after closer inspection, turned out to be a marking in her fur.

"You're adorable, missy, with that black smudge," she said, tapping the kitten's nose with the end of her finger. The kitten nipped at her fingers with her tiny teeth, and Anna laughed and moved her hand from side to side playfully as the kitten tried to grab hold.

"I think I'll call you Cricket since you resemble a cricket leaping from place to place." She scooped up the kitten and, sitting down in the chair at the table, dipped her cloth into the warm water to begin wiping the kitten's eyes clean. At first Cricket flinched, but Anna's touch was soothing and she was able to wipe all the fur down. Afterward she dried and buffed the kitten's long hair with a towel.

"This has to be the fastest bath in history, because you're no bigger than a mite!" she told the kitten.

It was at this point that Edward strode back into the kitchen, not smiling as he had when he'd left. He paused as if to say something then looked as though he thought better of it.

"Look." Anna held the kitty up. "Isn't she pretty with all these markings? And she's clean now." But he only stood with his hands in his pockets. "I've decided to name her Cricket. What do you think? *Goed?*" Something was wrong with Edward. Had something happened while he was in the backyard?

"Doesn't matter since you won't be keeping her. Look, Anna, I was thinking . . . you can't continue to bring animals home with you."

"But you said —"

"Never mind what I said. I had a weak

moment. You tend to do that to me." He folded his arms across his chest.

She wrapped the kitten in a towel and held her close. "I don't understand."

"For one thing, I don't like cat hair floating in the air."

"Okay. I'll keep her combed and will dust every day."

"I don't like having the dogs inside because they run all over the house and get into mischief."

"I promise to keep them on the porches or in the yard."

He paused, his jaw set in a firm line. "I don't like the excrement they leave in the backyard. It causes flies, and that's not sanitary."

"I'll pick it up and discard it, and I promise to keep the yard clean of the mess."

"And . . . I don't like sharing *you* with them." His eyes became steel-gray points as they honed in on hers.

Aha! Now she was beginning to get to the root of the problem. He was jealous of her time spent with them. *My goodness!* Would he be this way if they were to have a baby?

"I see . . . Then I'm very sorry I disobeyed your rules. I wanted to help Moose and Cricket escape a worse fate." As if in response, Cricket purred so loudly that they both could hear her. "You have to admit, she's a darling little kitty." Anna stared down at the kitten perfectly content to sleep in the towel in her arms. "As soon as I get more nutrients into her, she'll fill out and I can find a home for her."

"Tomorrow." His answer was firm. "She looks content enough. She's warm, fed, and bathed. That's hardly what most street urchins receive."

Anna stroked Cricket's back. "Edward, did you even listen to the reverend's sermon today?"

"Of course I did." He turned at the kitchen doorway to face her with a scowl. "Why?"

"The reverend said we are to care for animals as well as our fellow man," she said softly, not wanting to sound like it was a reprimand.

Edward pursed his lips. "That doesn't mean you personally have to start caring for every stray one that crosses your path."

"But what if I feel I must in my heart? What then?" She eyed him with a level gaze.

He drew in a deep breath. "I'm not sure. I'll have to consider that. But now I'm going to go read the newspaper."

Cricket purred, burrowing against Anna contentedly. Anna felt her husband's displeasure and blinked back tears. She thought that when he'd allowed Baby to stay, they'd agreed that the house belonged to both of them. Could it be a reminder was needed again? Perhaps she needed to give him more of her undivided attention.

She bent down and tucked the kitty into the bed. She was already looking healthier with clean fur. Anna removed her apron, smoothed her hair back in place, and unbuttoned the top button of her crisp blouse. She needed to spend time with her husband.

Edward lowered the paper when he heard Anna enter the room. He hadn't been able to read the first line with all the angst he was feeling about the dilemma with the pets. He realized it was her nature to have such empathy, but he wanted a wife who spent her free time with him. Not three animals. The sooner she got rid of the kitten, the better.

"Cricket is fast asleep. Thank you for feeding the dogs for me. I appreciate it." She sat down next to him on the couch, her hip touching his, and he felt warmth spread down his leg.

He laid the newspaper aside. "I didn't mind. But Anna, you really must find a home for the kitten in the next couple of days." He shifted to better see her face, and his eyes slid down to the narrow V at the top of her blouse, exposing the graceful curve of her neck as her chest rose and fell gently.

"I know. You told me. Do you remember what you said when you changed your mind about me keeping Baby?"

He groaned and rolled his eyes, knowing full well what he'd said.

"I've been thinking . . . until I can find homes for Moose and the kitten, what if I had a small area in the barn to put them in for part of the day?"

He looked at her sweet face full of hope. She reached out and ran her fingers lightly along the back of his neck where his hair curled, stroking it gently. He felt instant desire flash through him, and he had to control where his thoughts were taking him.

"There's not much space in the barn —" he began.

She leaned in and rested her head on his shoulder. "Would you at least think about it, please? It'd only be for a short time, I promise."

The sweet fragrance of her hair tickled his nostrils, and he longed to remove the hairpins and run his fingers through the silkiness of it. "You hardly know anyone around here, so how do you intend to find them homes?"

"I'll figure something out." She lifted her head, then kissed him sweetly on the mouth. "How about we take a walk?"

That was not what he had in mind, but at least he would be with her. "Okay."

She took his hand and rose. In the hallway, still holding her hand, he started for the front door, but she pulled him in the other direction. "Not that way — I meant a walk to the bedroom." Anna's lips tilted into a delicious, tempting smile.

His legs almost folded like gold chains at the end of a watch fob when she gave him that kind of look, but he was only too happy to follow her upstairs to their bedroom, where the afternoon sun slanted warmly across their bed.

18

The snow was nothing more than a memory Monday morning, melted by the brilliant sun and dripping off the roof by the time Anna stepped out to do her marketing. She breathed deeply of the invigorating, fragrant air and sauntered down the sidewalk, happily humming to herself. She didn't mind the chill, and as long as the sun shone, she was in good spirits.

After she'd fed the animals, she'd added a paintbrush and a tube or two of paint to her shopping list. Then she picked up the wicker basket and went to tell Edward she was leaving. She peeked into his work area to kiss him goodbye, but grew puzzled when he quickly hid something under a muslin cloth and had a peculiar expression on his face. He probably thought she would break something he was working on *again,* or he was going over his list. Soon she planned to tear her list in half, and he'd be glad to get rid of his too.

It hadn't gone unnoticed by her the night before that just after he'd left her breathless from his kisses, he'd removed his trousers and shirt, then carefully and deliberately folded each piece and draped them over the back of a chair before climbing into bed. Goodness! If he chose to do that every time, she might be fast asleep by the time he finished. Why, he'd even made sure the sheets were tucked back in place properly this morning when she was making the bed.

She smiled. That was just part of who Edward was, and there was no hurrying him or changing him. *Mmm, I wonder . . .*

The market was a few blocks away, and the walk would do her good as she planned what to buy. Her thoughts kept straying back to last night. She loved being held in the curve of Edward's arm after they'd doused the lights. A satisfying ending to a perfect, lazy Sunday. There had been no more mention of using the barn for the dogs, but she was worried about them when winter set in — although, if Edward had his way, Moose and Cricket would be gone.

A voice behind her called out, and she turned around. "Anna, wait for me." Callie scurried up the sidewalk to Anna, her shoes tapping out a sharp staccato.

"Good morning, Callie."

"Morning." Callie paused a moment to catch her breath. "I saw you and thought we could walk together. I was on my way to pick up a few things at the mercantile."

"That would be lovely. I'm about to do the same."

"I saw you leave church early yesterday. What in the world were you doing with a cat in the sanctuary?" Callie asked. She and Anna fell into step together and proceeded down the sidewalk.

Anna giggled. "It seemed the kitten found me." She related how the cat got tangled under her skirts.

"So what did you do with the kitten? I'll bet Edward was none too happy." Callie grinned at her.

"You've got that right. But let's just say with some friendly persuasion, I was able to take her home and get her cleaned up. But the worst part is that I'd already rescued an old dog earlier. I'll tell you all about that later. Maybe we could have tea after we complete our shopping?"

Callie hooked her arm through Anna's. "Sounds like a perfectly good idea to me."

Edward placed the mother-of-pearl watch face and clasp he was working on inside a piece of soft chamois, slid it into his jeweler's case, and locked it. He felt like he could conquer the world after the wonderful evening spent with his sweet wife. She never ceased to amaze him. She had a certain childlike quality but became very much a woman when she was in his arms. The effect she had on him was astonishing, but it was good. It was hard to say no to her, and he found himself taking a walk out to the barn to consider allowing her a small area to pen Baby and Moose — and Cricket, though he hoped not for long.

Cricket! What a funny but appropriate name for the kitten. Only Anna could come up with something like that.

Cloud, his dappled gray horse, greeted his owner with a snort as he walked past. Edward patted him on the neck and held out a carrot for the horse to gobble down. "I'll turn you out to have a little freedom here in a minute. Most of the snow's gone and you'll be fine," he said to his horse as though he were a friend.

He guessed his feelings about Cloud weren't much different from how Anna felt about Baby. Now that was a switch in thinking for him. A horse you needed, but a dog? Then he remembered how badly he'd wanted one as a child. His father had told him to put such foolish notions out of his head. He snuffed out the vision of his father sprawled out in a drunken stupor on the couch as quickly as if he were dousing a fire. It was best to put it behind him, but it wasn't an easy thing to do.

Edward shuffled over to the other side of the barn. He reckoned it was feasible to section off a small spot, but he didn't want to tell Anna just yet. He didn't want her to think he gave in too quickly. Maybe he could pick up some wire after he stopped by the bank today. He lifted the latch from the stall and led Cloud outdoors, then headed back inside.

Edward was busy with his regular customers and the morning flew past quickly. He had a meeting with Waldo Krunk at the bank, so he flipped the sign on his shop door from OPEN to BACK SOON and turned the key, knowing Anna wouldn't be back until later.

Callie suggested they have tea at the Red Rose after they completed their marketing since it was just across the street.

"Then I shall have to get back home," Anna said. Both of them left their purchases to be picked up on their way back.

"What's your hurry, Anna? It's not like

you have children at home that need looking after."

Anna felt her face warm. "At least not yet."

"How I'd love to have that to look forward to," Callie said as the waitress seated them at a table near the window.

Anna stared at her friend as she spread her napkin in her lap. "Callie, don't you have a beau? A woman like you should be inundated with marriage proposals." Anna meant it. She enjoyed Callie's easy, friendly manner, but she also gave Anna a sense of calm and centeredness.

"There have been a few, but I think they're only after the money that my father left me." Then she chuckled. "If only they knew . . ."

"Knew what?" Anna pressed.

Callie sighed. "Truly, most of the money is gone. In fact, I've considered selling the house, but I'm not sure where I'd go if I did. The only job I've ever had was keeping the books for my father's law practice, and it's hard to get someone to hire a woman in such an environment. Besides, jobs are scarce."

The waitress brought a teapot of fine rose porcelain and placed it on the table along with their cups. "Will there be anything else, ladies?"

"That will be all, thank you." Anna smiled up at the waitress, who bobbed her head at them and then scurried away to her next customer.

Callie poured their tea while Anna thought of what to say. "I don't want you to leave, Callie. We've just become friends. If you don't mind me asking, what happened to the money?"

"I don't mind. My father was generous to a fault. He had a tender heart and was always lending money to friends, never expecting them to repay, and so they didn't."

Anna stirred sugar into her cup of tea. "That's really not a fault, though. It sounds to me like he was tenderhearted. Better that he was generous than a tightwad, as long as his own family was cared for," she said. The noise of the restaurant patrons faded into the background as she focused her attention on her friend's earnest face.

Callie nodded. "Oh yes, of course he took care of us, but people took advantage of his kindness. The house is paid for, but it requires a lot of maintenance. Most of which I'm not able to do."

"I wish I could be of help, Callie. Oh! I

just had a thought. Have you ever considered renting out a room or two? It's a large house."

"No, not really. I'll give it some thought, though. Now enough about me, I want to hear all about married life. Is it wonderful?" Callie's eyes sparkled.

Anna laughed. "Yes, it is quite wonderful . . . at least for the most part."

"You seemed inseparable at the rodeo when I caught a glimpse of you," Callie teased. "Are you implying not every aspect is great?"

Anna ran her finger around the rim of her teacup thoughtfully before answering. "It's just that Edward and I are different personalities, though we do care deeply for one another. He's just so . . . so . . ."

Callie raised an eyebrow. "Particular?"

Anna laughed again. "How did you know?"

"We grew up together, remember? Edward's a good man, but he doesn't like anything in his world out of order. Correct?"

"Exactly. We got off to a bad start the very first day when he handed me a list."

"A list?" Callie's eyes widened. "A list of what?"

Anna shrugged. "You know. Things I was

to accomplish each day. Like washing, cooking, cleaning —"

"Are you serious?" When Anna nodded, Callie continued, "Ridiculous. Yes, those things must be done in every household, but one certainly doesn't hand it to his new bride!"

"He did. But then I'm not perfect either. I didn't tell him about Baby, my dog, until she arrived at the door. And since then I've rescued another dog and that kitten at church."

"Do tell. I can't imagine Edward giving in to that at all. He's too fastidious," she said with a grin.

Anna told her how Moose protected her and how she persuaded Edward to let him stay for the time being — and Cricket too. "Oh, we butted heads a bit . . . but the making up was grand." Anna thought back to Edward's gentle touch and warmth filled her heart. "I admit, I'd much rather be painting or be outdoors, but I won't have time for that."

"I'm sure marriage is give-and-take. My mother always told me to let the man believe that the things he opposed at first, but later agreed to, were his ideas all along." She giggled. "You'll just have to find time to do some of the things you like."

Anna nodded her agreement, then suddenly noticed the restaurant was very full now. She was mildly surprised when she saw Daniel walking in their direction.

"Hello, Anna, Callie." His rich baritone vibrated from deep within his thick chest. With his striking good looks and muscular frame, he seemed to fill the dining room. Ladies' heads turned as he walked past, his boots pounding loudly against the hardwood floor.

Callie nodded in greeting.

"Hello, Daniel," Anna said. "I so enjoyed your performance in the rodeo. I had no idea you were such a wood craftsman *and* a cowboy."

He laughed good-naturedly. "It's a side interest. Ever since I was a kid I've enjoyed horses, but I enjoy creating with my hands too."

"And you do that well," Callie murmured. She lowered her eyes.

Anna noticed a faint tinge of pink in her friend's cheeks. *So . . . she likes Daniel, but does he know?*

"Would you care to join us?" Anna asked.

"Oh, no thanks. I'm here to meet up with my dad today. Just wanted to say hello to two of the prettiest ladies in the room," he said. His eyes wandered over to Callie, and

Anna saw the corners of his mouth give way to a soft smile.

"Ha! I'm not sure about me, but I agree that Callie is a beauty." Anna knew she was matchmaking, but she couldn't seem to help herself with the possibility of the two of them courting. "Wouldn't you say?"

"She is lovely indeed," Daniel replied.

"Thank you," Callie said shyly. "You and Anna have something in common — she likes animals too. In fact, Edward has allowed her to have a couple of dogs and a kitten." Callie repeated what Anna had told her about the pets.

Daniel's eyes widened, then he slowly turned to Anna. "You must have cast a spell over my friend." He grinned.

"Hardly that. I convinced him that it's the humane thing to do," Anna quipped.

Daniel shifted his weight, moving aside to let a waiter with a heavy tray pass. "I agree with you about that. Maybe you should consider organizing a sort of shelter for forgotten animals."

"What a wonderful idea." Anna was thoughtful for a moment. "I don't know. I'll have to talk to Edward first. I'm not sure he'd let me go that far."

Callie bobbed her head in agreement. "I wouldn't press my luck just yet."

"Oh, I have a feeling you can get him to listen to any idea you have, Anna." Daniel tipped his hat. "I'd best be on my way."

Callie touched Daniel's sleeve. "Daniel, I was wondering if you'd like to visit our literary circle."

Anna saw him flash Callie a broad smile. It was obvious to her that he was interested in her friend.

"Well, I guess so. I don't do a lot of reading, but maybe I should begin." He chuckled.

"We'll look forward to seeing you on Friday then."

"All right. I'd better go now and meet my father."

"Of course," Anna said, one eye on Callie. It seemed the cat had gotten her tongue.

Daniel moved away, and Anna turned to her friend. "Callie, I think he likes you."

"What? Me? Never."

"Yes he does. I saw the way he looked at you. That's more than a friendly hello."

"If that were true, why hasn't he ever asked to court me? Goodness knows he's had lots of opportunities."

"I don't know . . ." *But I intend to find out.* Anna gathered her reticule. "I really have to go now. I hadn't meant to take so much time. But I'm so glad that we met up, and I hope we can get together again soon." She pulled out the money and laid it on the table for their bill.

"I'll get it this time," Callie protested, pushing the money back into her hand, but Anna refused.

"No. Let me treat today, Callie."

"Then next time we must take the streetcar downtown to 15th Street and have tea at the Denver Dry Goods. It's on the fifth floor, and it's exquisite."

"Sounds wonderful. Let's go pick up our purchases now so that I don't get into trouble with my *list*!"

Callie laughed, and as they left the restaurant chattering, Anna caught a glimpse of Daniel across the room, gazing at Callie.

19

Waldo Krunk was leaning back in his leather chair, feet propped up and puffing on a cigar, when Edward was shown to his office. He made no move to get up but indicated to Edward to have a seat. He blew a circle of smoke rings into the air, then swiveled around in his chair to eye Edward.

"Thanks for coming, Edward. I have something I'd like you to do for our bank."

Edward admired the fact that he got right down to business. "And what is that, Waldo?"

"We've just purchased a new vault that should arrive from New York any day now. I think you might be just the man we need." Waldo swung his feet down to the floor to sit in a more dignified manner. "You see, we've decided to replace our old vault that uses a combination with one that uses a timer. It's been around for years, made by a man name Sargent. It comes preassembled

190

by the manufacturer."

"I'm not sure I follow you."

"This vault is a combination lock and timer. Once it's installed, I want you to service it and make doggone certain that the timer is exact and that it works properly at all times. I thought of you because of your experience with watchmaking." He paused and took a puff from his cigar. "In other words, you will be responsible for the maintenance on the lock."

Waldo had Edward's undivided attention now, and he felt honored that Waldo had thought of him. "How exactly does a timer work with a combination?"

"The safe door can only be opened after a set number of hours have passed, making it impossible for a bank employee to open the lock in the middle of the night even under force. Do you follow?"

"I do now." Edward relaxed a bit.

Waldo reached into his desk drawer and handed him an envelope. "Take this home and look it over. It describes the mechanism, which I'm sure you'll understand easily. If you decide you want to do this, then I'll need you to sign an affidavit that you'll tell no one — and I mean no one — the combination or how the timer works."

Edward took the proffered envelope. "I'll

do it. I enjoy any kind of work that deals with intricate mechanisms, big or small." He stuck the envelope in his coat pocket.

"You'll be paid by the month for maintaining the lock once a week to ensure its effectiveness."

Edward rose. "I appreciate you thinking of me for the job."

Waldo reached out and they shook on the deal. "By the way, how's that new wife of yours? She's a feisty little thing. She gave me a browbeating about some ol' mongrel dog that hung around here."

Edward winced. "Well, sir, the dog — she calls him Moose — actually saved her life, so we have him now. But she's looking for a home for him."

"You don't say? Well, I'll be." Waldo tapped his fingers to his chin. "Now, why don't I take you for lunch?"

"Thanks, but I've had mine, and I'd better get back to the shop. Send me word when the safe arrives, and I'll be right over."

"I'll do it. Have a nice day."

Edward passed through the hallway to the lobby of the bank and on out to the sidewalk. It was a crisp, gorgeous Colorado day, just the kind he loved. One of the things he loved about the weather was that hours before it could be cold and snowing and then, just as fast, clear and pleasant. Of course, in the dead of winter there would be a few days that snow wasn't so obliging and most folks hunkered down indoors. But at least he'd be with Anna. He strode over to his horse, anxious now to tell her about his new client, and to see her bright blue eyes light up when he got home.

"Edward!" Daniel called out to him. He turned around and waited for his friend.

"You stashing more money in your bank account?" Daniel asked, resting his elbow against the hitching post. He gave Edward's horse a friendly pat and fed him a sugar cube from his pocket.

"You always carry sugar or carrots in your pocket, don't you?"

Daniel chuckled. "As a matter of fact, I try to. Where would we be without our best friend?"

Edward leaned his head back with a smile. "Well, if you believe what Anna says, then a man's best friend is his dog."

"A *dog*? Then she hasn't spent much time around horses, has she?"

"Apparently not. Where are you off to?"

"Back home. I came to meet up with my father and have lunch."

"He still giving you a hard time about moving back to the ranch?"

"He'd like nothing better. But for now, I have a good business making furniture. And besides, I enjoy it. But I'm not crazy about renting the small house I'm in, that's for sure."

Edward scratched his chin. "Mmm . . . I see."

"I've been saving when I can for my own house, but that's in the future at this point."

"Just like marriage?"

Daniel laughed again. "I don't know who'd have me, to tell the truth. But I have hopes."

"You do? Are you telling me that you have your sights set on someone?"

"Could be."

Edward clapped his friend on the back. "You sure are being tight-lipped. Can't you let me in on your secret?"

"You already know her. It's Callie."

"You kiddin'?"

"No, I'm not kiddin'." Daniel straightened up with a serious look at him.

"Well, I'll be danged. Does she know?"

"Of course not. She's not going to look at me. Heck, I don't even have a steady income. I work on commission, remember? With all her money and that fancy house, I don't believe she'd give me the time of day."

It was Edward's turn to laugh. "Daniel,

let me tell you a few things. When a woman is attracted to a man, it doesn't matter if he's rich or not. The other thing is, you're second-guessing her. Why don't you ask her for a ride out to your family's ranch? What do you have to lose? Nothing, except maybe a chance at love with a pretty nice lady. Look at me — I took a chance."

Daniel poked his finger in Edward's chest good-naturedly and said, "You're right as usual, friend. Maybe I will. But you've got the prettiest woman in these parts."

"I have to agree with you on that, so keep your thoughts to yourself — I'm not going anywhere. We get along just fine," Edward said.

"Ha! I know how particular you are, but I'm tickled to see you hitched and finally giving in a little."

"Giving in? Who gave you that idea?"

"I ran into the ladies having tea, and Anna said something about taking care of animals."

Edward pulled his shoulders back. "She did? Well, I guess it's true. I've let her have two dogs and a cat . . . for the time being, that is."

Daniel cocked an eyebrow. "Is that a fact? Wonders never cease."

Edward folded his arms. "See what I mean

about women? They can turn you inside out! Guess I'm proof of that. But I've got to get going. My shop's locked up and I'm behind." He climbed on his horse's back. "By the way, that was quite a bit of horse riding you did at the rodeo. Impressed the heck outta me, that's for sure. I didn't know you had such muscles either. Want to tell me how to get my upper body stronger?"

Daniel stared up at him. "Are you serious?"

"Yes . . ." Edward's voice trailed off.

"I do a few things to stay healthy, plus I'm outdoors every chance I get. You know, you could stand a little more sun yourself. Being inside makes you pale. Stop by sometime after supper. I'll show you my tricks."

Edward almost felt offended, but knowing his friend like he did, he knew Daniel's comments were just observations. "I think I will. You have me curious now. See you soon." Daniel nodded, and Edward tugged on the reins and set off for home.

Once there, he put his horse away and gave him oats and fresh water, then took the back steps to where Moose got up to greet him with a friendly lick. Baby jumped up, barking until he gave her a pat on the head. The kitchen door was locked. Hmm, Anna must still be out shopping. Well, he mustn't fuss if all the chores weren't done. He knew she'd get to them eventually.

He pulled out his key, opened the screen door to push open the wooden door, and stiffened. Cricket had dumped over the flour bowl that held the rising dough Anna had left on the table. The cat looked at him and meowed, then jumped from the table. After a hard landing, she ran underneath the kitchen cabinet to hide. Flour was on the floor and the pretty bowl was split in half. The dogs flew past him, barking at the cat. It was utter chaos — the dogs yapping and sliding around in the flour and the cat hissing to high heaven.

This is not good! Not good at all. Edward clamped his jaw tight. That had been his mother's prized bowl. He leaned down to pick up the pieces, muttering under his breath, and remembered how she'd allowed him as a child to lick the bowl after the cake batter was poured.

"Blasted cat! Good thing you're underneath that cabinet, or I'd be tempted to put you there right now!" *I must be crazy for even entertaining the thought of buying wire for pens in the barn.* Just as well — he'd forgotten to purchase it after talking to Waldo anyway.

The swinging kitchen door opened, and

Anna waltzed through and set her groceries on the table. With her hands on her hips, she asked, "Just who are you talking to, Edward?" Then she looked around at the mess he was standing in and gasped. "Oh no!"

"I was yelling at Cricket!" Edward said. "Apparently she felt the need to check out the bread dough you left rising. Of course, the bowl shattered in the process." He continued to pick up the broken pieces of the bowl, and after she got the dogs calmed down and pushed them back out onto the porch, Anna bent to help.

"I'm sorry. I left her fast asleep this morning with a full tummy. You know how frisky kittens can be." Anna tried to smooth the situation over, but anger was written across his handsome face.

"You should have put her pallet on the porch with the dogs."

Just when I was going to tell him about my idea to start an organization. She wouldn't say one word about it for now. Paw prints from where the dogs had traipsed through the flour were everywhere. Her heart sank as she went to get the broom and began to sweep up the floor. "Edward, I will finish. Don't you have work to do?" she asked when she heard the doorbell to his shop ring.

"Yes, but I want to talk to you about this later." Edward set the broken pieces of the bowl on the table and hurried to his shop.

After cleaning the floor and putting away her marketing supplies, Anna got down on all fours and looked into the far corner under the cabinet. Cricket was cowering there, her large eyes wide and luminous in the dark. "Cricket, sweetie, come on out. Your enemy is gone now." But Cricket wouldn't budge. So Anna laid down facing the opening of the cabinet and reached her arm in until she came in contact with Cricket's fur. Finally she pulled her out, all the while cooing and speaking softly to the frightened kitty.

Anna pulled Cricket to her chest and rubbed her bony back until the delighted kitten purred with contentment. "What you need is something to eat. I think oatmeal would be just the ticket!" She grabbed her apron and put Cricket in the deep front pocket, filled a pan with water to boil for oatmeal, and began to snap the fresh green beans she'd bought. When the water boiled, she added oatmeal and hummed a tune while the tiny kitten stayed curled inside her apron pocket. Poor little thing. Edward's yelling had scared her. How was she going to win his heart over when it came to the helpless creatures? He had finally taken to the dogs, but was she asking too much to get him to care about the kitty?

Her mind had been working overtime on the way home after Daniel had made his suggestion. She wondered if he could construct a couple of small individual pens at one end of the barn. Next time she went out, she'd drop by and ask him. No harm in that, right?

Once the oatmeal cooled, she added a teaspoon of sugar and a tad of milk and set it on the floor near the back door. She pulled Cricket out of her pocket, gave her a swift kiss on the forehead, and placed her in front of the dish. Smiling to herself, she watched the kitten lap the oatmeal right up, then went back to getting supper started. She needed to see what else she must do before the day was over. Moose and Baby were standing at the screen door, gazing at her for their share of supper, tails wagging. She had to laugh. It was almost like having children, but not quite.

20

"Today I had tea with Callie at the Red Rose," Anna said, clearing their dinner plates after they'd finished eating. Edward shoved back his chair to help. "She was doing her marketing too. I really enjoy her company. She invited Daniel to the reading group." She tried to ease into conversation and tell him about her idea.

"Good. I'm glad she asked him. She's a lovely woman, and I'm glad you'll be friends. I've known her since we went to grammar school." Edward helped to stack the dishes in the sink. "Supper was good. You know, you're a pretty good cook." He winked.

Good, she thought. *Maybe he's not mad anymore.* "I'm surprised you didn't take her as your wife," Anna said. She had wondered about that from the first day she'd met Callie.

"Oh, she's sweet, but she's like a sister to

me. We've spent a lot of time together, though. School, church functions, and the like. My mother would have been pleased if I'd been serious about her, I think."

"I'll just bet she would." Anna conjured up a picture of the two of them and envied all the time they'd spent together. Callie probably knew him better than anyone other than his mother when she was alive.

"Jealous?" Edward teased.

"A tiny bit," Anna admitted.

"Well, don't be. I never had *those* kinds of feelings for her." Edward took the dish towel from her and laid it on the sink, pulling her to him and planting a kiss on her brow. "With you . . . well, it's different. You and I have our differences, but I think we're working through them. Except for the cat . . . or maybe animals in general. You really must get rid of Cricket. She's nothing but a mischief maker." He glanced over at the cat curled in a ball and fast asleep.

Anna stiffened. "That's how kittens are — frisky! Edward, I plan to find her a home, but don't you see I must first get her healthy? You really frightened her. I wanted to . . . I wanted to talk to you about an idea that Daniel gave me."

"Daniel?" Edward gently pushed her back. "What does he have to do with this?"

"He stopped by our table today while we were having tea, and I mentioned his skill as a horseman. Then Callie told him how I like animals too and had rescued Moose and Cricket."

"Oh great, Mr. Muscle Man himself."

Anna wasn't sure why he said that. Envy? Jealousy? "Daniel's your friend, Edward," she pointed out, but continued on. "He suggested I think about starting an organization to help abandoned or mistreated animals. I must confess I had it on my mind all the way home today. I began to get excited about the possibility." She suddenly felt breathless trying to blurt it all out at one time.

"Just stop right there, Anna." Edward held his hand up. "I can't let this continue. Before I know it, our home would be overrun by strays." Whereas only moments ago he'd been smiling and flirting with her, his face was now an immovable mask.

How could he be so stubborn? "I promise that won't happen. If you let me have a small area to keep them in, then when I come across another animal in a situation, I'll have a place for them. Besides, if I have an organization, then I'll be able to garner interest from like-minded people. I just know it. I'll print up flyers to announce —"

Edward stood with his legs spread apart, hands on his hips. "And with all that you'd be involved in, how would you have time to run the household?"

"Do you mean finish that stupid list every day? Am I not doing that faithfully?"

"It's not a stupid list. It makes sense to have things itemized that *must* be attended to on a regular basis, or life is chaotic!" He stared at her as though she'd grown two heads.

"Chaotic only in your mind, Edward. But you didn't answer me. Aren't I doing what is required on that list?" She folded her arms across her chest, trying to keep her composure. She didn't want to have another spat just when everything was falling into place in their relationship — or so she thought.

"I suppose, most of the time. However, you do get distracted easily. Why can't you let someone else start a club for mistreated animals? Why does it have to be you?"

She struggled to keep angry tears back. "Because I care?" She threw the question back at him.

He appeared at a loss as to what to say. "But I don't, so we have a problem, don't we? In fact, the cat can sleep in the barn, starting tomorrow! I'm going to bed." He started toward the hallway.

"We're not finished talking, Edward," Anna said.

"*I* am. I have a lot that must be done tomorrow."

"Edward!"

He paused and turned around, the muscle in his jaw twitching. "What?"

Anna fished in her apron pocket and pulled out her list. "This is what I think about the list you tied me to." She ripped the paper into pieces, and it fluttered to his feet. As she watched his expression, she added, "And I suggest that you do the same thing with your list!"

His mouth fell open for a moment, then clenching his fists to his sides, he strode from the room. Anna stared after him, trembling in fury.

Anna walked over and picked Cricket up, holding her tightly before sitting down in the rocking chair by the fireplace. "It's going to be a long night, Cricket, but I'll figure out some way to keep you inside until you're healthy," she whispered in the kitten's ear. She'd never before seen that look in Edward's eyes, and it frightened her. She knew she'd probably acted immature and childish, but why was he so against having animals around? The more she thought about it, the harder she rocked. Somehow they would have to compromise. But how?

When there were only embers of fire left in the grate, she finally put Cricket down and, with dragging footsteps, made her way to the bedroom. She was glad Edward was already asleep so she could do some thinking — if he was in fact asleep. But just in case he wasn't, she quietly opened the bureau drawer and pulled out her least becoming nightgown of heavy flannel. She didn't feel amorous tonight.

Edward heard Anna come to bed but didn't so much as acknowledge the fact. If she wanted to be a little spitfire, then so be it! He lay on his side on the farthest edge of the bed, staring at the wall and making certain his body wouldn't come in contact with hers. That was all it would take and he would be undone by those luscious blue eyes. He had wanted to tell her about the job at the bank, which he'd felt so proud of, but now it didn't seem important to tell her.

Was he being too unreasonable? Maybe he deserved to have the list be torn into pieces. In the beginning, he thought it would make things easier for her if she knew what he expected. His mind drifted to his own list. He would never show it to her now, but he'd never intended to in the first place. *But you never asked her what she expected of you, did you?* a quiet voice in his spirit reminded him.

Edward sighed. No, he hadn't. *I need to start all over again.* He wanted to roll over and draw her to him, but something held him back. It was the whole thing about insisting on the pets and an organization that was going to take time away from him. He finally shut his eyes after what seemed an interminable amount of time, and he was soon dreaming . . .

Young Edward brought the dog home, despite his father telling him there would be no pets in the house. Sneaking the puppy to his bedroom at the back of the house, he figured his dad would eventually give in once he saw the cute puppy.

During the night his father heard the puppy's bark and stormed into his room, yelling and demanding to have the dog. Edward handed it over, and his father tore from the room and shoved the dog out into the cold rain. It was raining so hard that Edward couldn't see, but after his father left, he went outside, calling the puppy's name. But there was no answer. The storm was getting worse, the winds increasing.

Finally, he heard the puppy's bark and ran

toward him just as the high winds brought down a huge elm tree right in front of him, one of its heavy limbs falling onto the puppy. The boy sat in shock on the ground in the pouring rain next to the unmoving puppy, wet and matted, vowing he'd never forgive his father — and he'd never again let himself care about an animal that much.

When Edward awoke from the dream, he was sweating, and he mentally shook himself, throwing an arm over his head and eyes. It had been a long time since he'd had the dream. A sliver of light shone through the slit between the curtains, and he could hear Anna's deep, even breathing. He eased out of bed and slid on his pants. He'd hardly slept at all and needed a strong cup of coffee. If he hurried, he'd have time to catch the sunrise from the porch and have his coffee undisturbed.

In her sleepy state, Anna rolled over and automatically felt the spot next to her. She found it empty and cold. Then she remembered their quarrel the night before. She eyed the mantel clock over the fireplace and groaned. It was past seven and Edward would be furious with her. By now he'd most likely be working in the shop. She had come to no good conclusion about their argument, and if the previous night was any indication, she would be getting the cold shoulder today.

She drew on her robe and was grateful that Edward had installed a modern water closet with running water. After splashing water on her face, she ran a comb through her hair and quickly braided it. The eyes staring back at her in the mirror looked hollow and were tinged with dark shadows from lack of sleep.

She must hurry out, feed the dogs and the kitten, and face the day. No list to tell her what she was to do. If she planned her day just right, she could go back to the park with her watercolors.

She headed to the kitchen and poured her coffee, wishing she could talk to Greta or Catharine and get their advice about men. She felt totally ill-prepared for times such as these — even if she was falling in love with Edward. She made herself a piece of toast and decided that after she fed the dogs and Cricket, she'd get dressed and walk down the hall to his shop. He'd mentioned that he had a lot to do, and up till now she hadn't actually met any of his customers. She was too busy trying to accomplish all the tasks on his list.

Much later, after she'd dressed in a gabardine dress of mauve smartly trimmed in cream with a silky lace jabot, Anna tapped on the door to the shop, even though she knew it wasn't locked. She heard Edward say, "Come in, Anna."

She slowly stepped into his workshop, careful not to bang the door against anything lest she knock something over again or break something.

"I'm sorry to interrupt your work," she said tentatively.

He had a blank look on his face. "You're not a bother — really," he said quietly.

His answer was noncommittal as he continued with his task. He wore a band around his head that held his magnifying glass, and he was leaning over underneath a bright light that he used for working.

"Look, Edward . . . I'm sorry about —"

The bell above the door jangled and swung open, and Polly and Patty Holbrook bustled inside.

"Morning, ladies. I have your string of pearls, Patty."

"Hello again, Anna," Patty said.

Polly nodded to Anna and Edward. She was the quieter of the two, and Anna liked her. Funny how twins could be so similar in looks but so different in personality.

"You look absolutely stunning, Anna,"

Patty said. "Are you on your way out?"

Oh great! Thanks for exposing my purpose in dressing up a little. "Nice to see you both again," Anna said. "I'm not going anywhere, except to start the laundry. It's an all-day chore, as you probably know." Out of the corner of her eye, she saw Edward turn toward her as though he'd just noticed her dress. *He probably thinks that since I tore the list up I'm not going to do my part.*

"Yes, we do know," Polly interjected before Patty could respond. "But it must be done, so we just try to sing and our work goes faster," she quipped with a giggle.

"Mmm . . . I see. I'll try to remember that when it's too cold to hang the laundry outside."

Patty laughed, then walked over to Edward. "Did the string of pearls turn out all right?"

"Yes they did, and I think they look nice now that they're restrung and cleaned." He took the pearls out of a black velvet draw bag and laid them on top of it to show off their beauty.

Patty clapped her hands. "Beautiful! They were my mother's and I wanted to give them to Sarah for her birthday." She smiled broadly, examining the strand, then showed it to Polly, who, after bending as close as

211

she could to the pearls, finally murmured her agreement.

"I noticed my eyesight is failing and I need to get my glasses exchanged for stronger lenses," Polly said.

"Well, at least your eyesight is not near as bad as poor Harvey Thompson. I heard while I was out shopping that he's nearly gone blind!" Patty said.

"You don't say!" Polly exclaimed. "That's too bad."

Anna shook her head. "Yes, it is. He's in our literary circle. This must be a blow to him." She was conscious of Edward's eyes on her without even looking at him. Was he willing to compromise now since their quarrel?

Patty bobbed her gray head. "Oh yes, dear. It is. He lives alone now that his wife has passed, and not being able to get around will destroy his independence. And he's not even as old as we are."

"Tsk tsk." Polly tapped her finger to her chin.

"I knew his eyesight was diminishing, but I didn't know of all this before. I wish there was something we could do for him," Edward said. "Maybe one of you ladies could go over and read to him."

The ladies twittered between themselves,

giving the idea consideration.

The shop door opened again, and Anna looked up as another customer came in. Edward excused himself to help the customer while the ladies chatted.

"Say, Anna, I wondered how well you knew Daniel Moore. Sarah noticed him at church, and I was thinking we might introduce them — that is, if he isn't seeing anyone. Do you know?" Patty's brown eyes twinkled behind her spectacles.

"Well, uh . . . to tell you the truth, I don't know. Maybe Edward does." Anna groaned inwardly. Since she knew that Callie liked Daniel, she was going to see what Edward thought about having a dinner party with a few guests. She reckoned she could include Sarah as well.

"Well, when you do, just let us know," Patty said, then slipped the pearls into the pouch and pulled the drawstring. She handed Anna the bills to cover the cost and declared they must be on their way, as the church social group was meeting right after lunch.

Anna wasn't sure what to do with the money, so she folded the bills in half and set them under a crystal paperweight. "Thank you, ladies. Hope you'll return. Edward has some exquisite timepieces, I've

213

noticed."

"Anna, you should come over this afternoon yourself. We'll be making plans for our next fund-raiser," Polly suggested in a softer voice. "We'd be glad to have you."

"Sometime soon, I promise," she replied, then walked with the two ladies to the door. After they waved goodbye, she turned around to see Edward watching her with a thoughtful look. She gave him a timid smile, and his lips formed a stilted half smile back at her. It looked as though she would have to be the first one to make a move, although she felt like she'd been pushed into a corner without him willing to compromise. They couldn't continue walking on eggshells like this indefinitely. She decided she'd slip away and start the wash, then whip up the apple dumplings he liked. Stupid list or not, chores still had to be done.

"Anna," he said barely loud enough for her to hear when she started for the house. She stopped and turned to look at him, seeing that his eyes had taken on the shade of steel.

"*Ja,* Edward?"

"I don't know what to say except . . . I'm sorry I lost my temper. You must think I'm a slave driver." He sat on his stool, his shoulders slumped, and she knew he was referring to the list she'd shredded last night.

"Edward." She licked her lips. "I'm the one who lost my temper. I'm sorry too. Perhaps we can work this out?" She longed to feel his arms around her, holding her tightly.

As if he'd read her thoughts, Edward stretched out his arms, saying, "Come here, Anna." His voice was low, husky, and inviting. Anna didn't hesitate. She practically ran to him, slipping between his legs on the stool.

As he wrapped her in his arms, drawing her hard against him, she heard him sigh heavily and felt his breath on her temple. "What am I going to do with you, little one?"

21

By week's end, Anna had convinced Edward to proceed with her idea for caring for Cricket and any other abandoned animal she might come across in the future. She'd melted in his arms, and his heart had been melted by her gentle persuasion — of that she had no doubt. But still she wondered why he'd gotten so angry in the first place, considering she'd caught him a few times talking to Moose and Baby. She was convinced that she'd get him to open up about it one day, but for now she was satisfied.

He'd brought her flowers several times this week, and one day she found a sweet note pinned to her apron pocket that read:

Forgive this bumbling bridegroom for his pitiful attempts to prove his manhood by placing inexcusable demands on you for how to run the household. It's hard for me to let go of old habits,

216

but I'll leave those details to you, the real lady of the house.

Love, Edward

She smiled as she thought back to their fights that always ended in forgiveness and tender shows of affection. She thanked God for her husband, who was growing dearer to her with each passing day.

Anna began ironing but then decided to take a walk outdoors with the dogs. One day soon, she was going to take her easel to the park and spend some time painting that beautiful scenery. Edward was busy in his shop with a customer, and since it was a crisp fall day, she clipped leashes on both dogs, threw her shawl about her shoulders, and closed the door quietly behind her.

The fresh balsam fir scent tickled her nose, and the sky was clearer than a baby's blue eyes as Anna strolled down the street with no particular agenda. It was more like the dogs were leading her, pulling against the leash, sniffing here and there, delighted to be with their mistress for an afternoon stroll. She allowed them to dawdle along while she considered having guests over for dinner.

Tonight was the literary circle, which only met twice a month. The other thing she had on her mind was an idea that had been brewing in the back of her head. Ever since Patty related how Harvey was having an eyesight problem, she wondered if somehow she could teach Moose to fetch or be a guide to Harvey around the house or even outside. She'd seen an older man back in Cheyenne walking with an ordinary-looking dog that took orders from his master and walked closely by his side. If she could teach a few things to Moose, he'd be not only a big help but a great companion for a lonely man.

She decided she'd give it a try. The old saying "You can't teach an old dog new tricks" echoed in her mind. However, Anna never gave up anything easily. She bent over and gave Moose an affectionate pat on his neck, and he looked up adoringly. His large, sad eyes tore at her heart. How in the world could people abandon such a gentle creature? It pleased her to see that his ribs were no longer showing through his hide the way they had when she'd rescued him. She hugged his neck, then Baby clambered against both of them for her own attention, making Anna laugh.

She'd walked a couple of blocks and was about to turn back when she saw Pearl with Harvey promenading down the sidewalk in her direction. It thrilled her to see Pearl's arm through the crook of Harvey's elbow, guiding him on the walk before they crossed the corner to where Anna was. *How sweet.* She called out to them. "Hello!"

They stopped to greet her. "A fine morning for a walk, Anna," Harvey said.

"That's why I'm taking advantage of it with my two favorite critters. Let me introduce you to Baby and Moose. Moose is the bigger dog. I've had Baby since she was born."

Pearl said hello. "I didn't know you had two dogs, Anna." She let the dogs sniff her fingertips.

"My, that's a big dog you have there." Harvey scratched Moose behind the ear.

"*Ja,* he is, but despite his size, he's gentle." Then she giggled. "Not like Baby, who thinks she must be the center of attention all the time."

"They're both fine dogs," Pearl declared.

"Yes, they are. Poor ol' Moose here was abandoned, I think, and was roaming the streets of Denver until I brought him home to care for him."

"What a kind thing to do," Harvey commented. "But I'm afraid there's a lot more of those like him, you'll discover."

Anna hesitated. Should she mention her

plans? "Actually, I don't mind if I do discover them. I believe since they're dumb animals, it's our responsibility not to mistreat them."

Pearl drew in her breath. "You don't say? Then you might want to check the library, Anna. I have a publication on a society for the prevention of mistreatment of animals, I believe."

"Really? I'd be very interested to see it, Pearl."

"Stop by later today at the high school. That's where our library is until a proper building is built."

"I will. Thank you for telling me."

"You are most welcome. I believe it's a wonderful thing you're interested in doing," Pearl said.

"I'd better get back home now. I'll see you, Pearl, when I can get away later, and then I'll see you both tonight at our literary circle."

Harvey took her hand, giving it a swift kiss. "Bless you, dear girl. Until later then."

Anna murmured goodbye, then turned back the way she came and they did the same. She'd had no idea that someone had actually formed a society for mistreatment of animals and was excited to think she could learn more that could be of help to her.

She walked past Daniel's house on the way home, debating about asking him to section off a part of the barn, since part of her agreement with Edward was no more animals allowed in the house. He was a busy man, and she hesitated asking him, but he was so handy with building materials that she thought he'd be able to do it quickly. Still . . .

While she paused, pulling the dogs against their leash to halt them, she saw Daniel and another lad hauling a beautiful dresser down the steps and into the yard. She assumed the empty wagon parked out front was their destination. They paused to catch their breath from the weight of the dresser, and Daniel straightened and mopped his brow, then glanced over to the fence and caught her eye.

She lifted her hand in a brief wave and heard him say, "Take a break, Jimmy." He walked over to the fence.

"I see you're out letting the dogs walk you," he said teasingly.

She laughed, knowing his observance was correct. "Yes, I am."

"Is there a problem?" He leaned forward to rest his arms on the picket fence so he was almost eye level with her.

"Oh no . . . well, at least not today." She smiled. "I have something to ask you. You can refuse —"

"Me?" Daniel said. "Now, I'm not in the habit of refusing a lady *anything.* What can I help you with?"

"I have a small project if you're interested. I can't pay much, though. What I need is someone to create a couple of pens inside the barn for my dogs. I don't think it'd take you long." She held her breath for his answer. This would appease Edward and give the dogs a nice warm place before the weather turned cold.

"That couldn't take more than a couple of hours. I could do it after lunch if that would work for you."

"You could?" Anna's arm was jerked by Baby, who saw a chipmunk scamper across the grass. "That would be wonderful. Are you sure you can spare the time?"

Daniel straightened with a chuckle. "One · thing I like about what I do is that I set my own hours. Trust me, it'd be a pleasure to do something for my friends. No pay is needed. I can bring some sturdy scraps of wood and some wire that I already have on hand."

"Then say you'll have dinner with us and

a few of our friends in two weeks." It would be natural to have guests over, and she would have Callie and Sarah along with Edward's sister and husband.

"Now, that I can do. I need to get back to loading this dresser for delivery. Have a nice day."

"You too, Daniel."

This was perfect! Simply perfect! Turning to the dogs, she said, "Let's get home now, I've got lunch to prepare." She hurried down the sidewalk thinking that her walk had produced two very good things. Good things indeed.

Edward locked the door to his shop and flipped over the sign. It had been a good day with several new customers — one who ordered a grandfather clock that Edward promised could be made by Christmas. Those kinds of orders brought in a good commission, not to mention the job he had for the bank vault's timer. Everything was moving perfectly along again. Today he'd even had time to work on putting the final pieces together for the watch he was making for Anna as a surprise.

Funny, he hadn't smelled any lunch and he was hungry. Where in the heavens was she now? *Calm down,* he told himself. *She must be out in the backyard with the dogs.* Cricket greeted him with a meow when he entered the kitchen, where he found the cooking pots cold.

He'd agreed to let Cricket stay in the kitchen because she was sickly, and now she wobbled over to him, arching her bony back against his pant leg and leaving her long hair clinging to the fabric. Against his better judgment, he picked the kitten up and looked into her sleepy green eyes. He had to admit, she was a pretty kitty. She nuzzled his cheek with her head and he couldn't help himself. He hugged her to his neck and was standing like that when Anna returned from her walk.

22

Not long after lunch, Daniel showed up, rumbling down the back driveway with his wagonload of supplies. He drove to the backyard, pulling up by the barn, and began to carry wood inside. Anna was secretly glad that Edward had already left when Daniel arrived, lest he put up a fuss. They hadn't actually talked about carrying out her plan when they'd made up — they were too busy enjoying tender kisses while Edward locked her into a tight embrace. She blushed at the thought and was glad that Daniel couldn't see her face when she stepped out the back door to greet him. She called out and waved, hurrying down the stairs.

"Can I be of help?"

"Just bring me that hammer and saw, if you don't mind. I'll get the rest."

Anna followed him inside the barn, leaning the hammer and saw against the wall.

"How about at this end here? Will that be

okay?" Daniel rested his hands on his hips, surveying the space with a critical eye.

"*Ja!* If you could give me two or three pens, I'd be eternally grateful." She watched as he started measuring the space.

"I think I can make at least four of them for you. But you don't have four dogs, do you?"

"Oh, that's wonderful, Daniel. And to answer your question — no. At least not yet. But if another lost or hurt animal crosses my path, I will."

"I see . . . and Edward is in complete agreement with this?" He quirked an eyebrow at her. She assumed he was waiting for her response before he began. After all, he and Edward were best friends, and she knew he'd be loyal.

"Um . . . yes. We've talked about it but haven't worked out all the details yet. But don't worry, he doesn't want my pets or strays inside. Now, if you don't need me for anything, I have an errand that I must run."

"I'm fine here. I'll be gone before you return, I'll wager," he said. He was already bent down on one knee to mark a piece of wood with a pencil he'd stuck over his ear.

"Okay. I'll let you know when the dinner party will be, and I look forward to seeing you tonight at the literary circle." She went back inside, gathered up her coat and purse to leave, then decided that she'd put Cricket on the back porch in the sun. She scooped the kitty up still curled in her bed and set her outside the back door. Cricket probably wouldn't wander as little as she was, so Anna wasn't concerned that she might leave the porch.

She'd have to catch the streetcar to take her to Denver High School at City Park because Edward had taken the horse and buggy with him to town. But it wasn't long before she saw the high school come into view at 19th and Stout, so she hurried off the streetcar down the sidewalk to the school. It was already in session, and Anna stood gazing up at the large, impressive multistory building of brick with its own clock tower. She wondered how many students attended. Climbing the massive stone steps transported her back to the time she'd attended high school, which seemed like a long time ago but was only last year. She'd enjoyed her time living with Clara in Cheyenne and commuting on most weekends to the farm where her sister Catharine lived.

Once inside, she walked up to the office and swung the door wide. A few women were busy at several desks. A cheerful woman with shocking red hair greeted her with a wide smile.

"I wonder if you could direct me to the library," Anna said. "I need to speak with Miss Brooks."

"Of course. The library is on the second floor, first door on the left." Her red curls bobbed as she spoke.

She thanked her and started up the expansive mahogany staircase. The door was already open, and she quickly spotted Pearl holding books ready to be shelved. She loved the smell of books and suddenly felt right at home. The light shone through the ceiling windows onto the rich hardwood floors. It was quiet, of course, and several students were sitting at various tables speaking in low voices, apparently working on projects together. Pearl looked up and smiled as soon as she saw Anna.

"I was wondering if you'd come." Pearl set the books down on the long counter next to her. Behind it sat another lady typing faster than Anna had ever seen anyone type, and she marveled at the woman's speed.

"Anna, this is Mabel, my assistant."

Mabel barely paused long enough to murmur hello, then went right on back to her typing.

Pearl motioned for Anna to follow her to

her office. "Anna, I pulled a publication or two with articles that I thought might interest you about an organization called the American Society for the Prevention of Cruelty to Animals." She handed her some magazines. "And another article is about a woman who started the Women's Humane Society in Pennsylvania."

Anna glanced at the magazines. "Thank you for taking the time to do this for me. I do appreciate it."

"You're welcome. You may take those home to read as long as you return them." Pearl kept her voice low.

"I promise I will." Anna chewed her bottom lip.

"Is there something else I can help you with?" Pearl cocked her head.

"I want to tell you about an idea that's been going through my mind, if you have a moment."

Pearl indicated that Anna take a seat as she walked over to her desk. Anna couldn't help but notice the top was neat and organized much like Edward kept things. "I'm all ears."

"Well . . . Patty Holbrook mentioned Harvey was losing his eyesight." Anna paused. "I noticed how you guided him this morning on your walk."

Pearl pursed her lips together. "This is true, though I believe he's too proud to admit it. I think he can see peripherally somewhat. But what does this have to do with you?"

"One day while I was shopping in Cheyenne, I saw a blind man with a dog that guided him across the street and stayed next to his side. Well, I got to thinking that maybe I could teach Moose how to fetch and when to cross the street and things like that."

Pearl's eyes flew open. "What a brilliant idea! And it would be good for Harvey — if he would agree."

"Not only would it help him, but Moose could be a companion to him since he lost his wife."

Pearl leaned back in her chair with an astounded look. "My my, but you're surprisingly resourceful. I think it's a marvelous idea if you can train the dog — at least to do a few things. That would be better than nothing."

Anna blushed and didn't know what to say. *Did she think I'm not very bright?* She stood, preparing to leave. "Thank you. I just wanted to get your thoughts about my idea before I approached Harvey. But I can't do that until I experiment with Moose. I'd better be off now." She turned at the doorway.

"Oh, by the way, Edward and I are planning a dinner party soon — we would enjoy it if you would attend."

Pearl stood as well and walked her to the door that led out to the hallway and stairs. "Sounds like fun. Count me in. I'm glad I could be of help, Anna. Let me know if there's anything else I can research for you. This is a wonderful thing you're doing."

"Thank you again. I'll see you tonight at the literary circle." Anna clutched the magazines to her chest and descended the stairs, then walked out into the fresh air. She felt excitement bubble up and decided she would read on the ride home. God had given her a purpose other than taking care of the house.

She didn't have long to wait before a streetcar, crowded with passengers, came grinding to a halt at the corner. After she found a seat, Anna was fascinated by what she read. The society was formed in New York back in 1866 by a man named Henry Bergh who was impassioned about animal mistreatment, pointing out to Manhattan's powerful business leaders that it was a matter of the conscience and a moral question at best. He later established the first shelter for mistreated animals.

She could almost feel Bergh's passion in

the article seep straight into her heart. He must have been a kindhearted man indeed, she thought. She read the next article about a woman in Pennsylvania who started the Women's Humane Society in 1878.

Anna was encouraged by what she read and was done by the time she disembarked at the corner of her street. Wait until she told Edward! She hoped it would help her cause all the more.

There would be just enough time to finish her ironing and prepare a quick but light supper before they headed off to Callie's for the literary circle.

Edward returned with his load of lumber to surprise Anna with some pens for the animals. He'd left a note on the door for customers that he'd be back soon, so he decided that he'd hurry up and unload the supplies. Tomorrow morning he'd get up early and start on the project.

He was feeling pretty good about the fact that he would surprise Anna, which would show her he was willing to go the extra mile for her when it came to her passion for help-ing animals. Anna really had a tender spot for them, and he shouldn't be complaining that she wanted to do something useful. Besides, their making up had almost been worth the argument. He'd love nothing better than to figure out ways that he could make her fall in love with him the way he knew he was with her. She had seemed pleased with the flowers, so this should be a feather in his cap. Then on a special occasion, he would give her the pendant watch he was crafting especially for her.

He jumped down from the wagon and strode over to the barn door. Funny, it wasn't closed. He would've sworn he'd shut the big double doors. He pushed them back to give him plenty of room to carry in the planks, but what he saw made him stop dead in his tracks.

He couldn't believe his eyes, and he blinked to be sure he wasn't hallucinating. Right before him were four neat wood and wire cages with hinged doors. The frames were connected by a bolt in the front and one in the back. Where in the world had these come from? Anna had gone ahead and took it upon herself to do this, he was sure. But why? Did she think he wasn't capable of building them?

His neck stiffened and he felt his face burn as anger flooded his entire being. He strode over to the back door, nearly stepping on Cricket as he stomped up the steps.

"Anna! Anna! I need to talk to you," he

yelled. She wasn't in the kitchen. He stormed down the hall and saw her entering the front door.

"Oh, Edward. I can't wait to tell you what I've learned today with the help of Pearl —" She stopped short when her eyes met his. "Edward, whatever is the matter?" She put some magazines on the hall table, then removed her coat and threw it on the table as well.

He followed her motions with his eyes, wondering if she would ever learn to put anything back in its place. But now was not the time to mention that.

"Well? I'm waiting."

He folded his arms, spreading his legs apart slightly. "Anna, who built those pens while I was out?"

"Ack! I was going to tell you as soon as you returned. Daniel was kind enough to do this for me."

Keep your temper under control, he told himself. It was going to be hard to do right now when he felt like wringing her pretty little neck. Her pale cheeks shone pink from the cold and her blue eyes glittered . . . but her innocence wouldn't bear any weight in this matter. Not this time.

He sucked in a deep breath before he opened his mouth again. "Why did you do that? We hadn't agreed on using part of the barn yet."

"I thought I was helping you out by not having you worry about it. You have much better things to do with your time than try to build dog pens."

"Are you saying that I'm not capable of doing so?" Her statement made his blood boil, but not in the usual way.

"Not at all! I — I guess I should have told you first. I asked Daniel this morning."

She licked her lips, but she'd have to do better than that for him to forget his anger. "So now I have to return all the supplies that I got to build the pens for you." Edward's jaw worked as he uncrossed his arms and clenched his fists.

"You did what?" Anna clamped her hand across her mouth in surprise. "Edward . . . I don't know what to say . . ." Her voice trailed away and tears filled her eyes.

"It doesn't matter now, does it? I wanted it to be a surprise, but it looks like you took matters into your own hands as usual." He turned on his heel and clomped out the back kitchen door, letting it slam behind him. He heard one of her decorative plates shatter on the floor. Good! He hoped it was in a million pieces.

Edward decided to allow Cloud the freedom of the backyard after he unharnessed him. The dogs were clearly happy to have a horse to harass. He wished he was no more than a dog, with nothing on his mind but a tasty bone to chew. He washed up, then went back to his shop, passing through the kitchen but pretending not to see Anna bent over the stove.

He was just about to unlock the front door to the shop when he changed his mind. He stuffed the key back into his jacket pocket. It was still early. If he delayed reopening for another fifteen minutes, it wouldn't make much difference. What he had to do wouldn't take long. He trotted down the front steps and picked up his pace once he was on the sidewalk, the houses and people becoming just a mere blur. He was trying to keep his usually methodical brain from coming apart and going in different directions with negative thoughts.

He marched up to Daniel's house and rang the doorbell. Moments later, his friend greeted him, a big grin on his unshaven face and a wood planer in his hand. "Afternoon, Edward. You here to learn my secrets to adding some muscle to that lean frame of yours?" he teased.

That's all it took for Edward's blood to simmer again. "Hardly," he answered. "I

236

may not have your brawn but I can rival your intelligence."

"Whoa. I didn't mean that as an insult. Please, step inside."

"No thank you. What I have to say can be said right here on the steps."

"Edward, something botherin' you? You look a little angry. Hope it's not with me —"

Edward put his hands on his hips. "Oh, it's with you all right. What do you mean by running over to *my* house and building pens in *my* barn? Tell me that, will you?"

Daniel's eyes narrowed, but he faced Edward square on. "Edward, I did what I could to help you out."

"I don't need any help, for your information!" Edward raised his voice, and Daniel's neighbor, who was just leaving his house, turned to look.

Daniel shoved his friend through the doorway with an irritated glare in his eyes. "Keep your voice down and tell me what burr you got in your saddle today. I've known you for years and I know when something is wrong."

"I wish you'd talked to me before you took it upon yourself to build pens in my barn! That's what." How could he stand there and pretend to act innocent?

"That's what's eatin' you? For goodness' sake, man. Your wife asked me, and she said it was okay with you."

"She did, did she? Well, it's not all right with me. You still should've consulted with me. How long have you known Anna?"

"About a month."

"Exactly. And how long have you known me?"

"Since grammar school, I reckon. Look, I'm sorry, Edward. Do you want me to go tear them down now? 'Cause I will."

Edward sat down in a nearby chair, his shoulders slumped forward. He leaned over and put his face in his hands, then swiped his eyes before answering. "I'm sorry for railing at you. It's just that I wanted to surprise her, and I left work early to go buy the supplies."

Daniel took a step near his friend, laying his hand on his shoulder. "I understand why you're angry now. I'm really sorry if I caused grief between you and Anna. I was just trying to lend a hand."

Edward stared up at his friend. "I . . . I guess I realize that now, but I let jealousy and my emotions get the best of me."

"Look, don't let it worry you. Do you have time for a quick cup of coffee with your old friend?"

Edward stood facing him. "I'm sorry, Daniel. It's just that you seem to be everything I am not — good-looking, strong physique, charming, a fine woodworker, a cowboy . . ."

"But you have Anna, Edward. Don't ever forget that. I have no one."

"I guess I still have her, but she's pretty upset with me right now."

"You know you have her. She adores you. Don't sell yourself short." Daniel stuck his hand out. "It's settled now?"

Edward took his hand in a firm shake. "Settled."

"Now, how about that coffee?"

"I'd love to stay, but I must go reopen the shop. I'm late as it is." He strolled back to the still-open front door, then paused. "You say you have no one, but goodness, man, haven't you ever seen how Callie looks at you at church?"

Daniel stopped dead in his tracks and scratched his head. With narrowed eyes, he looked at Edward. "Really? I can't say that I've noticed her looking at me, but I *have* been looking at her for some time now."

"So why aren't you courting her?"

"I'm not rightly sure, Edward. We have a good friendship, so I didn't want to jeopardize that — plus I figured that she had

239

plenty of beaus more in her class, if you know what I mean." He leaned against the door and crossed his arms.

"Then you're a downright knucklehead, I tell you." Edward stepped outside.

Daniel followed him out to the porch. "Maybe that's why Anna invited me to a dinner party yesterday. She said others would be there."

"Hmm, I didn't know we were having a dinner party. I think she wants to play matchmaker with Callie. Get you two together or something like that." Edward chuckled.

"I'm glad to hear you laugh, ol' friend. Hey — go easy on your sweet little bride. She's still young and just full of ideas and pure excitement for living."

Edward smiled at his friend. "I know. I think I've expected way too much. I tend to do that, don't I?"

Daniel laughed outright. "Yes. I'm glad to hear you finally admit it, though."

Edward shook his head. "It isn't easy."

"It never is easy to admit our faults or apologize."

"Now you sound like a preacher," he teased.

"Maybe that's another thing I can add to that illustrious pedestal you have me on."

Daniel laughed good-naturedly.

"See you tonight," Edward said, then hurried down the walk.

When Edward entered his house, he admired how the floors shone from the light coating of linseed oil. He could smell the fresh scent of lemon and beeswax on the furniture. The sun shining through the sheer curtains gave the furniture a basking, homey glow. He'd love to stop and sit a spell in his easy chair, reading the paper, but since he'd gotten a late start, that would have to wait. He knew Anna was getting better at some of the household chores, just not all of them all of the time or on a timely basis. Sometimes her head was in the clouds. Whether it was her personality or her youth, he wasn't sure. But one thing he knew for sure — he hadn't told her directly that he appreciated her efforts.

The rest of the day, Anna busied herself with the remaining chores and later took a coffee tray to Edward. He was waiting on customers, so she discreetly put it on his counter until he could take a break. She wondered if at some point he might let her work alongside him. It looked to her like he could use her help at times. But she slipped out the way she'd come, shutting the door between her and the shop.

Anna decided they could have leftover ham slices for supper before they left for the literary circle. Her other chores were done, so she decided to spend some time writing to her sisters. She quickly found pen and paper at the secretary in the living room and enjoyed the sunny view of the street from the window as she composed her thoughts for her letters to Greta and Catharine.

Anna and Edward sat through an uncomfortable silence for most of their light supper, until Anna thought she was going to scream. She realized that neither of them wanted to budge. Finally she had to say *something* to break the ice, but even now she didn't think Edward appeared mad — more thoughtful than anything else.

She sucked in a deep breath, then dabbed her mouth with her napkin. "Edward, it was pretty busy today with customers when I popped in."

"Yes, it was for a little while," he said.

Tread lightly, but don't bring up animals yet. "If you need me to help out from time to time, I'd be happy to."

He looked up from his plate, his eyes looking directly into hers for a long moment before answering. "Maybe. I think you might be a distraction for me and then I couldn't get any work done."

He almost chuckled, she thought. *If only he would.* She couldn't gauge his thinking with his passive expression. She still felt really bad that he'd wanted to surprise her. "Edward, I'm sorry that I let Daniel do the work without checking with you first. It won't happen again."

"I sincerely hope not. We need to be partners, not enemies."

"Does that mean I'm to consult you on everything that happens in our household?" Anna could feel her angst rise. "Am I not allowed any freedom to make decisions I think are best sometimes?"

"I think that would be better, Anna. That way there will be no misunderstandings," he said.

She started picking up the dishes and carried them to the sink. He'd put her in her place like some lord of a medieval castle. Well, it wasn't going to work — not for her, not ever!

23

It was a crisp, cool evening with a full moon casting long shadows on the sidewalk as Anna and Edward made their way to the literary circle at Callie's. Edward wondered what the others in the group thought as they'd read *Pride and Prejudice.* Callie greeted them warmly, taking their coats, and led them to the parlor where the others were already sipping hot coffee.

"So nice to see you again, Anna. Did you get a chance to read the articles I found for you?" Pearl asked after they'd greeted everyone.

"Yes. I read them on the way home. I didn't bring them because I wanted to make a few notes, if that's all right."

Edward's forehead wrinkled. "What articles?"

"Oh, didn't Anna tell you? There are societies formed for the mistreatment of animals. I thought they might interest Anna and help her with her cause. Such a marvelous idea she has, wouldn't you agree, Edward?" Pearl smiled at him.

"Well, er . . . I'd have to know the particulars first, and we haven't had a chance to discuss it yet," he answered stiffly, then glanced at Anna. She sat perched primly on the edge of her chair but refused to give him any eye contact. She was being so contrary today that if he threw her in the river, he was sure she would float upstream. And yet, even so he was enchanted by the curve of her cheek where her lashes lightly touched. He glanced down at her shapely fingers and remembered the feel of them slowly circling his chest. Suddenly he felt desire for his wife. *Good grief, man. Quit letting your mind wander.* From the mood they were both in now, it would take awhile for them to iron out their differences before either felt like being intimate again.

She was talking to Chris, and Edward knew that his charm wasn't lost on Anna. Better that Chris keep that for another young lady.

"Everyone get a piece of Pearl's scrumptious pie?" Callie shyly glanced over in Daniel's direction and he nodded.

Harvey nodded too, smacking his lips. He turned to Pearl and said, "You've outdone yourself again, Pearl."

Pearl gave him a sweet smile, making Edward wonder if there was more than met the eye between the two of them. Funny, he'd really never given much thought to others' attachments until he was attached. He wondered if that meant he wasn't a good friend.

Callie continued talking as they all sat in somewhat of a semicircle. "Since Anna was our newest member, she got to choose our reading material this time, which, as you all know, was *Pride and Prejudice.*" She turned to Anna. "Would you like to start the discussion with your thoughts about the story?"

Anna blushed prettily but spoke clearly. "It's such a romantic book." Her eyes softened as they slid over to Edward, and her look pierced his heart as she began to speak. "The novel centers on the belief that a single man with a fortune must be in search of a wife, but as the story progresses, it's more the woman in want of a husband." Pausing, she glanced at Edward again, then back to the group. "Marriage should not be based on class or prejudice but on the depth of feelings of acceptance and true love. Money and possessions do not ensure happiness. Only real love can accomplish that."

Edward shifted in his seat to better see

Anna. She spoke with such passion. It was no wonder that she cared so much about animals. He felt his heart skip a beat. Tonight he would talk to her and get everything between them all worked out, or so he hoped.

Daniel shifted his gaze in Callie's direction. The look wasn't lost on Edward, and he hoped that Callie was aware of Daniel's interest.

Callie set her teacup aside and leaned back on the settee. Her book began to slide, but Daniel quickly leaned over and was able to catch it before it fell to the floor. Callie turned bright pink and murmured her thanks, then recovered her composure.

"As I read the story, I really identified with Jane and the way she lost her heart to Mr. Bingley," she said. "The story depicted different segments of love — courtship, marriage, struggles, and acceptance of not only others but ourselves."

Pearl pursed her lips. "Mmm, information that we can all use at one time or another. I found it to be a wonderful story. I was happy to discover that Mr. Darcy finally declared his love for Elizabeth and it was reciprocated in the end."

"I think Mr. Darcy was too hard on Jane, trying to protect his friend Mr. Bingley.

Don't you think?" Callie looked around at the group, then gave Daniel a shy glance that made him squirm in his chair.

"Yes, he was, and I agree you *are* like Jane — kindhearted and proper," Chris said.

Callie cleared her throat, turning pink. "Well, thank you, Chris, for saying that." But her eyes were on Daniel.

"My pleasure."

Harvey added his thoughts. "Mr. Darcy was disapproving of Bingley's infatuation with Jane and seemed to have much disdain for her high-strung mother and her frivolous sister Lydia. It was so conniving of him and Bingley's sisters to invent a plot to have Bingley removed from the situation in order to save him from making any kind of commitment to Jane."

"Yes, indeed," Pearl said. "Caroline was snobby, perhaps because of her money. My heart twisted when Jane mistook Bingley's leaving for rejection and became depressed. I confess, I felt depressed myself." She frowned.

Edward was starting to become more uncomfortable with all this intimate talk about feelings and romantic love.

Callie turned to Edward. "You've been awfully quiet. Do you have any thoughts you'd like to share about what you read,

Edward?"

Edward pulled himself up from the slump he'd sunk into while the others were talking. "I confess I felt somewhat divided when Mr. Collins, their cousin, was rejected by Elizabeth when he proposed marriage. That's a blow to a man's ego, but I suppose he deserved it since he was little more than an opportunistic clergyman."

Chris laughed. "However, it's just like a man to feel dejected and turn right around and marry her friend."

"I wouldn't blame Elizabeth one bit, since his proposal was given in such a condescending manner," Anna interjected.

"I'd never even read this novel until now, but I'm glad that I did. It may help me whenever I find the right lady. Hopefully I won't make the same mistakes." Daniel smiled directly at Callie, who looked away shyly, then cast her eyes back to Anna.

"I wouldn't mind having three marriageable daughters." Harvey smiled at Pearl, a twinkle in his eye.

Pearl laughed. "And tell me — what would you do with an impetuous daughter like Lydia who elopes with a penniless army officer?"

There was a rumble of laughter through the group.

Harvey humphed. "Well, I'd like to think I wouldn't be married to a woman like Mrs. Bennet, who was narrow-minded and given to palpitations."

Pearl gave him an endearing smile.

"This has been a lively discussion on love and marriage, and we may have to continue our discussion at our next meeting. There's so much more we could talk about," Callie said. "I'm glad you chose this book, Anna. Do you have any ending thoughts?"

"*Ja.* I think the course of Elizabeth and Darcy's relationship was truly decided when Darcy finally dealt with his pride and Elizabeth overcame her prejudice. This ultimately led them both to surrender to their love for each other."

"I couldn't agree with you more." Pearl nodded. "I believe I fell in love with Mr. Darcy." She sighed dreamily.

It occurred to Edward from reading this book that marriage was not supposed to be hard but a partnership that grows out of love and enjoyment with each other, as God had designed. Anna had made him proud tonight. Very proud.

"This was a delightful read and a change from our normal pace of adventure," Pearl said. Turning to Edward, she added, "You have a very romantic wife, you know."

250

Edward merely smiled. "I think I see that now."

Anna tilted her head at him with what he hoped was affection.

"Christopher has chosen *The Adventures of Tom Sawyer* by Mark Twain for our next read," Callie said. "I haven't read it, but I bet some of you have."

"Sounds good. I'm about to have another slice of that pie, Pearl, if you don't mind. It's not often that I get to taste homemade cooking." Harvey stood, and Pearl took his arm affectionately with a pat and led him to the sideboard.

"Well, I guess we're through until the next time," Callie added. "Help yourself to more tea, coffee, or what's left of Pearl's pie."

After chatting for a few minutes as they retrieved their coats and said good night, the group parted for the evening. Anna noted that when Edward helped her with her coat, his hand lingered on her shoulder. She could feel the strength of his fingers through the coat's material, transporting her thoughts to that leisurely morning they'd spent in their bedroom. She took a deep breath, lifting her eyes to his piercing gaze — and they held. She knew at that moment that everything would be all right somehow.

Walking home, Edward kept his arm about her waist when she mentioned that it was colder.

"I'll keep you warm tonight, Anna," he whispered as they sauntered along. "When we get heavy snowfall, I'll drive us to the meetings if need be."

Anna shook her head. "No, I find it very invigorating to walk outdoors in all kinds of weather, except blizzards or bad lightning, of course. I'll dress warmer."

"You know, Anna, you surprised me with your choice of books."

"And *you* surprised me with your knowledge and interpretation of the book. I'm glad I married a smart man!"

He chuckled. "I'm not so certain about that, but I'm pleased that you think so." He paused under the streetlight, turning her toward him. The shadows from the swaying elm tree branches and leaves made an interesting pattern against the starlit sky in the enfolding darkness, outlining their forms. "Anna, will you forgive me for acting like a jealous child earlier? I have so much to learn about you and how to be married, I guess."

She took his hands and brought them to her lips in a brief kiss. "Yes, I will. It's not only you, Edward. I let my passion for animals overtake my good judgment momentarily. We should've talked this through. But you must try to understand, I truly *want* to have an active part in doing something for helpless animals. I would never keep you from doing something that you felt was very important. In fact, I'd try to find a way to support you, even if I disagreed."

He tapped her nose with his finger. "I don't doubt that you would, my sweet one. I guess I've been bullheaded in my opinion of your idea, but let me tell you a little about why I probably was dead set against it."

Anna was confused. "*Was?* Does that mean you've changed your mind now?"

"I have a clearer picture of your heart tonight," he answered huskily. "If anyone can change my mind, it's you. Around you, I come undone like a bad watch spring!"

Anna had to laugh at his analogy.

"Come, you're shivering. When we get home, we'll have some hot chocolate. It's time I tell you a story."

Back at the house, Anna made hot chocolate, checked on Cricket fast asleep in her bed, and smiled. Moose and Baby seemed comfortable enough on the back porch for now, but Edward had left the barn door ajar for them earlier.

Once they were ready for bed, Edward tucked warm quilts around her while she leaned against the fluffy pillows in their massive cherry bed and unpinned her hair. A crackling fire burned in the bedroom fireplace, casting a soothing yellow-golden glow on their skin.

Edward sat cross-legged, looking comfortable in his long handles. With a cup of chocolate between his large hands, he faced her and shared his story of losing his dog. "I still have an occasional bad dream about the incident, and it haunts me still."

"Ack! Edward . . ." Anna spoke softly, tasting the salty tears streaming down her cheeks and onto her lips before they fell onto Edward's forearm. Such childhood sorrow was mirrored in his face when they locked eyes. "Now I understand why you never wanted any dogs in your home." She grabbed his hand, rubbing her thumb across the back of it, and he reached up to wipe the tears from her cheeks with one thumb, never taking his eyes from hers.

"Yes." He spoke so quietly that the snapping of the logs in the grate startled her. "I suppose you're right. I tried to block it out, but earlier this week I had the dream again. I haven't for a very long time."

Anna had never seen a sadder look before. She took their cups and set them on the nightstand, and without a word she pulled him to her bosom. He willingly relaxed against her, allowing her to caress his head and face and kiss his eyelids. He breathed deeply and evenly, closing his eyes as a small tear trickled out. No words were needed between them. Just the night sounds of a distant carriage passing by with the steady sound of clomping hoofbeats, and the wind's gentle stirring through the trees outside their bedroom window.

24

Saturday was always a busy day for Edward's business, and he was glad that Anna suggested she greet any customers while he handled orders or repairs for his regular clients. He watched her with a close eye and was impressed with her friendliness and how she put customers at ease, even making jewelry suggestions. But he also noticed her plain working clothes were beginning to show wear. He made a mental note to take her shopping at The Denver after he closed his shop today. He'd decided when he woke up this morning that he would begin closing his shop at one o'clock on Saturdays from now on. He had a wife now, and it was very clear to him that he wanted to spend all his free time with Anna. In fact, he didn't want to let her out of his sight!

In her arms the previous night had been the most secure he'd felt in many years. His way of coping with most things in life was to be pragmatic and try as best as he could to keep things in strict order so he wouldn't have time to think. His method had always worked for him since he was a child, but Anna's approach, which at first he'd thought flighty and unorganized, could be another way of enjoying life.

All of this ran through his mind as he adjusted the suspension on a pendulum for a customer's mantel clock. Just as he looked up, he saw a young man from the bank hurry in.

"Mr. Parker!" The young man eyed the customers briefly, removing his hat. "Can I have a word with you?"

Anna observed them from across the room, and Edward remembered that he'd forgotten to tell her about the bank vault job. He gave her a weak smile. It wasn't that he meant to keep it from her, but it had happened at the same time as their spat about the animals.

"Yes, please step into the hallway with me." Edward motioned him out.

Once they were out of earshot, the young man said, "Mr. Krunk wants you to come to the bank as soon as possible today."

Edward took his pocket watch from his waistband. "I have another thirty minutes before I can close my shop, but tell him I'll be there soon after one o'clock."

"The bank closes at 1 p.m. on Saturdays, but he'll be there waiting on you — just knock."

"Thanks for bringing me the message. I'll show you out."

After the man left, Edward waited on a wealthy gentleman looking for an anniversary gift for his wife, but he was aware of the quizzical look Anna shot him. After a moment, the gentleman chose a brooch for his wife and Edward rang up the purchase. That left one customer still with Anna, but it wasn't long before the woman chose black jet earrings with a matching necklace. It had been a profitable morning indeed, and Edward was sure Anna's presence had boosted the business.

Once the shop was empty, Edward quickly flipped his sign over, pointing to the Monday opening time at 9 a.m., and locked the door.

"Why are you locking up so early, Edward?" Anna asked.

Edward waltzed over and took her arm. "I decided to close at one on Saturday from now on. I want to spend time with my beautiful wife. Though I might work later hours right before Christmas."

Anna stared at him in surprise. "That's

wonderful, Edward. So how are we going to spend the afternoon? I was thinking of going to the park and paint —"

"Nope! Not today — maybe Sunday afternoon." He guided her to the hallway. "We're going into town and I'll explain on the way. I'll go hitch up Cloud while you gather our coats."

"Ooh, I love surprises!"

"Then scoot," he said, giving her backside an affectionate slap.

"You'll pay for that later," she teased with a twinkle in her blue eyes.

"I sure hope so." He laughed. He watched her hurry off, then raced to the barn in the bright sunshine and declared to the dogs, "It's a gorgeous day, don't you think?"

Moose raised his head from where it rested on his outstretched paws, then promptly settled back down and closed his eyes. Baby barked a happy greeting, following Edward around inside the barn. Edward couldn't help but admit that he was growing fond of the dogs — all because of Anna.

Fall had crept quietly into Denver this week. Leaves were beginning their gradual change to red, gold, and orange. The brief snow earlier was a thing of the past today as Edward guided Cloud down Main Street to the bank. He told Anna about the new part-time job.

"That's quite an honor that they trust you enough to monitor the combination for the vault." She snuggled close to his side, and he loved the feel of his leg touching hers. She looped her arm through the crook of his as he held the reins.

"I admit it was a surprise, but I'll find this an interesting side to my normal work. I'm going to drop you off at the Denver Dry Goods, then join you later, if that's okay. You can look around for some new dresses. I'll meet you when I'm through, and we can go up to the fifth floor for a late lunch, then finish shopping. Sound like fun?"

"*Ja!* But I really don't have to have new dresses."

"But I say you do. You've been working hard to please me — now let me have the privilege of pleasing you!"

She smiled up at him while he maneuvered the wagon between the throng of horses, carriages, and pedestrians as well as the streetcar. "You'd better watch out or you'll spoil me rotten."

He looked sideways at her. "It might become my favorite pastime, you know."

"Not to change the subject, but I want to have a dinner party. We can ask all our friends and your sister and her husband, even Patty, Polly, and Sarah. Won't that be fun?"

He grunted. "It could be, but that's a lot of people to cook for . . ."

She gave his leg a pat. "Not to worry about that. I intend to ask everyone to bring a dish. Then we would have plenty."

"Then I say, let's do it."

"All right, I'll plan and invite everyone. We'll make this a casual, fun time."

He pulled the carriage to a standstill in front of the massive, red-brick building of the Denver Dry Goods. Helping her down, he gave her a quick kiss on the cheek, promising to return within a half hour.

Waldo Krunk's assistant unlocked the bank door when Edward arrived, then walked him to Waldo's office where he was pacing the floor, waiting.

"Come in, Edward. Have you met Leonard? He's the assistant manager for the bank."

Leonard reached forward and shook Edward's hand with a firm grip. He was a tough, wiry-looking man but flashed Edward a warm smile.

"Good to meet you. Waldo seems to think you can keep our timer in good shape."

"I believe that I can. I read over the material you gave me, Waldo."

261

Waldo patted him on the shoulder. "Shall we go get started then?" The vault was only a short few steps away, tucked into its own separate small space. "It's best that we do this setup after hours in order to keep others in the dark about the combination."

The vault, whose door of reinforced steel and concrete stood wide open, held cash of an undetermined amount as far as Edward could tell. He gave a low whistle. "I don't think I've ever seen so much money in one place at one time."

Waldo humphed. "Well, Edward, that's just the way we'd like to keep it, right, Leonard?"

"Right, boss."

Edward stepped closer to the vault, examining the mechanism of the combination lock and timer and flipping the dial to see how smoothly it worked. The walls were about a foot thick, he surmised, and the door itself about three and a half feet thick. He was very impressed. The three men decided on the combination, but once that was determined, Edward set the timer. The vault door could only be opened after a set number of hours had passed, when the bank opened the next morning, making it pretty hard for anyone outside of them to open it up after hours.

When they were finished, Waldo shook Edward's hand. "Appreciate your help keeping this mechanism running correctly, Edward. It'd be best if you could drop by once a week to check it out for us."

"I'll do that, Waldo. I appreciate your confidence in me."

Waldo turned to Leonard. "You can go on home for the day now, Leonard. Thanks for staying late."

Leonard nodded. "My pleasure. See you next week, Edward." He left the two of them alone and headed out.

"How's that new bride of yours adjusting to life in Denver, Edward?" Waldo asked.

"Funny you mention that, Waldo. It seems she is on a crusade to save orphaned or abused animals."

Waldo leaned back, giving out a big belly laugh. "Ha! I did tell her that I'd be her first benefactor! She's got spunk, I'll give her that." He reached in his suit pocket and pulled out his checkbook, scribbled out a check, and tore it out. "Here, Edward. Give this to her. I don't want her badgering me about that ol' dog that hung around."

Edward happily took the check and looked at the amount. "My goodness, Waldo. Thank you. She'll be mighty pleased. Why, she's already had some cages made in the barn to get started, but she'll put this to good use, I'm sure." He folded the check and stuck it in his pocket. "Speaking of Moose, she intends to train him to be a companion of sorts for one of our friends having vision problems."

"You don't say? She's a very bright woman then. I like that. Someone I wouldn't mind having on my staff, if she decides she'd like to be a clerk and earn some money."

Edward chuckled. "I hardly think that would interest Anna, but thanks for the offer."

Waldo and Edward walked out together, and Waldo locked the bank door as Edward climbed back into his carriage to go have lunch with Anna. He hoped she was enjoying her outing. He'd been extremely pleased that she'd offered to help him in the jewelry shop. Now, he could hardly wait to feast his eyes on her lovely face again.

The time flew past while Anna shopped, delighted by everything she saw in the magnificent store. The store was busy with people out for their weekend shopping. The displays were nice and several things caught her eye. Never one to fuss much with her clothes, Anna preferred clean, simple lines. She finally chose two dresses, one with a matching woolen cape perfect for the colder weather. The other thing she took note of was a set of beautiful Blue Willow dishes. Besides the fact she loved the beautiful blue and white pattern, it held a soft spot in her heart. Maybe in the future she could own a set, but she knew for now that was out of the question.

She had the clerk wrap the dresses for her, charging them to Edward's account. Surely Edward would be outside waiting on her, she thought. She wished she had a watch, and finally she spotted a clock above the elevator. Two o'clock. Edward should arrive any moment, so she decided to wait near the front of the store and observe the shoppers. As she moved closer to the door, she nearly walked straight into Patty Holbrook, Polly and Sarah behind her.

"Excuse me! Oh, it's you, Patty." Anna reached up to steady Patty's hat, greeting the ladies. "Out for some shopping today?"

"Hello, Anna. So nice to see you again," Patty answered for the group. "Yes, we thought a bit of fall shopping was in order. And yourself?"

Anna blushed. "Yes, Edward decided that I needed a couple of new frocks. But I'm glad I ran into you. I'm having a little get-together a week from next Friday at six o'clock and wanted to invite all of you."

"Oh, we'd love to come! Wouldn't we, Aunties?" Sarah turned to her aunts for approval.

Polly smiled. "We wouldn't miss it. What do we need to bring?"

"I was going to ask everyone to bring a covered dish — is that what they call it? That way I can invite all of our friends."

"Yes, we can do that. Polly is a wonderful cook and Sarah is becoming quite the chef herself." Patty beamed.

"It's a good thing then, because I'm still learning to cook, I'm afraid." Anna giggled slightly.

"But you will learn eventually. Besides, this will be less work for one person." Polly patted Anna's arm affectionately.

"Thank you all for your vote of confidence. I see Edward is coming and we're having lunch, so excuse me."

"Ahh . . . a little romance in the afternoon, perhaps," Patty teased and Polly elbowed her.

"Patty, don't embarrass the young bride," she reprimanded her sister.

Sarah smiled. "We'll be looking forward to your dinner party, Anna. Thank you for asking us."

The older ladies would've stood gabbing,

but Sarah guided them by the elbow farther into the dry goods store, giving Anna a conspiratorial wink. Anna liked her a lot. But knowing that the aunts had all but handpicked Daniel for their niece, she was worried. Especially now that she knew Callie was interested in him. Hmm, she'd have to put her thinking cap on.

"My, but you look deep in thought," Edward said, walking up to her. "What's in that pretty little head of yours?"

She squeezed Edward's hand as he took her package. "I'll tell you at lunch. I just ran into Sarah and her aunts, so I invited them to our dinner."

"Is that a fact now?" Taking her arm, he steered her in the direction of the elevator. "I'm not sorry I missed them this time. I want our lunch to be just me and you."

He punched the elevator button. The door opened and the young male operator dressed in a dark suit and a jaunty hat asked them what floor they needed.

"Tearoom, please," Edward answered.

"Yes, sir. That will be on the fifth floor." He closed the door. "Coming right up."

Anna had never seen a pair of shoes as shiny as the elevator operator's. She'd only had one other elevator ride in her young life. This one was the second, the first being the bank building in Amsterdam.

"Did you enjoy the store and shopping?" Edward took her hand once they were inside. "The Denver is considered the largest dry goods store west of Chicago."

"I had a good time. It's so large I hardly knew where to look. I hoped I picked two dresses that are to your liking."

Edward looked down at her, his eyes narrowing, and whispered, "Something silky as well, I hope. I've heard they have exquisite lingerie."

She shoved him playfully on the shoulder. "Not this time, but perhaps later I'll spend more time looking around."

When the elevator stopped, the operator opened the door and wished them a nice lunch.

25

Anna threw the newspaper down the sidewalk, then walked Moose with the leash to where it landed. She let him sniff it first, then picked it up and threw it over and over again, repeating the word "fetch." By the time Moose figured out that she wanted him to go pick it up, Edward's morning paper was beginning to look ragged. Anna rolled it back up and threw it again, waiting to see what Moose would do. This time, after a thoughtful sideways cock of his large head, Moose put the newspaper between his powerful jaws, trotted over to Anna, and dropped it at her feet.

"Good boy!" She clapped her hands together, then reached into her apron pocket for a snack of jerky that she'd picked up at the grocery. Moose lost no time in gobbling it right down and looked for more. "I'm so proud of you! You're not lazy after all. However, before you can earn another treat, you must learn when to cross the street." He barked and Anna laughed, giving his head an affectionate pat.

It had taken a couple of days to get him to understand retrieving. She knew Moose liked lounging on the front porch in the sun and only moved when he saw Anna approach. Anna just shook her head at him and sighed. She'd had to put Baby in one of the pens in the barn earlier when she'd started trying to teach Moose, because she'd thought they were playing.

She spent the next hour teaching him when it was safe to cross the street. She did this by demonstration, keeping him by her side and using the word "stay," and he began to catch on quickly.

Anna had read everything that Pearl had given her and was glad when Edward agreed to let her write up a notice for her special meeting for a society for prevention of cruelty to animals. He'd had it printed for her and helped her hand out the flyers to people on the street who might be interested. She went one step further and ran the ad in the newspaper as well. She was beginning to get excited about it and thanked Edward over and over for agreeing to let her try this new venture. She couldn't help but wonder if he really was only giving in and hoping that nothing would come of it. But ever since he'd told her about the loss of his dog, it had softened his heart and broken down the barriers he'd put in place. It only made her love him more.

Sarah waved to her from across the street and walked over. "I've been sitting on the porch watching you and Moose, and I must say, Anna, I'm impressed. Who says that you can't teach an old dog new tricks!"

"Thank you. It really wasn't hard, considering I've never done this before. I believe Moose has a touch of arthritis, but then so does Harvey."

Sarah laughed. "Then they should be good company for one another. Does he know about Moose?"

Anna shook her head. "Not yet, but I'll ask him soon enough. Pearl thinks this will be good for Harvey."

"I think those two have some affection for each other, don't you?"

"*Ja,* it seems that way. They would make perfect companions."

Sarah lowered her eyes and looked at Moose, giving him a scratch behind the ears. "I want the kind of love someday that you and Edward have."

"Really?" Anna almost laughed but knew Sarah was serious. "Everything is not perfect, even though that's the way Edward wants everything in his life. That's just not real. We're still getting to know each other, but I hope it will be a true love . . . a lasting love."

"You seem wise beyond your years. I do see your love for Edward in your eyes and his for you."

They both strolled down the sidewalk, Moose by Anna's side. "When the timing is right, the right person will come along and sweep you off your feet. Just like that!" Anna snapped her fingers.

Sarah grinned. "But that wasn't the way it was for you and Edward."

Anna giggled. "Hardly. I was a mail-order bride. I was living with my sister and her family on a farm near Cheyenne but felt I needed to have my own life — to make my own future. Edward and I cared for each other through our short correspondence. We actually got off to a bad start and mixed like oil and water, but we're connecting on a deeper level now, and our love continues to grow."

"You know, my aunts seem to have singled out Daniel Moore as a love interest for me," Sarah confided.

Anna pretended that she didn't know. "I see . . . Well, sometimes people have good intentions, and their hearts are in the right place, but how do you feel about Daniel?"

Sarah's face turned pink. "Oh, I like him well enough. He's very handsome and we've talked at church socials, but I'm not sure how he feels about me."

"You'll get the opportunity very soon to figure that out at my dinner party next Friday night."

"I'm very nervous about it," she said, lowering her voice.

"Don't be afraid. Just come with the intent to enjoy yourself among friends."

Sarah nodded. "I'd better get back now, or my aunt Patty will come looking for me. It was so nice talking to you. Good luck with the dog and Harvey." She crossed the street back to her aunts' house, and Anna urged Moose back toward home. She decided that at her dinner party, she would try to let things unfold in the way they should and not involve herself with matchmaking, especially now that she knew Callie cared for Daniel.

She had plenty to do before her guests came for dinner next week, but she'd put off some of her regular chores, much to Edward's chagrin, to hand out the flyers. Edward had taken time off after supper the night before to let their friends know about the dinner and what to bring. It would be nice if Edward would install a telephone, especially for times like that. She'd have to work on him and convince him that the newfangled contraption, as he called it, was moving ahead with the times. She still intended to paint a picture while at City Park before the weather turned too cold — but then painting a snow scene would be quite nice too. Perhaps Sunday afternoon? She certainly hoped so.

Later in the afternoon, while supper was simmering on the stove, she was about to mop the kitchen floor when she heard the doorbell. Edward was still in the shop. Lately he'd been working a half hour later than usual. She dried her hands and placed the mop back in the bucket, then hurried to answer the door. It was Sarah.

"Sarah, hello —" She stopped when she saw Sarah holding a dog with thick golden hair in need of a good grooming.

"Anna, please, you have to take care of this puppy. He looks rather sickly to me."

"Please, come in." She guided Sarah to the kitchen. "I was just about to mop the kitchen floor," she said, removing two of the upturned chairs that were on the table. "Certainly not my most favorite chore. How did you happen to have the dog?"

"He followed me home this afternoon while I was out at the pharmacy for Aunt Patty. I don't know what to do for him, but I'll bet you will."

Anna leaned over the pup in Sarah's lap, examining his eyes and mouth while she held him. The pup was scratching vigorously at his hindquarters and whimpered as Anna gently looked between the folds of his dull fur and gasped at the sores along his back and tummy.

"Goodness! This poor dog is in sad shape. You were right to bring him to me. He must be a stray, and there are plenty of those in this town, I'll wager. I'll feed him then clean him up. I'm glad we have some pens made up in the barn."

"I'd stay and help, but I have to get Aunt Patty's medicine to her. She was feeling poorly today."

"Don't you worry about a thing. Just take care of your aunt, and thanks for being kind to a helpless pup. We need more people concerned like you. Matter of fact, I'm having a meeting to start a society for the prevention of cruelty to animals next Wednesday night. Why don't you stop by?"

Sarah handed the pup to her, her hand lingering on his face, tears in her eyes. "Edward gave us your notice. I'd be happy to attend."

"Are you sure you might not want to keep this dog? Seems he's stolen your heart already."

"True, but I don't think my aunts would let me have a pet. Well, I must go now. Thank you, Anna. No need to walk me out."

With a wave she was gone, and Anna turned to the pup. His sad eyes stared at hers. "We are going to feed you, clean you up, and hopefully find you a good home . . . maybe even Sarah's home." The dog's tail thumped hard against the floor as she talked, but he went right on scratching. She had just enough time to feed him, then after supper she'd give him a bath. She hoped he'd get along well enough with the other dogs and Cricket.

Edward eyed his wife when he came in for supper. He chuckled at her bare feet, and she explained that it was the best way to mop and she liked the way the cool floor felt. He kissed her soundly on the mouth, and she slid her arms around his neck, eager to return his kisses.

Finally, she pulled herself away from his warm embrace. "Supper is getting cold."

Her ragged breathing was a good sign, Edward thought. It thrilled him that their kisses caused such a reaction in both of them.

He gazed at her across the table when they sat down to eat. Her cheeks were flushed, some of her hair had come loose and brushed across her narrow shoulders, and her apron stretched tightly across her chest. In the beginning, her disheveled appearance had bothered him, but lately he'd had a slight change in attitude and found her natural look very appealing. Of course, he wouldn't want her to go out in public that way, and he'd yet to see any of the new dresses on her. He guessed he'd have to remind her to wear them instead of letting them hang in the closet with the tags still on them.

"How did your day go? I haven't seen you since lunchtime." Edward set down his fork.

"I've had a very busy day teaching Moose to retrieve, and I must say, he caught on quickly enough."

"I'm impressed. Waldo said he is too, after I told him about your venture. In fact, he said if you ever want to be a clerk in the bank, he'd hire you in a minute."

Anna sputtered, her mouthful of food almost choking her. She took a sip of water, shaking her head. "I have no desire to work in the bank. It's way too confining." She scratched her arm, then her side.

"That's exactly what I told him. Oh, I forgot to give you something last week. It totally slipped my mind." He pulled out the check from his vest pocket. "I'd forgotten it in my vest. It's your first benefactor's donation."

Anna's head jerked up. "What? You must be kidding."

"Nope." He handed the check to her and watched her eyes go wide with excitement.

"Oh my! Edward, this will help me get started with my society chapter for animals. That was mighty sweet of him."

"That's because he admired your spunk when you stood up to him concerning Moose."

"Well, for goodness' sake. I hardly know what to say."

"Write him a thank-you note and tell him that I forgot to give the donation to you last week."

"Oh, I will right after supper . . . as soon as I clean up a new boarder."

"Come again?"

"Sarah brought me a wayward dog that followed her home, and I've fed him, but he needs a thorough washing, I'm afraid." Anna tried to reach behind her to scratch her back.

"Anna, you've been scratching ever since I sat down to eat. Maybe you're allergic to the dog."

"Oh, it's nothing but dry skin, I believe. I'm going to bathe him right after supper. At least he was welcomed by the other dogs and cat, which I'm grateful for."

"From the looks of it, you'll be needing a bath as well."

"Then I'll need someone to wash my back . . ." She gave him a seductive half-lidded gaze that made his legs go weak.

"Have no fear, I seem to be free this evening."

"Perfect! I'll clean up the dishes and go bathe the dog." She rose and started clearing the table. "You be thinking of a name for the new pup. We can't call him 'dog' forever."

"I'll have to go check him out to see what would fit him, but I might have an idea."

Anna had finished bathing the dog in a large galvanized tub in the backyard, hurrying so he wouldn't get chilled by the autumn air. She felt sorry for him with all the redness beneath his coat. At least it was a shiny sandy gold now that she'd towel-dried him. He had a sweet face, and she talked to him throughout the process while Baby and

Moose watched close by. She tried to gauge his age.

Edward walked into the yard just as she was finishing up brushing the pup's coat. He knelt down beside them, allowing the pup to lick his hand. "Mmm . . . he's a really pretty dog, Anna. Still not fully grown."

"He's a whole lot prettier now. Have you thought of a name?"

"How about Frankie? That's what I named my dog . . ." His voice cracked. "In fact, he sorta reminds me of him."

"Then Frankie it is!"

"We need to put them all in the barn tonight." He glanced up at the clouds. "I think we may get a change in the weather tonight. Possibly rain."

"Okay, let's do that. I need to get cleaned up."

He pulled her to a standing position and held her at arm's length, his eyes sweeping down her. "I couldn't agree more."

Anna could hardly wait to bathe. It delighted her when she stepped into the bedroom to see the hip tub filled with water and bubbles, a fire burning in the grate, and candles burning on the mantel. She turned to give Edward a brief kiss. "Edward, you're so sweet to me. I can't wait to strip off these

280

dirty clothes." She turned her back to him. "Would you mind undoing the buttons for me?"

"It would be my pleasure, m' lady," he whispered in her ear.

The warmth of his fingers caressed her back, making the very skin underneath his fingertips feel sensual. But the trouble was, she was still itching — and now in more places. She heard him gasp as her dress and undergarments hit the floor.

"Anna! Mercy! You're covered in red welts!"

"I am?" She looked down the front of her body. "Goodness! I am!"

"I believe you got this from that dog. Probably fleabites. That explains all the itching."

"What do I do for it?" she asked, scratching her chest and arms.

"I'll run over to the pharmacist. He won't be happy to see me at this time of night, but he'll know how to treat the itching. Meanwhile, let me help you into the bath. That will help soothe the itching."

He helped her into the tub, then scooped up her clothes. "I think these will have to be disposed of. Then you'll have no excuse not to wear the new dresses you bought. I won't be long."

He hurried out and she heard the front door slam behind him. She wasn't sure she'd ever seen him move so fast. The water was relaxing, and by the time Edward returned, she was just getting out of the tub.

"I've got a tincture of clove oil that will stop the itching for you and keep the welts from getting worse. The pharmacist gave me some powdered pyrethrum to sprinkle on Frankie tomorrow." He watched as she patted herself dry, desire reflected in his eyes despite her red spots.

"Do you mind applying it?" she asked, lifting the hair off the nape of her neck.

"Not at all. You'll smell good enough to eat — like my mother's mincemeat pie." He chuckled as he opened the bottle, releasing the fragrance of cloves. Taking a piece of cotton the pharmacist had provided, he began applying the oil. "Here's one, and here's one, and here's one . . ." He wiped the spots gently, his eyes smoldering as the towel she held lightly to her chest slipped a little. "You're beautiful even with red dots all over. Turn around and I'll get the backs of your legs."

She chewed her bottom lip as his head was bent over her legs. She couldn't stand it another minute. She dropped the towel next to him and Edward looked up in surprise, fire in his eyes.

He lifted her in his arms and carried her toward the bed. "I think we'll finish here, my sweet." His voice was low and husky as he reached out and fondled her clean hair between his fingers, breathing in the smell of it.

He lovingly lowered her to the bed, whispering sweet words that fueled her desire for him. And for a time, Anna knew what blissful happiness was.

26

Immediately after church services, Edward and Anna set off for Denver's City Park instead of having lunch with Ella and Ernie. She'd packed sandwiches and cookies for a picnic. The weather couldn't be more spectacular, with the crisp autumn sunshine and a breeze that required only a light coat. The park was beautiful this time of year, abounding with families — some pushing prams, others picnicking or strolling the grounds surrounded by spruce, fir, and elm trees in brilliant orange. The Rocky Mountain range dressed with snowcapped tops created the perfect setting for Anna's painting. Edward lounged on the blanket after eating, watching her profile as she began to paint what she saw. Occasionally, someone walking past would slow down and crane their necks to take a look at her canvas, but she only nodded sweetly and continued with her painting.

Edward's chest swelled with pride as he watched Anna. God had sent him a gift, and he was afraid if he blinked, all the happiness would disappear. He appreciated her keen mind and the rather funny sense of playfulness that kept him both mystified and enamored by her charms. Her profile made a beautiful picture in itself, and he wished he could paint her as she was — contented with brushes in hand, deep in concentration, wearing her blue dress with delicate lace edging the cuffs. But for now he would commit the image in his memory to enjoy later.

An hour or so later, Anna turned, flashing him a beguiling smile. "Are you tired? The sun makes one sleepy, doesn't it?"

"Yes, it does. Why don't you stop for a bit and come sit beside me?" He patted the blanket next to him.

"All right." She laid her paints and brush next to her canvas, then moved next to him. He drew her head to his shoulder, enjoying the smell of her hair.

"I enjoy looking at your pretty face," he said, running his finger along her cheek and jawline. "Your painting is turning out nicely. Let's hang it in the living room."

"I'm glad you like it, but it'll need to be framed first."

He kissed the tip of her nose. "What other talents have you hidden from me, my sweet one?"

Anna grabbed his hand, kissing his fingertips. She loved his hands. "I can't give away all my secrets too soon, you know."

"True, I wouldn't have anything to look forward to then, would I?"

"Besides, you seem to hold a few surprises yourself that I'm slowly discovering." She wrapped her arms about her knees, watching all the activity in the park. "I like watching people who are enjoying a day away from their normal cares of the world. Especially the families with children. Don't you?"

"I rather enjoy watching you," he replied, then looked out across the grassy park. "But you're right, people-watching can be an interesting pastime. Perhaps someday we'll be watching our children play in the park."

"*Ja,* that would be so special. I want a little boy who looks just like you." She turned toward him and looked into his gray eyes, seeing his love within their soft gaze.

"And I intend to have a little girl who looks just like you — even if it means a lot of trying to get it right."

Her bottom lip trembled. "Which will

make life all the more fun!" she teased back. As she turned back to the scenic lake, her heart stilled. Carriage rides were available for riding through the park, and one was just passing by them. The driver was yelling at the nag pulling the now-empty carriage and lashing out with the sharp sting of his whip.

"You good-for-nothing beast! At this rate, we'll never get around the park!"

Anna hopped to her feet, and Edward rose as well. The horse was old, and anyone could see that it was worn from years of service. It had a limp and was thin, with graying whiskers.

The driver, mindless of an audience, got even angrier when the horse refused to budge, and he whipped it again. Anna shuddered but then drew her shoulders back, daring to interfere.

"Sir!" She marched over to him.

The driver, an older paunchy man, glared at her. "What do you want? A ride? Well, I don't think we'll get far with this piece of horseflesh, but tell you what — I'll give you a ride around the lake for half price."

By now, Anna was at the mare's head and saw sores around her mouth where the bit was wearing against skin that sagged from age. Her coat was dull and lifeless, and

Anna wondered when was the last time she'd been groomed.

She reached up and stroked the mare's face, seeking the sad eyes that were no longer bright. "It's not a ride I want." She turned to face the driver and sensed Edward coming to stand next to her. "It's compassion. How about retiring the horse? She's worn out." She stood tense, her hands on her hips.

"Ha! You must be joking. This ol' nag still has another year in her yet. She's just being ornery today and wants more oats. She's grown lazy."

"The horse does look worn out, mister," Edward added, studying the horse closely. "Something's wrong with her hind leg."

"Well, see here — it's none of your business what I do with my property!" He twisted in his seat above them, then spat a stream of tobacco not far from where they stood. "When I'm done with her, it won't be a sweet green pasture — it'll be the glue factory!" He laughed heartily.

How disgusting, Anna thought. She faced Edward. "Edward, we must do something."

She could tell he was hesitating to get involved from the contemplative look on his face.

"I don't know, Anna. The horse is his

property, not ours."

"But don't you see how he's treating her? He's abusing the helpless horse. In all good conscience, Edward, I can't let this continue. I just can't."

A small group of people were beginning to form near them, but Anna didn't care. "I'll take that horse off your hands and turn her out to pasture to finish out her days, if you'll let me," she said to the driver. "And I'll take good care of her too."

Confusion registered on Edward's face. He would eventually understand, but at the moment, her concern was for the crippled horse.

The man lowered his whip with a frown. "I can't just give my horse away. She's my livelihood. What do you take me for? An idiot?"

Anna's heart pounded. "I'll give you fifty dollars for her. You'll still have your carriage." She waited, hoping he might consider her offer.

"I can't buy a horse for fifty dollars. Make it a hundred and you got yourself a deal." He smiled through his tobacco-stained teeth.

"Okay. One hundred dollars — but the horse goes with me now." Anna tried to sound more confident than she felt.

"What the devil?" Edward sputtered, taking a step toward her. "The horse is so old she can barely walk!"

"Please — I'll use the money Waldo gave me if you can supply the rest."

Edward rolled his eyes, then sighed. "All right, but we can't make a habit of this, Anna. Understand?"

She nodded gratefully while he took the bills out of his wallet. The driver hopped down from his perch rather quickly for someone his age and snatched the money in his fat little hands. He stuffed the bills in his coat pocket. "Good deal. Now I'll unhitch her and she's yours, lady," he said. When he was done, he left the carriage and started walking away, whistling a tune.

"What's the horse's name?" Anna called out.

He yelled over his shoulder, "Belle!" and then sauntered on his way. Anna wouldn't be surprised if the man used some of the money for spirits, considering his eyes were bloodshot and drooping. But it didn't make any difference to her.

Edward took the bridle and nudged the horse toward where their carriage and Cloud waited under a shade tree, but it took Anna's soft cajoling to inspire the horse to walk.

"We'll tie her behind the carriage so she won't be straining," Edward said. "Then once we get her home, I'll have Daniel come over and take a look at her leg."

When they got Belle over to their carriage, Anna took Edward's hand. "Thank you. I couldn't let this go or my word about forming the society wouldn't mean a thing, Edward. I hope you understand."

He squinted in the sunlight. "I'm trying to. I understand that you want to help animals, truly . . . but we can't walk the streets of Denver and assume authority over pets and livestock. If we did, then the day would never end."

"I know that. But I'll have others who'll get involved. And you're right — I can't possibly take every animal in, but when the Lord places an opportunity to do good right in front of me, then I have to take a stand."

Edward only grunted, and she felt his eyes on her while she packed up her paints and rolled her brushes in the canvas to be cleaned when she got home. Somehow, she felt like he was less than understanding — even though he did pay the man for the horse. Of course, she'd put him on the spot. Well, everyone had their own gifts and talents from God, and Anna intended to develop hers.

291

■ ■ ■ ■

They drove slowly so as not to stress Belle's leg, and by the time they reached home, the sun was beginning to slide behind the purple mountains. Edward got Belle settled in the barn, and Anna gave her fresh oats and water while the dogs yapped around them, creating noise and confusion. He wasn't sure what in the world they would do with an old horse, and now he had to go see if Daniel could come over and examine her. Belle didn't appear to be very hungry, despite what the man had told Anna. The day had started off nicely until the affairs of rescuing the horse had gotten in the way. He'd planned a romantic evening at home before the workweek started.

As he put Cloud in his stall, he eyed Anna. She went about the barn humming a hymn, then took a curry brush to the tired Belle, talking to her in soothing tones. He felt a little envious of the attention. When it came to the animals, Anna became very focused, unlike the way she handled her chores around the house. He'd observed that she was easily distracted if it wasn't something *she* wanted to do.

He sighed. Maturity would help her focus.

He was sure that if he hadn't said yes to bringing Belle home, Anna was feisty enough that she would have done it anyway. *Nothing in life is ever perfect, even when you strive hard for it to be,* he told himself. Sometimes he felt like he'd lost all control. He swallowed his disappointment and set off to fetch Daniel.

"The horse has arthritis for sure," Daniel said after examining the horse. "There's not a whole lot you can do for that. It's part of aging, but no tellin' what kind of hard labor this horse has been through in her lifetime. You might try some warm compresses, and I'll bring over some liniment in the morning now that I know what's wrong." His brows drew together as he ran his hand along the horse's flanks. "Her breathing is shallow. There could be something else going on here."

"Thank you for coming over," Anna said, stroking Belle's head. "I'll bet she was a beauty at one time."

"I agree. You're so kind to want to take care of her in her last days." Daniel turned to leave. "Be seeing you in the morning then."

Edward thumped him on the back. "Appreciate it, Daniel."

"Daniel, could Edward walk back with you and get the liniment now instead of waiting until tomorrow? I'd like to see if I can give her some kind of comfort tonight, if that's all right with you, Edward."

"Sure, Anna." Edward nodded in agreement, and they started toward Daniel's home. Anna noticed that the two men paused and said something to each other, but she couldn't hear what.

They probably think I've lost my mind today. She turned back to Belle and saw that the bucket of oats was still more than half full. Maybe the horse would feel like eating later. Her breathing sounded a little labored to Anna. Cloud stuck his head across the stall door and nudged Belle's nose, neighing loudly. It made Anna smile. Belle tossed her head at him, pawing the straw with her forefoot. The horses had their own way of communicating, and watching them make friends warmed her heart.

She hugged her arms about her and said a brief prayer for Belle, then went back to the kitchen to heat up supper.

27

Anna fell into bed and was asleep the moment her head hit the pillow. Later in the night she woke up, dreaming about the man lashing Belle with his whip while she struggled to take the whip from his hand. It was hard to shake the feeling the dream had over her, but it was also good to know it was just a bad dream.

She moved closer to Edward, but if he felt her against him, he didn't give any sign. Soon she drifted back to sleep, lulled by the moaning wind outside· and the heat of Edward's back against her.

"Anna. Anna. Wake up." Edward gently shook her shoulder and sat on the edge of the bed.

"What?" Anna forced her heavy lids open. "What?" She saw Edward swallow hard, pursing his lips together for a brief moment. "I'm sorry if I overslept. I'll get —"

"I hate to tell you this . . . but Belle died

during the night." Edward's face was solemn.

Anna jerked up in the bed and clutched Edward's arms. "No! Please tell me you're joking."

"I wouldn't joke about a thing like that, Anna. Daniel warned me last night that Belle's breathing was shallow, and he wasn't sure how much time she had."

She put her hand over her mouth, stifling a cry. "Oh no!" She couldn't hold back the tears. Edward handed her his handkerchief.

"I'll go over and see if Daniel can help me dispose of her. We'll have to get some help. Thin as she was, the weight is more than the two of us can handle."

She yanked the covers back. "I'll get dressed and come help."

"You'll do no such thing. That's not a good idea. I'll handle this, okay?"

She leaned back on the bed frame, quietly crying. "I just can't believe she was that close to dying. Poor thing! At least her suffering is over now."

A meow sounded from the door as Cricket waltzed in and hopped up on the bed. She tried to get as close to Anna's face as she could, as though to comfort her. How did the kitten know she was upset? She saw Edward frown, but she didn't want to start arguing this morning. Bad enough that he'd given her money for the horse. The kitten settled in her lap and purred loudly.

"I guess I left the back door open. She's wanting her breakfast."

Anna wiped her tears. "I'm sorry . . . I'll take her back outside, Edward," she said, running her hand down the cat's fur. Cricket arched her back with each of Anna's strokes.

He sighed heavily. "She can stay this time. It seems she wants to comfort you."

"Thank you. I had a bad dream about Belle last night. I should've guessed how really sick she was."

Edward stood, hands on his hips. "At least you didn't have time to get attached. 'Course, we're out that hundred dollars now," he said with a tight look. "I'm not convinced that you should take in any more strays, Anna." His face was serious and his eyes looked tired, which meant he hadn't slept well. "There's coffee on the stove. I'm going to go round up some help. Don't come outside now, you hear? I'll see that your dogs are fed this time."

"What about your customers? Do you want me to open the shop?"

"No. Mondays are always a bit slow. I'll be back soon."

Anna hugged the purring cat, then noticed

how much brighter her eyes were now than when she'd first brought her home. Most likely responding to the good care she'd been given. Too bad it came too late for Belle. She understood that everything died in time, but that didn't keep her from wishing it weren't so.

She put Cricket on the floor and shuddered at the cold beneath her feet. Quickly she pulled on her dressing robe, then shoved her feet into slippers. A fire would've been nice in the bedroom this morning, but under the circumstances, she knew Edward hadn't had time. She needed a cup of his strong coffee. Cricket was right on her heels, anxious for her breakfast.

Avoiding looking in the backyard, Anna took her coffee and stood by the front living room window. The wind swirled the leaves along the sidewalk and lifted them into the street. She enjoyed the fall most of all seasons. Somehow it invigorated her with energy, but today that energy was sadly lacking. She sighed. She would have to be happy with the fact that she'd tried her best with Belle. There would be other animals she could rescue, she was certain. Wednesday night was her first meeting, and she had to admit that she was more than a little anxious about it. What if no one came?

Edward's wagon, with several other men in the back and Daniel in the front with him, passed by the front yard. They turned down the drive to the back, but she refrained from running to the back window to watch. It would do her no good — only make her sadder.

Dreaded laundry awaited her, but it was better to get a head start while she had time on her hands. She shouldn't be complaining since Edward was willing to get involved with the horse and dispose of her in the first place. She just hoped he wouldn't go on and on today about the money spent. She knew his mood last night was an indication of his displeasure. She noticed how easily he'd clammed up instead of talking with her. She thought they'd worked this all out, and she knew he was working hard at accepting animals, period. Why, just look how he'd allowed Cricket to stay inside today, she mused, looking fondly down at her furry little body weaving in and out of her legs. Anna smiled. In her heart, she knew that she wanted to keep the kitten, but she didn't want to bring that up just yet.

Lord, am I doing the right thing? I feel certain that You laid this on my heart to do. I guess I'm wavering now. How can I be sure this idea was from You and not just something that I wanted to do on my own? I can't do this without Your direction to guide the work. I'll be listening. I need to hear from You. Amen.

Praying always made her feel better, but it would help to keep occupied. She would wait until Belle was gone before doing the wash, but at least she could gather up clothing and do any mending.

As usual, Edward's dirty clothes were folded in a neat pile ready for washing; hers were thrown on the floor of the closet. She carried the clothing to the kitchen, heated up another cup of coffee, then looked for any buttons missing on his shirt or pants. Edward was good at removing anything from his pockets, but one pair had a folded piece of paper. She took it out and stared at it, then reached for a chair and eased herself down to sit. It was his list. Her eyes scanned the list then went back and read the items one by one.

Compliment her every day.
Start helping her with chores when you
  have the extra time.
Bring her flowers.
Tell her romantic things.
Take her on a picnic.
Talk to her about her desires and goals.
Tell her you love her!

Tell her you want her to have your children.
Work on the surprise gift.
Try to relax a little on the chore list.
Let her make some decisions.
Plan a trip.

Anna's heart was deeply moved and filled with fresh love for Edward, causing her eyes to fill with tears. She had no idea that his list was drastically different from hers. Now she felt awful about the times she'd brought up his list in a hateful way. No wonder he never said anything. *Oh, God . . . I'm still learning how to be a wife.* She felt incredibly naïve and unprepared to manage her feelings adequately. And today, even though he'd been against buying the horse last night, he still did it — for her!

How in the world was she going to make it up to him? She'd have to think of something special. She could start today by making those apple dumplings she'd promised him. It was the one thing she cooked best, and the cool weather called for a warm dessert and a delicious roast.

A couple of hours later, after she'd cored and peeled the apples and cut up potatoes and carrots for the roast, Edward wandered in, looking dirty and tired. "I'm going to get cleaned up and get to work now. Most of my morning is gone." He washed his hands at the sink, then turned to face her. "Daniel's father let us have a spot on his land to bury her. But I don't intend to have to do this again. Ever." He was curt but civil.

"*Dank U wel,* Edward." She choked out the words.

He didn't respond or reach out to touch her. Sweeping his eyes over her robe, he glanced down at her feet, where Cricket sat on her haunches, quietly licking her paws. "There's no need for that." He simply shook his head and turned on his heel, leaving her feeling deflated and lonely.

Edward didn't stop for lunch, so she didn't bother to interrupt him in his present state of mind. Sometimes it was best to just let him be. She donned her work dress before going outside to start the wash. She wondered what she'd do when there were more than just the two of them to wash, cook, and clean for. How would she manage or have time for her society?

For that matter, how did any woman manage so many things that had to be done? If she worked from sunup to sundown, she'd never accomplish everything. Maybe a lot of women felt that way too. She truly could appreciate everything her mother had done for her, and how Catharine had taken care of her and Greta. She had to face the truth — she'd been nothing more than a selfish child most of the time. Now she was a wife and a woman. She would not get discouraged or resentful. She was determined to do what had to be done first, and eventually the rest would fall into place.

Anna quit ruminating and complaining, finished the wash, and then played a game of fetch with the dogs with an old ball she'd found in the barn. Moose lumbered around the lawn slowly to get the ball, but Baby was faster and bounded back to drop the ball at her feet, making her laugh out loud. Moose wagged his tail, Frankie barked at Anna in anticipation of the next game, and Baby yakked to get Anna's attention.

"You silly dogs, I have no more spare time." Finally tiring them out, she hurried back inside to check on the roast.

No more than five minutes later, she heard the doorbell. She wiped her hands on her apron and went to answer the door. Through the glass she could tell it was no one she knew, so she opened the door slowly. "Can I help you?"

"I'm sorry to disturb you. You are Anna Parker, aren't you?" The well-dressed lady a few years older than herself greeted her.

303

Anna could see her carriage parked outside the fence.

"I am Anna. Do I know you?"

The lady gave her a bright smile. "No, you do not. But Pearl told me about your endeavors to start a society for the protection of animals. I'm very interested. Unfortunately, I won't be able to attend your first meeting."

Anna opened the door wider and tried to pat her hair into place. "Won't you come in? Please excuse my appearance. I've been doing the wash."

The lady stepped into the foyer. "There's nothing wrong with good, honest work, Mrs. Parker. Let me introduce myself. I'm Mary Elitch. I really just wanted to drop by and give you a donation to help with your endeavors. I'm a very busy person, but I take note of people who are always striving to do better for our city and any helpless creature." She handed Anna a thick envelope of fine stationery.

Anna gasped. Was this an immediate answer to her prayer this morning? "I don't know what to say, Mrs. Elitch, except that I'm eternally grateful to you for being a benefactor. Your donation will be put to good use, I can assure you."

Mrs. Elitch's soft laughter rang out in the

foyer. "I'm sure it will, but please call me Mary. I'd love it if you and your husband would stop in to our restaurant for dinner sometime, compliments of the house."

"That's very generous of you, Mary. I was just trying to come up with something extra nice to do for my husband. I think that will be it."

She smiled broadly. "Then there you have it. Our restaurant is Tortoni's, on 15th and Arapahoe. I believe you will find it delightful."

"Thank you so much! You're a very gracious lady, I can tell."

"And I can tell that you are a determined young woman to take on this much-needed responsibility. My husband and I are working on gardens to share with all of Denver, complete with wholesome, clean entertainment for everyone. That's part of the reason for my donation. You see, I'm very fond of animals, tame and wild, and intend to have them in our gardens when they open. Naturally I don't like to hear of anyone mistreating them."

"Your gardens sound wonderful! And I feel the same. Animals are helpless creatures that need someone to advocate for them." Anna liked Mary Elitch right away. She seemed to be a genuinely lovely and generous lady. "Would you like to have some tea or coffee?" Anna asked her.

"Oh no, dear. But I'll be seeing you around. I wish you all the best and thank you on behalf of all the abandoned or abused animals that I am sure will find their way to your front door." She squeezed Anna's hand and was gone in a flash to the awaiting carriage. The driver took off down the street while Anna stood there in total disbelief. Mary Elitch was a true visiting angel. She could hardly wait to tell Edward.

28

Edward sighed, sipping the strong coffee, then picked up the watch that he'd made for Anna and turned it over. The gold metal felt warm in his hand. He hadn't given her a wedding present and wanted to do something special just for her. It had taken him awhile to engrave the initials and the Scripture from the Song of Solomon on the back. He tried to work on it between customers. He'd thought of the idea of the Scripture when Anna first suggested reading the Song of Solomon. He was proud of his workmanship and at the time thought it was a perfect gift, but now he wasn't so certain. Lately it seemed rescuing animals had taken over their life, using up all of Anna's spare time. And spending money that he really didn't have on an old run-down horse hadn't set well with him.

He'd always been able to concentrate fully on his work and details, but now he noticed that he was totally consumed with thoughts of Anna. Her presence . . . her indomitable spirit . . . her laughter . . . His constant desire for her flooding his mind made it very difficult for him to want to do anything else. *What is wrong with me?*

You're in love, a voice inside his head told him. Was this the way men acted when they were in love? Perhaps so. Trouble was, Anna irritated him some of the time with her different ways and ideas. God knows he was trying to change just a little, but he wasn't really sure that he wanted to. Did he?

Anna had been so happy when Mary Elitch gave her a donation, which in Edward's mind meant that people were beginning to take notice. Truth be known, he wasn't against the animals per se, just a bit jealous of all her involvement with them, and he felt foolish because of it. He knew he'd have to attend her first meeting — there was no way around that.

He put the watch away as a couple of customers arrived. He'd have to decide on the perfect time to give it to her.

By supper time, Edward was starving, and the delicious scents from the kitchen tantalized him. He knew the smell of apple dumplings meant she'd been trying to get back into his good graces, but he'd been

308

stubborn, not appreciating her efforts, and allowed his ego to get in the way because he didn't feel in control in his own home. Well, he'd had enough of the pouting. Besides, it was getting him nowhere. He locked up the shop and headed toward the kitchen, anxious to see what his little lady had cooked up.

She had her back to him and was stirring something in a pan in the oven. Roast? He hoped so. He was ravenous . . . and watching her now, he was ravenous for her as well . . .

The roast looked like it should, Anna thought, but would it be tender? This was her first attempt at the dish. Patty had told her how to prepare it when Anna stopped in to say hello to her, Polly, and Sarah. Every afternoon they sat enjoying their front porch, since soon it would be too cold.

Earlier that day, she had walked over to talk to Callie, and soon the friction between her and Edward came tumbling out.

"It's all because of me, Callie," she'd told her. "In his mind, I'm forcing the issue of animals on him. I don't mean it to seem that way, but I do have this passion in my heart for dumb animals."

Callie raised an eyebrow, pelting her with

questions. "More passion for *them* than your husband? How much time are you spending on this society for abused animals and tending to the dogs and cat?"

At first, Anna was offended by her questions. "I don't spend *all* my time taking care of animals. I do many things to take care of Edward and the house!"

Callie's stare was frank. "Are you sure?"

Anna chewed her bottom lip. "I suppose you're right . . . I don't even keep the house clean enough for him, that's for sure. I'd rather be outside painting or tending to the dogs."

"I don't mean to be hard on you, Anna, and I'm hardly an expert on marriage. I could be wrong, but from what I've observed from my friends, when women get married, their husbands become their first priority. Men tend to be egotistical when it comes to wanting your undivided attention . . . if you get what I mean."

Anna looked out Callie's large picture window. "I do. Lately we've been a little off-kilter and I hate it. I need to feel his strong arms about me, holding me tight." She told Callie about the fleas with the latest dog rescue, buying Belle, and the horse's death. "That's when we started acting stiff with one another, hardly speaking at all. Then I found *his* chore list, which wasn't a chore list at all." Anna's voice cracked with emotion.

"What was it?" Anna had Callie's undivided attention now.

"A list of ways to romance me."

"Really? That in itself was romantic, don't you think?"

"Yes. To tell you the truth, I felt awful."

"Then my suggestion is to search your heart and see if you can compromise. If you hate housework so much, why not hire someone to do some of the more unpleasant chores for you?"

"Good suggestion, but I don't know if Edward would agree to that after spending money on that old horse. He's so fastidious, you know."

Callie laughed. "Yes, I do know! Even more reason to hire someone else to do that for both of you."

Anna rose to leave. "I'll give it some thought and let you know how it goes. Sometimes I need an outside opinion to help me see clearly."

Callie walked her to the door, her arm circling her friend's waist. "You love him very much, don't you?"

"Yes. I've fallen in love with him, Callie."

"Then let him know. My mother always

said never go to bed angry. I'm not so sure that isn't in the Bible somewhere."

"*Ja,* it is." Anna pulled her jacket on. "And that's as good a place to start as any." She ruminated on their conversation all the way home, determined to be a better wife.

Now here she was attempting to make amends by trying her hand at roast beef and potatoes. She heard Edward behind her and straightened, spoon in hand. "Would you care to taste the gravy?"

Edward stepped up to where she stood at the oven, blowing gently on the spoon to cool the gravy. While she held the spoon, he took a taste and smacked his lips. "It's good . . . it's *very* good. Maybe a tiny bit more salt? You're becoming quite the cook."

She felt heat spread across her face and neck. Her sister had once said that a way to a man's heart was through his stomach. "I'm trying to. Patty gave me the recipe for making roast beef. It's not nearly as good as my sister Catharine's, but I don't think it's bad either."

He took the spoon from her hand and laid it on top of the stove, then took her hands in his. "You look cute when you're all flushed from the heat of the stove."

"Thank you. But I always seem to look a mess when you're around," she replied, pushing the hair back from her brow. After thrusting her hairpins back into place, she began to button the top of her housedress where it exposed part of her décolletage. The heat from the oven had made her warm, and her bodice clung with dampness.

He caught her hands. "No, don't do that. It's better left unbuttoned for now." He kissed her fingertips.

What had caused this renewed playfulness in him? Her heart thumped. "Why don't you wash up? Then I'll serve our dinner." She shoved the oven door closed, and then he grabbed her arm, forcing her to look at him.

"Anna," he whispered, then pulled her against him, pressing her body into his. "I've suddenly found myself not very hungry, at least not for food."

Before she could utter a single word, he began kissing her brow, her eyes, her lips, then lightly planted kisses on her throat and on down to the V where her breasts swelled at the top of her blouse. Her breath felt like it was cut off as her arms caressed his back. She searched for an excuse for him to stop, but nothing came to mind. She licked her lips while he locked eyes with her. He had a way of making her go weak in the knees with every tender kiss, and every place his fingers

313

touched made her skin tingle. Whatever had caused his attitude change, she loved it!

"Edward —"

"No, don't say anything. Just let me hold you as I've longed to. Please."

His breathing was ragged, his palms pressing into her shoulder blades, bringing her closer to him. The tension in her body relaxed as she leaned back against the counter, tilting her head back while he feathered kisses along her neck again. He nipped at her moistened lips until she returned his kisses with a fervor of her own.

Supper would have to wait . . .

It was much later when together they heated up supper for an unexpected, cozy candlelit dinner. Edward had stoked the fire, which warmed the room comfortably. He pampered Anna by fixing a plate for her for a change, then fed her forkfuls of his potatoes as they laughed and joked about their sudden tryst while all their differences melted away. They were sitting side by side, and it felt as if nothing could separate them or the feelings they had for each other.

Anna pierced a slice of beef with her fork as Edward opened his mouth wide to receive it, never taking his eyes off of her.

"I'm sorry for my attitude after Belle died.

I shouldn't have gotten mad at you, since I did agree with the situation."

Anna stroked his jaw. "I'm sorry too, because I forced you into buying her when I know you really didn't want to. Sometimes I'm impulsive, I guess."

He laughed. "You think maybe more than a little bit? Honestly, Anna, I admire you for what you're doing. Not many people would do those things. To be perfectly honest, I was feeling jealous of your time setting up the society," he admitted.

"My dearest, you never have to feel that way again. I promise to not neglect you — at least not intentionally. Otherwise I'm doing the same thing that I'm trying to save the dogs from, aren't I?"

Edward's eyes twinkled in amusement. "Are you comparing me to your dogs?" They both chuckled, then finished eating. "You made a wonderful supper," he said. "Sorry it was I who caused it to grow cold, but you have to admit, dessert is always better . . ."

Heat flooded her face, but she gazed into his steel-gray eyes. "Maybe we should always have dessert first, then."

"Watch out what you promise me — you may live to regret it." He pushed his chair back. "I'll feed the dogs. I'm sure they're starved. And you can stack the dishes and feed that weakling you call a cat that sleeps all day," he teased.

Anna swatted him with her napkin. "You know you like her. I've seen you talking to her, but go ahead and pretend. I won't share your secret with your men friends." She put the dishes in soapy water to soak.

He laughed heartily, then strode to the door. "I'll be back, and perhaps there's time for a little more fun . . ."

Anna shook her head, poking her tongue out at him. He began to chase after her but she ran off.

29

Ominous afternoon clouds descended Wednesday, threatening the first measurable snowfall of the season for Denver. Anna hoped it would hold off until the next day since tonight would be her first meeting to form a chapter for her society. She had butterflies in her stomach and was excited about the prospect and the chance to meet new people. What would they think of her? Or of her crusade to save Denver's abandoned and homeless animals?

Today she'd stayed busy cleaning the parlor until the windows shone, only to be disappointed as the gray skies hung heavy and the wind blew in over the mountains. In the afternoon, she baked spice cookies and prepared hot chocolate. The spice fragrance permeated the house with an inviting, homey smell, but more than once she had to swat Edward's hand to keep him from eating the cookies.

Now, as she pushed back the sheers, she watched large drops of rain begin to fall. She usually loved the smell of rain and enjoyed the sound as it came harder, but today she worried about the meeting.

She tried to distract herself by thinking about Edward, busy as always in the shop. Their relationship had taken a marked turn for the better — each promising to come to the other when they felt there was any kind of problem arising in their relationship. Life was good, their love was growing deeper, and the intimacy . . . well, Anna held those precious times fondly in her heart. Edward always made her feel beautiful and desirable even when she looked a little bedraggled. She vowed to work on her appearance in the future. She wasn't lazy, it just wasn't a priority to her. But she could tell when she did style her hair and press the wrinkles from her dress, Edward was very pleased. Most of the time she only did that for church.

Callie's influence was taking hold on her too. Anna secretly admired how Callie seemed to always look perfect. She was someone Anna wanted to emulate in fashion, if she ever set her mind to thinking about it. Today she wore a demure navy Woolsey dress with a conservative high neckline. It was full at the shoulders and bustled at the back, and her hair was braided tightly against her head. She wanted to look as mature as possible, but she worried that the braiding was out of style in Denver. She would ask Callie to help her when she took Edward to the restaurant. She was keeping one of her new dresses for that special evening.

The time passed slowly after their early supper. She kept watching the clock and pacing until it was time for folks to arrive. The rain had turned to sleet then tiny flakes of snow. "Will anyone come, Edward?"

She jumped when the doorbell rang, shattering the silence. "I'll get the door. You just steady yourself," Edward said. He gave her a brief kiss on the brow.

Anna heard a conversation in the hall while she waited.

"Hi, Sarah," Edward said. "Come right in and let me take your coat. The weather change was a big surprise."

"Thank you, Edward." Sarah removed her coat, and he hung it on the coatrack then showed her to the parlor.

Anna greeted her. "Sarah, I'm so grateful that you came. The weather will keep many away, I'm afraid."

Sarah took a seat. "Oh, I wouldn't miss

your meeting, Anna. It's very important and I want to support you if I can. Aunt Patty and Aunt Polly send you best wishes, but the weather is a little hard on their rheumatism."

A moment later the bell rang again, and Edward shot Anna a wink. When he opened the door, Pearl and Harvey tramped in, stomping their feet as snow blew into the foyer. Anna hurried over to them and helped Edward with their coats. "Bless you for coming in this weather. Go warm up by the fire. Edward made us a nice one."

"We certainly shall," Harvey said.

While Anna hung up their coats, she watched how sweetly Pearl was guiding Harvey by the elbow.

"We've got hot chocolate to warm you, and Anna made delicious spice cookies," Edward added as he led the way to the fireplace.

Pearl removed her gloves and stood with her hands stretched out to the fire. "Hello, Sarah. It's nice to see you again. I hope your aunts are doing well."

"They are doing fair to middling. I think Anna's idea is a good thing, don't you?"

"Yes, indeed I do."

Harvey nodded his agreement. "If anyone

can get something done, it will be spunky Anna."

Anna could hear their chatter from where she stood waiting for Ella and Callie as they met at the same time on the sidewalk.

"I'm glad I only had a short distance to walk," Callie said. "These are tiny flakes now, but if the snow continues and the temperature drops, we'll have to shovel for sure in the morning." She brushed the snow from her cape, Ella right behind her.

"Ella, so glad you came. Where's Ernie?"

Ella shook her head. "He dropped me off and will pick me up later. You have his support, Anna, but he hates meetings," she said, leaning over to give Anna a swift peck on the cheek. "Where's my brother?"

"Edward's in the parlor. You know the way." She watched Ella disappear down the hallway, then directed her gaze back to the street out front. To her surprise, she made out Waldo Krunk and a woman on his arm coming up the walk. His wife?

"Good evening, Anna. I'd like you to meet my dear wife, Leola. Leola, this is Anna, the little whippersnapper I told you about."

Leola was an attractive woman with a soft face and an expression of friendliness. "How do you do, Anna. It's a pleasure to meet you. Waldo told me all about you." She stretched out a gloved hand to Anna, who shook it.

"And you as well. Thank you so much for coming to the meeting. Please follow me," she said. A huge gust of wind slammed the front door shut as she took Waldo's hat and their coats.

They scurried to the parlor where everyone was gathered, sampling the cookies and hot chocolate set up on the sideboard. Soon Edward ushered in Reverend Buchtel, or Hank as he liked to be called, and his gracious wife, Mary. Anna was pleased to no end to see them in attendance. Given the weather, this was turning out better than she'd hoped. There might be fewer people than what she wanted, but still . . .

"I'll go get more hot chocolate and then we'll get started," Anna whispered to Edward. "I don't see anyone else arriving."

"Do you want help?"

She smiled up at her handsome husband. "I'll get it. Please, just entertain our guests."

She scooted to the kitchen, refilled the pot of hot chocolate, then stopped to give Cricket a stroke down her back. Clasping her hands together, she paused to say a prayer that the meeting would turn out to be worth everyone's time and for the right words to say to the small group. Even now her mouth was dry. She got a sip of water, braced herself, then marched back to the parlor, pretending to be in complete control.

Two other people had come in while she'd been in the kitchen. A young lad who looked to be thirteen was seated next to his mother. The group was mainly composed of women, but that was okay. Perhaps a good thing. Women usually got things done, she thought. Anna walked around refilling a few empty cups, then walked over and introduced herself to the newcomers.

"I'm Jane Wallace and this is my son, Alan," the woman said. "We admire your efforts and want to see what we can do to help."

Alan nodded but was quiet and appeared a little shy. Jane was a petite woman with graying hair at her temples and frank brown eyes that expressed warmth of character.

"I so appreciate both of you taking the time to come tonight," Anna said. "I guess it's time to get started."

She moved to stand in the front of the room and took a deep breath. "Please continue with your refreshments while I talk. First, thank you all for coming out, even with this change in the weather. You'd probably rather be curled up by your own fireplaces. But I appreciate it from the bottom of my heart. You see, animals will always have a spot in my heart. When I see a dog, cat, or any other animal treated in a less than humane way, I feel I must speak out and do what I can to help their unfortunate circumstances. I feel that it's our responsibility as citizens to look after all homeless creatures in Denver, therefore making it safer and, in the long run, healthier for both humans and animals."

Anna could see the group's interest, and someone responded with "Amen."

She continued. "Henry Bergh was an activist who touched Americans' hearts and consciences with the idea that animals should be protected from cruelty. He started the first American Society for the Prevention of Cruelty to Animals, or ASPCA, in New York in 1866. Other societies began springing up around the country. He paved the way a long time ago for what I'm proposing. Legislative laws that he wrote were subsequently passed, and his tireless work and efforts instituted the ASPCA. I have just recently learned about all his endeavors by reading articles Pearl was kind enough to supply to me.

"It's my desire to rescue as many wounded and abandoned or abused animals as possible in this city. That will be a big undertaking, I know, and I'll eventually have to house them somewhere besides our barn." She gave her husband a lopsided smile, and the group laughed. "But that is where I'll need eager volunteers to help me out. I can't pay anyone, of course, so I need willing hearts. To add to that, we will need to have several fund-raisers to help us get our society off the ground."

She paused and looked out at the familiar faces, realizing that they were here because they were genuinely interested to see what she had planned. She noticed now that Daniel had slipped inside and was sitting next to Callie. She was happy to see him here.

"In Proverbs chapter twelve it says that a good man regards the life of animals, but the mercies of the wicked are cruel. I'm not quoting here, but I think that means we are to be the caretakers of the animals that God has put on this earth. I for one want to be able to say I tried to do this. I've read about so many cruel actions against animals that they're hard to believe. In fact, I'm already housing two extra dogs and a kitten in our barn, and I took in a very old horse that died from such treatment."

There was a gasp from the group, but she continued. "If you share my same passion, please join our society, which will be a chapter of the American Society for the Prevention of Cruelty to Animals. Please add your name to the paper Edward is going to pass around. Are there any questions?"

"I have one." Sarah raised her hand. Anna nodded. "What can we do to raise money to house and feed animals that come to us?"

"That's a good question, and the floor is open for any suggestions." Anna directed her gaze to the group.

"I'm sure we can get the church to hold a bake sale, with the proceeds to go toward the cause," Mary answered. The reverend nodded his agreement.

"Great idea," Anna said.

"I could offer to shovel sidewalks for those who needed help and donate what I earn. Of course, it'd be after school." Alan glanced at his mom for approval, and she smiled at her son, touching his hand affectionately. Anna could tell she was proud of him.

"Why don't we try to have an auction?"

Anna turned to Edward. "An auction? What would we auction?"

"Oh, things like handmade items, some nice or new furniture." Edward shot a look at Daniel. "I would be willing to donate a watch or two and maybe a piece of jewelry."

Cocking his head toward Edward, Daniel remarked, "Thanks for offering pieces of my furniture." He laughed. "But I have to admit, it's a good idea."

"The jewelry is an excellent thought too," Pearl added.

Callie leaned in toward the entire circle. "What about a ball?" she suggested. "You could invite as many of the important people as possible and charge for admission, which would become a donation."

"That's another excellent idea," Harvey commented. "Women love nothing more than an excuse to dress up!" He chuckled. All the men added to his comment and the women started chatting.

Anna clapped her hands to get their attention. Their enthusiasm made her heart swell with pride. This was more confirmation of the work God had led her to do.

Finally everyone quieted down, and Anna said, "I believe we've heard some great suggestions, so I think it'd be a good idea to appoint someone now to chair the fundraiser. Who would you like to nominate?"

The room was quiet for a moment and the wind could be heard howling outside. "I think Mary could handle the job," Daniel said.

Mary, who'd been quiet for most of the

time, replied, "I'm honored that you have confidence in me, but with supporting my husband in all the church responsibilities, I'm afraid that I wouldn't be able to follow through."

"I agree with that my dear," Hank added.

"Well then, Sarah, what about you? Would you be interested?" Anna questioned.

"Me?" Sarah's face reddened. "Well . . . I guess I could. I've never done anything like this before."

Leola leaned over and patted her arm. "It'll be a great way to meet people and get you involved. I think you'll do all right. Remember, we'll all be your underlings, and of course you'll have Anna, who will be in charge."

Sarah smiled brightly. "Then I'll give it my best."

"Wonderful," Anna said. "I think we're finished for now. I'll send out a letter to each of you outlining our goals and commitment. Once again, thank you for attending. You don't have to leave if you'd like to stay around and chat. There are more cookies and hot chocolate to warm you before you face the cold again."

The group clapped their hands in appreciation, and Anna felt grateful to know them. Everyone rose and stood about chatting, so she made her way over to Harvey.

30

"Your spice cookies are now my favorite cookie!" Harvey exclaimed to Anna.

"Then I shall wrap up a few extra for you to take home. But for now I want to talk to you about something."

Harvey focused on her face, his eyes narrowed, and paused with a cookie halfway to his lips. "Of course, Anna. What is it?"

"I couldn't help but notice you seem to be having some problems with your vision," she said quietly.

"Er . . . yes, I am. Hate to admit that I'm growing old, but it's true. The doctor has told me that I'm losing most of my eyesight, but I see somewhat peripherally — for now."

"Can I make a suggestion then?"

Harvey shrugged. "I don't see why not. Pearl adds her two cents when she can." He chuckled. "Really, she has been very kind to try and help me."

"I've been training one of my rescued

dogs to fetch and how to tell when to cross the street. Simple things like that. I don't really know what else to teach him." She gave a slight laugh. "However, I wondered if you'd be interested in having him as a sort of companion and friend, but also to guide you when you're walking, especially outside the home."

Harvey's mouth dropped open. "You're serious? Well, my goodness, I never thought of anything like that. I guess I could give it a try. I had a dog years ago."

"Perfect. Once I introduce you to Moose, you'll like him, I'm sure. He's an older dog, and I've had him only a few weeks, but he's sweet and affectionate."

He laughed. "Then we'll be perfect for one another." Harvey cocked his head at her. "But won't you miss him?"

"Of course, but I can come visit, can't I? I can't keep all of them, you know. Besides, this is what it's all about — finding good homes for these animals, right?"

He nodded. "Indeed, you're right, and of course you can come and visit . . . that is, if he likes being with me."

"Oh, I can assure you he will. Just give him a bowl of food, a warm fire, and a place to sleep." Anna grinned, and Harvey smiled and finally popped the cookie into his mouth. "You can take him home tonight if you'd like."

Pearl and Edward walked up. "I couldn't help but overhear the last part of your conversation, Anna. Such an excellent idea for Harvey." Pearl beamed at them.

"It's still snowing out, so we have the dogs in the barn for tonight," Edward said. He laughed. "Anna already had a dog. Then she found Moose, and then Sarah brought her another one."

"Sounds like the program is already under way then," Pearl stated. "I'm sure there'll be many more animals to come."

"Let's hope so. Edward, can you go get Moose for Harvey?" Anna asked.

"Yes, of course. I'll be right back." Edward nodded. "Unless you'd like to come with me, Harvey."

"That's a good idea — I'll come with you. Pearl, can you wait for me here?" Harvey asked.

"I surely can. I'm glad you're going to take Moose with you. I promise not to move from this spot." Pearl clasped her hands in front of her.

Anna turned to Pearl. "If you'll excuse me, some people are leaving now, and I want to wish them goodbye."

"Go right ahead, Anna." Pearl flashed her a smile.

Soon Harvey and Pearl left with Moose, and the last ones to leave were the reverend and his wife. "I completely admire what you're trying to do, Anna." Hank helped his wife with her coat.

"Thank you, Reverend — Hank. I have a theological question for you, if I may?"

"Of course, but I may not know the answer." He smiled down at her.

"Do animals go to heaven? I was thinking about Belle, the horse we rescued. It started me wondering about that."

Hank gave her a mild look of surprise. He hooked his thumbs in his pants pockets, spreading the coat he'd already donned, and paused as if contemplating his answer. "I'm not 100 percent certain, Anna, but Scripture is full of places where God cares for animals throughout history. In Genesis, when a rainbow appears, it's an everlasting reminder of the covenant between God and all living creatures of every kind on earth. And God opened the mouth of Balaam's donkey to speak, which saved Balaam's life. To me that speaks to the importance of animals in creation."

"Yes, I've read that," Anna said.

Hank went on. "Your question is a deep

one, but I'm reminded from the book of Luke that at Christ's coming, all flesh will see the salvation of God. Therefore, I see no reason that He couldn't re-create animals. As to our pets, remember that God is the giver of all good things, and it would be a simple request for Him to give to us if it would please us."

"My, my. Your answer has given me hope. Why don't you do a sermon about this?"

He grinned. "I just might do that in the future. But we'd best be on our way now. If Mary and I can help in any way, please let us know. As a matter of fact, why don't you let the church be your meeting place? I think you might have more people attend if it was closer in town."

Anna's heart sang. "Oh, that's so generous of you! I think that would be better."

"Then I'll see what room isn't being used and let you know. How's that?"

She folded her hands together. "Perfect. I can't thank you enough. Of course, if more people don't turn out, we won't need that much room."

Hank strolled to the door where Mary was waiting. "Oh, I have confidence in you. See you soon."

Later, when Edward and Anna were nestled under a heavy quilt with the snow outside softly falling, they talked about the meeting.

"I'm very proud of my little wife. You were wonderful tonight."

Anna laid her head on his shoulder. "Thank you, but I must admit that I expected more people. Most of the ones who came were our friends. At least everyone present signed up."

"Don't worry. Things will change as word gets around. You'll see."

"And at least something came of rescuing Moose. I think Harvey was pleased, don't you?"

Edward stroked her arm lying across his chest. "Without a doubt. Moose will be a good companion for him, but I have a feeling pretty soon he'll have to share Harvey with Pearl," he said matter-of-factly.

"You think so?"

"Just a matter of time, my dear."

"Mmm . . . I'll miss Moose, but I'm glad we found each other," she mumbled.

"I am too, my sweet one," he answered, holding her tightly. "I am too."

The city awoke to a mere trace of snow, but it was very cold. After pleading with Edward, Anna was allowed to bring Baby and Frankie into the kitchen to stay warm. It

335

was hard to say no where she was concerned. It was funny how swiftly he'd been willing to change some of his habits to suit her. He liked to call it compromise. Daniel teased him that he was tied to Anna's apron strings.

Edward made sure that wood was stacked right outside the back porch as he left to walk over to Daniel's. He was interested in learning what he could to build stronger muscles and gain strength, now that Daniel wasn't always working out at his father's ranch. Mainly, Edward wanted to be stronger than he was. His kind of work didn't lead to staying in shape.

Walking the few blocks, he enjoyed the crunching sound his shoes made against the snow as cold, refreshing air filled his lungs. He decided that later in the year, with more snowfall, he would pull the sleigh out to take Anna for a wintry ride. For now he knew that the snow they'd just had was a brief warning of things to come.

He rapped sharply on his friend's door, and moments later Daniel's cheerful face smiled back at him. "I see you finally decided to come by," he said.

Edward followed his friend inside. "You always look fit as a fiddle, and with my job, I'm not. I decided that I was too young to be flabby. So here I am."

Daniel gave a hearty laugh. "You are not flabby, Edward, and you're *not* old! But maybe I can show you what's helped me. Ranch work used to keep me fit, but making furniture doesn't. Let's go out to the barn where my secret is kept."

Edward was puzzled but followed him outside. The barn held Daniel's horse, but mostly he had old and new furniture in various stages piled around.

"I discovered a few of these things when I went to New York to visit my grandparents last year." He pointed to wooden clubs that looked more like bowling pins to Edward. "These are Indian clubs that were used by the British army, believe it or not, to keep the men in good physical condition. I'll show you how to use them in a moment. I got this idea on how to make dumbbells there too. Pretty clever, I think." Daniel lifted the dumbbells.

Edward took a closer look. "Well, I'll be. Church bells at either end of a metal rod. Clever, very clever."

"Yes, it is. All I had to do was remove the clapper. I made two sets, one with larger bells for a heavier weight after the first one became easy to lift. I'm thinking about buying a bicycle too, but since winter's coming on I'll wait until spring. It's good exercise, plus it gets me outdoors on the weekends that I don't run over to my dad's ranch." Daniel strode over to a box and lifted something out. "I just ordered these. Took a couple of weeks to get here. They're kettle balls — really nothing more than a painted cast-iron ball with a handle for weight lifting. Just another way to exercise when I'm bored with the wooden clubs. So what do you think?"

Edward stared down at the equipment and scratched his head. "I'm downright impressed, Daniel. I admit to you that at first I was jealous, but I'm glad I had the nerve to tell you."

"Besides gaining strength, if you do this often enough, you'll gain stamina . . . if you get my drift." Both of them laughed.

"Let's get started then. I told Anna I'd be back in an hour."

Daniel clapped him on the back. "Plenty of time." He demonstrated how to swing the clubs in a certain pattern — in a circle, behind him, overhead, and in forearm swing circles. "You'll do these in a couple of sets. Here, it's your turn. Take your time. Oh, and by the way, next time wear some loose clothing — it'll be easier to execute the rhythms."

By the time Edward had run through the routine with Daniel's instruction, he was sweating, but he actually felt good too. If this could work for Daniel, then it could work for him.

When he was finished with the set, he wiped his brow with his handkerchief. "Whew! That's some kind of work, but not bad."

"Glad to hear you say that. Let's move on to the next. I'm thinking of adding some ropes over the rafters with sandbags attached for weight. Just another way of working a different group of muscles, I think."

Thirty minutes later, both men were tired but enjoying the camaraderie that the time together allowed them. They guzzled down tall glasses of water in the kitchen.

"You are welcome to come over anytime to do this with me, or you can pick your day and just go on back to the barn and help yourself."

"I'd like to give it a shot, especially if my biceps and shoulders are gonna look like yours!"

"It can help, that's for sure, and you'll see results in no time at all." Changing the subject, Daniel asked, "How's married life?"

Edward stared at his handsome friend. "I'll tell you, we got off to a rough start, but it couldn't be better. She's sweet, smart, and opinionated, and fun too. To tell you the truth, I don't want to spend one minute away from Anna."

"That's great news, Edward. I truly am happy for you. Now if I could just get the courage to ask Callie out . . ."

"Why not try to work up the courage at our dinner party tomorrow night?"

"Mmm . . . we'll see."

"That young Sarah also seemed to be looking you over as a prospect last night at the meeting. Must be nice to have two women interested in you," Edward teased.

"Aw, I don't know if Callie's interested. Sarah seems nice after I talked with her at the meeting, but . . ." He looked out the window.

"But?"

"There's something that I can't put my finger on about Callie. I'm drawn to her for some reason. Maybe it's because she has such a cheerful spirit."

"You won't know what it is about her until you try to court her. Don't waste any more time thinking about it, Daniel. I have a feeling she'll say yes."

31

It was apparent that word had gotten out about Anna's chapter of the ASPCA, whether from her flyers, her ad in the newspaper, or word of mouth. A number of people stopped by with small donations to support the cause or brought another stray or wounded animal. It was also obvious that she and Sarah alone would soon not be able to handle all immediate requests or rescues. They would need help, especially in transporting and taking care of the number of stray dogs. Anna hadn't stopped all morning long, what with visitors appearing at her doorstep and keeping track of the animals' care.

She'd walked across the street to see if Sarah had any free time to lend a hand, and in a matter of hours she was thankful Sarah had become her assistant. Another dog had been found by Alan, and he'd dropped it by on his way to school. Too bad he wasn't already out of school or she would've claimed him as the official dogcatcher. She would have to see about hiring someone for the job, and that would mean they needed another wagon — one that was enclosed. Anna decided to talk to Edward for suggestions.

One thing both Anna and Edward were concerned about was the noise from the dogs barking. If she had more strays, the neighbors would soon be complaining — and rightly so. To date they had five dogs and a goat to feed, and that didn't include Baby.

Sarah had a list to keep track of each dog or other animal by its color, since neither of them were knowledgeable about the different breeds. Anna made a mental note to order a book on dog breeds. Or she could see if there were any in the library.

"Anna, how about I check with some of the local restaurants and cafés and see if they're willing to let us have their scraps to feed the dogs and cats and anything else that comes our way? At least until we can order something to feed them from the general store."

"Sarah, that's a brilliant idea. But how are we going to be able to pick up the scraps?"

"Well . . . couldn't Alan after school?"

"I don't know with his schoolwork, but his mother might be able to lend us a hand. We need to check on that."

Sarah made notes in her tablet as Anna talked. "Suddenly I have so many things to figure out, but these donations will certainly help. Tomorrow we need to go to the church to plan the bake sale and find out where we can meet in the building. I don't think I have time to wait until the reverend lets us know — there's so much work to be done. I also need to write up a newsletter for our chapter. I believe Edward has a typewriter." She laughed. "Trouble is, I'm a slow typist. One finger at a time."

"You're so funny! You'll manage, and I can help if need be. We'll have to work fast to get a lot done, since winter is right on our heels. It'd be good if we can find a space or building to rent soon for the animals." Sarah got up from the desk. "I'll leave now. I believe I can persuade a few people to allow us to collect their leftovers for our shelter."

"Shelter? Hmm . . . Sarah, I never thought of that, but you're exactly right — that's what it really is, isn't it? A shelter." Anna admired how Sarah's brain worked.

"Yes. We'll have to think up a name for it."

Anna giggled. "Hold on — we don't even

have the building yet." She rose as well, stretching her back. "I've got so much to do, and I have the dinner party tonight as well."

"I'll be right here to help. It should be fun. Perhaps we can generate more ideas, since almost everyone who attended the meeting is coming to dinner."

"You're right."

Sarah grabbed her coat, then slipped on her gloves. "I'll be back in no time."

Anna gave her arm a squeeze. "Sarah, thank you for stepping right in to help me today. I think I suddenly realized what a huge undertaking this could become. I can't do it alone."

Sarah's hazel eyes were warm and crinkled at the corners when she smiled. "You won't have to, Anna."

"That means a lot. Now I'm going to see if I can interrupt Edward long enough to find out if he knows of anyone I could approach who would be willing to drive a wagon to pick up stray dogs or cats. It will be me in the beginning, I'm afraid, but somehow I don't think that will set well with him," Anna admitted.

Sarah frowned. "Mmm . . . I can hardly see Edward letting you become the town dogcatcher." She tied her bonnet and scurried on her way.

Edward had several customers he was busy with, so Anna decided to wait until he was free, although she was mentally going over things to be done and plans for tonight's dinner party. Perhaps she should've waited. Too late now.

She walked over to assist a young lady at the jewelry case, and it wasn't long before Edward was finished.

"Thanks for your help, Anna," he said when they were finally alone. "You look like you have something on your mind."

Anna took a deep breath and told him everything she and Sarah had discussed. Edward folded his arms and leaned against the jewelry counter, listening.

"I think I'm going to need your help," Anna said.

"That's an awful lot of wants. What do you think you need first?"

"An enclosed wagon for picking up strays."

"Who's going to be doing the driving?"

Anna chewed her bottom lip. "Me," she whispered.

"No, that's not going to work. I won't have my wife driving through the streets of Denver looking for animals, and that's that!" He spread his hands in exasperation.

Anna had expected this reaction, but she'd have to convince him that without the means to hire someone, she would have to be the one.

"Edward, I must be the driver for the time being, until my chapter has the funds to hire someone. Don't forget this was all my idea. I can't push it off on someone else. Sarah is already helping as much as she can." She paused. "Very soon, I can see us needing a larger space, since the barn is filling up fast."

"So I've noticed. I've seen all the activity from my work area. May I remind you that someone will have to be out in the yard to dispose of the animal excrement?"

"I did that right before Sarah came over. I must admit, I need another set of legs and arms, and if I could grow them I certainly would."

Edward rubbed his chin. "Let me think on it. I have to run into town and check on the bank vault timer later this afternoon. Maybe I can think of something. For a shelter, you'll either have to have a benefactor or lease an old building that's not being used. Waldo might have some notions about that since he knows just about everyone in town."

She threw her arms around him, and he received her embrace. "I knew you would help me! Now don't be too long. Our dinner guests are coming at six o'clock sharp!" She pulled away as he tried to plant a kiss on her lips. "No time for that now. I've got a million things to do!"

He shook his head, laughing, as she spun around and flew from the shop just as another customer arrived. Sometimes she resembled a little waif — apron half-tied, hair escaping its pins, her mind going a mile a minute. As soon as he finished up for the day, he'd head on over to the bank. Maybe even stop to pick up some flowers for her table for the dinner guests tonight. Nothing made him happier than pleasing Anna. He just hoped dogs didn't take over their life. But one thing was clear to him — if a woman wasn't happy, then no one was happy!

Downtown Denver was the hub on Friday evenings for many folks dining out or going to the theater, and the busy streets were no exception when Edward hopped on the street-car into town. That would be quicker than taking time to saddle up Cloud, and it was too far to walk there and get back in time for their guests. From the looks of things, the parlor wasn't as tidy as he'd like it, and Anna would need some help getting last-minute things done before everyone arrived. His father would've laughed at him, but Edward didn't care. He was learning that when two divided the chores they went faster, leaving him and Anna more time to spend together.

" 'Bout time you showed up. We like to close the bank at five o'clock sharp, especially on Fridays," Leonard said, leading him past the only teller still there closing up his window for the day. Edward nodded at him and noticed the teller looked nervous when Leonard spoke to him in passing. Leonard fancied himself as the next president of the bank when Waldo retired, and in Edward's estimation, he liked being in charge. As long as Edward had this job, he would be cordial and get along with him.

Waldo was chewing on his usual cigar and greeted him heartily. "Howdy, Edward. Good to see you again so soon. I have to say I'm glad I attended Anna's meeting, even if my wife had to twist my arm. Very informative."

"Thanks for saying that, Waldo. She was tickled that you and Leola came. She's already working hard at getting this whole thing started. Matter of fact, I'd like to ask if you know anyone who might have an old building to lease. The number of animals has started to rise and soon my barn won't be able to hold them. Sort of a shelter for them. Nothing fancy."

"Can't say right off for sure, but I can inquire for you. I do know of a customer of mine who's closing his account to move to Wyoming. He owns a warehouse on Broadway. If he doesn't already have it leased, I'll ask."

Edward thought for a moment. "It depends if we can afford the rent. It may be a stretch for us until we get funding under way."

"I can always float you a short loan to help you get started. Matter of fact, my customer is leaving because a fire destroyed part of the building and merchandise, but the damage could be easily repaired . . . at least I think so."

"Hmm . . . maybe Daniel and I can do the work, which would save us a lot. I'll tell you what — you find out what you can, and we'll see if we can swing it."

Waldo clapped him on the back. "You've got it. And just for the record, I'm proud of you for standing by Anna's endeavors. Now go on and check that timer so we can all call it a day, son."

Edward nodded, feeling proud from Waldo's compliment. He walked toward the safe, where Leonard was putting the last stack of money and bonds inside.

He turned to Edward. "All done for the day, Edward. I'll leave you to set the timer. See you next Friday."

"Good night, Leonard." Edward could hear him telling Waldo goodbye before walking down the hallway and out the front door.

Edward spun the dial around, checking the mechanism on the combination, and then made sure the timer was working properly. Behind him, he heard a movement as he closed the vault door.

"Excuse me, Mr. Parker?" It was the teller he'd seen when he'd arrived earlier. He was a swarthy-looking man — hardly the look of a teller — but then it wasn't his business if the man looked more like a rough-edged miner than a businessman.

"That's me," Edward answered as he stood.

"My name's Calvin. I overheard you mention to Mr. Krunk something about needing an empty building?"

"I did for a fact. Why? Do you know of one?" Edward thought it unlikely that he owned anything, but maybe he knew of someone who did.

"I might. Friend of mine on Colfax can't come up with his rent, and he's fallen on hard times with his business. His lease is about up, so I could ask for you."

Edward was curious as to why Calvin wanted to help him. "What's in it for you, Calvin? You don't know me at all."

Calvin scratched his beard. "To tell you the truth, my friend told me he'd give me half the money for the rest of the lease if he could find a buyer for the remaining months."

"I see. Well, find out what the remaining balance is and when his lease is up, and we'll go from there. You know where to find me," he said. They walked to the front of the bank, where Waldo was putting on his coat and hat. "I'm kinda pressed for time tonight." He thought it was a stroke of luck that he might have not one but two places to tell Anna about.

"All right. I best be hurrying home, don't like to keep the missus holding supper too long for me." Calvin lifted his coat off the coatrack and said good night to Waldo before hurrying down the steps.

"Have a great weekend, Waldo. See you next week," Edward said, tipping his hat. Since he'd never taken his coat off, he headed out right behind Calvin with rapid strides toward 17th and York. He hoped Park Floral was still open. He had his heart set on surprising Anna with flowers.

Sure enough, he made it just before his friend John Valentine was about to flip the sign to CLOSED. "Wait, John! Please!"

John smiled through the glass showcase and swung the door open. "We're just about to close up shop, Edward. You almost missed me. What can I do for you?" John stared at Edward through his round spectacles.

"I know you don't work in the floral shop usually." Edward struggled to catch his breath.

"Ha! I'm here and there. I have to stay on top of everything, you know, and make sure my helpers here are getting the job done. So what can I help you with, son?"

"I just want to get Anna some flowers for a dinner party that she's having tonight. You know, a bouquet for the table, maybe?"

John twirled his mustache between two fingers. "Step on in. Everyone else has left, but I'm sure I can put something together for you right quick. I have some pink and white chrysanthemums. How would that work?"

"Perfectly!"

"Okay, I'll just wrap them up for you."

The fragrant smell of flowers and greenery pervaded the room. There were boxes, paper wrappings, leaves, flower stems, and crushed rose petals scattered on the floor and counter.

Edward glanced at his watch. It was 5:45! He'd have to hurry. He watched while John took his time laying the flowers neatly onto stiff paper, jawing about something with the city ordinances. Edward was really in no mood to talk and only grunted in agreement.

John tied the paper with bright red ribbon and handed the bundle to him. Edward grabbed it, slapping some bills into John's hand. Waving to his surprised friend, Edward took off running for the next streetcar at the corner and reached it just before it took off again.

It was colder now as dusk descended on the city, and the streetlight cast a warm glow on what little snow still lay on the sidewalk, making it sparkle like diamonds on a woman's necklace. He should've been home to light the fires for their guests before now. He hoped the exercises he'd started doing would eventually be beneficial for helping him run from the bank to the florist and then to catch a streetcar.

He smiled. It had been a good day. A good day indeed!

32

What was keeping Edward? Anna fumed. She'd spent the afternoon baking enough apple dumplings to feed an army, then tried to straighten the house while Cricket, under her feet, tried to catch her swishing broom, making a game of it. The kitten made her laugh, but she had no time for such folderol. Good thing she'd gone ahead and fed the dogs and put them in the barn, since Edward was still out.

Passing the hallway mirror, she saw her reflection and decided she needed to stop now or there wouldn't be time before guests arrived to change her work dress and freshen up. *Oh, why did I plan a party so soon after my meeting?* Of course, she hadn't expected things to move as fast as they had, but she was very pleased and only hoped she could iron out all the things she'd discussed with Sarah and Edward.

Once she had pulled her hair back into a

chignon instead of braided cornrows for a change, she donned one of her new dresses. A soft shade of pink moiré silk, the dress had sleeves that ended at the elbow, with two rows of lace that fell from the sleeve's hem. *Very feminine,* she thought as she turned this way and that in front of the cheval mirror. The bodice itself, made of piqué, had tiny tucks and folds, creating a basket-weave effect that ended at the hip and made her waist appear wasp thin. Touches of black velvet trim on the shoulder and the edging of the bodice and hem created a lovely balance between light and dark. Next time she would ask Callie to help her with her hair.

She had no sooner finished her toilette than the doorbell rang, announcing the arrival of her first guest. She hadn't made a fire in the living room yet, and with the type of dress she was wearing she would be chilly for certain. That would simply have to be Edward's job — *if* he ever returned from town.

She sprinted from the bedroom to answer the door. It was Patty, Polly, and Sarah, all laden with dishes of food.

"Patty and Polly, I'm so glad to see both of you. Sarah told me you've been under the weather lately." She greeted the older ladies with a brief hug as Sarah winked at her from behind.

"Thank you, I'm feeling much better. We've brought baked chicken and saffron rice," Patty said.

"Mmm, smells wonderful!" Anna peeked into the dish as Patty lifted the lid proudly.

Polly sniffed the air. "Whatever you cooked for dessert smells heavenly. Something with cinnamon, I'll wager."

"I made Edward's favorite, apple dumplings," she said, showing them to the dining room. "It's the only thing I can cook really well. Let's put the food on the sideboard. That way each person can fill their plate. Maybe a little unconventional, but —"

"It is for a dinner party, so it's a good idea," Sarah agreed, smiling.

"Oops! There goes the doorbell again. Excuse me, ladies, make yourself at home in the living room. There's coffee and tea on the teacart in there." She hastened to the door to greet Callie, Ella, and Ernie, who'd all walked over together, and within a few minutes the living room was full of guests. Daniel and Chris arrived, but still no Edward.

The sideboard was quickly filling up with delectable dishes. Sarah offered to fill the water glasses while Anna stuck the rolls that

Ella had baked into the oven to keep them warm.

Anna walked back through the dining room to make certain the silverware was at each place setting, then paused to admire Sarah's outfit. "I declare, Sarah. You look lovely tonight in that shade of rust. It sets off your complexion."

"Thank you, Anna. You look lovely too. I wasn't sure what to wear. I'm not trying to impress anyone."

"You will! Did you meet Christopher? He wasn't at the meeting, but I'll introduce you."

"Is he the man who walked in with Daniel? No, I have not met him."

"Then come with me." Anna took Sarah by the elbow. "I think you might find him very interesting."

The front door flew open and Edward raced in, a large bouquet of flowers in his hand. "I'm sorry I'm late," he said as he handed Anna the flowers. "These are for the table." He gave her a peck on the cheek.

Anna looked at her husband in surprise. "How pretty! I was wondering what happened to you."

"I'll tell you later. Let me start a fire in the living room." He tore off his hat and coat, hung them with the others, and strode to the fireplace.

Harvey and Pearl arrived along with Moose. "I hope it was okay to bring him," Harvey asked while Moose danced around Anna, licking her hands and barking.

Anna giggled at the way Moose's tongue tickled her hand. "Shush, Moose. Quiet down. Yes, Harvey, it's okay. How's it working out with you two?"

"Just fine. He's pretty smart, but most of all it's good to have a companion — one that will fetch!"

"I'm so glad for you."

"Thank you for being so thoughtful to think of this in the first place. Though Moose may have to compete with someone else soon."

"Is that right? Might that companion be someone I know?"

Harvey nodded in Pearl's direction and her face turned pink.

"Ooh. How wonderful for both of you! But I hope you'll keep Moose. He needs a good home."

Pearl nodded. "You can take comfort in that. We both adore him already!"

"Oh, that does my soul good. Why don't you join the others? I want to put these flowers in the dining room."

Moose stuck close to Harvey's side, and

Anna quickly said a silent prayer for God's creatures everywhere.

Dinner was a smashing success with a variety of good dishes to choose from. The flowers added the perfect touch to the white Battenberg tablecloth, and the tall tapers burning on either end of the table gave a cozy glow. Candlelight looked best on everyone, making them softer, more approachable, Anna thought. The only thing missing was her family — and her mother's Blue Willow china.

For a moment, she felt very sad that her family couldn't be here with her. Peter, her brother-in-law, had given her a Blue Willow teacup and saucer for her hope chest. But it would be so nice to have her own set. Maybe for Christmas? Hardly! She could see how every little cent would go toward the shelter now — if Edward agreed, that is.

She was reminded of all the new friendships she'd formed so quickly. God had truly blessed her and had given her a wonderful husband. Perhaps her sister Greta could visit for Christmas, since she lived closer. Anna would mention it to Edward, who was presently sitting at the head of the table.

His gift of flowers had caught her off guard, but then she remembered his list.

She still hadn't told him she'd found it. Best not to mention a word, lest she embarrass him. He certainly had changed from who he'd been when she'd first arrived. Even now he was watching her, and she smiled at him. She knew the admiring look was all about the new dress with the off-the-shoulder neckline. He nodded his approval, making her feel quite desirable.

"So what do you think about that, Anna?" Callie asked, drawing her back to the present.

"I'm sorry, I'm afraid I wasn't paying attention." Her face turned warm.

"Chris asked if you'd like him to be your first official dogcatcher."

Anna directed her gaze to Chris. "Really? Do you mean it?"

Chris shifted in the small dining chair that he seemed too large for. "Yes, but with my job, it couldn't be full-time. More like a volunteer."

Anna knew that he worked for the *Rocky Mountain News* as a journalist. "I would be forever grateful, Chris."

"I'll even interview you and write a story about your chapter news. I'm sure I can get the boss to put it in the paper."

"Chris, that would be such a great advertisement." Edward set his forkful of food down. "Thank you so much. We won't forget it."

Chris waved his hand. "Bah. It's all in a day's work for me."

"Just the same, we can't thank you enough," Anna added. "Now to find us a covered wagon of sorts . . ."

Ernie cleared his throat. "Anna, I'd like to donate that to you for all your efforts. I'll even have a sign painted on the side so there'll be no mistaking who the ASPCA is." Everyone around the table twittered with surprise. A covered wagon was not cheap.

Tears of joy filled her eyes that he would do that for her. "Ernie, God will bless you for it."

Ella beamed at her husband. "You have such a generous heart, Ernie." She squeezed his arm.

"Aw, you two cut it out! I'm just wanting to help, that's all."

"Then I'll throw in a horse for you so Chris will have something to drive," Daniel offered.

Anna caught her breath. "*Uff da!* Now I'm really going to cry." She popped up from her seat and raced to each of the men to give them a hug, and they patted her affectionately. "I know now what friendship is

361

all about." She looked around the table. "I just want to tell all of you how much you've come to mean to me in such a short time since I arrived. I was lonely at first, but you've helped me in ways you couldn't know."

Polly sniffed into her napkin, and Harvey seemed to have something in his eye as he dabbed it with his handkerchief.

"You've given us much as well," Sarah declared. "Not only friendship, but something to focus on that can help our community."

"Yes, and I am grateful!" Callie said.

"Oh, you women are getting sappy now." Edward humphed. "I say we bring out the dessert."

Everyone laughed, and Anna just shook her head. "Of course you would be thinking about your stomach!" she teased.

"Oh, wait! There's something I've been thinking about since you started all of this, Anna," Edward said. "I'm going to have a telephone installed so you'll have a way to keep track of everything without having to leave the house."

Anna scrambled over to kiss him soundly on the mouth. "Edward, you never cease to surprise me. *Dank U wel!* A telephone is going to be a great help to me, and to Sarah."

He patted her hand. "You're welcome. *Now* can we have dessert?"

"I'll help you with that." Ella pushed her chair back and followed Anna into the kitchen. "Anna, you have brought sunshine into our lives and Edward's. I just want you to know that. I know we don't see each other very often, but I'm really happy to have you as my sister-in-law. You can count on me when you need something — anything. Just let me know."

Anna took her hand, looking into Ella's friendly face. "Ella, it's all of you who've made me feel wanted. Truly, I mean that. I wasn't sure I'd be accepted at all."

She gave Anna's hand a squeeze. "Anyone who can make Edward smile the way he's been smiling lately is worth their weight in gold! Now let's deliver his dumplings before he has a fit."

Anna's heart was fair to bursting with the outpouring of love from everyone. Would it always be this way? She sure hoped so.

During dessert, Ella addressed the group. "I think Anna's dinner was a good idea. We should consider rotating once a month and do this again. Any takers?"

"My sister and I would be honored to be included in you young people's get-togethers," Patty agreed.

"Age will not be a discriminating factor at any of my dinners," Callie inserted. "It's a marvelous idea."

Everyone began talking at once. Ella tapped her water glass with her fork and they quieted down. "Sounds to me like we're all in agreement. Whose house is next?" She looked around the table.

"I'd be glad to host. All of you know I can't cook a lick, but I can make coffee." Daniel grinned.

"Great! You're next. Let the rest of us come up with a menu." Callie turned to Anna. "What about a parlor game, Anna?"

"Uh, I don't know any, but if you'd like to lead one, then go ahead," she answered.

"Okay, let's retire to the living room and I'll give you all the rules." Callie pushed back her chair. "But first we need to carry our plates to the kitchen sink in gratitude for Edward and Anna's hospitality."

Later, after everyone played charades and laughed until they couldn't anymore, they bade Anna and Edward good night. Their spirits were high and unaffected by the blast of cold air as they stepped outside to leave. Anna gave Moose a hug around the neck when he left with Harvey and Pearl, reminding him to come back anytime for a visit. Edward wrapped his arms about Anna's shoulders as they stood waving goodbye to their last guest.

"We couldn't have had a more perfect ending to a day. Don't you agree?" She looked up at her husband.

"It was a very nice time and I think enjoyed by all."

As they readied for bed, he told her about the possible buildings he'd found out about and would be checking into for a shelter.

"But how will we afford the rent, Edward? I don't have enough donations for that." She didn't want him to know how excited she was at the possibility of a real shelter for the animals.

"It'll all work out. More advertising will help too. Let's just wait until I know what the asking price is before you start worrying, okay?"

Anna pulled back the sheets and climbed into bed next to him. "But how will we be able to make a building into a shelter?"

He pulled her against himself, and she laid her head in the crook of his arm. "I have a feeling Daniel and I could paint and fix up what's needed and others would volunteer. I'll help when I can. I think that's the least of our problems."

"Speaking of Daniel, it looks like he and

Callie are getting to know each other better."

"Yes, it does look that way. And did you see how attentive Chris was to Sarah?"

"I did. I think it's wonderful. I'm getting to know her and I enjoy her company, not to mention her help and sharp ideas." Suddenly Anna felt an icy cold foot on her leg. "Ohh! Your feet are freezing!" She tried to move away, but he caught her by the arm as she feigned a struggle.

"Then I guess you'll have to warm me up! Come here, my sweet one." He chuckled. They held each other for a long time until Anna could no longer keep her eyes open.

33

After breakfast, still basking in a glow of love and contentment, Anna nursed her mug of hot coffee to warm her hands. Cricket curled up in her lap, purring contentedly, while she and Edward bounced around ways to spend their Saturday.

"I have an idea. Why don't we take a ride out to the country and have a picnic?" Edward said. "It'll warm up like it always does. We can take the dogs and let them have a good romp with total freedom."

"Can we? That would be wonderful. A change of scenery would be nice."

"Sure thing. Why don't you pack some sandwiches, and I'll feed the dogs and hitch up Cloud?" Edward rose.

"Edward, you have nearly taken over the job of feeding the dogs, and I want to thank you for doing that when I haven't even asked you." She stroked his arm.

"I don't mind, really. But we'll have to

clean up a little around here. Tomorrow's the Lord's day and no housekeeping —"

The doorbell sounded, interrupting him and startling Cricket. She leapt up from Anna's lap and ran underneath a nearby cabinet.

"Are you expecting anyone?" Anna frowned, hoping that whoever it was wouldn't stay long. She was excited about Edward's plan.

"No, I'm not. I'll go see who it is."

Anna followed closely behind him and could see through the glass on the door that it was Waldo and the sheriff. *What in the world?* Maybe they were dropping off a stray dog?

Edward swung open the door. "Morning, Waldo."

"Edward, I . . . hate to disturb you, but we must have a word with you." Waldo glanced worriedly at Anna.

"What's this about?" Edward cut the sheriff a hard look. He was middle-aged with a long handlebar mustache and a weather-beaten face, and he didn't look any happier to be at Edward's than Waldo.

"My name is James Archer," the sheriff said. "I have some questions for you."

Anna stepped close, holding on to Edward's arm.

"You can ask whatever you want in front of my wife, Anna," Edward said.

"Ma'am." The sheriff touched his finger to his hat brim. "Edward, where were you last night?"

The sheriff's question caught him off guard, but Edward answered respectfully. "I was home with my wife. We had a dinner party, and it didn't break up until very late. Why?"

Waldo shifted on his feet. "Can we come in, Edward?"

"Why, of course." He moved aside and they all stood in the foyer. "Is something wrong?"

"Where were you before dinner, and what time was that?" the sheriff asked.

Edward thought a moment. "I was late coming home. I was at the bank with Waldo, then I picked up some flowers for Anna's dinner table. Why?"

"I'm sorry, but I'm going to have to take you in for questioning. The bank was robbed last night after you and Waldo left. And you were the last one there to secure the safe, according to Waldo."

"What?" Anna gasped.

"I'm sorry, Edward, but it's true. When I got there this morning, all the money was gone! You and I were the last ones to leave last night," Waldo blurted out all in one breath.

"Are you insinuating that I would take the bank's money?" Edward snapped. "I set the timer before I left. No one could've opened it until 8:30 this morning!"

"Calm down, Edward. I'm sure there's been some terrible mistake," Anna piped up.

The sheriff stepped forward. "You can come peacefully, or I can haul you in." He pulled out handcuffs from his coat pocket and dangled them in his hand.

Edward wondered if he were in a nightmare. It sure felt like it. "Waldo," he pleaded. How could Waldo believe he'd do something like this? Preposterous! He and Waldo had been friends a long time.

Waldo could barely make eye contact with him as he spoke. "I'm sorry, Edward. Really, I am, but I don't have any choice. There are no other suspects. You were the last one in the bank's vault."

"There'll be no need for handcuffs. Let me get my coat." Edward turned to Anna, placing his hands on her shoulders. "Try not to worry. I'll explain everything, and we'll take our picnic when I get back, you hear?" He saw the worry in her eyes.

She nodded. "Let me go with you."

"No," he said firmly, then kissed her brow and reached for his coat. The three of them hurried down the steps.

Anna put a fist to her mouth, stifling a sob as she leaned against the cold door. How could her world crumble in a matter of minutes? How could anyone believe Edward would steal anything entrusted to him? But she would do as he said — go ahead and make the sandwiches and dress for an afternoon outdoors. She just had to believe it would all be resolved in a matter of hours.

She forced herself into action. Standing here in shock wouldn't accomplish anything and wouldn't help the situation. She donned a brown tweed skirt with matching bolero jacket, then set about making the food as Cricket sat on her back haunches watching her every move. She found the picnic basket in the pantry and wrapped the food in clean linen napkins, then placed it on the table to wait until Edward returned.

It would be a good time to write her sisters while she waited for the time to pass. She sat at the writing desk near the window so that she could see outside. This would be a perfect time to have that telephone Edward had promised.

Her mind kept coming back to the bank

robbery. Edward *was* very late last night. And where was he getting the money to pay for a telephone? For that matter, how had he planned on paying for the rent on a building? He'd made it clear from the beginning that his jewelry business wasn't as lucrative as he'd like.

Stop it! Don't even entertain such a thought, Anna chided herself.

After she'd written letters to her two sisters and to Clara, Catharine's mother-in-law, the morning had worn on, and by eleven o'clock, there was still no sign of Edward. Anna's heart fell. She was about to go hitch up the wagon and drive downtown when she saw Sarah coming up the walk. She hurried to meet her, swinging the door wide.

"Sarah, I'm so glad to see you! I need a friend right now." She pulled Sarah inside.

Sarah gave her a puzzled look. "Anna, are you all right?"

"Edward was taken to the sheriff's," Anna blurted out. "The bank was robbed after he set the vault timer last night! Edward hasn't returned and I'm not sure what to do next. I —" Her breath caught, and she looked away to keep Sarah from seeing the tears that threatened.

Sarah took a step closer and placed her

arm around her. "I'm so sorry, but there has to be some misunderstanding. How long has Edward been gone?"

"Since right after breakfast! I'm so worried. What if they've arrested him?"

Sarah's face was etched with true concern as Anna looked to her for help. "Want me to go with you to the sheriff's? Then you can see what's going on and perhaps set your mind at ease."

"Would you? I'm sorry, I didn't even ask if there was something you needed."

"Nothing that can't wait. Grab your coat and let's go."

"I'll go harness Cloud so we can take the wagon."

"I'd help you, but I need to let my aunts know that I'll be gone a little while or they'll just get worried."

"All right. I'll be out back. Meet me there," Anna said, donning her coat.

While she was harnessing Cloud to the wagon, the dogs yapping at his heels, a nagging thought occurred to her. She hadn't really known Edward very long. How could she be certain that he wouldn't do something unscrupulous?

Because you know him! a voice inside her said.

Anna shook the negative feeling aside and

climbed aboard the wagon.

Sarah came puffing up to the wagon. "I tried to hurry so I could help you. Sorry, but Aunt Polly wanted to know what I was in such a hurry for, so I told her," she explained, taking her seat next to Anna. "My aunts will be praying."

Anna nodded, then picked up the reins and yelled, "Giddyup," urging Cloud to trot out of the yard and down the street. She caught a glimpse of Patty waving from her front porch. It did her heart good to know that others would pray for her husband.

Edward sat across the cluttered desk from Sheriff Archer, who'd spent all morning questioning him thoroughly about the night before. He'd told the sheriff the same thing over and over again. *How can this be happening to me?*

Edward sighed. "Why don't you believe me, Sheriff?"

Archer pushed back his chair and fumbled around on his desk until he found a round ring of keys. "I want to, but it's really not up to me. I'm afraid I'm going to have to hold you until I get further evidence that you weren't involved in the robbery."

"You've got to be kidding."

"Sir, I don't kid about such things." He

motioned for Edward to follow him.

"Aren't you going to question anyone but me?" Edward rose, shoving his hands in his jeans pockets. Best he keep them there or he might swing a fist in his anger.

"That's my job, not yours." He shoved Edward to the back side of the room and into a cell. "If you're innocent, then there's nothing to worry about, is there?"

"How do you propose I clear my name from this jail cell? I told my wife I'd be coming back."

"Well, you were wrong. Best you spend some time sitting there contemplating your fate." Archer slammed the metal door shut, then turned the key in the lock. Edward was the only prisoner in the stark cell block, and he was glad. He didn't want anyone to know that he'd been there.

"Then at least let my wife know I'm in your cell, would you?" Edward heard Archer's boots on the floor as he walked back to his desk.

"I'll have my deputy let her know," the sheriff offered.

Edward heard the front door close and looked at his surroundings. A cot with a questionable mattress was pushed against the wall, and there was a chamber pot nearby. *Such luxuries,* he thought. He finally

375

sat on the edge of the cot and leaned over, putting his head in his hands. It bothered him a lot that his friend Waldo thought he might be responsible for the robbery. It bothered him even more that his reputation would be ruined, and he was devastated to consider what Anna must think.

He went over the trip to town in his mind more than once. He'd been in good spirits and looking forward to Anna's dinner party. That was all that had been on his mind. *Think, think, Edward.* But he was tired of thinking. And here he was, stuck in this dingy cell on a glorious day, charged with a ridiculous crime. He should've allowed Anna to come too, but he really figured once he told Archer what he wanted to know, he'd be back home. He rubbed his temples — a headache right now was not welcome.

In the quietness he heard the front door open again. *Archer must be back,* he thought. But the footsteps were too light to be Archer's.

"Edward?" He recognized Anna's voice immediately.

"Back here, in the corner cell." Edward hurried over to the cell door.

Two sets of footsteps rushed to where he was. He saw Sarah and was glad she was with Anna. He hated seeing the concern on his wife's face.

"Edward!" Anna gasped. "I thought the sheriff was only going to ask you questions!" She wore a brown cape with a hood covering her head, making her appear small. She thrust her fingers through the bars to touch his hand, her eyes filling with tears.

"Me too. Hello, Sarah. I'm glad you came with Anna." Turning his gaze back to Anna, he said, "He just keeps asking me the same questions over and over. He hasn't officially arrested me — he's just holding me for now. Besides, I already told him I left the bank right behind the teller."

"What can I do to help you? Anything, just tell me. I feel helpless."

"Should we get you an attorney?" Sarah added.

"The only one I know is Harvey."

Sarah nodded. "I'll go after him."

"His office is just down the block, but he's only open a half day on Saturday, so he may not be there." He told Sarah where Harvey's office was located, and she murmured to them that she'd return soon — hopefully with Harvey. Then she was gone, leaving them alone to talk.

Edward held Anna's small hand tightly in his. "I'm sorry about the picnic. I wanted us to do something fun."

"I know, and we will."

"It'll all get worked out soon. I just need some advice, that's all."

"I hope you're right. It seems like a terrible dream." She paused, then taking a deep breath, she asked, "You were the last one in the room, right? Do you have any idea who might've done this?"

Was that doubt he saw reflected in her eyes? Didn't she believe him? "Anna! You *do* believe I had nothing to do with the robbery, don't you?" His heart caught in his throat. He must have a wife who believed in him.

"I — yes, of course I do, Edward."

He flinched. "You hesitated."

Their eyes held.

She stiffened. "No, I —"

"You did," he stated flatly, dropping her hand. He suddenly felt sad and hurt. But her solemn face gave away the truth.

"Yes, I'm sorry, I did have doubts at first. You seemed to know how we could get the money for the shelter, and you were planning to get us a telephone. But I can see in your eyes right now that you are innocent without a shadow of a doubt. I'm sorry, I didn't mean to hurt your feelings. I believe you, Edward," she whispered, pressing her

378

cheek against the metal bars.

"You must know I would never lie to you, Anna." He stood stiffly but looked away, not wanting to meet her questioning eyes — the ones he'd let himself believe in. He'd thought he and Anna were indeed a perfect match. But something had just happened here — broken trust.

"I said I'm sorry." She pulled back, staring at him. "Edward . . . do you . . . want me to leave?"

Edward tightened his jaw, then turned to look at her squarely. "That's up to you, Anna."

The front door rattled, and they turned to see Sarah and Harvey march in with Moose, who ran straight up to Anna. She gave him an affectionate hug.

"Edward, what in high heaven has happened?" Harvey asked. "When Sarah told me about this, I couldn't believe it!"

"It's true — Archer and Waldo think I robbed the bank last night."

"Hmm, I see. I want to talk to you and Waldo," Harvey proposed.

Sheriff Archer strolled in. "Guess you didn't hear me come in." He eyed Sarah, then looked back to Harvey. "I see we're having a group meeting."

Harvey inclined his head slightly. "Should

that matter?"

Archer sniffed. "Not as long as you're not conspiring on how to get him out of here."

"Not conspiring, but I know his rights. You haven't charged him with a crime, so you can't hold him against his will."

"I'm well aware of the law and don't need you to tell me."

Edward knew Harvey didn't take kindly to that remark by the stern look that crossed his face. "Your shiny badge doesn't mean a thing to me." Harvey's voice remained calm and collected.

The sheriff anchored his thumbs in his hip pockets and rocked back on his heels. "And just who are you?"

"Harvey Thompson, Edward's attorney. I'm asking you to release Edward unless you have some evidence other than hearsay to keep him here."

Archer scratched his head. "I suppose you're right. I can let you talk to him, but I haven't decided if he's going to be charged or not. I still have some investigating to do." He strode to his desk for the keys, then came back and unlocked the door.

Anna moved toward Edward, but he turned away to follow Harvey.

"You can have a seat by my desk and ask him anything you want. I'll take notes."

Archer glanced back at the women. "You two ladies can have a seat over there." He pointed to some chairs a few feet away. Anna and Sarah complied.

Archer sat behind his desk, propping his feet up and leaning back, a tablet and pencil in his hand. "Have at it, Mr. Thompson."

Moose settled in next to Harvey's feet. "Edward, let's start with when you were at the bank. Sarah told me on the way over here that you left right behind the teller. Is that correct?"

"Yes. Waldo was the last to leave."

Harvey paused. "So where did you go from there?"

"I hurried to catch the streetcar to my friend's floral shop, Park Floral, to get flowers for the dinner party we were giving. Which made me later getting home than I expected."

"So you won't mind if I check this out with them?" Archer inserted.

"No, I don't mind. The owner actually put the flowers together for me since they were just closing up shop."

"What's his name?" Harvey was taking notes.

"John Valentine."

"Then after you picked up the flowers, where did you go?"

Edward sighed. "I caught the streetcar at the corner for home. After I got off, I sprinted the rest of the way to my house."

"Or had time to sprint back to the bank and unlock the safe and take the money!" Archer said.

Edward nearly came out of his chair with a clenched fist. "I did not!"

"Calm down, Edward." Harvey patiently took his time. "We won't get very far if you can't stay calm. Back to the bank. What do you do there?"

Edward leaned back farther in his chair. He was already tired of repeating these facts, but maybe Archer had missed something, so it was good that he was also taking notes. "Waldo hired me to set the vault's new timer on the combination, which allows the vault to open only after a certain time has lapsed, and only by people who are privy to the safe's combination."

Harvey's brows knitted together. "And you are one of them?"

"Yes, I have to be in order to secure the lock."

He saw Anna lean forward to hear every word that was said. His mouth was dry now. "Could I have a drink of water, please?" he asked Archer.

Archer let his legs plop to the floor. "I

382

reckon." He strode over to a cabinet that held a pitcher and bowl on top. He poured himself a glass first and slugged the water down, then took another glass and filled it for Edward. Manners weren't his forte, Edward thought. Gratefully, he took the water and drank it right down, then set the glass on the desk.

"What did you and Waldo talk about before you checked the lock?" Harvey continued.

"Let's see . . . Oh yes. I mentioned that Anna needed a place to have a shelter for her rescued animals." Archer frowned, so he explained the situation.

Archer tapped his pencil against his leg. "So that money would more than supply the lease for a building, wouldn't it? Let me remind you there was no sign of forced entry."

"Look, if I had the money, would we be sitting here like three old maids chatting?"

Archer sneered. "No need to get wise with me, son. I'm only trying to get the facts."

"I've told you the facts! I've had enough, and I'm going home. You have no evidence to charge me with." He stood up and Anna popped up from her chair. Sarah stayed seated, watching.

"Please, Edward. I have a few more questions for you." Harvey got up to give him a gentle push on his shoulder. Edward and Anna sat back down and Harvey continued. "After you two talked about leasing a building, what did you do after that?"

Edward retraced his steps in his head. He remembered that the money had already been counted for the day and Leonard was there in the room, putting away the stacks of money and bonds.

"I recall Leonard, the assistant manager, was in the room, and the safe door was open. He'd just finished stacking the money. He told me he'd leave me to set the timer, and then he was gone. I heard him tell Waldo goodbye."

"So you set the timer?" Harvey asked, pushing him to remember the details.

Edward's hands tightened. "Yes, I was checking the combination — oh! I just remembered that the bank teller was still there too. He walked into the room where I was, so I closed the door to the safe."

"What did he want?"

"I thought it was odd, but he told me he'd overheard me talking about renting a building and he had a friend who needed someone to take over his lease. I told him I was interested, then he said he'd let me know the details when he could."

"That was all of the conversation?" Harvey leaned closer.

"Yes. Then we both walked toward the front of the building and told Waldo good night. The teller went one way and I went the other. I hurried away to get to the florist, like I told you." Edward's head was pounding now and he was done. He had nothing more to add.

"What's the teller's name?"

"I think he said Calvin . . . yes, that's right. Maybe you should be talking to him, Sheriff." He stood, ready to leave.

"I certainly will." Archer nodded. "You can count on that."

"Unless you have something else to ask, I'm leaving now. You know where to find me," Edward said through tight lips.

"Wait just a minute," Harvey said, pressing a finger thoughtfully to his lips. "You said you closed the safe door when Calvin entered the room, but did you actually *set* the timer?"

The only sound in the room was the ticking of the schoolhouse clock behind Archer's desk as they waited for Edward's response.

34

Edward froze, feeling the blood drain from his face. For goodness' sake! In his haste, he *hadn't* set the timer, only closed the door. He swallowed hard before facing Harvey.

"I don't recall actually setting the timer at all." Edward ran his hands through his hair and shifted on his feet. "I don't even think I turned the combination around so the door would lock, much less set the timer! I can't believe it, but I think I got distracted when Calvin started talking about the building. I was in a hurry with other things on my mind. This is not like me at all. I always do things by the book." He glanced over at Anna, whose face was pale.

Edward sat back down in the chair and stared at the floor, spreading his hands wide in frustration. "I'm responsible for the bank robbery, but I did *not* take that money!" He would never be trusted now. He'd left the safe open — an easy target for any thief who was determined to get inside the bank. *How could I have been so careless?* What would this mean to the hardworking citizens who trusted their money to the bank? He had to find that money.

Archer grunted. "Well, now. That puts a different light on things. But from the look on your face along with your own admittance that you forgot to set the timer, I think you're telling the truth. I'll let you go tonight, but make yourself available for further questioning if needed."

Harvey gave Edward a sympathetic look, but it didn't make him feel one bit better. "You'll have to explain to the bank about what you *didn't* do, Edward." Turning to Archer, he said, "Sheriff, I think you'd better talk to Waldo about this Calvin fellow. Seems Calvin made doggone sure he distracted Edward long enough to keep him from setting the lock. You'd better make sure he hasn't skipped town by now."

"I'll head over there now," he said, lifting his hat off his desk.

"There's no need. The bank closes at one on Saturday," Edward reminded him.

"Right you are. Then I'll go have a word with Waldo at home about his bank teller. If we can't locate this Calvin, he may be our man. I need to be hot on his trail."

Before leaving, Edward shook Harvey's hand, thanking him for the questions that had made him think through the events. "I owe you."

Harvey chuckled. "No you don't. Besides, your wife gave me the gift of ol' Moose here," he said, scratching the dog behind the ear. "We'll talk again."

With the afternoon almost gone, Edward turned the wagon toward home. Sarah sat in the back, but Anna was so grateful she'd been with her today. She glanced at her husband's profile, noting the solemnness of his face. He looked straight ahead, and though she tried to make casual talk, he barely said a word. It was clear that her doubts about him being the robber had created a wedge between them. The look Edward had given her earlier chilled her. Would this affect their marriage to the point that he would ask her to leave? She tried to steady her hands in her lap. She wouldn't let that happen. He had to forgive her. Oh, why had she ever doubted him?

"Edward, we can still have our picnic tomorrow after church as long as the weather stays nice. I'm sure your name will be cleared when the sheriff completes his investigation."

Edward grunted, guiding Cloud around muddy holes in the road. "Let's hope so."

She placed a comforting hand on his forearm. "It's going to be all right. Harvey impressed me today, and I'm glad he was there to jog your memory."

"You mean make me remember how careless I've become, don't you?"

Anna wasn't sure what to say, knowing that he felt completely responsible for the robbery. "You have to forgive yourself, Edward. No one can be perfect. If everyone was perfect, there would be no need for the Savior, would there? *He's* the only one who's ever been perfect. Even the best people mess up sometimes."

"Well, I don't!" he said, his voice rising. "Ever since you became my wife, I haven't been able to concentrate the way I used to, and you've changed everything about the way I used to live. And those dogs you dragged into the fray . . ."

Anna felt like shrinking into the wagon seat. Pain pierced her heart. What must Sarah think? "I'm sorry you feel that way, Edward. I hoped that I was making your life happier," she choked out.

He slowed Cloud as they neared Patty and Polly's driveway and looked over at her. "You do . . . you did, but now . . ." He

389

pulled against the reins, stopping Cloud in front of the house.

"Can we talk about this later, please?" Anna didn't want to make Sarah feel any more uncomfortable than she surely already was.

Sarah hopped out. "Anna, I'll talk to you tomorrow." With a brief wave, she scampered up the front porch steps, where Patty and Polly sat waiting in their rocking chairs, no doubt anxious to hear the news.

Anna and Edward waved, then drove around to their barn. While Edward unhitched Cloud and put him in his stall, Anna fed the dogs their supper. She had no idea what she and Edward would be eating — the sandwiches sitting on the kitchen table were many hours old and most likely dried out by now. But the truth was Anna was no longer hungry.

Edward was still in a bad mood when they left for church the next morning, so Anna dared not mention the picnic. Instead they would have lunch with his sister. Some members stared coolly at them, and others barely nodded hello. They had a right to be angry.

Anna prayed fervently that Edward would forgive himself. Casting a sideways peek at him, she saw his lips moving. More than anything else, she wanted the Lord to bless their marriage and asked for guidance. Even after a rough start, they'd finally come to understand each other better. Wasn't that what marriage was all about? Love? Acceptance? A helpmeet?

"I want to go have a word with Waldo," Edward declared to her as the service ended. "He's just walking out to leave." He held her elbow, hurriedly guiding her past the crowded aisle to reach the Krunks.

"Waldo! Wait!" Edward called out, pulling Anna down the wide concrete steps and into the courtyard.

Waldo and his wife paused, then turned around. Anna knew this would be hard for Edward, so she promised to hold her tongue.

"Hello, Edward," Waldo said.

"I guess by now the sheriff told you that I forgot to set the combination and timer. I don't suppose you'd ever forgive me, but you know that I didn't steal the money from the safe."

Waldo let out a deep sigh. "Archer did tell me. I could hardly believe it. I trusted you to handle that with the utmost professionalism."

Edward stared down at his feet. "I'm truly sorry."

"It seems that my teller Calvin went back in with his key, and since the safe wasn't locked, he took everything and is nowhere to be found. Probably left on the last train out of Union Station."

Anna squeezed Edward's hand.

"I don't know how to make it up to you," he said.

Waldo shook his head. "Fact is, you can't. I just hope the posse can catch him and I get my money returned. I'm sorry this happened too — but you no longer have a job with my bank."

"If you'll just give me another chance, Waldo, I promise you the checks and balances for the safety of your vault will be given my utmost attention and detail."

Anna felt sorry for Edward. It pained her to hear him grovel like this.

Leola gave her husband a pleading look. Waldo shifted his stance and looked down at his boots. "I don't know, Edward. This is the worst thing that I've had to deal with in my banking years. I had to face all the people and tell them their money's gone." Waldo shook his head.

"I don't know what else to do, other than go after the man myself."

"Now, Edward, don't go breaking down like a cheap watch! You're a better man than that." He pursed his lips, his jaw twitching. "Oh, all right! Against my better judgment, I'm going to let you try one more time — only because we're friends. But I'll be with you when you set that timer. Understood?"

"Yes, yes! Of course." Edward stuck out his hand, and after a second Waldo shook it.

"With that responsibility, I expect you to check the timer several times a week and make sure the combination is up to snuff. Agreed?"

"Agreed. I promise you, I won't disappoint you again." He pumped Waldo's hand.

Waldo smiled. "You can let go of my hand now, Edward."

Edward dropped his hand. "Pardon me, but thank you for being willing to give me another try."

Waldo clapped him on the back. "I'll see you Tuesday at five o'clock then?"

"I'll be there — and no distractions."

Anna smiled her appreciation at Waldo, who smiled back, tipping his hat. Then he and Leola strolled down the sidewalk to their buggy.

"Feel better now?" Anna turned to her husband.

"Yes, I do. Let's get on over to Ella's.

Wonder what's for lunch?" His unsmiling face belied his cheerful speech.

"I'm sure it's something delicious. It always is." She took his arm while walking to their carriage. Although he'd apologized for what he'd said on the ride home last night, she still had a wounded heart. And though she'd apologized for doubting his innocence, he had remained distant. *Lord, give us strength,* she prayed as they rode in silence to Ella's.

Lunch was good as usual. Edward took two helpings of fried chicken. Too bad he didn't eat heartily like that when *she* cooked, Anna thought. Very little was mentioned about the bank robbery. Anna had felt the cloud of suspicion from a few of the church members who'd given them a wide berth at the service, so she was sure Edward must have been aware of it too.

It was always enjoyable to have a leisurely Sunday dinner with Ella and Ernie, and when Ernie suggested that Edward needed to see his new hunting gun, Ella and Anna were left to talk while washing the dishes.

"Ella, you know Edward better than I, being his sister. His ego is terribly bruised, and I don't know what to say to help him." She dried the dish Ella gave her and stacked it with the others.

Ella brushed a fallen curl from her brow. "Give him some time, Anna. He's worried about his reputation, but as soon as they catch Calvin, people will forget. Thank God Waldo is going to give him another chance." She looked at Anna. "But it's more than that, isn't it?"

Anna's bottom lip trembled. "Yes."

"Come, let's sit at the table and talk while the men are occupied."

Anna plopped into a chair and sighed deeply. "I think he believes that he forgot to lock the safe because of me."

Ella laughed heartily, but seeing Anna's frown, she quickly stifled her laughter. "I'm sorry, but that struck me as funny."

"Let me explain and maybe you'll understand." Anna briefly told her how Edward had said he'd been more distracted with his work and other things since he'd married her. "He feels I'm to blame that he forgot to lock the safe. He told me that since he married me he's been too distracted . . . He said some very unkind things to me." She stared down at her hands in her lap. "I suppose it's the truth. I am a distraction to him, but I thought we were both having fun in our relationship and making progress."

Ella's curls bounced when she shook her head. "Edward has always thought he had to be perfect to earn our father's respect. Father was hard on both of us growing up, but harder still on Edward, which in Edward's mind meant that everything had to be perfect or it wasn't worthy. He wasn't able to relax and had very little fun in his life."

Anna was reminded of the incident with the puppy and Edward's father, and it made her heart ache. "So why does he blame me?"

"I suspect it has a lot to do with his own expectations of himself. Perhaps the bank robbery will turn out to be a good thing."

"How do you mean?" Anna raised her eyes to look at Ella, whose thoughtful expression conveyed genuine concern for her older brother.

"He has to realize that just because things aren't perfect in his life, that doesn't mean they're not worthy of consideration or value. That is one of the reasons he is so particular about his timepieces. He thinks they must be simply perfect — and for keeping time they are. But *real* life cannot imitate inanimate objects."

"Mmm . . . I can see that in him. I know I've been a huge disappointment to him in many ways. It's a wonder he tolerates me at all."

"Let me guess. That list he gave is part of

the problem?" Ella arched an eyebrow.

Anna laughed. "How did you guess?"

"As a boy, he wrote lists for everything. He marked items off one by one and was quite pleased when he'd accomplish a task. He simply could not move forward with a new task unless another one was completed." She giggled. "I remember his room was always in perfect order, and he could tell you exactly how many steps it was to the schoolhouse door." She placed her hand over Anna's. "Anna, however peculiar his habits are, you've made him change some of his thinking so that he can relent a tiny bit for the first time in his life. I'd go so far as to say you've brought him a lot of joy in a few short weeks. I call it love. Love makes one do strange things that are sometimes totally out of character."

"Love?" Anna was shocked, since she hadn't heard that word from Edward.

"Yes, my dear, love. Hasn't he told you?"

Anna's heart beat fast. "Well, not exactly."

"Do you love my brother?"

Anna was surprised at her direct question. "I didn't in the beginning. I had affection, yes. But I've known for some time that I do love him — really love him."

Ella smiled at her. "Then the two of you will be all right. Just give love time to blossom even more."

"You've made me feel better and helped me understand him. But what if he continues to think that *I'm* the problem and that this is too much change for him?"

"I know one thing. He told me you seem willing to do most of the things he expects of you. You both have to be willing to risk small changes to accommodate each other. I don't mean in everything, because that would change who you are, but the give-and-take every single day — that's what marriage is about. I think Edward may be a mite jealous of all the attention you give to your animal rescue work too. Just be sure and keep him the focus of your marriage, and the rest will fall into place. That's when he'll want to do everything to make *you* feel happy. Respect him first. That's what men want and need — respect. Everything else is icing on the cake."

Edward handed Ernie back his new gun. "Very nice, Ernie."

Ernie grinned, then placed the gun back on the wall.

"I'm going to find him, you know," Edward said.

"Who?"

"Calvin. I have to do something. It's my

fault, and I had so many cold stares today I thought an ice storm had moved into the sanctuary."

"I'll go with you." He reached for his gun again.

"No, I have to do this, Ernie. I'll find him, and he'll give that money back or I'll wring his scrawny neck!"

Voices coming from outside alerted the women that the men were on their way back, so their private conversation would have to end. Ella gave Anna a sisterly hug — like Catharine or Greta would have done.

Anna patted Ella's hand. "Thank you for your wisdom. I count you as my sister," she said.

Ella smiled. "Me too!"

Anna watched as Edward flipped his saddle-bags across Cloud's back and tightened the cinch under the horse's belly, then slid his carbine into its sheath. She'd been surprised when he'd woken up early and dressed in jeans, boots, and a hat he'd borrowed from Daniel, then declared he was going to find Calvin.

"There's no way I can talk you out of do-ing this?" she asked.

"Not a chance. I have to track down

Calvin as soon as possible. He's already got a two-day head start on me." Edward stood with one hand on his hip and the other holding the reins.

"But this is the sheriff's job."

"That's true, but I can't stand by when I'm responsible for the people of this town losing everything they had in the bank." Edward drew on his leather gloves, not meeting Anna's eyes.

"Where will you go first?"

"I'm not convinced that he's left this area. He could be lying low anywhere. I put the 'Closed' sign over the shop door until I return."

"Please be careful, Edward." Anna touched his sleeve. Was he not going to kiss her goodbye?

"I will. Keep the doors locked." He threw his leg over Cloud's back, then tipped his hat to her and gave Cloud a tap on his sides.

So, he's still angry with me. She lifted her hand in a wave, watching as he rode away, and said a silent prayer for his safety. She wished he'd asked Daniel to go with him.

Edward rode out of Denver, heading toward the foothills. He had a hunch from his brief meeting with Calvin that he wasn't a rugged outlaw. More like a man looking for a way to get rich fast if the opportunity presented itself.

If it wasn't for tracking Calvin, Edward would've enjoyed the brisk fall morning. He rode for miles, keeping his eyes peeled for any sign of tracks or movement, hoping that he could pick up on something Sheriff Archer had missed.

He felt bad that things had turned out the way they had with him and Anna, but he hadn't felt like kissing her goodbye. He'd seen the hurt reflected in her pretty eyes, but he was hurt too. He wasn't sure what to do about it. He hoped the good Lord would give him guidance — after all, he really loved Anna. *But have you told her?* he asked himself. He reckoned he hadn't, but how could he now?

The higher he pushed into the foothills, the colder it became. The wind rose and he buttoned up his coat. Cloud's nostrils expelled steam as he labored up the steep incline. When they'd made it to the ridge, he reined Cloud in and scanned below the trees and thickets as far as he could see. Wasn't Daniel's father's ranch nearby? If so, Edward figured he probably had a line cabin somewhere close. He could stop and let Cloud rest. He patted the dappled gray, admiring his strength. He knew that his horse was from good stock, but he didn't want to push him too far.

It was another mile or so before Edward spotted the line cabin in the distance, tucked beneath a thicket of spruce and aspens. Perfect timing. He needed to dismount and stretch his legs. As he drew closer, he spied sudden movement at the cabin door. He squinted and made out a man's figure, so he slowed his mount behind a stand of trees to watch without being seen. He'd figured on the cabin being empty. Could this be who he was looking for?

The man turned and looked around, scanning the landscape. It *was* Calvin! What a stroke of luck. But why in the world would he have stopped here? And how had the sheriff missed him? Edward didn't have to consider the thought for very long. The man strode over to a small pile of firewood and hoisted a few logs onto one arm just as a young and very pregnant woman walked out of the front door and said something to him. She went back inside, leaving the door open.

Edward slid off the horse's back, looped the reins around a branch, and lifted his carbine. He didn't intend to use it, but it would make a statement if need be.

Calvin started back to the house, and Edward called out, "Calvin!" as he moved from the shelter of the trees.

Calvin dropped the wood, sprinted to the house, and slammed the door. The next thing Edward saw was the barrel of a gun poking out the front window. "Who are you and what do you want?" Calvin yelled.

"You remember me — Edward from the bank. Why don't you come on out peacefully and let's talk about that money you stole!"

"I didn't take any money! Who do you think you are — the sheriff?"

Edward took a couple of steps into the clearing.

"You'd better leave now!" Calvin fired a shot at the ground in front of Edward, but Edward stood his ground.

"I'm just a common citizen who wants to see that the people of Denver get their savings back. Let's talk about it, Calvin, like adults."

"I'm leaving Colorado for good! I worked hard all my life and never got anywhere. Then Waldo hired Leonard over me, after I gave five dedicated years without a raise, 'cause he was Waldo's nephew. I don't need them!"

Edward heard loud arguing, and suddenly the young woman burst through the door and ran down the steps. She stood wringing her hands in her dirty apron.

"Please, don't hurt Calvin, mister!" she cried. "He really is a good man."

"Jenny! What are you doing? Get back in here!" Calvin now stood at the door.

Jenny turned to her husband. "Calvin, I can't do this. *We* can't do this — running from the law. Please give yourself up!" She was sobbing now, holding a supportive arm under her belly.

"Not a chance! Get back inside, woman."

"Calvin, she's right. You can't keep running, and it looks like you have a baby on the way. Is this the way you want to start off raising your child? Teaching him or her to be dishonest?" Edward kept perfectly still, his hand still on his gun, not sure what to expect from a man he knew little about. He glanced at the young woman who stood between him and Calvin.

"He's right, Calvin," Jenny said. "Please come to your senses."

"Calvin, I had five hundred dollars of my own savings in the bank vault too. If you hand the money over to me right now, I'll see that it's returned to the bank, but I'll give you my five hundred dollars to start a new life with your missus and child. I'll even give you a day's head start. But that's all I'll promise. A second chance — no strings attached. What do you say?"

"Say yes, Calvin, please —" The woman gripped her abdomen and expelled a loud moan, one arm flailing out into the air. "The baby —"

"Jenny!" Calvin tore down the steps to reach his wife. He grabbed her about the waist and supported her to keep her from falling to the ground. "Honey, is the baby coming?"

Edward scurried over to help, and when Calvin didn't object, they helped Jenny inside the cabin and eased her onto a lumpy cot.

"Jenny, are you all right?" Calvin patted her hand. Edward took a step back.

"I'm okay. It could be false labor, the baby's not due for a couple more weeks." She took his hand. "Just give him the money. I never wanted any part of this," she pleaded. "For me . . . for the baby and us."

Calvin's shoulders slumped over, and he sighed deeply, stroking her brow before whispering, "For you." She squeezed his hand, then closed her eyes. Edward wasn't sure whether she was sleeping or only resting as Calvin pulled a thin blanket over her.

Calvin motioned for Edward to follow him to the other side of the room. He reached behind the wood stacked by the fireplace, dragged out two saddlebags stuffed with the stolen money, and handed them to Edward. "I reckon it's time to settle up."

Edward thought of Anna and how he hadn't kissed her goodbye. "Yes. And it's time I settle up too."

35

It was well after supper time when Edward arrived home. Anna was relieved to see him and rushed out to meet him.

"Edward, I'm so glad you're back. I've been so worried." Which was true. Anna could hardly concentrate all day, but she'd managed to bake pork chops and whip up a batch of biscuits. Supper that she couldn't eat because of the lump in her throat.

She watched him wearily dismount, and she took the reins. "Did you find him?"

"I'll tell you everything once we're inside."

He looked tired, and she couldn't read his expression. Had he given up chasing Calvin? "Why don't you let me put Cloud in the barn and feed him for you. Go get cleaned up. I've kept your supper warming in the oven."

"No, I —"

But Anna wouldn't hear his protests, giving him a shove toward the house. "I won't be long."

He shrugged but didn't argue.

In the barn, Anna removed Cloud's saddle and blanket and lifted the saddlebags from his back. Funny, she hadn't noticed them this morning. They felt heavy, and as she slung them onto the straw barn floor, the buckle on one bag snapped open. To her surprise, money flew across the stall like drifting leaves.

What in the world? Where had he gotten that money? He certainly hadn't found Calvin or they would've been together. Had he really robbed the bank then went to retrieve the money from where he'd hidden it? Her heart sank. It really was Edward's word against Calvin's. There was no proof that Calvin was the thief, other than the fact that he'd left Denver. But this explained why Edward had the money to order the phone for her and rent the building for the animals. She just didn't want to believe it to be true.

With an aching heart, she gave Cloud his oats and a brief brushing, then decided she would ask Edward. She scooped up a handful of bills and marched to the kitchen.

He was eating, though his plate was almost empty now. Anna waved the bills in the air as she entered the kitchen. "Edward, where have you been hiding the money? Was this whole thing about going after Calvin just a plot to take the focus off yourself?" Her bottom lip trembled.

"What the devil — where did you get that?" Edward shoved his chair back.

"In *your* saddlebags! When were you going to tell me that you took the money?"

His face flamed, and his eyes narrowed in disbelief. "Have you lost your mind, Anna?"

"I may have, by trusting in what you wanted me to believe." She dropped the money on the table. "That's why you didn't bring Calvin back — because he didn't do it and you have the money," she said through tight lips.

"And here I was feeling bad that I hadn't kissed you goodbye!" he said. "How could you begin to believe that about me? I thought this was settled."

"But is this the bank's money?"

The look on his face sliced her heart. "Yes, it is. But I don't have to stand here and listen to your accusations!" He strode to the back door, then paused. "Either you believe me, Anna, or one of us needs to leave."

Anna's heart pinched. She knew he meant it. She'd made another rash assumption and blunder. Why hadn't she asked him to tell her what happened first? It wasn't like her to be so impulsive — or was it?

She rushed over to his side and took his arm. "Edward, please forgive me. I tend to overreact before I ask questions. Impulsiveness is a bad habit of mine. Will you ever forgive me?"

Edward sighed heavily, taking her hand. "Anna, if we are to have a committed marriage, we have to believe in each other and support one another. I hoped you knew me better by now, and it really pains me to hear you still harbor these doubts about my honesty."

"I am sorry, truly. Please, can we sit down? Then you can tell me what happened."

"Are you going to listen to me this time?" He stared down at her.

"Cross my heart."

Edward told her what transpired with Calvin and how he'd convinced him to give Edward the money. "That's why I have the saddlebags of money, because I promised him a head start. My plan is to turn the money in tomorrow afternoon, and tell the sheriff that Calvin hightailed it and I lost his trail. That's more than what he was able to do himself."

"I was so worried, Edward. But I'm proud of how you handled this — giving him and his wife a chance to start over. From what I've heard around town, he wasn't a bad man. I think that's why everyone was so shocked."

"I don't believe he was. Truth is, good men make bad mistakes sometimes." He squeezed her hand. "I accept your apology, Anna. But we were both wrong. Let's make a promise to each other that we will try to communicate better instead of second-guessing what the other one is thinking. Is that a fair deal?"

Anna moved closer, and he encircled her waist with his arm. "It's a fair deal. Let's never go to bed angry. I think we need to seal the deal with a kiss."

He pulled her onto his lap. Her kiss was long and sweet. Strange how he craved her kisses and her presence each day. She was his sunshine, and he did not want to live without her. "Anna, you do know I love you, don't you?" he asked hoarsely.

She flashed him a bright smile. "I suspected it, but it sounds good to hear you say it because I love you too! I'd go so far as to say we're perfectly matched." She closed her eyes, pressing her lips to his again.

"Then you shall hear it more often if I get that response every time." Edward felt contented to have her in his arms and leaned closer, kissing her throat and nibbling at her ear. She giggled with abandon while receiving every kiss and touch that he happily bestowed on her.

Fierce winds blew across the Front Range, with brisk temperatures prevailing. Anna and Sarah sat in the living room with a pot of hot chocolate, planning the bake sale at church to raise funds for the shelter. Anna was having her hot chocolate from the Blue Willow cup and saucer that her brother-in-law Peter had given her one special day in Wyoming.

She ran her finger around the rim of the china cup, fondly remembering eating all their meals off Blue Willow china. One day she hoped to own a set like her mother's and Catharine's.

"That's such a pretty china cup," Sarah commented.

"Yes, it is. One day I'll have to tell you the reason I have only this piece."

"I'd like to hear it." Sarah blew on her hot chocolate. "I'm so glad that you pushed me into agreeing to chair the fundraiser for you. This is going to be a fun event. What are you planning on bringing, Anna?"

"Apple dumplings, of course! What about you?"

Sarah tapped a pencil to her chin. "I'll bring a lemon pie." She wrote their items on the list. "I'm sure Aunt Patty and Aunt Polly will bake a cake and maybe a pie or two."

"Trouble is, we won't know what others are bringing until Saturday when we have the fund-raiser." Anna took a sip of her hot chocolate and stared at her friend over the cup's rim.

"Ah, I'm a step ahead of you. I posted a sign-up sheet right after church. I'll check it this afternoon to see if anyone volunteered. Maybe then we can sort of estimate what we might take in."

Anna shook her head. "My, but you're the best chairperson I could have! Right after work today, Chris is going to bring the wagon around. He painted the sides with 'ASPCA' in red. We'll take our first ride after supper to see if we can round up any strays. Want to come?"

"Not this time. I'll leave that up to you. My true forte is organizational skills."

"As well I can see, my friend. You're an answer to prayer, I tell you!"

The wind howled down through the chimney, but Anna felt cozy inside her home —

warm and safe, unlike the dogs that roamed the streets of Denver. With winter coming on, the animals would need shelter. She hoped that they could raise enough money to afford the rental Edward was able to secure through Waldo's client.

"How's the new space coming along?" Sarah inquired. "Chris told me he was working with Edward and Daniel to change the inside of the building to accommodate animals."

"Chris, huh?" Anna teased. Sarah's pale skin turned bright pink, but Anna continued. "Yes, they're working on it every evening and coming home late. I try to have supper for all of them before they go over there. Say, why don't you come back about supper time and help out — you could be around Chris. And don't tell me that doesn't appeal to you."

Sarah pursed her lips. "I won't lie . . . Yes, I'll come over. Anything I can do to help."

The telephone rang, and Anna walked over to the desk to answer it. "Hello," she said. She was still not used to having it and marveled how she could talk to someone by a piece of wire and cables. It was all too much for her to grasp. Still, she enjoyed the novelty of having it, even if she had to share the line with several other people.

The operator connected her. "Anna, hi. It's Mary Buchtel here. I wanted to tell you that the sign-up list is growing larger every hour, so I have an idea. Why don't you bring a dog or cat or two to the fund-raiser, to generate interest in adoption of the abandoned animals? What do you think?"

"Excellent idea. I don't know why I didn't think of it myself. I've concluded that God has abundantly blessed me with smart, caring volunteers!"

"Great! One or two should suffice, I think. I must go now, but just had to share my idea with you."

After Anna hung up, she said a silent prayer for her volunteers and for the input they were having. It may have started off as her chapter, but she could see how quickly it was becoming the people's cause. What a blessing this was turning out to be!

"I'm beginning to get used to having a telephone now," Anna said to Sarah.

"As we get busier, I think it's going to be worth having it. I wonder what they'll invent next?" Sarah giggled. "Something to send a man to the moon?"

Anna laughed heartily. "You're too funny. How outrageous. That will never happen."

Sarah smiled. "That's for sure. Look, I'd better get back home, but I'll try to return to help you feed the men. I'll even clean up so that you and Chris can go ahead and leave."

"Oh, would you? That would help me out so much, Sarah. And I think I'll ask Callie if I can invite you to our literary circle."

Sarah's eyes brightened. "Oh, would you? I'd love to come. I read a lot, especially in the winter."

"Then I'll ask. I'm sure it will be fine. Chris is a member, if you didn't know."

"Are you playing matchmaker?" Sarah wagged her finger at Anna.

"Could be. But I'm not so sure that I need to." Anna raised an eyebrow at her friend.

Sarah shrugged and smiled, then put her coat on, promising to return around five or so.

As Anna set the table, the telephone's constant ringing kept interrupting her, but that turned out to be a good thing. Several people had called to pledge their donations for the animal shelter. Someone asked where she could drop off a housecat, and another person had found a small dog running loose in his grandma's yard. She kept a list of the names and told them where to mail their donations.

Excitement filled her as she stirred the thick stew on the stove and poured the batter for corn bread into a skillet. Things were beginning to happen and donations were coming in! She wondered how people had heard that she had a telephone. Then she laughed. Callie had told her that Eloise, the local operator, knew everybody's business.

It wasn't long before all the men showed up for supper, just as she took the corn bread out of the oven. She wondered if Sarah was still going to come over.

"My goodness! It sure smells good in here." Daniel strode in with Edward. Chris was right behind him.

"Do we have time to let you stop and take a peek at the newly painted wagon?" Chris asked Anna. "I'm not the best artist, but I'm cheap."

"And free, I might add." Edward grinned then threw a look her way.

"I'd love to see it. Lead the way!" Anna said.

They all followed Chris down the hallway and out to the front sidewalk where he'd parked the enclosed wagon. In bold, bright red letters across the side was painted "American Society for the Prevention of Cruelty to Animals." Anna was so impressed that she jumped up and down — just like a child, Edward thought.

"It's perfect, Chris! Thank you!" Anna flung her arms around Chris's waist.

"You're mighty welcome." He seemed somewhat surprised at her reaction. "Tonight we'll take her out and see what we can rescue."

"You did a really fine job, Chris. Thank you," Edward said, wishing his wife would let go of Chris's waist. Now why was that getting under his skin after their talk? *Because you're jealous.*

Daniel gave the wagon a closer look. "The wagon's in good shape. The wood's not too worn, but if you need any of it replaced, let me know. I'd be glad to work on it for you."

"I'll take you up on that. Ernie was the generous one. All I did was paint the signage." Chris directed his gaze from Daniel to Sarah coming across the street. "Hello there, Sarah. Come to admire my handiwork?"

"Indeed, it's very nice, Chris. I actually came to help Anna so the two of you could leave right after supper."

"Sure you don't want to come along?" He gazed at her while she looked over the wagon.

Sarah blushed. "I'm sure. I'm only here to help out in the kitchen. Maybe another time?"

"I'm gonna hold you to that, my fair lady." Chris followed her inside.

"Let's go eat before the food gets cold. Come on!" Anna started up the steps.

Edward noticed that Chris couldn't take his eyes off Sarah. She was comely and had a graceful way of walking and speaking. He knew all of that wasn't lost on Chris, and if he had to guess, he thought his friend was already lovesick for her. Was that the way he looked to people when he was around Anna? Could be.

"I've eaten already, but I'll serve everyone, then clean up afterward." Sarah donned an apron as soon as they got to the kitchen and began to ladle generous portions of stew into bowls.

Anna sliced the corn bread and slathered it with butter. She kept noticing how Chris's eyes stayed on Sarah every time she was near, but she thought Sarah put on a good act of pretending not to be aware of his lingering looks. *He's a man who's set his sights on Sarah for sure,* she thought. Anna sighed. She was glad her new friend was finding a beau, and it appeared as though her other good friend Callie was happily courting Daniel. They were seen together everywhere.

"Are you sure you won't eat with us, Sarah?" Anna asked as she took a seat at the table.

"There's an empty chair right next to me." Chris grinned, patting the chair.

"At least have a slice of Anna's corn bread. It's the best!" Edward clapped eyes on Anna. His compliment surprised her.

She murmured her thanks, then looked away. His compliment made her skin tingle. Catharine and Peter loved each other, and Catharine had been a mail-order bride, but they'd corresponded more than Anna and Edward had. She and Edward exchanged only a few letters, so Edward's admission now filled her with renewed hope for a wonderful life with him.

"Oh, all right. Just one tiny piece," Sarah said. Chris pulled out the chair next to him, and Sarah took a seat.

Daniel looked over at Anna. "Had any more donations lately?"

"As a matter of fact, two dear benefactors this morning. I'm so tickled that people are willing to help my cause. The telephone is turning out to be a great way for me to talk to people about it, otherwise I might not ever hear from them."

"Telephone? How lucky you are." Chris finished off his second helping of stew.

"Yes, thanks to my sweet husband, who's given me his support." Anna shot Edward a shy look.

"And I'm happy to do so." Edward stood. "If you're ready to leave, Daniel, I am. I've got lots to paint while you finish the cages."

Daniel popped up, giving a bow to Anna. "I must say, supper was delicious. Edward's been holding out on me." He chuckled.

"Thank you, Daniel."

Edward bent to give her a kiss on the cheek as he passed by on his way out.

"See you later, Chris. You and Anna be careful now."

Chris nodded. "Don't worry, I'll take good care of your pretty little wife."

The streets of Denver were less crowded now as Anna and Chris drove slowly down Colfax Avenue with the soft glow of the streetlights creating eerie patterns on the street. Since it was dusk, Chris drove slowly, and they both kept their eyes peeled for a stray or wounded dog or cat. Anna also made note of the cabs drawn by horses to see if the horses looked well cared for. So far, the ones they'd passed looked okay.

They made small talk as they went along, noticing the stares of curious passersby when they saw the writing on the wagon's cover. "I wonder if we shouldn't turn down one of the side streets, Chris," Anna said. "I'm not sure at this time of the day if we'll see anything on the main street."

"Good idea," he answered, and with a light touch to the horse's reins, he guided him down a side street. It wasn't long before they saw a limping dog on the sidewalk, but when he heard the wagon wheels rumbling toward him, he ran for cover. Chris stopped the wagon. "I'll try to go after him. He looks injured."

"No, let me, Chris. I sometimes have a way that seems to soothe an animal's spirit." Before he could answer, Anna climbed down quietly and moved toward the large planter that the dog hid behind.

"Come now, I'm your friend. I'm here to help you." She took a couple of slow, cautious steps toward the shivering dog. She wanted to make sure that he wasn't rabid and didn't have any white foam coming from his mouth. But from what she could see, there was none. She stretched out her hand as she drew closer. "See, I'm not here to harm you."

The small dog made whimpering sounds, which encouraged her to step closer. "Poor baby. You're hurt. I want to help you." The dog sniffed her hand timidly but stayed down. Carefully she stretched her hand out farther and touched the top of his head.

The hollow look in his eyes made Anna's heart melt. That look was one of pain. Taking her time as the dog lay on the sidewalk behind the planter, she examined a wound on his leg. The bleeding on his front leg was from some sort of injury, but the wound wasn't too deep. She couldn't tell if anything was broken or not. She would have to carry him in her apron to the wagon — if he'd let her.

Anna heard footsteps behind her and turned to see Chris. "I thought you might need some help," he said.

"He's hurt all right. We need to get him to the wagon. I think I can lift him. I'll check the wound better once I'm home. It doesn't appear to be too serious, though." Anna continued to stroke the dog's back, and his whimpering ceased.

"Let me carry him. He seems docile enough." Chris knelt down beside the dog, petting him to let him take in his scent. "There now, fella." He spoke softly, then in a quick movement scooped up the dog and carried him to the waiting wagon. "Anna, will you open the door for me?"

Anna quickly stepped to the back of the wagon and opened the door. Chris had placed some straw and old, raggedy blankets on top of the floor of the wagon. Gently he laid the dog on a blanket, then turned to her. "I think he'll be okay while we drive through a couple other streets, don't you?"

She gave the dog a scratch behind the ears. "Yes, we must get moving. I promised Edward I wouldn't be out too late."

36

Daniel dropped Edward off at home, where he found Anna in the kitchen, tending to another dog with Cricket curiously looking on.

"You're home." Anna looked up but stayed seated on the floor with the dog's leg in her lap. A bowl of water and peroxide was next to her. "We found this poor fella limping down the street. I'm cleaning his wound."

Edward knelt down for a closer look. "He must've gotten hit by a speeding stage or wagon, but it doesn't look too bad. Want me to help?" He was really tired from painting the walls and sweeping up the floor of the shelter, but he'd help if she needed him.

"I think I can manage." She continued dipping the cloth into the warm water.

"Once you clean his wound with peroxide, I have some ointment that you could put on it. But I believe you should cover it. Was he the only stray you found tonight?"

"*Ja*. And he had no collar. I'll introduce this new boarder to the others and get them settled for the night." She squeezed the water out of the rag then swabbed the wound with peroxide.

"So what are you going to call this dog?"

"Hmm . . . What do you think of Scruffy? He looks a little rough around the edges."

Edward laughed. "I think it's a good name for him."

"How did it go at the shelter tonight?"

"It went well. Daniel finished the cages while I finished painting. Tomorrow I'll take you over there and you can see for yourself how it's shaping up." He stood. "But to tell you the truth, I'm pretty tired. I'm going to go wash up. Oh, and thanks for feeding everyone with your stew and corn bread. It was really good."

Her eyes traveled up until they met his. *How could any woman have such beautiful blue eyes?* The smile she gave him made his heart lurch. She titled her head to one side, staring up at him.

"What?" he asked when she continued to stare. Cricket began sniffing him and rubbing against his pant leg.

"You do look a little worse for wear, Edward." She snickered. "You're doing so much for me, and if I forgot to tell you, I

426

truly appreciate all your hard work to help with the shelter, especially after you've worked all day. Maybe I can give your shoulders a rub later." Her enticing look was full of promise.

"Sounds wonderful." He resisted the urge to sweep her into his arms and apologize again, and instead left to get cleaned up. He wouldn't want to have her subjected to his smelly and dirty clothes, but later he would make things right. While he was painting he'd spent some time praying for guidance for his marriage and his strict habits. It was crystal clear that he needed to tell her he was sorry.

As he stripped off his clothes, stained with paint and perspiration, he regarded his body with approval. The efforts of exercising with Daniel were beginning to become apparent. He had more muscle tone, and he figured that was the reason he was able to work the long hours that he and Daniel had been putting in lately. Would Anna even notice? Probably not — there wasn't *that* much difference.

He hurriedly washed and donned clean long handles because he wanted to be wide awake when she came to bed. He didn't have long to wait.

He lay in bed watching her as she took

her time to wash her face then her slender arms. The scent of the lavender soap she used tickled his nose. The moonlight outlined her curvy silhouette — ample breasts and long legs that ignited a fire in his veins, threatening to undo him. *Stay steady, Edward.*

"Anna?" He spoke just above a whisper.

"Mmm?" she answered as she untied her chemise, kicked it to the side, and slipped on her nightgown. She picked up her brush and ran it through her long hair while the moonbeams shone through the window, illuminating her with an angelic appearance. Only one light burned next to the bedside, and the embers in the fireplace had almost all burned out. She couldn't be more appealing than she was at this moment, sitting in front of the dressing table.

"Before I tell you how beautiful and desirable you are, I want to repeat that I did not mean what I said before. You remember — that you were the cause of my troubles. I know that's not the truth, and even if it was, it's worth it all to have you in my life. I mean that, and I'm trying to change."

Anna stopped her brushing and laid the brush aside. She didn't walk, he was sure, but glided like the angel he knew her to be to his side of the bed. Kneeling with her arms propped up on the mattress, she gazed lovingly into his eyes.

"I knew that, Edward, but I must admit, I wanted to hear you say it. You *have* changed! Think about it. When I first arrived, you didn't even want me to have Baby, and now you've come to not only accept the dogs but also help me with them. I'd say that's a huge improvement. And let's face it, I'm not perfect."

He took her hands in his, holding them to his lips. "Near to perfect, though. I don't deserve you."

She laughed. "I'm not sure you deserve all the anxiety that I seem to cause you, but we'll iron out our differences one piece at a time. That's what married folks do. Just focus on the promise we made about always communicating." She stroked his face tenderly. "I understand you much better now that Ella told me about your father. I'm so sorry your childhood was marred by alcoholism. How terrible that must have been," she said softly.

His heart filled with the knowledge that she could so easily overlook his inadequacies and flaws. That was one of the lovely things about her personality. Another woman would have packed her bags the first time he produced his list. Edward knew he was a lucky man to have found not only a wife full of compassion for people and animals, but one with spontaneity — a desirable trait — and one so understanding.

"It was terrible, but I'm learning to put some of it behind me now, and you've taken my mind off that." He wasn't surprised that Ella had revealed their past and was glad that she did. But he wasn't ready to talk about it. Not yet.

"Come to bed, Anna," he whispered huskily, then gently pulled her to lie across him. "I'm ready for my shoulder rub." He touched his lips to hers with a lingering kiss full of desire.

She gave him a lopsided grin and said, "And I'm ready to give it, kind sir."

Anna's dinner party had taken place instead of the literary circle meeting, and tonight the discussion was lively. Edward was teased that he and Anna had been too busy being lovebirds to read the required chapters — which was true. They'd both fallen into bed every night exhausted from the work of getting the shelter in operation. But Edward took their teasing good-naturedly.

"You know we're not the only two lovebirds in this room," he said, shooting a glance over to Daniel, who sat close to

Callie. "Are you two courting or what?"

Callie's face flushed bright pink, and Anna tried to shush her husband. Daniel took Callie's hand in his and gave it a squeeze obvious to everyone.

"We are for a fact courting, and I have to say I'm enjoying getting to know one of the kindest ladies in Denver." There was guffawing from the men and clapping from the ladies around the room.

"Oh, Daniel," Callie murmured. "You're sweet to say that."

Chris let out a whistle. "For goodness' sake, you two." He smiled at them.

Waldo walked over to Edward and Anna. "I just want to thank you again for finding that money, Edward. We're all very proud that you did what you could to apprehend Calvin. Who knows where he is now, but he still has to face the law when he's found. The sheriffs in other counties have been notified to be on alert for him. But the main thing is that people's money was restored — well, all but five hundred dollars." He paused, giving Edward an intense look, then glanced at the group. "In case you hadn't heard, Edward donated his own five hundred dollars that wasn't accounted for so the books would balance. I'm very grateful, Edward."

Edward nodded. "I'm sorry that I was part of the problem, but I'm glad to be a part of the solution."

Waldo clapped him on the back. "All of us make mistakes at one time or another, but we aren't always privy to what those mistakes are."

"Still, I'm much obliged for the second chance. Not many would do that after their bank was robbed." Edward was aware of Anna's eyes resting on him. He wanted her to be proud that he was her husband, and if looks said anything at all, hers said she was. There was applause from everyone, which made Edward grateful for his friends.

"We're happy to have Waldo join our group tonight, and I wanted to ask you all about allowing Sarah Holbrook to join us as well," Anna said.

Callie looked around the group. "Any nays?" There were none. "Any yeas?" All spoke or nodded their agreement, with Chris being the loudest of the group.

"Sarah will bring much to our group. She's very well read," Chris declared.

"Then, please, Anna, go ahead and invite her. I believe that ends our lively discussion of Tom Sawyer for the evening." Callie rose, indicating that it was time to break up the meeting.

With the discussion over for the night, everyone retrieved their coats. Waldo stepped next to Edward, who was helping Anna into her coat. "Edward, would you consider another part-time job? Say, maybe once a week — an hour of your time?"

Edward was surprised by the question. "You know that I'd be no good at working as a teller at your bank."

"No, no. That's not at all what I meant. I have a friend at Union Station, and he mentioned they needed someone to keep the correct time for the station's tower clock. Naturally, I thought of you."

Anna's face brightened when Edward glanced at her before answering. "I'd have to talk it over with Anna. You know I'm helping her out a lot in my spare time."

"That's true, but the shelter is ready for use, and I have Chris and other volunteers who will help me now. You don't have to ask me. I think it's a fine idea." Anna grabbed his arm affectionately and gave it a squeeze.

He smiled down at her. "Then I guess I can say yes, Waldo, if you're sure about this."

"As sure as the sun rises! I'll give you my friend's name when you're at the bank next. I believe he's anxious for you to start."

Edward held out his hand and shook Wal-

433

do's. "Thanks for putting in a good word for me. I'll make it up to you somehow, Waldo."

Waldo gave him a genuine smile. "No need to, son. As I said, everyone needs a second chance. I'll say good evening now."

"Good night, Waldo," Anna said, and Edward nodded.

They hurried home with the cold air nipping at their noses, eager to enjoy sitting by the fire.

37

Dazzling sunshine and crisp air made a perfect day that filled Anna with energy — and today she would need it. The bake sale started at two o'clock, and she was already wishing she had an extra set of hands. Still in her dressing gown, she pulled the living room curtains aside. Barren limbs, now stripped of their fall foliage, created a sharp contrast against the evergreens lining the distant hillsides. She was ready for that drive to the mountains outside of Denver. Hopefully Sunday would prove to be just as spectacular.

She finished her coffee, then donned a sage-green plaid dress with deep pleated cuffs and black trim lace at the hem. A deep rust ribbon held the pleated bustle at the top. A black feather adorned her plumed hat whose high brim was turned up. Very seasonal, she mused while looking at her reflection.

"You look wonderful, my sweet!" Edward said. He came up behind her, slipped his arms about her slender waist, and rocked side to side.

Anna loved the feel of his arms and stared at the reflection of the two of them — inseparable, they were. She couldn't be happier. "You don't look so bad yourself, dear husband of mine." He was wearing a suede coat the color of wheat with dark brown trousers. "I think we're going to enjoy the bake sale. I'm glad that I got up early to make the apple dumplings. I just hope someone wishes to buy them!"

Edward turned her to face him. "You must be kidding. Of course someone will buy them, and if they don't, I will. You know they're my favorite dessert."

She looked up, smiling back at him. He lowered his head to kiss her, lingering a moment or two until she gave him a gentle shove. "No time for tomfoolery now. We must get going. I promised Mary that I'd be there early to set up the tables."

Edward pursed his lips, making a pitiful pout. "I'm offended," he teased. "I'm ready when you are. Did you put Cricket in the kitchen? You know I don't like her to roam the house — all that cat hair . . ."

"Yes, I did." Anna tweaked his nose. "I'll

go get Frankie and Scruffy while you get the platter of apple dumplings." She scooted out to get the dogs, anticipating her very first fund-raiser.

Sarah and Mary, Pastor Buchtel's wife, were already at the church when they arrived. It had been decided the bake sale would be held in the church's courtyard. Some men were carrying tables onto the lawn where they would place the baked goods. Chris had parked the ASPCA wagon right next to the sidewalk for all to see, and Sarah had hung the banner she'd made across the wrought-iron gate to direct visitors to the fund-raiser.

"Hello," Anna called out, her hand gripped firmly around Scruffy's and Frankie's leashes while Edward parked their buggy.

Mary and Sarah looked up as Anna entered the courtyard. "Hi there, Anna — the star of the fund-raiser!" Mary said.

"I'm no star, but these fellas might be." She patted each dog on the head and they obediently sat back on their haunches. She rewarded them with a bit of jerky. "Good boys."

"Is the plan for someone to adopt them today?" Sarah asked, unfolding a tablecloth.

"I hope so. If not, then they'll just come

back home with me."

Mary gave the dogs a friendly pat. "Is the shelter finished?"

"Yes, and what a fine job Edward and Daniel did getting the place fixed up. Perfect timing for me to announce it today and beg for volunteers."

Mary smiled. "Great! Why don't you get the dogs settled, and then maybe you could help us tag the cakes and pastries as they're brought in."

"Absolutely," Anna replied. She was just turning around when Mary Elitch came walking up with a huge and beautifully decorated chocolate cake. "Goodness! What a pretty cake, Mary."

She beamed. "I had my chef make this especially for your fund-raiser." She handed it to Sarah for the table.

"I have a feeling Edward is going to be your highest bidder." Anna giggled.

Edward walked up at that moment. "Hello, Mary. Anna's told me about you. And she may be right — I love chocolate."

Mary nodded to him. "Edward, so nice to meet you. Your wife is really working hard to protect animals in our city."

He nodded. "She certainly is," he answered, flashing a grin at Anna. She was suddenly struck by her intense love for him.

"Mary, I could not have accomplished all of this unless Edward had been supportive of my plans. He's not only been supportive, but he's worked hard to get the shelter in shape with our friend Daniel's help."

"I see," she said, giving Edward a look of appraisal. "You're much like my husband — my partner in the Elitch Gardens. We're working hard to open soon. Surely you've heard about it?"

"Who hasn't? We'll be one of your first customers to visit the gardens," Edward said.

"That would be grand. Well, it was lovely to speak with you, but let me move aside now. You have a line of people coming in with their donations." Turning to Anna, she said, "I hope the fund-raiser is a huge success."

"You're not leaving, are you?" Anna frowned. She enjoyed Mary's effervescent personality and energy.

"Oh no. I'll be circulating around and about to put in a good word for you." She winked, then strolled away.

Sarah and Mary Buchtel were soon very busy receiving the baked goods. Anna wrote down every person's name and what they brought. When she had a moment, she walked over to where the dogs lay under a tree with seeming disinterest in all the comings and goings, and glanced over her prepared speech. Why did speaking always make her so nervous? A sudden gust of wind nearly tore her hat off, and her speech went flying away. She sighed, realizing she'd have to speak from her heart instead.

She looked up to see children running through the courtyard, the boys sometimes chasing the girls, who pretended not to care until the boys pulled their pigtails. She couldn't help but laugh as she watched their carefree ways. Secretly she hoped to have her own children soon to enjoy. She wanted a son who looked like Edward but wasn't nearly as restrained.

Watching him talking to Callie and Daniel and Pearl, she felt amazed at how far they'd come in a few short weeks. She felt sure God's blessing was as much upon their marriage as her endeavors to protect His creatures.

Chris stood by the now-laden tables — which bore every kind of dessert one could imagine — and flirted with Sarah. Anna was glad they'd started courting, but even happier that Sarah had turned out to be such a jewel. She wasn't sure how she could have accomplished everything without Sarah's help. She smiled at them and thought they made a good match.

Ella and Ernie waved to her from the other side of the courtyard, and she returned the wave just as Harvey, led by Moose, showed up.

Anna crossed her arms, looking with satisfaction at the crowd — some of whom she didn't know and others who had generously brought something to the fund-raiser today. She caught a glimpse of Patty and Polly talking with Pastor Buchtel, who signaled to her that it was finally time to begin.

"Ready, my little one?" Edward asked as he walked up.

Anna took a deep breath. "I think so. Wish me luck!"

Mary Buchtel rang the courtyard bell to get everyone's attention, and folks crowded around. Near the food tables, someone had set up a small podium for her to speak from to begin the fund-raiser. Edward kept his hand at Anna's elbow, steering her to the podium. He remained next to her as she began speaking.

"Friends, I'm so glad you all turned out today to be a part of the American Society for the Prevention of Cruelty to Animals. I'm Anna Parker, and this is my husband, Edward." She paused while there was applause from the crowd. Now that she was facing them, she was thrilled with the large turnout. "This wonderful organization started years ago in New York. The bake sale, or should I say fund-raiser, today will help our chapter for abandoned and abused animals. With the help of volunteers and citizens' generous donations, the chapter is ready to open its first animal shelter this weekend."

There was more applause.

"Thank you so much for your support, and if any of you would consider being a volunteer, please let me know after the fund-raiser. There are a lot of goodies for you to take advantage of. And if you look to your left, I have brought along two very sweet dogs that need good homes. To prove to you how valuable a dog can be, one that I've rescued has now become a seeing-eye assistant to a friend of mine. You can see Harvey sitting over there with his companion, Moose."

Suddenly everything became a blur before her eyes. At the mention of his name, Moose barked loudly at Anna and ran toward her, and then Frankie and Scruffy took off after him. But before she could reach out to pet Moose, he ran right up to the table next to her, his lumbering body stumbling over her feet. Being as tall as he was, he was the perfect height for his face to land smack-dab in the center of Mary Elitch's seven-layer chocolate cake. Before Sarah or Mary could move, the other two dogs ran barking toward Moose, enjoying the fray. They chased each other under the table while Moose turned his attention to Patty's lemon pie, making himself a nice white mustache of meringue, oblivious to the yells of the frantic ladies.

Slipping right past Anna and Edward, Frankie and Scruffy went barreling toward Moose again, landing hard against him. Moose's weight jarring against the table caused it to topple over. All the delectable desserts went sliding to the ground just as Frankie took hold of a corner of the table-cloth and dragged it through the yard. Moose and Scruffy followed, ears flying and tails straight out, as food containers rolled onto the grass.

All in a matter of seconds, the crowd gasped and yelled and Anna screamed, "Moose! Stop! Frankie!" She sprang into action with Edward at her side, trying to control the dogs before they ran pell-mell into a middle-aged lady leaning over to place a silver tray of cookies on the next table. She never saw Frankie coming toward her from behind. He jumped hard against her, and she fell onto the table, arms splayed out into pies, gooey cakes, and brownies. Her face landed with a splat right in a large bowl of creamy vanilla custard and whipped cream.

Chris, Daniel, and their helper Alan were in hot pursuit of Frankie and Scruffy about the same time that Edward caught up with Moose. Anna stood surveying the disaster with shock and horror, her arms akimbo, heart pounding, skirt twisted, hat askew, and hair a mess. How could this have happened? The fund-raiser was ruined! Sarah and Mary were picking up the flipped-over desserts with hopeless expressions. Mary shook her head, and the long look on Sarah's face said it all.

"Well!" The middle-aged lady, who was being assisted by Alan and Edward, attempted to wipe the creamy custard off her face, and Alan started laughing. Anna saw the look on the lady's face and shot him a stern look. He instantly clamped his mouth shut. Harvey stood shaking his head, apologizing to Mary and Sarah, whose hands were now covered with a variety of gooey delights.

"I've never been so humiliated in all my life. Trained assistant dog, huh?" the lady exclaimed. "Don't expect a donation from me, Mrs. Parker." Then she stalked off before Anna could reply. A few others began to leave. With no baked goods, there was no reason now for anyone to stay.

What could she say? No one would want to adopt Frankie or Scruffy now! She scolded the dogs, now that Alan and the others had them in control.

Anna began to cry. The crowd, quelled by the mishap, stood wondering what to do next, while some of the ladies who'd brought desserts quietly turned to retrieve their dishes, admonishing their children not to laugh.

Edward took her hand. "Anna, it will be all right. It's not your fault," he said gently.

The others nodded. "Folks won't blame you," Daniel said.

Edward gave her his handkerchief, and Anna wiped her eyes. Mary, the pastor's wife, was speaking from the podium, saying something about planning an event for next week, when Mary Elitch walked up to her.

"May I?" she asked.

Mary Buchtel nodded, an odd look on her face, as Anna watched.

Mary Elitch cleared her throat. "Please, can I have your attention for just a few minutes longer?"

Everyone who was left in the courtyard stilled.

"My new friend Anna has worked so hard to make our city aware of the needs of our animal friends. What started out with a vast variety of delicious-looking desserts was quickly ruined by three playful and, ahem, unruly dogs. But remember, these dogs weren't given a home with a master who trained them — they were dropped off in the cold streets of Denver." She paused. "Now, some of you know that my husband and I are working to create a theme park for families to enjoy. Part of the showcase will be animals — some exotic. God has blessed us in many ways, and I consider it an honor to contribute to the ASPCA. I will match dollar for dollar each and every donation you make today. But today only!"

"What?" Anna could barely speak. A twitter carried throughout the surprised crowd until it became a loud crescendo. Edward hugged Anna, and there was a hoot from Alan. Daniel and Chris clapped and others followed suit.

Mary smiled at Anna. "So if you want to contribute, please come now. If Anna will make her way to the podium, which looks to be the only thing still standing, she will be happy to tally up the donations. Then I will make my personal contribution."

Anna started to cry again and tried to pull herself together as Edward urged her to the front of the crowd. Amid thundering applause, dozens of people made their way forward. "God has answered my prayers," she whispered to Edward.

38

The fund-raiser results astounded Anna. Because of Mary Elitch's gracious offer to match donations, her ASPCA chapter had more than enough to hire someone to be at the shelter part-time to begin with. Although some left grumbling and complaining about the waste of time and food donated, Alan and his mother both agreed to volunteer a couple of days a week once things got under way.

"I'm not sure I've ever seen you look as happy as you do right now," Edward commented on the way home.

Anna tilted her head and gave him a sly look. "Are you sure about that?"

Edward's face reddened. "Well, I . . . uh . . . there were those other private times." He chuckled.

"That's better! I was beginning to wonder if those times had made any impression on you." Of course she knew that *he* knew what she was talking about.

She was in a great mood. Even the look of horror on Patty's face when Moose had taken a hunk of her lemon pie couldn't dampen her spirits now. She laughed.

Edward glanced at her. "What are you laughing about?"

"I was thinking about the look on Patty's face and the lady who fell into the custard. It's all so funny in hindsight." She started laughing hard, holding her sides, and Edward joined her. They cackled until tears ran down their faces.

"What a mess those dogs made!" Edward wiped his eyes, then nudged Cloud homeward.

"Didn't they?" She sobered. "I couldn't believe old Moose could even move that fast." She paused, licking her lips. "I was so afraid that after we cleaned up, you'd be telling me that you wanted no part of this crazy scheme of mine to rescue animals."

Edward pulled the carriage to the side of the road, draping the reins over the side as he twisted in his seat to face her. Taking one of her hands in his, he held her eyes. "Anna, I admit to those doubts in the beginning when all this started, but your genuine love for animals won me over. You know it's not that I never liked dogs before."

Anna started to speak, but he placed a finger over her mouth, shushing her. "I'm beginning to enjoy the dogs and yes, I'll admit, Cricket too. I admire what you're trying to do, and anything you're passionately involved in I want to know about and help with if possible. I'm starting to think you're a lot more complicated than I first thought. But I'm in this with you, and I couldn't be prouder!" He tapped her nose. "Now, not another word. Let's get these dogs home and feed that whining cat of yours." He chuckled.

Tears filled Anna's eyes, and she was speechless. She nodded, squeezing his hand.

The trolley stopped at Wynkoop and 17th Street. Edward quickly leapt off and, with a spring in his step, made his way across the street to Union Station. It was a magnificently large building, and he paused to gaze up at the massive clock centered high above the stone entrance. It read 10:25 as he pulled out his pocket watch. The clock was wrong — it was 10:30. The maintenance people clearly did need him.

He stepped inside the vast waiting area, looking for the main offices. This was the very place he'd first laid eyes on Anna, and he recalled how sweet and innocent she appeared. This would always be a special place to him.

He smiled. Things were working out very well at the bank, his shop was gaining more customers, and he felt confident once again — mostly because he'd married a gal who made him feel like there wasn't anything he couldn't set his mind to and accomplish. Who would've ever thought that a mail-order bride would turn out to be the person he truly wanted to spend the rest of his life with? He'd heard tales of other brides who came but then left just as suddenly. *Yes indeed, Edward, you're a very lucky man God has smiled upon.*

He pushed past the long line of folks waiting to buy train tickets or waiting for arrivals and saw the sign pointing to the offices upstairs. He was eager to get started on perfecting the time.

Callie was coming over any minute to style her hair, so Anna hurried through her chores, returned two phone calls, and fed the dogs and the cat. No one had adopted Frankie after the shenanigans that he and Moose pulled at the fund-raiser, but she hadn't placed him in the shelter because of Edward's growing affection for him. Maybe, just maybe, Edward would want to keep him as his own dog.

The doorbell rang, but when she answered it wasn't Callie. It was a special delivery.

"Are you Mrs. Edward Parker?" the man asked.

"Yes, that's me."

"Wait right here, I have a box to deliver to you." He looked down at his clipboard. "From a Mrs. Peter Anderson?"

"Oh yes. That's my sister." Anna couldn't imagine what Catharine could be sending to her.

The delivery man jogged back to his wagon and proceeded to haul a medium-sized box up to the porch. "If you'll sign here, ma'am."

"I'll be happy to." Anna scribbled her name. "Do you mind bringing it into the living room for me?"

"Not at all," he answered and carried the box inside. "Here ya go. Have a nice day."

"A moment, please." Anna walked over to her desk for some coins from her purse and handed them to the man. "Thanks so much."

"Much obliged," he said, tipping his hat, then scrambled down the walk back to his wagon.

She took the scissors from the desk and sat down on the couch with Cricket next to her, wondering what Catharine had sent. Her school mementos? Some clothes she'd left behind? She slit the cord, opened the box, and found a note from Catharine lying on top.

My dearest Anna,

I'm so sorry that I missed sending you a wedding gift, but I've never been so busy — I've been preparing a nursery for another baby!

I'm happy to hear about your plans for homeless animals. Do write me soon.

Best wishes for a bright future with Edward.

Love, Catharine

What in heaven's name did you send, Catharine? Anna set the letter aside, lifted the heavy paper, and found individually wrapped items beneath it. She unwrapped one of the lumps of paper and exclaimed loudly enough that Cricket jumped off the couch. "Oh my dear sweet heavens!"

She let the paper fall to the floor, revealing a Blue Willow plate — just like her mother's and Catharine's. Tears of joy sprang to her eyes as she recalled how Peter had given Catharine a set of Blue Willow dishes. Their mother's china had broken on their voyage to America, and Catharine had managed to salvage only a few pieces from the set.

Anna continued to unwrap the package to discover that it was a four-place setting — a starter set, but oh, how it made Anna's heart soar. She wished her sister had a phone so that she could call her personally.

Carefully she set the dishes back inside the box and carried them to the dining room table as Cricket ran ahead. She couldn't wait to tell Edward, but he'd gone to Union Station this morning and was now busy with customers in his shop, so she wouldn't interrupt. Tonight they were having dinner at Mary Elitch's restaurant — just the two of them. It would be nice to get away from all the demands they'd both had the last few weeks.

"Anna?" Callie called out.

"I'm in the dining room, Callie," she answered. She'd almost forgotten their hair date.

"The door was open, so I let myself in. Hope you don't mind," Callie said as she entered the dining room.

"Not at all. Come see what my sister Catharine gave me as a wedding gift."

Callie peeked inside the box. "Blue Willow dishes! They're lovely. What a thoughtful sister you have."

"*Ja,* she is indeed. Catharine was busy decorating a nursery. She already has twins, a precious little boy and girl."

Callie smiled sweetly. "So you'll be an aunt three times. Perhaps soon it will be you!"

"Not too soon, I hope. Edward and I are just now beginning to understand each other, I think. But of course I want to have his baby." Even the very thought of a baby of their own made Anna feel like crying. Who would the baby look like? Her or Edward?

Callie grabbed her hand. "In that case we'd better get started on your toilette and hair. I can see by your expression that you're somewhere in dreamland."

"Mmm, sorry. I was just imagining what our baby would look like."

They walked upstairs to Anna's bedroom. "I can tell you — precious!" Callie said. "Since your sisters aren't here, I want to be the surrogate aunt."

"Absolutely. I can think of no one better when that happens. But by then you and Daniel will be getting married. *Ja?*"

Callie's face colored a deep pink and she suddenly looked shy. "Well . . . er . . . actually, last night Daniel asked me to marry him." Her face glowing, she pointed to Anna's chair in front of the dressing table.

"*Uff da!* And you didn't tell me? Oh, how wonderful! Congratulations, Callie!" Anna gave her a big hug, then sat down and looked at her friend's face reflected in the mirror. "You will make a beautiful bride."

"Thank you, Anna. I'll need you to help me plan the wedding. It won't be a very large one, because neither of us have a lot of money, although I think Daniel thought my father left me well-off. But you know that's not true."

"Don't you worry. We'll make it very festive, and it'll be fun. Have you set a date yet?"

"Not a firm one. It'll be either Thanksgiving or Christmas. We're going to talk about it tonight."

"Oh, I can just envision it. If it's Thanksgiving we can decorate with fall flowers and vegetables. If it's Christmas — well, there's no end to ideas or colors I could come up with."

Callie giggled. "I knew you could, being the artist that you are. Say, have you painted anything lately?"

"No, I've been a bit busy, as you know, but I will have time to now that we have a shelter and someone to help me. Anyway, just let me know your wedding date, and I'll start giving you ideas."

"Oh my! Look at the time. We've got to get busy with your hair."

They chatted away about weddings, babies, and children while Callie curled her hair and created a style that Anna knew she'd never be able to duplicate. The time flew by, and Callie helped her with her dress since Edward would be closing his shop any moment and would want to change for dinner.

"Your dress is lovely, Anna." Callie stood admiring her.

"It is, isn't it? Edward has never seen this dress. I bought it from the Denver Dry Goods and kept it hidden for something special. You know we never went on a trip after we were married or anything like that."

"Go take a look at your beautiful self in the mirror. I promise he won't be able to take his eyes off of you!"

Anna stood far enough away to see herself from head to toe. Her blonde hair was swept up high, and Callie had curled pieces of it to hang here and there, with trailing wisps down her neck. Her dress, a deep royal-blue velvet, matched her eyes. The low sweetheart neckline was complemented by a bertha of antique lace veils and large balloon sleeves, and the skirt, with a slight train at the back, fell on godet pleats just above her black heels. The effect was a very pleasing one, she thought. What would Edward think?

"All I need is a piece of jewelry to match."

"Or a matching velvet wrap to keep warm. Maybe one day Edward will make you a choker to match the royal blue. You look like a princess!"

"*Dank U wel.* And thank you for doing my hair. I feel beautiful. I did buy the matching coat since it gets so cold at night now."

"Good. Now I must go. I want to hear all about your dinner tomorrow." After a quick hug, Callie proceeded down the stairs.

Edward almost lost his breath when Anna, a vision of beauty, floated down the stairs wearing a beautiful velvet gown, her coat draped over one arm. "You're breathtaking, Anna!" His eyes traveled from top to bottom, and he took her hands when she reached the landing.

"Thank you, my dear. I wanted to surprise you. By your expression, I'd say you like the dress."

Not wanting to rumple her dress or her hair, he leaned forward to give her a peck on the cheek. "I see, then, that you have excellent taste. The dress looks like it was made for you. I'll have to make a sapphire necklace to match the sparkle in your beautiful eyes. Let me run up and change, and I'll be right back down in a few minutes," he said, then bolted up the stairs.

Anna was certainly glad that she'd had the forethought to purchase the heavy velvet coat. The November night was very cold, and other than the light dusting of snow weeks before, tonight's sky with low-hanging dark clouds appeared to promise Denver's first real snowfall of the season. She sat as close to Edward as possible, a robe covering their laps.

When they arrived at Tortoni's on Arapahoe Street, they were both hungry and eager to have a night away from the house. Anna was sure Edward wanted a break from her cooking. Heads turned and every eye was on her when Anna entered the dining room. Delicious smells from the kitchen permeated the restaurant, making Anna's stomach growl and reminding her she hadn't taken the time for lunch today.

After they were seated, Mary Elitch bustled over. "Hello once again, my dears! Order anything on the menu you desire. Dinner's on me as promised, Anna."

"How kind of you to do that, Mary,"

Edward said, standing up and giving her a slight bow. "I've heard nothing but good things about your place."

She laughed good-naturedly. "They're all true! I'm only joking, of course, but I believe you will enjoy the food. And Anna, you look as fresh and beautiful as a columbine in springtime."

"Thank you, Mary. I don't believe I've ever been compared to a columbine. What is that?"

"It's my favorite flower here. It ought to be our state flower. Well, I'll leave you two alone now." She scurried off to greet her other customers.

Finally they were alone. Candlelight and crisp white linens set the tone for an intimate dinner for two away from the crowd, a beautiful view of Denver in the background.

"I feel like I'm Cinderella about to go to the ball. Everything's so perfect." Anna placed her napkin in her lap and glanced around the dining room.

"It's perfect because you're in the room. I saw how every man turned to gaze at you when we came in." He popped his napkin open. "But I'm proud to say you belong to me and not them."

Anna was secretly tickled. "A bit jealous, are you?"

"Probably . . . but don't let that go to that pretty head of yours."

"Oh, I almost forgot! Catharine sent me a starter set of Blue Willow china today as our wedding gift. Also, she's expecting again."

"How wonderful for them. That'll be three now, won't it? I can't wait to meet all of your family one day. I only have my sister and Ernie."

"You'll love them, I just know it."

"I'm sure I will." He smiled. "Let's look at the menu now. I'm starving."

Throughout dinner, Anna felt Edward's eyes lingering on her. The two of them took their time, oblivious to others nearby. The night belonged to only them, she thought.

They both ordered spaghetti and meatballs. Once, Edward leaned over to poke some dangling spaghetti into her mouth with his fork, and they both giggled like they'd just met. Then he wiped a fleck of spaghetti sauce from her chin. He was showing such a romantic side that soon she was thinking of no one but him.

"The food is great, don't you think?" he asked after they'd devoured the strawberry gelato.

"Mmm, wonderful. It's so nice not to have to cook tonight."

"Yes, I know, and now you're so busy. I worry you'll have too many irons in the fire. Perhaps soon with the money I'll earn from the part-time jobs, we could hire a housekeeper to help out once a week. Would that help?"

Anna almost choked. "Are you serious?" He really was working on that list of his, but she would never say a word about finding it.

"Yes. I've been thinking about it, and it would give you more time to spend running your chapter."

"Oh my goodness. It would. I don't mean to annoy you, Edward, but you're so particular . . ."

He grinned. "Yes, I suppose so, but you have to admit I've relaxed quite a bit where your housekeeping skills are concerned, and your cooking, well . . . you have improved a whole lot on that score."

"I'm sorry that I'm not the best housekeeper. It's just that so many other things call to me. I do the best I can."

He reached over and took her hand. "I know that. I've accepted that fact, and I'm learning to relax some of my standards, but it hasn't been easy for me."

"I've noticed the difference in you. And Edward, I'm so grateful for all your help with the animal shelter."

"Little one, I wouldn't do it if my heart wasn't in it. I don't want to see one single animal abandoned or hurt either, but it's funny how I never thought about starting something to remedy that. You are just amazing. I think God has His hand over you."

Anna's heart swelled. "I'd like to think He planted the notion in my head."

"Oh, one other thing. I want you to make sure that you leave yourself enough time to paint when you can. Everyone needs something of their own to help them relax."

"And you, Edward — what is it that you do?"

He pursed his lips while he thought a moment. "I wasn't going to tell you, but I've been running over to Daniel's, usually at lunch, and spending some time doing exercises. I enjoy it and actually look forward to it now."

"Exercise? Why do you need that?" So that's why he was always disappearing at lunchtime.

"Because I'm so sedentary most of the day from my work, and I'm getting soft. I needed something physical to do besides hitching up the carriage every now and then. It didn't help when I saw how you and other women seemed to admire Daniel's strength at the rodeo, so I asked him about it. He's got all kinds of contraptions to use."

She squeezed his hand and covered it with her other one. "I'm pleased that you want to look good for me. I thought you looked a little leaner and firmer the other night, but I couldn't imagine why."

Edward sat up straighter. "You mean you noticed?"

She giggled. "Of course I noticed. I always watch you get dressed in the morning, not to mention when we're in bed."

"Mmm . . . which sounds like a good idea about now."

She shook her head at him. "You're incorrigible."

"If you're finished with your dessert, I'd like to take you on a ride before we go home." He had a funny expression on his handsome face. Something was up his sleeve, she was certain.

It was a superb evening, despite the cold. A break in the thick clouds allowed the moon to peek through, making the night all the more romantic. Anna was warm under the robe as Edward guided the carriage through the streets of Denver. She was completely lost and clueless as to where they were going, so she sat back to relax and enjoy the ride, noticing much less traffic than they'd had earlier. They turned down 17th Street and drove a ways past the Oxford Hotel until she saw the lights of Union Station facing Wynkoop Street. It was a magnificent stone structure, and seeing it took her back to the first day she'd arrived in Denver with a mixture of anxiety and anticipation.

Edward drew the carriage up close to the sidewalk and parked. He hopped out, looped Cloud's reins over the hitching post, and returned to extend his hand to help Anna from the carriage.

"We're getting out here?" This was not at all what she was expecting.

"Yes," he said. He slipped her hand through the crook of his arm and pulled her forward to stand in front of the station brightly lit against the cold, dark sky. He pointed up at the clock over the center of the building. "Perfect time. See?"

She leaned her head back and gazed up at the clock. "That's a mighty big clock to have to work on. That's why they called on the best man for the job." She smiled at him. "I remember seeing it when I first arrived here."

He walked her inside the huge waiting

room framed by gigantic arched windows. The station was nearly empty at this hour. He guided her over to one of the long wooden benches that resembled a parson's bench except for its length.

Turning sideways on the seat to face her, he took her gloved hands in his. "Meeting you here that day changed my life, but I didn't realize it at first. I was so determined to keep things as they were that I almost lost sight of what was important — building our life together, as God intended. You are the very air I breathe, Anna." His voice was low and heavy. "I want to show you just how much you mean to me, but I feel inadequate — except to say I do love you very much!"

Anna thought her heart would burst from his admission of love. She loved hearing him tell her he loved her. Tears blinded her as she looked into the eyes she adored. She removed her gloves and cradled his sweet face between her hands. "Oh, Edward, my dear one, I think I loved you from the start, and even through all our difficulties, my heart knew the truth. Only after you put aside your own concerns about the animal shelter and offered your help and support for me did I fully come to realize what a sacrifice that was for you. That's when I knew I truly loved you. I *do* love you,

Edward, with all my heart!"

Anna was surprised as a tear slid from the corner of Edward's eye down his cheek. He quickly wiped it away. "Anna, I'm so glad you answered my ad for a bride. I'm so honored to be your husband that I'll do my best to make you happy. In fact, I have something to give you." He reached inside his overcoat pocket and pulled out a small velvet case. "I made this for you. There's not another one like it. It's for your eighteenth birthday. With everything that's been going on, there hasn't been much time for celebration. But I didn't forget it."

She took the box and slowly opened its hinged lid, marveling at the stunning gold watch in the shape of a heart, with a matching delicate gold chain cradled against the velvet. "How beautiful! Edward, this is exquisite!" She held it up, fingering the coolness of the gold metal and the scrolling under her fingertips.

"Turn it over," he urged.

Anna flipped over the watch to read the inscription on the back.

"I am my beloved's, and my beloved is mine." Sgs. 6:3

Forever yours — Love, Edward

Below that, he'd inscribed "E & A" in a beautiful script.

"This is the best gift I've ever received!" she cried, throwing her arms around his neck and hugging him hard.

"Even better than the Blue Willow dishes?" He laughed.

"Absolutely. Thank you, thank you!" She pulled back from the hug, but he wouldn't let her go until he kissed her soundly, lingering until she could hardly breathe. Finally, he placed the chain around her neck and stood back to look at her with an admiring gaze.

By now they'd drawn the attention of a few people in the station who were staring at their display of affection, but she didn't mind at all. Nothing could spoil this moment for her.

"Your timing is perfect, Edward. I just wish I had something to give to you," she said, nearly breathless. "The best I can do is give you my all — my love that will be forever timeless."

"And that's good enough for me. I guess you could say that it's timeless perfection at its best."

Stepping back outside, they walked arm in arm, her head against his shoulder, back to their waiting carriage. Anna paused to gaze up into the night sky thick with heavy, gray clouds, and whispered a prayer of thanks as delicate, fluffy snowflakes began to fall on her nose and eyelashes. Her heart was full of love and promises for the future.

AUTHOR'S NOTE

I once lived in Aurora, Colorado — a place that's considered the "Gateway to the Rockies." As long as I live, I'll never forget my first glimpse of the magnificent and panoramic view of the Rocky Mountains as they loomed before me when I first entered the city on Colfax Avenue. That view has long stayed in my heart, creating this deep love affair with the Rocky Mountains, Colorado, and the West. One of my favorite cities is Denver, so that's where my story is set. Two overarching themes, other than the romance in the story, are reflected in my love for all God's creatures and for all sufferers of any type of disorder that controls their life. I hope I was able to convey those in my story.

Denver gets its nickname, the Mile-High City, because of its elevation of a mile (5,280 feet). The mountain panorama that I spoke of is 120 miles long. The weather there is usually superb, having over 300 sunny days per year on average. It was the first large city in the world to give women the right to vote. Colfax Avenue, which I mention in the story, is twenty-six miles long and is the longest continuous street in the United States. Denver implemented America's first — and the world's second — electric streetcar system a couple of years before my story takes place.

The love for my own pets through the years is how I came up with Anna's desire to help prevent any cruelty to animals. Here are a few that I've had: Jody, a Shetland sheepdog that lived more than sixteen years; KatyKat, my sweetest cat that lived to be nineteen; Amelia, a calico that lived to be seventeen years old; and Snowball, my cat when I was six.

The rodeo scene reflects the many rodeos I've enjoyed, and now Denver hosts the largest rodeo every year — the National Western Stock Show. The announcer, Billy McKinley of Cheyenne, along with judges H. H. Metcalf, Carey Culver, J. H. Gorman, and P. G. Webster, were actual men at the 1887 rodeo, but since my story takes place in 1888, I used poetic license to include them.

City Park, where Anna sets up her easel, is situated between Broadway and York on 314 acres and was built in 1880. Denver has the nation's largest park system.

Although the Denver Public Library was established in 1889, books were housed in Denver High School until a library was built in 1910.

The Denver Dry Goods, a beautiful brick structure built in 1879, was where Anna shopped for her dresses. It was once the largest store in the Central West. It was also known as "The Denver." It was acquired by May D&F and eventually closed in 1986, then was turned into apartments in 1994. I had the privilege of shopping at The Denver back in the eighties when I lived in Colorado.

Mary Elitch was a real historical figure who, along with her husband, built the famous Elitch Gardens — a family theme park that opened two years after this story takes place. She was a lovely, gracious woman who loved animals, so for story purposes, I took the liberty of having her donate to Anna's cause. She and her husband did have a restaurant named Tortoni's on 15th and Arapahoe Street, where Anna and Edward have their romantic dinner.

Reverend Henry Augustus Buchtel was really the pastor of the historic Trinity Methodist Episcopal Church, the oldest church in Denver, where he served from

1886 to 1891. He became Colorado's seventh governor. His wife's name was Mary (not to be confused with Mary Elitch). The minister of music was Isaac Blake, another historical person in the story. Reverend Buchtel was able to save the fledgling church by rallying its members to commit to relocate from Lawrence Street to a new church on Broadway. The church's sanctuary originally opened for worship in December 1888, but I took the liberty of having it already open at the time of my story. The fund-raiser that took place there in the story is purely fictional, and I have no proof that Reverend Buchtel or Mary held a fund-raiser for the ASPCA.

The church's steeple is divided by three sandstone bands and topped with a cross and has stained-glass lancet and wheel windows. It was the tallest stone tower in the United States in 1888. The church is now called Trinity United Methodist and is on the National Register of Historic Places. It has some intriguing mysteries: Why did the glass artisan use a different color in a tiny piece of the rose designs? And who wrote the messages in the rafters that can only be viewed by climbing into the attic?

John A. Valentine, a Denver Realtor, did actually own Park Floral Company, where

Edward purchased his flowers. Valentine had a desire to send flowers across the country and later brought a group of florists together to form the Florists' Telegraph Delivery (FTD).

In 1866 Henry Bergh started the American Society for the Prevention of Cruelty to Animals (ASPCA), which Anna is so passionate about. For further reading and to find out how you can help prevent cruelty to animals, see www.aspca.org.

James Sargent invented the theft-proof lock, a combination lock that worked on a timer, which Edward was responsible for in the story. The safe could only be opened after a set number of hours had passed, thus a kidnapped bank employee could not open the lock in the middle of the night, even under force.

In the story, Edward mildly suffers from obsessive-compulsive disorder, which was considered religious melancholy in the seventeenth century. Concepts about it began to evolve in the nineteenth century, and the term OCD emerged in 1877. For further reading, see www.ocfoundation.org.

Harvey's visual problem was called age-related blindness years ago, but now it is labeled macular degeneration. Moose, once referred to as an assistance dog, is now called a guide dog. Moose is the real name of my son's dog, a Rhodesian ridgeback. That breed did not arrive in the United States until the 1950s, but I modeled Moose in the story after him because of his size and sweet personality. Sadly, my son's dog died suddenly a month after I finished this book.

Frankie, another dog in the story, was modeled after my daughter's dog, Frankie, a beautiful golden retriever. However, that breed didn't arrive in the United States until the 1890s.

ACKNOWLEDGMENTS

With gratitude to:

My family, who all mean the world to me.

My faithful readers and their encouraging cards, reviews, and emails.

My editors, Andrea Doering and Jessica English, and the entire fabulous Revell team working behind the scenes on my novels.

Kelly Long, my critique partner, for her insights and, as always, her prayerful support.

My church family at Johnson Ferry Baptist Church.

Natasha Kern, my agent, for her friendship and keen advice but being tough on me when it was needed.

Mag's Peeps, my personal prayer warriors — Sheri Christine, Karen Casey, Connie Crawford, Linda Hoffner,

Kelly Long, Gaye Orsini, and Lynn Underwood. A huge thank-you!

Last but not least, the one who knows me best, my Lord Jesus Christ.

ABOUT THE AUTHOR

Maggie Brendan is a CBA bestselling author, was a 2012 finalist for the Inspirational Reader's Choice Award and The Heart of Excellence, and was twice nominated for the RITA Award. She is married, lives in Georgia, and loves all things Western. She has two grown children and four grandchildren. When she's not writing, she enjoys reading, researching her next novel, and being with her family.

Maggie invites you to connect with her at www.Maggie Brendan.com or www.southernbellewriter.blogspot.com, on Facebook at www.facebook.com/maggiebrendan, or on Twitter @MaggieBrendan. You can also contact her at:

Maggie Brendan
1860 Sandy Plains Rd., Ste. 204
PMB #121
Marietta, GA 30066